"*The Tales of Tarsurella: The Wedding* was everything I expected it to be…and more! I laughed, cried, pondered, and squealed for joy! It was so exciting to visit new places, meet new people, and be so surprised with fantastic plot twists! Livy has such a gift for bringing characters to life as well as making them relatable. *The Wedding* did not disappoint in this area. I was able to relate to so many of the characters as they faced similar challenges as myself. They brought me so much hope for the future and reminded me to keep trusting God with my life story! Livy has really outdone herself with the third installment in *The Tales of Tarusrella* series."

~Holly, age 20, Arizona

"An absolutely stunning addition to a fantastically wonderful series! Livy has created characters and a world that feel so real, it doesn't seem odd at all to put Tarsurella on my Travel Bucket List!"

~Sarah, age 21, Michigan

"A third installment that will knock the crown right off your head! Every book in *The Tales of Tarsurella* series are like gems, each packed with purity, faith, family, friendship, royalty, and romance! In short, I love this book so, so much, and wish I could live in it!"

~Alex, age 16, Florida

"I haven't read a book so quickly in a LONG time! *The Wedding* was everything I hoped it would be and more. Putting a book back on a shelf feeling inspired, excited, and ready to take on the world is such an amazing feeling - and this novel gave me that. I wanted to cry, I wanted to squeal, I wanted to write, and change, and pray...I also really just wanted to go to Tarsurella."

~Riley, age 17, Texas

The Tales of Tarsurella

THE
WEDDING

OLIVIA LYNN JARMUSCH

The Tales of Tarsurella: The Wedding

By Livy Jarmusch

Copyright 2019 ©

Cover design by Victoria Lynn

Visit: www.victorialynndesigns.com for more information.

Crown Image Rights: <a href="https://www.freepik.com/free-photos-vectors/logo">Logo vector created by mariia_fr - www.freepik.com</a>

Chapter One

Dresses and Dreams

Vanessa Bennett floated on the cotton-candy clouds of a dream come true. Tucked within the most famous castle in the world, Vanessa held her breath with anticipation and wonderment. Like a little girl awaiting a grand surprise, she wasn't allowed to open her eyes. She squeezed them tighter, wrinkling her nose in delight. A cool waterfall of elegant, diamond-white, draped taffeta material tumbled over her head and down her legs. She touched an elated hand to her stomach, her fingers brushing against crystal beading. Excited chatter buzzed all about her ears as royal assistants buttoned up her gown and proofed the skirt. Vanessa couldn't believe it. She was standing in her wedding dress.

The surreal moment was flying by so fast. The entire morning had been a whirlwind of satin, lace, chiffon, and organza. Each quintessential material had been handcrafted by gifted artisans from across the globe, as each potential design had been critiqued and scrutinized to the point of flawless perfection for Tarsurella's future Queen.

Vanessa had quickly grown overwhelmed by the sheer amount of options—metallic beading, crystal rhinestones, delicate embroidery. Each offering was stunning; how would she ever choose? Thankfully, she didn't have to decide on her own. She had an entire party of people, waiting on just the other side of the lilac curtain, eager to give their vote.

Bridget, her beautiful and soon to be sister-in-law, tenderly lowered a sparkling tiara onto her head. "Vanessa. Vanessa, you are going to *freak* out!"

"Can I open my eyes yet?" Vanessa asked anxiously, resisting the urge to pop them open. Keeping them shut, as Bridget had insisted, was harder than she'd thought it would be.

Vanessa felt Bridget's hands touch her bare shoulders, carefully directing her to turn around. "Almost." Bridget cautiously turned the girl in her gown, so she wouldn't be facing the mirror.

"Ready for the big reveal?!" Bridget squealed, clasping her hands together with delight. Bridget could not get over how stunningly regal Vanessa looked in her gown. Bridget already knew, her brother was going to be love-struck.

"Are you kidding?!" Vanessa waved her hands excitedly, matching the emotion in her voice, "Say I can open, or I might explode!"

"Oh no, we can't have an exploding bride!" Bridget laughed, looking at Victoria Stefan, the proud designer who quietly admired her masterpiece. "Addison would *not* be okay with that." She giggled.

Victoria and Bridget exchanged excited glances. Victoria reached for a long, braided, white rope. Bridget grinned and reached for the rope on the opposite side. Together, they begin the countdown.

"On my count of three, and not any sooner, darling!" Victoria announced, "One!"

Vanessa inhaled deeply, nearly unable to contain her ecstatic anticipation.

"Two!" Bridget chanted.

"Three!" They all shouted in unison, and the lilac curtain fell away. Vanessa opened her eyes, greeted by the sight of a room full of her favorite ladies. Jubilant gasps and joyful tears were the first response. "Oh, Vanessa!" Mrs. Bennett cried, her eyes pooling, "Oh, just look at my little girl!"

"Miss Vanessa, you look like a Princess!" Nine-year-old Millie raved, "Addison is going to fall straight into his cake!"

All of Addison's sisters—Bridget, Hope, Chasity, Jillian, and Millie— lavished her with gleeful compliments, but Vanessa couldn't hear a thing. Lost in the dreamlike moment, Vanessa slowly turned around, catching a glimpse of her reflection in the mirror, seeing her dress for the first time.

Vanessa was speechless. The sophisticated gown sweetly hugged her chest with a fitted bodice, adorned with delicate lace and a handmade, crystal-beaded design. Victoria Stefan and her design squad worked dozens of hours on perfecting this original pattern. This one-of-a-kind piece flowed from an A-line into a cascading skirt, effortlessly ebbing into a semi-cathedral train. The fact that this dazzling gown had actually been made for Vanessa was too wonderful for her to process. And yet, a far weightier revelation was hitting her heart.

[3]

In just two months, Vanessa would be married. She was going to walk down the aisle and say "I Do" to the love of her life. Addison was going to be her husband, and she was going to be his wife. *And that*, Vanessa thought, fighting back tears of her own, *is far more beautiful than even the loveliest of dresses.*

"Oh Vanessa, you look so perfect!" Bridget squeezed Vanessa with an excited hug over the shoulder, then gently proofed out her dress further, enjoying the feeling of the taffeta running through her fingers. "I know you have two other dresses to try on, but this is just so *you*!"

Bridget couldn't stop smiling. Weddings were one of her favorite things *ever*. Bridget had gone through a phase in her life where she was a reality TV wedding show junkie. She consumed endless episodes of *Say Yes to the Dress* and *I Found the Gown*. She always dreamed of the day when her wedding-dress fairytale would come true. Today, she could live vicariously through her soon to be sister.

Bridget stepped back to give the girl some space, allowing Vanessa ample time to examine the dress without outside opinions. Bridget smiled at the room full of happy hearts, knowing that every woman present was just as excited as she. There's nothing women love more than trying on wedding gowns! Even little Millie was completely absorbed in the event. Bridget noticed that several of The Palace Staff had dropped by; maids and wardrobe assistants who wanted to get a special sneak peek at the gown *everyone* will be talking about. Even Deborah was there, fighting back tears. She handed a hankie to Mrs. Bennett. Bridget couldn't help but giggle and think, *These are the moments fairytales are made of. And we're all witnessing the unfolding of it.*

"I can't believe this is actually happening. It doesn't feel real," Vanessa finally spoke.

As magical as getting all dolled-up and wearing a sparkly dress could be, Vanessa wasn't referring to her gorgeous gown. Her disbelief was not so much with the expensive material or lacy bodice; but rather, the fact that her life had changed so rapidly.

One year ago, in June, she had just graduated high school. During that season of life, her mind was plagued with the ever-lingering question brought on during her Senior Year, "What are you going to do with your life?" She considered several options, including filling out college applications or taking a gap year to travel before pursuing her degree at NYU. She created a reasonable, carefully-thought-through, solid plan for her life. Going to college in New York and preparing herself for a career seemed like the perfect next step.

But apparently, God had a different plan.

After her parents surprised her with a trip to Tarsurella as a graduation gift, a whirlwind of events unleashed, and everything started to change. There she met the young, dashingly-kind Prince Addison, who was soon to become King. He offered her a mind-blowingly wonderful job opportunity at The Palace, and she packed up everything in her tiny closet and moved to Tarsurella.

It didn't take long for the intentional, freshly-crowned King to reveal his true intentions for asking her to come and work. He was interested in pursuing a relationship with her.

And now, here she was, standing in her wedding dress! The speed at which their relationship progressed nearly took her breath away. She *never* imagined that she would meet and marry her husband at such a young age. Vanessa always envisioned herself finishing her college education, traveling the world, or doing volunteer work for several years before settling down and becoming a wife. But if Vanessa knew anything about her future with Addison, she knew that there would be no 'settling down' about it! There were endless adventures yet to be lived, and now she would live them with Addison by her side.

"Believe it!" Victoria Stefan broke into Vanessa's reflective thoughts. "The wedding will be here before you can say 'Victoria Stefan is a genius'! Now, before you decide for sure whether or not this is the dress for you, there are several design elements we still have to discuss. We can add the shoulder piece to give you more coverage—a more modest, classy look, if you will. Or, we can bring the train out several inches, going for a very dramatic WOW factor. We can tier the skirt, adding more ruffles and really bringing new life and texture to the piece. Or, we can rework the bodice entirely, starting from scratch to try a lavishly-beaded waist line with pearls, or diamonds even! Or, what if we—"

Vanessa bit her bottom lip. As much as she appreciated Victoria's creative input and ideas, the buffet of options was just too much. Vanessa started to feel as if the dress might swallow her up, eating away at the simple and pure purpose of the wedding itself.

Royal weddings were quite the "to-do," and there hadn't been one in Tarsurella since Addison's parents were married twenty-five years previously. Needless to say, the citizens of Tarsurella expected nothing but the spectacular. Immediately after announcing Addison and Vanessa's engagement, the press bombarded Vanessa with wedding questions; badgering her about details, color schemes, and floral choices. The Tarsurellian newspapers and devoted fan magazines buzzed about the upcoming event, claiming that it would be the "Most Monumental Wedding in all of History!"

But unlike the rest of the world, Vanessa didn't care about the lace and glitter. To be completely frank, she didn't care if the silverware their guests dined with was plastic or gold, or if the kitchen served French

Roasted Duck or French fries. In her heart of hearts, her deepest thrill came from simply knowing their wedding date marked the first day of spending forever with the man God chose to be her husband.

Vanessa turned away from the mirror, removed her tiara, and ran impatient fingers through her long, brunette locks. "Victoria, with all due respect, I don't think I can answer these questions right now. I officially put Bridget in charge of gown design." She playfully placed her tiara on Bridget's head. "You two can decide which changes to make. I trust you."

"But wait, don't you want to try on the other two dresses?" Bridget asked, feeling confused as to why Vanessa would want to cut her amazing, dress-trying-on party short.

"I *really* like this one." Vanessa smiled, turning toward her mother and Addison's sisters. "What do you guys think?"

Mrs. Bennett was still fighting back tears. "I, I think it's the one, honey!"

All the other women nodded in agreement.

"Then it's settled." Vanessa grinned, relived that another massively-huge "to-do" could be scratched off her wedding check list. "This is the dress!"

"As much as I adore the other two designs, I think you're right, Ness! This one is just so perfect." Bridget sighed happily, "I think Addi is actually going to cry when he sees you walking down the aisle."

"He won't be the only one!" Mrs. Bennet called out.

"Aw, Mom!" Vanessa crossed the room, her long train dragging behind her. She closed the gap between them and squeezed her mother in a tight hug.

"You grew up far too quickly!" She sniffed, "It feels like just yesterday you were dressing your Barbies in white gowns and now, *you're* standing in one."

"I love you." Vanessa gave her mom one more squeeze, then pulled away from the hug.

"There's nothing quite like watching our little girls grow up." Deborah sighed, offering Mrs. Bennett a supportive pat on the arm. "Blink, and next thing you know, they're sophisticated, kind, classy young women." Deborah reached for Vanessa's hand. "Oh Vanessa, I am so happy for you! I can only hope that my daughter will someday blossom into a rose as lovely as you have become."

"Oh Deborah!" Vanessa could feel her voice shaking as fresh tears desired to surface. "You have been too kind to me." She hugged the woman, "Like a mother. Thank you."

Over the past several months, Deborah and Vanessa had formed a very special connection. Moving straight from her parents' home and all the way to a foreign country had confronted Vanessa with its own unique set of challenges, but Deborah made sure her time in Tarsurella didn't lack a motherly touch. Upon her arrival, Deborah loaded her freezer with delicious meals and made sure Vanessa knew she could always call on her for anything.

It made Vanessa's heart happy to know that Deborah and her mother were now forming a friendship as well. Even though her mom would only be visiting for two weeks, Vanessa was thrilled to have her parents here, meeting Addison and his family in person, and helping play a special role in all the important planning. They would of course fly back for the wedding in August.

"I hate to be the bearer of bad news, but the International Relations Banquet pre-party begins in just fifteen minutes," Deborah announced, glancing at her ever-handy clip board. "It's time for the girls to go get ready."

"Oh joy, dinner with a bunch of stuffy, embassy colleagues," Vanessa sighed, the sarcasm evident in her voice. As much as she adored everything about her future with Addison, she could do without the fake smiles and mind-numbing chatter of socially-required cocktail parties. "I'm sorry I can't hang out with you and Dad tonight," Vanessa told her mother. "But how about we grab some ice cream downtown afterward? There's a really cute parlor just a few blocks from my apartment."

"Sounds great, sweetie." Mrs. Bennett smiled, "And don't you worry about us. Your father and I will be just fine on our own. There's plenty around The Palace to keep us entertained! I'll take all the time in the Royal Spa I can get!"

"Alright, I guess we'd better get you out of this dress!" Bridget knew they didn't have much time before the banquet began.

"Do I have to?" Vanessa frowned playfully, "As long as I'm in it, I might as well get married right now!"

Bridget laughed. "Hold your horses, chicklet, we haven't even picked out your jewelry yet! Trust me, we need these next two months to prepare."

"Jewelry?" Vanessa laughed, following Bridget back to the changing area. "Who needs jewelry to get married?"

"The Queen of Tarsurella does!"

"Oh goodness, those words sound *so* strange." Vanessa shook her head, "Let's just focus on one new title at a time, okay? I'm still trying to get used to the word *bride*."

"Here's another new word for you. Sister!" Bridget closed the curtain and began unfastening Vanessa's hard-to-reach buttons. "And I'm thrilled that you get to be ours! Seriously, Addison couldn't have done a better job picking you out."

"Oh really?" Vanessa chuckled, "From what I remember, you were ready to claw my eyes out when we first met."

"Oh I was!" Bridget laughed, "And I feel so bad about that! But you weren't too crazy about me either!"

"It's amazing how God changed all of our perspectives." Vanessa shook her head in wonderment, truly amazed by everything God had done over the past year. "He had a far better plan than any of us did. Speaking of plans…" Vanessa slipped out of her gown and into a knee-length, blue, orange, and pink flower-print dress. "It may not be too long until we start planning *your* wedding."

Bridget held up an empty hand beside her face. "Still no ring. Nothing's official until he buys jewelry. *But*," Bridget squealed, unable to hide her gushing joy, "I have a feeling he may propose soon."

Vanessa floated onto the ivy-laced balcony alongside Bridget. A temperate, summertime breeze merrily skipped through the air, making contact with the girls' long locks. Vanessa inhaled, relishing everything Tarsurella had to offer, now that the cruel, cold winter had dissipated. Something about the summertime air made Vanessa believe that all was well with the world. The ideal temperature made it just perfect enough to be comfortable in her light floral dress without needing a sweater, or suffering on the opposite end of the weather spectrum, of merciless heat.

From their vantage point on the balcony, the girls could see the frivolous cocktail party below. Men in suits and their dolled-up wives, mindlessly mingled with one another, trailing throughout the gardens, admiring the flowers and nibbling on appetizers. Vanessa could only imagine what these wealthy dignitaries were discussing. Life at their lakeside summer homes, boasting about the accomplishments of their college-aged children, and low-key arguing about Tarsurella's future, she suspected. Vanessa wasn't looking forward to the company. Nevertheless, she knew Addison was required to attend engagements such as these, and now, as Vanessa was becoming such a huge part of his world, they would be required for her as well.

She glanced at Bridget, who cut her teeth on these kinds of parties. She was a sparkling socialite, a brilliant natural who knew how to take every awkward or painfully dull moment in stride.

"Ahem." Someone cleared his throat from behind the girls, causing Vanessa and Bridget to turn and see who wanted their attention.

Liam Henderson, the clean-cut, good-looking young man from Alaska who stole Bridget's heart, stood with an arm stretched out to her. "May I have the honor of escorting you to this banquet, madam?"

Bridget's blonde, expressive eyebrows shot up. She wasn't used to seeing Liam in a tuxedo. The rugged young guy usually preferred to wear denim jeans and plaid, enjoying the great outdoors from a saddle. The Tarsurellian Palace wasn't exactly his native scenery. Bridget giggled, knowing that Liam was only using fancy words for the sake of the character he was playing. Bridget decided to go along with it. "Thank you, good sir." She bowed melodramatically before taking his arm and allowing him to lead her down the staircase.

Vanessa couldn't help but giggle as well. The two were positively adorable together. Vanessa knew they would make an amazing pair. A power couple, even. With their fiery hearts of passion for Jesus, and their desire to honor Him in everything they did, Vanessa was confident they would make a huge impact on the world.

Vanessa filled her lungs with another deep breath, knowing it was time for her to take the plunge as well. She couldn't stay up on this balcony forever. She slowly descended the steps, all too aware of the questionable stares and unshakable attention. Now, as Addison's leading lady, the spotlight was always on her. Whether she liked it or not.

"Miss Bennett, you look lovely!" A familiar female face greeted her. Vanessa knew that she should know who this woman was, but she didn't. Was she the wife of the Ambassador of France? Or was she one of the gray-haired Parliament member's wives? "How are the wedding details going? Is everything all set for the big gala?"

"We still have two months, so we've got plenty of time to iron out all the kinks."

"Two months?!" The woman gasped. "Most women spend at *least* a year planning their wedding. Engagement is a time to enjoy, and not rush about. There's no need to run like racehorses to the altar!"

Vanessa flashed a fake smile, "Um, thanks for the advice. Hope you enjoy your evening!"

Vanessa offered a small curtsy before making a quick escape. Curtsying was just one of the many new social habits she had to adopt after moving from the States. For whatever reason, people in Tarsurella loved to curtsy. Vanessa still found it slightly awkward.

Vanessa made a beeline for the refreshment table, careful not to make eye-contact with anyone, knowing that if she did, she'd be forced to have the same conversation over and over again. Where was Addison? Chatting with these people would be so much easier with him nearby.

She reached for a small tea plate and eyed the lemon cookies. If she appeared distracted, perhaps no one would try to speak with her.

"Nice party!" a familiar, yet terribly annoying voice spoke from behind. Vanessa clenched her teeth. She recognized the antagonist. The voice belonged to Matt, a bothersome co-worker. He wasn't a fan of Vanessa. The feeling was mutual. "Did you bake the love muffins?"

Vanessa spun around, not even bothering to smile. "No." Her voice fell flat, knowing all-too-well where his joke was aimed. When she and Addison first started courting, she had baked muffins for everyone in her department. After Matt found out that the two were in a serious relationship, he titled them "love muffins." Several of the men she worked with got a huge kick out of the comment and thought it would be great fun to carry on the ridiculous joke, but Vanessa certainly didn't. Her co-workers could be so immature at times.

"Bummer." Matt shrugged, "Well maybe you can bake some going-away muffins for the wedding. Since that *will* be your retirement party."

Vanessa pursed her lips, growing angry with the contender who constantly pushed her to resign. "I told you, me marrying Addison is not going to change *anything* in the office. I said I would be in that department until I'm old and gray, and when I make a promise, I don't go back on my word. Don't think you're getting rid of me that easily."

"Rawr, don't have a royal hissy!" Matt threw his hands up in mocking defense. "I just thought, with you being Queen and all, you may want to focus on your family duties. Juggling school, a job, and you know, all that wife stuff, might be too much for you to handle."

Vanessa's glare intensified. There was nothing Vanessa hated more than people telling her she couldn't do something. Matt was a master at getting under her skin. Vanessa opened her mouth, ready to fire off a heated response, when someone else popped into the conversation.

"Oh my flamingos, it's Vanessa Bennett!" A young woman who appeared to be about the same age as herself, excitedly proclaimed, "I have been dying to meet you! I can't believe this is happening!"

Vanessa cocked her head toward the stranger, and Matt grabbed a pink macaroon and slipped away.

"I'm Kiki Kawaki, from *Tarsurella Teen* magazine!" Kiki held out an energy-charged hand, "Do you mind if I ask you a few questions? I know the official press conference isn't until after dinner, but I'm one of the smaller outlets, and I might not even get into the main press room! Our readers would just DIE if we could get a few quotes from you!"

"Well, I wouldn't want you to have dead readers," Vanessa giggled, "but sure, I can answer a few questions."

As much as she disliked talking to the media, this young girl seemed sweet enough.

"Oh my flamingos, yay!" She quickly dug into her purse, searching for her phone to record the conversation. "Okay, so my first question. Does the reason you guys are getting married so fast have to do with an underlying fear that the Kingdom is going to fall apart, and you want to experience some of the perks of being Queen before it does?"

Vanessa's smile disappeared. Her eyes widened in horror. Did she *seriously* just ask that question?

"Excuse me, Miss Vanessa, you're needed on the balcony for a photoshoot." Deborah suddenly broke in, rescuing Vanessa from the awful question.

Disappointment flashed across Kiki's deceitfully-innocent face.

"My apologies." Vanessa wrinkled her nose, abundantly relived she didn't have to finish the interview. "Say hello to your readers for me!" She waved a little goodbye, then followed Deborah toward the staircase.

"Thank you." Vanessa muttered under her breath, "That one came out of nowhere."

"There was a mistake in scheduling, and now the press and media have been allowed in early," Deborah explained regretfully. "They won't be joining you for the banquet, but they will be everywhere for the next hour or so. *Tarsurellian People* has requested a quick photoshoot with you and His Majesty."

"Good thing I brushed my hair!" Vanessa laughed, attempting to keep the atmosphere light. There was no sense in getting worked up over the little things. As irritating as it was to socialize with the likes of Matt and Kiki, she knew that there were worse things in the world. Once Vanessa reached the top step, all her minor irritations and foolish frustrations melted away. Standing before her, talking with several photographers, was her beloved Addison.

She watched him for a moment, as he chatted easily, soaking in his handsome features. Finally, he saw her. His stardust-speckled eyes twinkled with delight as he caught a glimpse of her. His inviting gaze welcomed her forward. She took several steps and reached for his hand. As their fingers clasped together in a warm embrace, she knew all was well.

"Perfect, perfect, let's get the shots now, before the lighting changes!" the snappy photographer instructed.

She stood happily beside Addison, smiling at the huge camera and attempting not to feel blinded by the large, circular light reflector aiming in her eyes.

"Oh, what naturals, look at those love birds!" The photographer appeared to be immensely pleased with their simple smiles. "Now let's get one of the two of you gazing into one another's eyes, that's it, look at each other like you really mean it!"

"We can do that." Addison laughed, his eyes twinkling mischievously.

Vanessa blushed. As much as she adored staring at him, it felt a little awkward acting so mushy-gushy in front of all the curious bystanders.

"Alright, now Your Majesty, take her into your arms and give her a nice, romantic kiss!"

Vanessa couldn't help but laugh.

Addison turned toward the photographer, "Hey, you know, as much as I'd love to, we're saving our first kiss until our wedding day. So, you'll have to wait until then."

"What?" The photographer's shock was evident. "You mean to say... the two of you haven't kissed yet?!"

"Nope." Addison's genuine smile didn't disappear, "We want to honor God with our relationship and maintain our standards of purity, so we're saving the PDA for the altar."

Vanessa beamed proudly, unable to stop her heart from admiring Addison in an even greater measure. He was so bold to explain their personal convictions to the photographer. And *that* was just one of many things Vanessa loved about him. Her mental list of all the reasons she adored him grew daily.

"Suit yourselves," the photographer shrugged, "but let me get one more shot. Let's do something zesty! Your Majesty, get down on one knee and act as if you're proposing again. Miss Bennet, give us your best shocked face."

Vanessa giggled and followed the photographer's orders. She drew a dramatic hand up to her face, while her jaw hung open, pretending to be blindsided by his outrageous request.

The small entourage standing nearby laughed and cheered, getting a big kick out of the scene. Finally, the photoshoot ended, and *Tarsurellian People* bid them farewell. Addison squeezed Vanessa's hand, silently thanking her for being such a good sport.

There was much Vanessa wanted to tell him, but she knew now wasn't the time. They were surrounded by people who were all eager to chat with His Royal Majesty. Finding alone time with Addison was growing harder and harder as each day passed. And so, she cherished each moment they spent together. Even if it was a moment like this, answering the questions of nosy reporters.

"Good afternoon, Your Majesty, Miss Bennett," a man with a pointy nose and quizzical brow nodded respectfully toward the King, then toward Vanessa, "I'm with TNN News. Can we get a quote on Prince Asher's upcoming trial? How do you foresee the outcome of Asher's trial panning out? Do you expect he'll be found innocent? Guilty?"

Vanessa tossed a worried look toward Addison. The poor guy had *so* much on his plate. As if running a country, planning a wedding, and courting his girlfriend wasn't enough, now he had this bothersome trial to contend with.

Vanessa knew this wasn't easy for Addison. Setting up the court date for his fifteen-year-old brother was something he dreaded. As much as Addison had been trying to protect Asher, the country demanded Asher be given no special treatment or excuses due to his famous last name. Asher must now experience the full weight of his consequences. His trial, which would happen in just three days, would determine Asher's entire future. The judge would decide whether or not the Prince was guilty for the terror attacks which ensued on the eve of Addison's Coronation.

Even though Asher had not planned nor wanted the attack, evidence proved he had aided and abetted, and he could potentially be charged as guilty, simply by clicking on the link which opened the door to the nightmare. Asher's assistance enabled the enemy to shut down their security system and flung open the door to the terror attack. Addison and the rest of his family had long since forgiven him, but the rest of the world still held an unmovable grudge.

"I believe our judge will make a just and fair decision, after looking at every aspect of the situation, and examining each detail very thoroughly. Then the people of Tarsurella will have to be at rest with whatever determination is made, whether they like it or not," Addison told the reporter. "Though I do not know what the outcome of this trial will be, it is my hope and prayer that after Asher's fate is determined, the citizens of this nation will finally understand that, unlike false propaganda buzzing around the media claims, we did *not* hide anything from you. I'm not showing favoritism to my brother, or anyone else for that matter. A crime is a crime, and it is up to our trusted justice system to determine whether or not Asher is guilty of accomplice. Because of the complexity of this situation, we didn't disclose details to the Tarsurellian people, not because we wanted to be secretive, but because sometimes we, as a family, appreciate a little bit of privacy." Addison's jaw was taunt, "It is my hope and prayer that after all this mess is over in a few days, the rebellious voices who are spreading rumors and lies will finally come to their senses and realize that our Royal Administration can be trusted. We would *never* do anything intentionally to hurt our nation. And if for some crazy reason you don't believe me, at least believe my father. He has spoken these same things to all of you, and you've trusted him for decades. I strive every day to follow in his footsteps, and as long as I'm in this position, I will see to it that our nation continues to move in that direction."

Chapter Two

Something in the Air

"Vanessa is *such* a natural when it comes to the press," Bridget complimented her from afar. "I know it can be overwhelming, and she's handling this all so well."

"There's nothing easy about marrying into a family like this one." Liam nodded from where they stood beside the snack table, "It's like living in a glass building, where everyone can see inside."

"Yup." Bridget sighed, feeling the occasional weariness of this lifestyle draining on her heart. "Every move is tracked beneath a microscope. Things were so great in Alaska." She turned to Liam with hopeful eyes, "Nobody knew who I was."

"That's because there was nobody there *to* know who you were." Liam laughed, making fun of his home state, "Unless of course you're counting the wild animals, but for the most part, they really seem to mind their own business."

"Yeah, I don't think any of those grizzly bears read *Tarsurella Today*!" Bridget joked.

"So, do you know any of these people?" Liam asked, changing the subject.

Bridget scanned the crowd, wondering if she might spot a familiar face. "Hmm... that's the Ambassador of France, and his wife. Their little girl should be running around here somewhere. Um, there's a man from Parliament, although I can't remember if his name is Mr. Fred, or Mr. Ned..."

"Anyone you can't wait to talk to?"

"Uh, no." Bridget's voice fell flat.

"In that case, I'm going to sneak you out."

"Excuse me?" Bridget was unsure of what he had up his sleeve.

"I hid a cooler in a tree beside the pond." He spoke quietly out the side of his mouth, acting as though he were conducting a top-secret operation. "Inside sources tell me those snacks are way better than these. We have exactly forty-two minutes before anyone will realize you're missing. Now, act casual and follow me."

Bridget couldn't help but giggle. As steady and serious as sweet Liam could be, there were also times he could really ham it up. This was one of those moments. She tried to slip on a straight face and follow his orders.

Liam was careful to avoid the main-traffic areas of the party, for fear of bumping into someone who desired to chat. He led her through the East Garden, then turned onto a path that led to the small pond just several feet away. Now they were out of sight of all party guests.

[22]

"I've gotta hand it to you, Mr. Henderson, you are quite brilliant." Bridget grinned, relishing the fact that they now had a few moments to spend alone together. Even though she got to spend an ample amount of time with her suitor, it was usually with the rest of her rowdy family, or on group dates with Bridget's besties, Kitty and Caitlin. It was a rare treat for them to be alone. Bridget glanced upward at one of the many trees scattered about the garden, spotting a familiar security camera mounted in a branch. Okay, so they weren't *completely* alone. Someone always had a watchful eye on the Princess. But still, this was the next best thing.

Once they reached the pond, Liam unloaded his pre-packed picnic. "Forget all that uppity, handmade pastry stuff. I brought the *real* snacks. Pringles, Oreos, pretzels, and gummy worms."

"Everything you brought the first time we went canoeing on your property."

"No ducks here though." Liam smiled, perfectly remembering the first real conversation he and Bridget shared. Princess Bridget had arrived at their family ranch in Alaska with a battered heart. It was shortly after the terror attack that rocked the Royal Family to their core. Bridget wasn't very kind to Liam, but Liam knew she was hurting. When Liam took Bridget for a canoe ride, the two were forced to spend time together and have a heart-to-heart chat. God used Liam to bring a fresh layer of much-needed healing to her soul. In the weeks and months to follow, God had used all the Henderson family to minister to her broken wings and get her flying once more.

Liam tossed Bridget the bag of gummy worms.

"The only ducks on our property are the ridiculous media-birds." Bridget shook her head, "Always digging for inside information, then quacking their little beaks about things they know nothing about. It's gotta be hard for Vanessa, trying to get used to all this."

"Like you said, she seems to be doing a great job making the adjustment." Liam removed the Pringles lid and popped a flaky chip in his mouth.

"It almost makes me think that if I get married someday, suddenly eloping and traveling to a top-secret location in the middle of the woods would definitely be the way to go."

"*If* you get married?" Liam asked jokingly.

"Hey, nothing's official until I have a ring!" she laughed.

"I know what you mean." Liam chuckled, "But still, I'm surprised to hear you say that. A spur-of-the-moment wedding in the middle of the woods? Really? This is coming from a girl whose been planning her dream wedding since she knew how to walk."

"As much as I *love* lace and lilacs and embroidered cloth napkins, the way Vanessa and Addison are handling everything is reminding me of what truly matters in a relationship. You don't need the perfect dress or a flawless table arrangement to have a beautiful wedding. And honestly, the way the press has been hounding Nessa and Addi, it's making the idea of doing something super-low key sound like heaven."

"It's true that Addison and Vanessa are under a lot of extra stress right now, but I think a huge load of that is coming from Asher's trial. Once that's out of the way, hopefully the media will calm down a little bit and give them some breathing room."

"I hope so too." Bridget nodded, "This is supposed to be the happiest time of their lives! I'd hate for the press to be a kill-joy."

"Freedom of speech is a strange animal." Liam popped another chip into his mouth, "We'd never want it to go away, yet some people sure abuse it."

"I know. It's so disturbing to see how the world is turning into an open forum of mean YouTube comments. The internet has allowed so many terrible people to share their awful opinions. And sadly, people are actually listening to them! I know freedom of speech is an essential human right, but I do wish there was a way to shut down trending bloggers and YouTuber personalities who flap their jaws about nonsense and spew out such ridiculousness. Just look at the social influence Liberty Stone had. After the backstabbing piece Luke wrote about Addison, even our most loyal citizens have grown suspicious of his integrity."

"They say the pen is more powerful than the sword. And it's true. The ability for young people to access so much information coming from so many messed-up sources on the internet has changed everything for this generation. But just because enemy forces are using it for destruction doesn't mean there isn't a way to use it for good. If the enemy can do *that* much damage with his words, just think about how much hope and restoration someone representing the Crown could do." Liam's eyes sparkled, pausing before adding his final sentence. "Someone like you."

"Me?" Bridget laughed, "I *hated* writing in school! You should've seen my English papers. It wasn't pretty."

"Somehow I find that hard to believe." Liam's eyes told Bridget that he believed a different story, "Every word that you've ever written for me has been powerful. Bridget, I think you have a gift for writing."

"And *I* think you're a bit biased." She shook her head. "I told you, English is not my friend."

"Who says you have to be an English guru, in the traditional sense of the word, to be a good blogger?" Liam asked.

"Blogger?!" Bridget's eyes grew wide, "Where is all of this coming from?" She laughed.

"I don't know, just dreaming." He smiled. "Thinking about all the epic ways you're going to change the world."

"You mean all the epic ways *we're* going to change the world," she corrected him.

Liam sat down on a grassy patch beside the pond, and Bridget quickly followed suit. "What do you see for us?" he asked, his voice full of expectation. "If there were no limits. Five years from now. Where do you want to be? If, Lord willing, this courtship leads to marriage, and we have the rest of our lives to live out God's story for us, what does it look like?"

Bridget couldn't stop smiling. She loved when Liam talked about the future. Even though he was very practical, sensible, and steady, he loved to think about the possible coming days, just as much as she did. They have so, *so* much to look forward to.

"I think, we need a log cabin," Bridget revealed. "In Alaska."

"Alaska?" Liam echoed. "Don't you want to stay here in Tarsurella? Where your family and your home is?"

"Of course, I would miss my family. But this isn't truly my home. My home is wherever you are."

"But you hated the winters up there. And what about the spotty Wi-Fi and staticky cell service? You'd be miserable."

"No, I wouldn't," Bridget insisted. "I know how much you adore Alaska. And as long as you're happy, I would be happy too!"

"That's not true." Liam shook his head, "I'm not your source for joy and happiness. I'm bound to disappoint you. Only Jesus can be that for you."

"I know." Bridget nodded, "But you know what I mean. The Bible says to leave and cleave, and if it's the Lord's will for us to be married someday, then I'm willing to leave my old life, pack up, and follow you. Wherever God calls you to be, whether it's here, in Alaska, or in some other country. I'm gonna be right there with you."

"My dad has this plot of land in the back of our property that we've been talking about for years." Liam excitedly turned to Bridget and revealed what was on his mind, "He always said that someday, if I want to buy it from him, he'd give me a deal on the land. We've been talking about me building a house back there. Right now, I can only manage to swing an acre or two, but that's plenty of room for a starter home. The land is already perked, and we'd have clearance to build, it's just a matter of saving up for the raw materials. I know a two-bedroom, three bath isn't a castle, but with your mad interior design skills, I think we could build a log cabin fit for a princess."

"That sounds *incredible*!" Bridget gushed. "But is two bedrooms going to be big enough? I have a *lot* of siblings. And I know they're gonna wanna come visit."

"That's right, we'd better make it four."

"And what about your desire to follow in your dad's footsteps and take in foster children? Is that still something on your heart?" Bridget knew that one of Liam's dreams was to bring hurting young people into his home, to help them find healing and freedom in Christ, just like Rebecca and Donald had done for him. Liam was a foster care child himself and had struggled with a rough and painful past.

[27]

"Absolutely," Liam nodded. "But what about you? Is that something God has placed on your heart as well? I know that ministering to troubled teens will be no small task. I don't want to pursue foster care unless you're one-hundred percent in."

"I can't say that I necessarily grew up with that dream, or that it was a desire I thought very much about before meeting you. But the more I hear you talk about it, the more I find myself being drawn into the idea. Your dreams are becoming my dreams, and I want to see them happen! Like I said, wherever you go, and whatever you do, I'm gonna be right there with you."

Bridget and Liam continued to daydream about the future, thinking of nothing but one another and the glorious days to come. Even the Pringles and gummy worms were soon forgotten as their words tasted sweeter than any old snack. They were blissfully unaware of the late afternoon breeze, or the sweet birds chirping from a nearby tree. They had also forgotten about the security camera, carefully monitoring their every word.

Up in the Security Tower, where watchful eyes observed the scene, nineteen-year-old Hanson Fletcher removed his earbuds and shook his head. He had had *more* than his fill of their nauseating conversation. Between this cheesy new couple and the deliriously happy King with his future Queen, Hanson was sick of all the Hallmark-squeaky-clean romance scenes.

"Alright man, I'm out of here." Hanson stood, stretching his arms toward the ceiling, relived to be done with his shift. "See you tomorrow." He told his partner, George, who would be forced to listen to several more hours of such conversations.

"Oh come on, don't you want to stick around for the next episode of *The Bachelorette?*"

"I'd rather get hit by a truck." Hanson's response was cold.

"Yikes. What's wrong, don't you feel all the *looovvve* floating around The Palace?" George enjoyed razzing Hanson. "Isn't about time for you to spark up your own summertime romance?"

Hanson rolled his eyes and turned for the door. "Later, George."

Hanson leapt down the steps, taking two at a time, *beyond* ready to be done with his workday. As much as he appreciated his steady job and the fact that he had a hefty paycheck coming in each month, day-to-day life in the Security Tower could get pretty drab. He had mastered the game of chess, as well as Speed and Euchre, and there wasn't much else to do in the Tower other than listen to music and chat with his fellow guards.

After enduring such a rocky childhood and dysfunctional home life, the steady pace of a constant routine was good for him and his mother. Hanson knew better than to complain. It appeared as though life was really turning around for them. Yet, despite all the good fortune and much-appreciated blessings that came their way, there was still something deeply unsettled in Hanson's soul. The restless wondering caused his mind to wonder about what things might be like if they were different.

Hanson pushed out the employee exit, and the late afternoon sunshine beat down on his black jacket. He jingled car keys in his pocket. Even though he distanced himself from The Palace, his thoughts remained up in the Tower. Princess Chasity had been mingling in the garden with a dapper, distinguished looking fellow. Hanson had an exclusive, somewhat abnormal, fly-on-the-wall view of everything Chasity did. And from Hanson's perspective, it seemed to him that this British guy, James O'Conner, had been hanging out quite a bit lately. Hanson knew the matter shouldn't concern him; Chasity should be free to chat with whomever she wished. Yet it did. It mattered far more than Hanson would ever admit.

Hanson sent a quick hand to smack a buzzing mosquito behind his ear. His reflexes were not fast enough. The mosquito took a cruel bite and left Hanson with an itch. He shook his head. *Yup, summer is definitely here.*

Hanson unlocked his silver Chevy Impala and turned on the radio. "We're only two months out from the big wedding!" an excited DJ announced. "Can you believe it, Patty? It seems to me like King Addison and his leading lady are flying down the fast track with this relationship! It feels like just yesterday we heard about this random girl from the States, and now we're mentally preparing ourselves for her to be our Queen! What's your take on this, Patty, do you think the couple is ready for this kind of commitment? I mean, how does King Addison know for *sure* this is the girl he wants to spend the rest of his life with and share his Royal title?"

Hanson tossed an irritated look at Scott, the DJ, on his favorite station. He placed an arm on the empty seat beside him and looked over his shoulder, slowly backing out of the tight parking space. "Oh, come on Scott, play some hits!" Hanson told the DJ, even though he couldn't hear him. "Nobody cares about the wedding!"

Hanson knew that wasn't true. *Everybody* cared about the wedding.

"This is obviously a massive decision for our young, inexperienced King. You can't help but wonder if this is more a political move than a true Royal romance going on here. I mean, King Addison has lived a very sheltered life, as all the young Royals have, and the prospect of finding that special person they want to spend the rest of their life with can't be as easy as it is for the rest of us. With all the political pressure and frustrated demands for change coming from fed-up citizens, I myself am quite shocked he's making another massive move this soon in his career. But on the other hand, from what we know about Vanessa, she seems to have some very liberal ideas about democracy, so perhaps they're seeing this union as some kind of peace-treaty to show the rebels that they're being represented by Vanessa's presence in The Palace."

Hanson flicked off the radio. Silence filled the car, and Hanson was alone with his thoughts.

He maneuvered his way out of the employee parking lot, wondering why the nation was consumed with discussing every tiny detail about the Royal Family's lives; forming long-winded opinions about people they've never even met. Even though Hanson hadn't spent much time with the Royal Family personally, he knew them far more than any of these radio DJs or press personalities. He'd heard hours and hours of conversation between the Royal siblings, their father, their staff, and their friends. It was strange knowing so much about this legendary family, and yet, they didn't know a thing about him.

Well, all except one. Princess Chasity.

Hanson sighed, silently chiding himself for thinking about her again. She had a strange way of appearing in his thoughts, abruptly and unannounced, sneaking in like a misty fog. His feelings for her were unpredictable, and memories of their interactions popped into his mind in the most unexpected moments.

Chasity was a one-of-a-kind young woman, Hanson was sure of that. She was beautiful and spirited, yet stubborn, opinioned, and at times, straight-up impossible. Chasity was like a wild thoroughbred. Absolutely enchanting, yet never in a million years would there be a chance at taming her. Hanson couldn't help but wonder what things could've been like if circumstances were different. If Chasity's last name was different, and if they'd met one another in high school or while attending university. Perhaps, in a different lifetime, Chasity's wild heart and Hanson's restless soul would've found one another. In a world where their social status and walks of life were not so vastly different.

Hanson knew better than to think like this, as it did nothing but create a dull, uncomfortable ache in his heart. Caring for Chasity was ridiculous. The Princess's life should be none of his business. Yet, try as he may, Hanson couldn't quite kill the dream. At least, not entirely

Hanson hadn't spoken to the spunky young woman in several months. After escorting Jane Akerly home to the States, there hadn't been a reason to pursue further contact with the Princess. Their interactions evaporated along with the snow. And as spring emerged at The Palace, so did a frequent new face–that of James O'Conner.

Hanson couldn't tell if Chasity was exactly interested in the young man, but they appeared to have a lot in common. Wealthy families, a genuine love for horses, and supposedly some warm, childhood memories. James hadn't pursued anything official, but Hanson knew how fast this family worked. There would be no messing around. If James was truly interested in a relationship with Chasity, it would be revealed soon. And why wouldn't he be? Chasity was an amazing catch. But was this stuffy British chap the right guy for Chasity? Hanson squirmed in the driver's seat. The thought of Chasity being with another guy made his stomach hurt. The sudden burst of jealousy was surprising to Hanson, as he thought he had already gotten over her.

But obviously he hadn't.

"You're gonna have to let it go, man." Hanson sighed, giving himself a quiet pep talk, hoping this would be the final straw. It was time he surrendered his affections and move on. "Chasity isn't just going to wait around in that castle forever. She's got a life to live. And, so do you."

All at once, a shocking thought arrested Hanson's heart. What if *he* could be the right guy for her? What if life was finally working itself out enough to give Hanson the opportunity to make his true feelings known?

Hanson's heartbeat picked up. It was ludicrous. Things could never work out between him and Chasity. At least, that's what he *had* thought. But now, with his father behind bars and the dangerous threats that once cornered him in a place of fear gone, Hanson saw nothing but blue skies for the future.

Hanson reviewed the facts. For starters, he had a secure and steady job. That had to be a plus, right? No dad was about to let his daughter start dating a dude without a job; at least any noble father, that is.

Secondly, Chasity's father already *kind of* approved of him, or else he wouldn't have been hired. Steve knew far more about Hanson than any father in the history of fathers knew about their daughter's potential suitors. And wasn't Princess Bridget dating a security agent as well? If the retired King had no rules against one daughter dating someone who worked for them, why would he for the other?!

Hanson scratched his neck, electrified with these new, exhilarating thoughts.

Everything was perfect! All the roadblocks had been cleared away, and there was nothing but a clear path to Chasity's front door!

All he had to do was buy some flowers, meet with her dad, plan a romantic date—oh, maybe buy some chocolates too, the Princess *loves* chocolate, ask her-

Hanson's phone rang, interrupting the excited flurry of thoughts which danced around his brain. He didn't bother to look at the caller ID. He quickly lifted the phone to his ear, greeting whoever was on the other end with a cheerful, "Hello?"

"H-h-Hanson," a quiet voice stuttered from the other end.

A deep chord of concern struck Hanson's heart. He recognized the voice. "Lilly?"

"I, I need you to come," she managed to choke out through what sounded like tears.

"What's wrong, where are you?!" Hanson couldn't hide the concern in his voice.

"I, I'm on Carlson Road, right by the old dairy farm." Lilly took a huge gasp for air, attempting to compose herself, "Hanson, I can't do this, I'm completely freaked out."

"Lilly, what's going on?" Hanson quickly turned on his blinker, prepared to take the back road to find his old friend.

"I just need you to come!" she cried.

"I'm on my way." Hanson reassured her, "I'll be there as fast as I can. But Lilly, I need to know, are you okay?"

"Yes." She sniffed, "I, I'm okay. But s-someone just tried to kill me."

Chapter Three

Promises Fulfilled

Hanson whipped down Carlson Road, bouncing slightly in his seat as his left front tire hit a pot hole. He was driving much faster than what was wise for a gravel road like this one. Tiny pebbles kicked up from beneath his tires and smacked the side of his car. But Hanson didn't dare slow down. Lilly's words shook him to the core.

Within seconds he spotted her sporty, bright-red convertible off to the side of the road. He pulled up behind her and hurried out. He opened her driver's seat door, and Lilly fell into his arms.

"Hanson!" she cried. Lilly's eyes were red and puffy from the fearful tears. "Oh Hanson, it was awful! I, I thought I was gonna die!"

"Shhh, Lilly, it's okay," Hanson attempted to comfort his friend. "You're okay now." His eyes scanned her car, searching for signs of any damage, or clues as to what might have occurred. "What happened?"

She timidly pulled away from his hug, wiping her eyes with her long sweater sleeve. She took a deep breath before sharing the terrible details. "I went to get fro-yo, then run a few errands, and the whole time I felt like someone was watching me. At first, I thought I was just paranoid, with the house empty and Dad gone."

Hanson frowned and scratched his bug bite. In the Spring, Lilly's father had gone to jail the same time his own dad had. The partners in crime were guilty for the disappearance of a man by the name of Walter Akerly. Hanson wasn't sure if Mr. Chesterfield, Lilly's dad, was *actually* guilty. It was very likely he had gotten innocently roped into one of Mr. Fletcher's schemes, then threatened with forceful ultimatums, spiraling him further into the mess than he had bargained for. Mr. Chesterfield had always been a generally nice guy, and even though Hanson was doubtful he was actually responsible for the crime, they could never be too safe. This spring, Lilly's and Hanson's fathers had been spending a lot of time together, and Hanson still hadn't figured out the extent of their plot. All Hanson knew was that Walter Akerly, the brilliant inventor of The Palace's Royal Security System and its powerful computer code, was a treasure that greedy Mr. Fletcher wanted to get his hands on. Miraculously, Hanson had found Mr. Akerly, held captive in Mr. Fletcher's basement, and was able to arrest the man to whom justice needed to be served. Sadly, he wasn't able to do it before Mr. Akerly disappeared again.

"But no, this stalker was real." Lilly continued, her throat gravelly, "Not just some figment of my imagination. I decided to take the back roads, and every road I turned down, this black SUV kept following me. I speed up, scared they might try something, and they sped up too. I was going like 70, and all of a sudden the driver started playing tag with my rear end, yelling at me to pull over or else they were gonna crash into me. I didn't know what to do, Hanson! The faster I went, the faster they came, until he got right beside me and held a gun out the window. I had to pull over."

"Who was the driver?" Hanson asked frantically.

"I don't know!" Lilly fought back tears, "Whoever it was, they wore a black ski mask. So did the person in the passenger seat. They got out and said I have sixty days left to live. Then they shot my front right tire, got back in the car, and buzzed off."

"Did you catch the license plate?" Hanson asked.

"They didn't have one."

"We need to call the police." He dug his hand into his pocket.

"Hanson, wait!" Lilly stopped him. "You can't! They said…." She took a deep breath, "They said if I get the authorities involved, they'll come back and kill me sooner."

A defeated look washed across Hanson's face. That threat sounded all too familiar. Hanson shook his head. No, it couldn't be. Hanson's dad was locked up. There was no way he'd be messing with them like this. Then again, Mr. Fletcher had promised his son that if he didn't do his evil bidding, Lilly was going to pay for it.

Just then, Hanson's pocket vibrated. He glanced at his phone, shocked to see the violent text message.

REVENGE is due to those who don't cooperate. You had your warning. You made your choice. Now, the promises will be fulfilled.

Hanson's heart stopped. His mind raced to his mother.

"Lilly, get in my car!" he quickly told her.

"Hanson wha—"

"Don't ask, just do it! We'll tow your convertible later!" He grabbed her hand and pulled her toward the car, fearful of what might come. He needed to get to his house.

Lilly scrambled into the passenger seat. "You're freaking me out!"

Hanson revved up the engine and whipped down the road.

"What's going on?"

"I don't know yet," Hanson huffed, "but we have to hurry. I don't think you're this guy's only target."

Hanson's tires squealed as they turned off the main road and into the familiar driveway. He dashed out of the car and burst through the black door. He didn't dare pause and admire the recent face-lift of his mother's comfortable, two-story town home. Just last weekend he had added two stylish front porch lights, which posed as faux lanterns, and a small iron rail to the cement porch. The worn-out home that Hanson and his mother had lived in for years was now looking quite spiffy, thanks to the recent spike in Hanson's paycheck.

He crashed into the entryway, not bothering to wipe his shoes on the 'Welcome' mat or toss his car keys into the open-mouthed cat jar where he usually stored them.

"Mom? Mom!" Hanson frantically called.

He quickly searched the kitchen, living room and pantry, all the while his heart kicking within his chest, stomach churning with dread. "Mom! Mom!"

He bounded up the stairs, just when Lilly entered the house. Lilly watched with wide, fearful eyes as Hanson disappeared to search the second floor.

"Mrs. Fletcher?" Lilly called in a strained tone. "Mrs. Fletcher, are you here?"

Hanson thundered back down the stairs, his eyes wild with concern.

"Hanson, don't jump to such terrible conclusions!" Lilly attempted to comfort him, "I'm sure she's okay. Maybe she just went out for an errand or something?"

"She doesn't have a car," Hanson told her all in one breath. "It's in the shop, and I *know* she didn't have plans to go anywhere today!"

Lilly frowned as Hanson hurried back into the kitchen. She quickly followed him, unsure of what else to say.

Hanson lifted the home phone from the counter up to his ear. "That's it, I'm calling for backup." The numbing feeling of panic and loss was all too familiar. Once again, he felt like the helpless little boy he once was. His stomach turned as his blood boiled with rage, sick to think of his father pulling the trigger on his mother. Vengeful thoughts burned from within. *If something happened to her, I will destroy him!*

Just then, the screen door snapped, cracking through the house like a whip. Hanson spun around, short of breath as his mother's familiar frame filled the doorway. He dropped the phone and rushed to give her a hug.

The sudden embrace nearly caused Mrs. Fletcher to lose her grip on a fresh basket of green beans plucked from the garden.

"Hanson!" Mrs. Fletcher chuckled, her voice light with surprise. "Well, my goodness, it's good to see you too!"

"Mom," he pulled away, his dark eyes holding all seriousness, "we need to leave."

"Whatever are you talking about?" She slowly took her floppy garden hat off and set her beans on the counter, fanning herself slightly, relieved to be back in the cool air conditioning

"Mom, I need you to trust me. Grab the necessities and let's jet. We need to go. Like, now."

"Hanson, slow down son, you're making no sense." She unwound her bun, and short black curls fell down her neck, "Would you mind pausing for long enough to take a breath and explain what's going on here?"

Hanson stared at the beautiful woman from whom he inherited his dark eyes, dark hair, and tanned completion. He had always admired her classic air of simplistic beauty. But far more than her stunning external features, she modeled a rock-solid strength which Hanson knew was the only thing that had gotten them this far. She was a fighter. She had raised her son as a single mom despite the hardships, challenges, and many, *many* unfair circumstances they encountered. She deserved better. He couldn't bear the thought of anything happening to her.

"I'll explain in the car, right now we just need to hurry." Hanson didn't have time for details.

"Oh no." Mrs. Fletchers voice dropped with concern, "Hanson. Please tell me it isn't—you haven't had a run-in with your dad, have you?"

Chapter Four

Sons of Liberty

"Vanessa, this place is looking *amazing*," Princess Hope told her soon-to-be sister-in-law. The girls continued walking as automatic glass doors parted for their grand entry. Deborah, Jillian, Millie, and several security guards followed.

"Wow, this building is huge!" Millie expressed Hope's exact thoughts. "You did a great job making this, Vanessa!"

Vanessa happily clutched a clipboard to her chest, delighted to be standing on the newly-installed and freshly-vacuumed carpet. Construction was nearly finished, and now the interior elements were being added. She looked upward, her eyes scaling the tall ceilings of Tarsurella's brand new, homeless shelter. The lobby was large and welcoming, with daylight streaming in from three rows of windows, each divided by white beams. The windows continued climbing up to the ceiling, bringing in as much natural light as possible. Vanessa adored the design. The unique architecture allowed everyone who would be served in this facility to feel the warm sunshine kissing their skin. Behind the front desk stood a tall, brick fireplace, which would be a welcome friend in the wintertime.

"Watching this develop from an idea into an actual building has just been incredible," Vanessa told the group, feeling just as giddy as she had the day before.

"Well, give us the official tour!" Hope smiled.

Vanessa was pleased to do so. They followed Vanessa down the long, slightly-curved hallway which was filled with windows and more natural sunlight. With only a few steps, they were standing in the cafeteria. But Hope had never seen a cafeteria quite like this. Eleven, large, beautifully-handcrafted cedar tables filled the ginormous space, with a full wall of French doors on the left, making it feel oh so bright and cheery. The doors opened to a patio, where even more hungry mouths could be fed in the summertime. On the right, a long, aqua-blue bar would be used to serve the neediest in Tarsurella.

"Wow, it looks good enough to eat in here!" Millie gave Vanessa an eager thumbs-up. "Now all we need is some of Clark's cake!"

"I'm so glad you guys came," Vanessa told Jillian, Millie, and Willie. "I wanted to create care packages for everyone who visits on opening day, and I've set out a table where we can decorate cards and write little notes for them! They're going to *love* getting special messages from the Royals! Think you can help me with that?"

"Yeah!" Willie chimed in, "I'm great at making cards!"

"Alright!" Vanessa pumped an excited fist into the air, "To the card-making table!"

Hope smiled as she watched the children follow Vanessa. "Look at her go." Hope laughed, grinning at Deborah. "She's going to make an amazing mom someday."

"Nobody can deny, they will certainly have the cutest kids in the Kingdom," Deborah chuckled before following the rest of the group.

Hope couldn't agree more. Instead of heading to the craft table, Hope wanted to explore further. "Hey, I'm gonna take a look around, okay?"

"Sure!" Vanessa called over her shoulder from where she sorted through a pile of stickers for the kids. "Just be careful of the bunk house area 'cause I think they're still doing construction."

"Gotcha." Hope winked, understanding that the Shelter was still very much a work in progress. The buzz of electric saws and mechanical nail-guns whirled in the background. Hope gingerly trekked down the hall, popping her head into a small room void of windows, but bright with a fresh splash of yellow on the walls. The smell of fresh paint filled her lungs. Hope knew the compact area would serve as a computer room where struggling adults could attend classes to earn their GED. Hope smiled, pleased at how Vanessa wasn't just bringing a temporary fix to Tarsurella's homeless problem. She was determined to bring innovative, lasting answers that would assist in solving the core of Tarsurella's homeless crisis, rather than just cover it up with a Band-Aid. Vanessa's dream of providing classes, resources and opportunities to help those struggling on the streets was finally coming to pass, and Hope was thrilled to be part of a project like this.

She continued walking, entering her favorite room of them all–the library. Hope sighed happily, knowing that soon the empty walls would be covered with books. She couldn't wait for the first shipment to come in, for the bookshelves to be built, and for Vanessa and her to start stacking the shelves! Hope's throat constricted, as she thought of how much her mom would've *adored* Vanessa. A twinge of pain shot through Hope's heart, saddened by the fact that their mom wouldn't be there to see the wedding of her firstborn son.

Hope left the library, shaking off the unexpected sadness that had abruptly pounced upon her. Many years had passed since her mother's tragic death during childbirth, yet Hope still missed her dearly.

She continued her self-led tour back to the kitchen filled with sparkling stainless-steel appliances. A handful of volunteers were unloading a food truck. She paused, happy to see the back of his head. Luke Myers.

The energetic young man quickly maneuvered bags of dinner rolls onto the counter, working at the end of a well-oiled assembly line. Luke had been volunteering in this capacity his entire life, and he was incredibly efficient when it came to moving food around.

Hope hopped into the line, grabbing the rolls he placed on the counter, and slid them into the bread box.

"Oh hey!" Luke grinned, sounding surprised to see her working alongside him. "I didn't know you'd be down here today."

"These days you can find Vanessa and me in either of two places," Hope responded in a chipper tone, delighted by his refreshingly-boyish grin. "Wedding planning or working on the Shelter. I can't believe it's opening in just a few weeks! There's still so much to be done.

"Yeah, I wish I had more time to help out. But this is the restaurant's busy season. Dad has me working like a dog."

"Yup, The Palace's tourists are just as thick as the mosquitos." She noticed his slightly tanned skin, wondering if he had been spending much time outside. Apparently so. He wasn't nearly as pale as when they had met last winter. Because of the warmer temps, he had also ditched his signature blue beanie. As goofy as it was for her to think so, Hope kind of missed it. "What else have you been up to? Besides working?"

"Uh... you know," Luke hesitated with his response, "just... stuff."

"Stuff?" Hope echoed, adding a laugh. "That's descriptive. I would expect a little something more, coming from a writer."

"What, you want me to give you a detailed outline of my day, starting from the moment I wake up to the second my head hits the pillow at night?" Luke tossed her a playful glance.

"No," Hope continued stacking each new bag of rolls that came her way, "I just want to know why you've been blowing me off so much lately."

Luke was a strange puzzle that Hope couldn't quite seem to make sense of. A few months ago, he had agreed to meet with her on a regular basis and share his progressive ideas about democracy, their nation's politics, and the things he believed to be wrong with Tarsurella. Luke had been causing quite a stir, being a huge megaphone for a movement of young people who believed Tarsurella needed to see change. Luke's fiery writings had done much damage to the Royal Family's reputation. But even though his political beliefs didn't make much sense to her, Hope wanted to know more about them. As much as her family didn't approve of the rouge horse, she knew Luke wasn't stupid. Even though she didn't agree with many of the bold statements in his writing, she couldn't ignore the fact that he was both brilliant and talented. Strangely, it caused Hope to wonder if there *was* something wrong with the way her brother ran their country. Her desire to humbly learn was harmless, right?

But Luke hadn't been making things easy for her. After just two meetings, he dished out a handful of reasons why he needed to cancel.

She hadn't seen him around much since. And now, Hope was suspicious. What *was* he spending all his time doing?

"I'm not blowing you off." Luke's cheeks flushed with a touch of red, "I told you, I'm busy."

"So what about tonight? You were *just* starting to get into why you believe it's wrong for one person to have all the power, and how our monarchy is taking advantage of the middle class—or something along those lines? I wouldn't know, because you never finished explaining it to me."

"I can't tonight." Luke handed Hope the last bag of rolls, "I've got a meeting."

"A meeting?" Hope's left eyebrow arched. "For what?"

"*Wow,* you're nosey." Luke shook his head. "I just have a thing with some friends, okay?"

Hope threw up her hands in mock surrender, "Fine. I get it. None of my business. Have a great summer." She turned to leave.

"Hope," Luke groaned quietly, "wait!"

Hope stopped, an impatient hand on her hip.

"Don't take this the wrong way. I enjoy hanging out with you. It's just… how can I say this? My friends are *not* exactly members of your fan club."

"I get it. Hanging out with me is like walking behind enemy lines. From your friends' perspective, talking to me is like mingling with the bad guy." Hope folded her harms, "And if that's how you feel about this, then whatever. Just as long as you don't go around complaining that the Crown won't listen to you, when you've got someone right here who gives you a direct line to the King."

Luke stuffed his hands in his pockets, leaned his head back and sighed. He looked back at Hope and took a step closer, lowering his voice. "Talking with you about this stuff is a huge risk." His eyes narrowed, "But if you really want to know what's going on, come to this address tonight at seven."

He slipped a business card into her hand. Hope glanced down and flipped it over. The words read, *Sons of Liberty, Media Movement.*

"Liberty?" Hope echoed. "Luke, I thought your dad made you shut down that blog and—"

"Shhh!" Luke hushed her. "You can't tell anyone about this. This is a secret. I'm trusting you. Tell a soul and we're toast."

"I don't know if I can come." Hope crunched on her bottom lip and tapped the card in her hand. "It's so hard for me to get out of The Palace and—"

"Fine, then don't!" Luke abruptly snatched the card out of her palm. "I never should've told you in the first place."

"Luke, why does everything have to be so dramatic with you?!" Hope snapped back, her patience wearing thin. "I didn't say I wasn't coming! I said I *might* not be able to. Gosh, what is with your moodiness? You're so intense about everything; you think it has to be all or nothing! But why can't there be some middle ground here? Why can't I just think about this and decide whether or not it's something I want to do? You're so melodramatic."

"Hope. I'm sorry." Luke brushed a frustrated hand through his hair as he rocked on his heel. "But if you understood the delicacy of this situation, you'd get why I'm a little bit worked up here!"

"You're right, I don't understand it at all." Hope shook her head.

"Then, whatever," Luke grabbed an empty box before heading to the food truck, "just come to the meeting."

He vacated the kitchen and just like that their conversation was over. She let out a frustrated huff. Why did she even bother to communicate with Luke? He was such an unpredictable firecracker! Hope decided to head back to the craft table, choosing to put Luke and this whole ridiculous meeting out of her mind. Talking with him was such a waste of time and energy. *Besides*, she added bitterly, chiding herself for ever secretly thinking anything could work between them, *he's not even that cute without his stupid beanie.*

Hope joined the crew just in time to catch Millie going crazy with glitter, while Willie drew one-eyed octopuses on each card.

"Whoa, Millie, that's enough glitter!" Vanessa jumped in, nervous that the tiny, gold sparkles would eternally imbed themselves into the wood floors.

"You can never have too much glitter!" Millie announced, proud of her glammed-up masterpiece.

"Millie, you're getting it everywhere!" Jillian scolded her. "*Except* on the card where you're supposed to!"

"Here honey, let's dump some onto this extra sheet of paper." Quick-thinking Deborah sprang into action. "My little Pearl has the same love for glitter as you do," Deborah laughed. "We've had to learn some tricks for getting it out of the carpet."

"I thought you said Pearl was older?" Jillian asked, not being able to match the image of 'little Pearl' with what she had heard previously about the girl. "Isn't she like a freshman in high school?"

"Well, yes." Deborah shrugged, "But she still has an unhealthy obsession with glitter. She's one-hundred-percent girl, that's for sure!"

Just then, Steve entered the cafeteria with three familiar security guards. Hope looked up, surprised to see her dad. "Dad!" Millie squealed excitedly, "What are you doing here?"

"I've been hearing so many wonderful things about this project, I thought I'd come down and take a look at it myself! And wow, Vanessa. The things I've heard don't even describe the half of it! It looks spectacular!"

"Aw, thank you." Vanessa blushed, "A lot of amazing people poured their hearts into this project. I'm so humbled to work with such a talented and motived team."

"*We* are the blessed ones to have you leading the charge," Steve smiled. "Goodness, Addison sure made the right decision in hiring you as head of the Homeless Committee. But, he made an even better decision in asking you to join the family!" Steve winked.

"Daddy, look at my glitter card!" Millie proudly held the card beside her face, "Do you think the homeless families will like it?"

"And look at my octopus!" Willie added, grinning through a freshly-lost baby tooth in the bottom row.

"They'll love it." Steve kissed Millie on the top of her head, then playfully tasseled Willie's red locks. "Well, are you all ready to head home? It's such a beautiful summer day, I'm going to throw some burgers on the grill and we can have a good ol' BBQ."

"Yay!" Millie cheered, "I love when we grill outside!"

"How would you like to join us this evening, Deborah?" Steve turned to their faithful staff member. "It's nearing the dinner hour. Perhaps you'd like to stay and spend some time with the family? You could even bring Pearl if you like."

Hope glared at her father. Why was he inviting Deborah to their family dinner? Sure, they all adored Deborah, but they had never hung out after business hours. It just wasn't proper for staff to mingle at Royal Family events. Then again, over the past few months, things had been changing. Clark, their Head Chef, occasionally conversed with Steve, and even attended Jillian's birthday party. It appeared as though the social barriers were being slowly torn down, and everyone was coming together as equals. Hope loved it. But still, it was a bit odd to see her dad offering such an open-armed invitation to Deborah.

"Oh, I would hate to inconvenience you," Deborah quickly responded. "And I wouldn't want to barge in on your personal family time."

"Nonsense," Steve waved his hand through the air as if he was swatting a fly, "it would be a pleasure for you to join us."

"Well, I suppose I would enjoy that!" Deborah nodded humbly. "Thank you, Your Majesty, it is an honor."

Hope thought she detected a hint of color in Deborah's cheeks. Was she feeling flushed? Was she truly *that* touched by Steve's invitation?

Her dad was grinning as well, ear to ear, a jolly happiness and ray of light shining from his eyes. Hope did a double-take. She hadn't seen her dad looking that electrified in a long time. Not since... not since her mother was alive.

Chapter Five

London Love

"Your Majesty, Prince Asher."

Addison looked up from his pile of paperwork. His dark-haired, long-limbed fifteen-year-old brother stood in the doorway of his office. Asher sported a pair of swimming shorts, a navy-blue tank top, and a tropical beach towel draped over his shoulder. Addison smiled at his younger brother, feeling as though he had gotten even taller since yesterday. "I see you dressed up for our meeting."

"I was just headed to the pool." Asher's bare feet entered the office, and one of King Addison's many assistants left the room and shut the door behind him. Addison had asked for a private audience with his brother.

Asher walked over to the globe on Addison's monstrous desk and spun it with his finger. "Am I in trouble?"

"I've been putting this off for as long as I could, but I think we're just gonna have to bite the bullet and talk about this." Addison sighed, leaning back in his black swirly chair. "The trial is in three days."

Asher's auburn eyes met Addison's. Asher's jaw tightened. He knew this was coming.

"Our team has hired one of the best lawyers they could find. I want you to meet with him tomorrow and go over some things. If you tell him the entire story, he'll be able to pick out important information and use that in your defense. I know it's not easy to talk about. But the judge is going to be asking you a lot of hard questions, and Daniel Lee, your lawyer, recommends that we fashion your answers to be presented in the best possible light."

"So, you want me to lie?" Asher asked with an uplifted brow, shocked that his brother would suggest such a thing.

"No, of course not!" Addison shook his head, "Just... I don't know, Mr. Lee can explain it better than I can. It's just.... we just want to be as careful as possible about what you say."

"Addison, I'm not going to twist the truth. And I'm not going to hide behind any false innocent act either. If I'm guilty, then I'm guilty."

"But you don't *have* to be guilty." Addison insisted, "If you just listen to Mr. Lee's tips, we can figure out a way to work the odds in our favor. He thinks you can be proven innocent."

"But I'm not innocent!" Asher barked at his brother, his guilty conscience reeling. "You want to talk about innocent? *Innocent* people were killed because of me! I'm not just gonna sit in court and pretend I don't know what I did! If they send me to jail, then I'll just have to deal with the punishment—God knows I deserve it."

"Asher, don't talk like that." Addison's voice was soft, "You've gotta let go of your guilt. You did *not* know that you were opening the door to warlord terrorists. You had no way of knowing the events that were going to unfold. We've all forgiven you, Ash! God has forgiven you. Isn't it about time you forgave yourself?"

"I… I know God can extend grace." Asher's voice cracked a little as he spoke, spinning the globe once more. "But I also know that sometimes you have to pay a price for your actions. And all I'm saying is… I'm not going to hate you if this fancy lawyer guy doesn't work, and the judge doesn't see things the way you do. I mean, the country would be a whole lot happier with me locked-up anyway."

"That is *not* true."

"It is too, and you know it! I know what's happening out there, Addison! I'm not a little kid anymore, so quit treating me like one! This country is fed up with the way you're trying to cover for me, and they're not going to be satisfied until I spend time in juvie!"

"Their opinions do *not* matter," Addison spoke through clenched teeth, hating the fact that this conversation was even happening. *For goodness sake, he's only fifteen-years-old! He should be outside playing basketball and doing flips off the diving board, not worrying about whether his sophomore year is going to be spent in jail.* Addison's eyes burned with determination. "We're not gonna let you go to jail, Ash. I won't let it happen."

"You need to stop protecting me." Asher shook his head, "If you underhandedly rig this trial to work out in my favor, then everything they're saying about you is gonna be true! It'll just be another reason for the rebels to become all-the-more outraged. Our people don't trust you right now. So, quit trying to put my problems before all of theirs."

[53]

"Family always comes first," Addison firmly insisted. "No matter what."

"But maybe it shouldn't." Asher stood up and readjusted his pool towel. "At least, maybe not this time."

Meanwhile, in the United States...

Jane Akerly carried a cardboard box filled with books into her new bedroom. The heavy box tumbled out of her arms and onto the empty mattress. She scowled at the wooden walls surrounding her. It wasn't so much that she hated the room itself. But she severely detested the reason *why* she was there.

"Alright, all we need is a few buckets of paint, some sheets for the bed, a quilt from downstairs, and we'll have this place all spiffed up in no time!" a chipper voice chimed in from behind. It belonged to Cassidy Tyson, the aunt of her close friend Charlie. She sounded disgustingly optimistic. But Jane knew this couldn't be her real home. It never would.

"How. Can. You. Have. This. Many. Books!" An airy voice was heard huffing and puffing its way up the stairs. Jane knew the voice belonged to her scrawny little friend, Charlie. Sure enough, floppy-haired Charlie popped around the corner and his wobbly arms dropped the box of books on the floor. "I know all about the enchanting high you get from reading so much fiction, but the next time you want to haul so many novels up two flights of stairs, get a pulley up to the window or something! Aye, that's actually not such a bad idea... it could be like a dumb-waiter, used to transport heavy objects to the attic." Charlie placed a thoughtful hand on his chin and examined the wall closest to him, "Hey, Aunt Cassidy, how do you feel about me cutting a hole in the wall?"

[54]

"Absolutely not!" Aunt Cassidy wagged a finger in his direction, "The only holes I'm allowing in this room are the tiny nail pegs for Jane's posters!" She smiled at Jane, "I want you to make this room comfortable, honey. I know it isn't home, but we might as well make it as cozy as possible."

Jane wished she could smile back, but she could not. "That won't be necessary." She crossed the room to pick up the books Charlie had spilled all over the floor, "I'll only be here for a little while."

"Oh Chickadee," Aunt Cassidy sighed, wishing there was some way to make things easier for the poor girl, "I know how much you want your father to return. But he's been missing for months. Everyone involved with this case has been counseling us to move forward and accept the fact that perhaps he—"

"No!" Jane abruptly slammed one of her books on top of the other. "He is *not* dead. Nothing has suggested that he is, and there's still a whole team in Tarsurella looking for him! Unless they have some kind of proof, I refuse to believe it. I'm not going to lose hope. I'm not." Her bottom lip quivered. Jane took a deep breath, attempting to keep herself from losing it.

"I know, honey." Aunt Cassidy nodded, fighting back tears of her own. She lowered her voice in humility. "I know this is hard. All I'm suggesting is, sometimes we have to adjust to change, no matter how hard it may be. And I want this room to be as comfortable as possible for you, while you *are* here."

Jane continued stacking her books, refusing to look up. She knew what Aunt Cassidy really meant. She'd overheard the conversation with her social worker. She knew how dire the situation was. Everyone wanted to paint Jane's blue skies of hope with a depressing shade of gray. They wanted her to believe that her father might be dead. They wanted her to get a grip on reality and begin the grieving process, in hopes that she would heal and move forward with life. But Jane knew that would be impossible. She couldn't accept it. Her dad wasn't gone. She wasn't an orphan. She wasn't going to enter the wretched foster care system and be bounced around from house to house, like an unwanted rag-doll in the giveaway box at Goodwill. She stood her ground for months, refusing to leave the house. Eventually, her social worker came with a complementary police officer, just to get the point across, and sent her to live with Charlie and his Aunt.

Jane had to believe he would return home. Surely, in just a few days, she would get the call that Dad was on his way, and someone would shake her awake from this unthinkable nightmare. She would dash through the airport and catapult herself into his arms. The hug would feel like a peppermint ice-cream cone on a hot afternoon, everything her heart craved and silently begged for. They would climb into his goofy little car and bounce home, laughing and chatting all the while, as Dad excitedly yacked about his latest idea for a breakthrough invention. Jane would tell him about the *Young Novelist Writers Contest* she entered and explain her story in a ridiculous amount of vivid detail. He would smile and nod and tell her she's sure to win. They would turn the latch of their locked door and burst out laughing, as Dad stubbed his toe on one of the many random items he had left carelessly lying around. Jane would pour them each a bowl of Fruity Pebbles, and they would sit on the couch, competing with one another to see who could slurp their milk the loudest, boasting loudly about the delightful fact that they don't need to use their manners.

Jane knew all of this to be so. As ludicrous as it sounded, it would happen. It absolutely *had* to happen. She had no intention of things working out any other way. She wouldn't adjust to a life without him. She wouldn't accept the haunting suggestion everyone kept making. She knew that her fragile heart wasn't capable of enduring such heartbreak. And so, she wasn't going to think about it.

"Well, is there anything you'd like me to do, to help you decorate?" Aunt Cassidy asked eagerly.

"No, thank you." Jane slowly stood up and maneuvered her armful of books onto the bed. "I think I'd just like to be alone for a while."

"Oh. Of course, Chickadee." Aunt Cassidy's voice was tight with sadness, "Come on Charlie, why don't you help me with lunch? You're a fabulous pancake-maker."

"The secret to great pancakes is really just knowing the right altitude and angle at which to flip them," Charlie explained as the two headed for the door. "You see, it's kind of like an eatable science experiment, except your elements are each ingredient and—"

Aunt Cassidy closed the door behind them, giving Jane some privacy.

Jane sighed and stared helplessly at her pile of books. They were not going to assist her right now. Normally they were grand tools for forgetting her worries and slipping away into a fantasy world, but she knew that today, reading just wasn't going to cut it. She uneasily scanned the room, detesting it all the more. She made her way to the window, sitting on the ledge, wondering why Aunt Cassidy always called her a chickadee. She wished she was a chickadee. Or any kind of winged bird. She would rise in one breath and break through the glass, soaring far, far away from Ohio.

With her wings, she would ride on the flowing wind currents and soar to Europe. There, she would find herself in a different world entirely. She would land in London, just beside the Big Ben clock tower, and people-watch for a while. She would absorb every moment among the flow of bustling traffic, entertaining herself with deep, probing thoughts, wondering where each character was going and what might happen when they each returned home to their little abodes. Once she grew tired of watching the masses pass her by, she would go exploring, meandering the sparkling streets fresh with rain puddles, searching for an adorable café serving tea and scones. But it wouldn't take her long to find it, because the entrance is already vivid in her imagination. She would know that green door anywhere. She had been there countless times. The café is the backdrop for her short story, *London Love*.

The fictional story had been stirring in her heart for months, long before her dad disappeared. Her imaginary London adventures had become so vivid. She could taste the rain, smell the scones, and see the face of the dashing young fella' who greeted her in the café. For months, this story pounded on the doorposts of her brain, begging to be written. But writer's block had held an iron grip on her imagination. Every time she sat down to type, the words wouldn't come. After her dad disappeared, she went to Tarsurella, met the Royal Family, and returned home. Even then, the story remained within her. *London Love* was like her shadow. There was no way she could escape the characters flooding her mind. And one day, they finally broke loose.

Jane quickly rose from the window seat and opened a box of belongings. She dug beneath a pile of sweaters until her fingers gripped her leather journal. She hugged the precious book to her chest, returned to her seat, and opened to a monumental entry.

It finally happened. Her hazel eyes scanned the familiar writing. *The characters who have been following me around for years, lurking in the shadows, dancing in my mind, demanded they see the light of day. I've never written so fast and furiously! In just two days, the mini-masterpiece was complete. The words so effortlessly flowed, bringing the perfect*

[58]

ending, just in time for the Young Novelist Writers Contest! Though I might've wished for more time to edit and polish the piece, with trembling fingers I emailed the manuscript for the contest and crossed my heart with an uncanny amount of hope. I haven't the faintest idea if my material is good enough to hold a candle in such a prestigious contest. I'm competing with thousands of authors all across the United States. BUT, if by some delightful spark of a miracle, I'm chosen as a finalist, I would win an all-expenses-paid trip to London! There, I would be given the once-in-a-lifetime opportunity to compete with teens from all over the world for the chance at a REAL publishing deal! The possibilities are far too delightful to process. I want to squeal just thinking about it! Going to London would be an absolute dream come true. And a publishing deal with an international publishing house? It makes me dizzy just thinking about it!

Jane looked up from the journal in her lap, nervously glancing toward the mailbox. The finalists of the competition would be contacted this week. The website stated that winners would receive an official document in the mail, congratulating them on their placement, and giving further details. Jane lifted an excited hand up to her mouth, anxiously biting a nail. She had already checked the mailbox three times today. She knew her chances of winning were nearly impossible, but she couldn't stop herself from dreaming.

Jane found herself growing happier with each fantastical thought, allowing her mind to meditate on what might happen if she won. Her daydreams quickly gained speed, whisking her mind up, up and away, far from her stuffy old bedroom, transporting her into a blissfully perfect world, across the sea.

"My personal favorite is the lilac and chiffon gown." Bridget's voice sparkled with excitement, "The lilac has such a whimsical, fairytale feel, which could be mind-blowingly beautiful for your happily ever after. I adore everything about the cocktail length and sweetheart neckline."

"But what if it's breezy?" Hope asked. "The chiffon looks so loose and flowy, I'd be freaked out that my skirt might fly up during the reception! What about the longer gowns? They're so elegant and sophisticated. They definitely feel more wedding-ish to me." Hope quickly flipped through one of many catalogues piled before them, trying to find an example of what she was envisioning. "Like this! The satin, A-line with the draped bodice. It's just so feminine. And what if you did like a light, aqua blue?"

Vanessa finished sipping on her lemonade and leaned over to examine the picture. She opened her mouth to speak, but Chasity beat her to it.

"The blue is pretty, but what if you did more of a mint green? You could do a pastel theme!"

"Yes, and then the cocktail-length dresses would be perfect!" Bridget chimed in, not yet ready to give up her opinion.

"But mint would be just as pretty in a full-length gown, if not more." Hope added.

"Ohhh, have you looked at these?" Chasity pointed to a new discovery in her catalogue, "It's overlaid with this flowery, patterned lace!"

Hope wrinkled her nose, "That's still too modern. Your gown is a bit more traditional, isn't it, Vanessa? Maybe another reason to go with the full-length gowns."

Vanessa's eyes dashed back and forth between the girls, attempting to keep up with their spirted comments and dozens of suggestions.

"The real question is, what's going to look best with our shoes?" Jillian perked up, wanting to be part of the conversation too. She relished any amount of time she got to spend with her older sisters. Spending time on the patio looking at bridesmaid's dress ideas with the girls was definitely something she wanted to take full advantage of. "Just look at these stilettos with gold rhinestones! I am completely fangirling right now! Daddy doesn't let me wear heels unless it's a special occasion. Vanessa, please choose these so that I can have a pair!"

Vanessa laughed. "Oh goodness. I have to pick out *shoes* too?" She shook her head, feeling overwhelmed by her ever-increasing wedding check list, "Maybe we should just go barefoot. That's *much* simpler."

"Speaking of heels, I hear Deborah." Hope tossed a smile over her shoulder as Deborah clicked across the patio.

"Good afternoon, ladies." She greeted them with a formal introduction, then steered the conversation in a more casual direction, "Oh, what kind of fun are we up to today? More dress shopping?"

"Bridesmaids' dresses." Vanessa sighed, wishing her excitement was even half as much as those around her, "But at this point, I'm considering just having them each wear whatever they like. Even if it's sweatpants."

"I know the process can be a little bit stressful, but if I may offer you a small piece of advice, I'll pass on to you what my mother told me." Deborah smiled, "Delegate, delegate, delegate! The less you have on your mind, the better off you'll be."

"That's really good advice." Vanessa smiled, then reached for Bridget's hand. "I seriously don't know what I'd do without Bridget here. She's been amazing. And much more fun to work with than our official wedding planner."

"We all want to help in whatever ways we can," Hope offered. "But it's true that Bridget definitely has a knack for these kinds of things. Planning flower arrangements and coordinating color schemes was instilled in her from birth. She gets it from our mom." Hope looked back at the page, "On second thought, maybe you should go with Bridget's suggestion for the dresses. I trust her. I probably don't have a clue what I'm talking about."

"Me neither! Up until last year I still thought I wanted to get married on horseback." Chasity laughed.

"I still have an uncanny talent when it comes to picking out the right shoes," Jillian winked.

"I'll let you girls return to your fun in just a moment, but first I have a message for Miss Vanessa." Deborah turned to the young woman who would soon become their Queen, "The Royal Social and Public Relations Committee has requested you respond to the invitation to attend Tarsurella's grand, annual Belington Derby on Saturday. Shall I respond with your RSVP?"

"A horse race?" Vanessa questioned. "On Saturday? Geesh, I dunno. There are still so many last-minute things to do to prepare for the Shelter's opening, and then with wedding planning, and my parents being here, and still trying to squeeze in time to see Addison... that really doesn't seem like good timing."

"The *Belington Derby* is amazing!" Chasity perked up. "Our family goes every year."

"And by amazing, she means it's another stuffy, high-class social event, with all the most important so-and-sos from Tarsurella wearing fancy hats and gossiping about everything under the sun." Bridget rolled her eyes, "Trust me, Vanessa, you can skip it."

"Bridget!" Chasity argued, "The *Belington Derby* is run by the finest and fastest thoroughbreds in Tarsurella! If the only thing you notice at the race is everyone's fluffy hats and sparkling champagne glasses, you're totally missing the point!" Chasity turned back to Vanessa, "Don't listen to her. It's actually really exciting. You've never seen horses like these before. Watching them thunder around the track, as their chestnut coats burn with glory from the sun, striving toward the winner's circle... it's so thrilling. Last year, *Reckless Road Rage* was the unsuspecting underdog who completely blew everyone away!"

"Is Addison going?" Vanessa asked.

"Sadly, no," Deborah reported. "He has a full schedule of meetings that day. But it would be greatly frowned upon if you don't attend."

"Deborah's right," Hope sighed. "As petty and drab as the racing world can be, it would look really bad if you didn't attend. *The Belington* is pretty much *the* event of the year. It would be expected of the Queen-to-be to show up."

"Tell you what, as much as I'm *not* looking forward to it," Bridget told Vanessa, "I'll go with you. That way you don't have to suffer through it alone."

"Yes!" Hope grinned. "I mean, we can all go. We can hate it together. Sisters are really good for that kind of thing."

"Aw, thanks you guys." Vanessa smiled before turning to Chasity, "And I'm sure it's just as fun as you've described. I'll try my best to enjoy it." Lastly, she turned to Deborah, "Yep, yep, sign me up! Although, make sure I'm not cross-scheduled for something else that day. As much as I'd like to, I still haven't figured out how to be in two places at once."

"Wonderful! I'm sure the committee will be very pleased to hear that. Now, one last thing. Jillian, this is for you." She handed her a sparkly envelope.

"For me?" Jillian asked as she flipped the envelope over. She quickly opened it, wondering what could be inside.

"It's an invitation for Pearl's birthday party!" Deborah explained, "I know the two of you haven't met yet, but your father and I were talking, and thought it would be great fun for all of you to begin getting to know one another."

"Um, didn't you say Pearl is older than me?" Jillian asked, slightly confused as to why she would be invited to this stranger's birthday party.

"She'll be turning fourteen. Which really isn't too far off from your lovely age of twelve!" Deborah smiled, "The two of you actually have quite a lot in common, and I think you'd greatly enjoy one another's company."

Jillian was still puzzled. It didn't seem to be adding up. She decided to say thank you and accept the invite anyway. Once Deborah completed her tasks, she scurried off to do her next job. When she was out of hearing distance, Hope was the first to speak.

"Well, that was a little strange. I know Deborah said her daughter has always been a huge fan of our family, but what made her suddenly decide to invite Jillian to her party?"

Bridget's eyebrows knitted together. "That is odd. First Dad invites her to our family cookout, and now they want to get their daughters together? I get that we're being more friendly and lenient with staff lately, but something about this seems a little more than just being friendly."

"I don't want to jump to any conclusions," Hope started slowly, "but did you see how happy Dad was last night with Deborah there? He was pretty much glowing. You don't think Dad could actually be… interested in her. Do you?"

Everyone was quiet, contemplating the wild suggestion.

"I know I haven't been around for very long," Vanessa started, "but from what I've seen of Deborah, she's absolutely spectacular. And she's beautiful, too. It wouldn't be totally outlandish to consider that he might be attracted to her."

"Well, I sure hope not," Jillian spat out, unashamed to state her bold thoughts. "Because whoever this Pearl chick is, she is *not* going to be sharing my last name."

Chapter Six

To Freeze Time

Vanessa blinked and scratched her scalp. Her eyes were starting to feel like mush, so she turned them away from the screen and reached for her glass water mug. She cracked her knuckles. *Come on girl, you've got this. Only three more grants, four safety forms, and two inventory checklists to finish. You're so, so close.*

She glanced at the clock, greatly displeased with the numbers frowning at her. The pounding stress pressing into her forehead increased as she quickly sat her drink down, and she silently commanded her fingers to keep typing.

"Miss Vanessa, do you have a moment?"

Vanessa sighed impatiently, doing everything within her power to keep her irritation calmly bridled. *I am not going to explode, I am not going to explode. Lord, help me! I've got to finish all of this tonight!* She calmly folded her hands in her lap. She looked over the edge of her cubical to where Deborah stood.

"I just spoke with your wedding coordinator, and she wants to run a couple things by you."

"Can't this wait until tomorrow?" Vanessa placed an impatient elbow on her desk. "I have some really important forms that *need* to get done if we want clearance to open the Shelter on time."

"Stacie said it was extremely important for you to answer these questions tonight, before you meet with her tomorrow at two. She just wants you to confirm your wedding colors, let her know what you're thinking for the bridesmaid's dresses, and discuss possible reception venues. Of course, it will be in The Palace, but she wants to know if you'd like the reception set up indoors, outdoors, in a ballroom, the East Gardens—"

"I don't know!" Vanessa tossed her hands in the air. "And at this point, I don't even care!" She pushed herself back from her desk in a sudden burst of distress, her chair wheeling several inches across the floor.

Vanessa's head fell into her hands, embarrassed with her sudden outburst. "I'm so sorry." She whined, hiding beneath her hands, "I can't do this. I just, I can't."

"Oh Vanessa dear, it's okay, you're okay darling!" Deborah abandoned her clipboard and threw all Royal protocol out the window. She forgot her role as hired administrative assistant and stepped in as a thoughtful mother-figure. She knelt beside Vanessa's chair and tenderly patted her on the arm.

"I promised myself that I wouldn't be bridezilla!" Vanessa burst out. "And look at me! I'm so irritated with all these stupid wedding questions that I don't even care about any of those annoying little details! Deborah, I can't think about wedding stuff right now! I *have* to finish this paperwork!" Frantic with the pressing deadline, she attempted to roll her chair back up to her desk, but Deborah stopped her.

"Vanessa, stop. Take a breath. You're pushing yourself *way* too hard. Forget about the deadlines for just a moment and take a little bit of pressure off yourself. You're okay. Nobody's expecting you to be perfect through all of this!"

"Yeah, nobody except for me," Vanessa grumbled.

"I know how challenging it can be to live with yourself when you're a type-A perfectionist," Deborah smiled knowingly. "But something I've learned over the years is that you have to know when enough is enough. I know you want to be superwoman and do everything to please everybody; that's only natural for someone with a heart as big as yours! But it's okay to stop every now and then, to take a few moments for yourself. Now, is there anything I can do to help you relax? Chamomile tea, a hot bath? Should I schedule a massage, or an afternoon in the spa?"

Vanessa sighed, tired shoulders slumping, "I appreciate your concern, but I'm okay. As long as we can place those wedding questions on hold and I can knock out my to-do list in the next forty minutes, I'll be fine. Addi and I have a date planned, and I'll totally unwind then."

Deborah didn't appear too convinced, "Of course."

Vanessa flashed a stressed smile. "Now if you'll excuse me, I *have* to finish these forms."

Vanessa squeezed Addison's hand, foolishly hoping the gesture could express how much she loved him. But who was she kidding? Not even the sweetest of romantic expressions or flowery words could aptly convey how she felt about the young man walking beside her. Every attempt she made to convince his soul of how much she loved him was but a faint whisper. She could have stood on top of a mountain, screamed at the top of her lungs about her undying admiration and eternal affection, and it wouldn't even begin to touch what bubbled up inside her heart. Even if the finest poet wrote a song on her behalf, penning it just for him and gathering up the greatest orchestra in the world, that too would fall short of what she was feeling right now.

She peered happily toward the tangerine sun that would soon set. The sky was painted with brilliant streaks of purple and blue, with just a finger stroke of pink. Vanessa knew that God's brilliant display of majestic creativity was placed there to remind her heart just how deeply she was loved by Him. Vanessa smiled, relishing the feeling of awe that she was somewhat, in a pathetically small way, able to understand how God must feel as He is bursting with love for His created ones. Vanessa wished with everything inside her that there was a way she could adequately voice and express the way she treasured and adored the one standing beside her. And with each passing day, it was becoming more and more clear that God had the same struggle. *Although*, she thought with a fresh dose of wonderment, *God is never short on language, words, or miraculous signs—his heartbreak only comes from the fact that we're not paying any attention.*

In that moment, as she and Addison strolled contentedly along the bank of the pond, she could feel God smiling down upon them. She relished the feeling of Addison's warm hand covering hers and squealed somewhere deep inside as she thought about their soon-to-come first kiss.

"I wish there was a way to freeze time." Vanessa sighed, sharing her thoughts with Addison. All the stress piled upon her shoulders from the course of the day had melted away. "Because this? This is perfect."

Addison looked into the face of his fiancé, his eyes glowing with love. "I couldn't agree more. If it were up to me, I'd ditch this whole palace for a week and run off somewhere to spend all our time together. It's disappointing how crazy-hectic our schedules are."

"Tell me about it," Vanessa groaned. "Between wedding planning, work, and administrating the opening of this homeless shelter, I feel like I'm gonna go gray!"

Addison and Vanessa plopped down onto a bench in unison. Several birds tweeted happily in the background, and Vanessa relished the calming effects of the still pond before them.

"You know how amazing I think you are, right?" Addison turned toward her and released his lavish compliments, "I've never met anyone with a mind as amazing as yours, not to mention the relentless determination to conquer a project and completely smash it out of the park. Vanessa, you shatter everyone's expectations. But are you sure you're not pushing yourself too hard? I mean, the things mentioned on your list are a lot, but you didn't even state one of the most important changes–becoming Queen."

"That still sounds so strange to me. Queen." Vanessa shook her head, unable to mesh with those odd words, "I'm still trying to get used to the fact that I'm going to be your wife. I don't want to get distracted by the titles. I mean, I know helping you run the country is a huge deal and all, but for now, I just want to focus on the season we're in and enjoy it, you know? These moments are going to fly by *way* too fast."

"Really?" Addison asked with a laugh, "Sometimes I feel like they're not going by fast enough. I'm ready to be married, like, yesterday."

"Well, I can't argue with that!" Vanessa laughed, her eyes twinkling with a playful tone of good-natured mischief. "Does this mean we're eloping? I say we sneak out, cross the border, find a random preacher to perform the ceremony, and then I can toss that wedding list out the window!"

Addison laughed, "Oh no, don't tempt me." He smiled and patted her hand, "I want to rush just as much as you do. But we have to remember that there's purpose in the process. We need this time."

"I know." Vanessa sighed, smiling once more, appreciating his strongly-anchored wisdom. Vanessa agreed whole-heartedly. Their engagement was a special time for their hearts to grow closer, their roots to grow deeper, and for the foundation of their relationship to become solid. They couldn't build a fireproof home without a strong rock below.

"Ness, I think I know you well enough to know that you're the kind of girl who, once she commits to something, isn't going to back out, or even admit that she needs help. But I want you to be totally honest. Is this too much for you? The job, the Shelter, the press interviews, and social appearances? Do you need to start weeding out your schedule a bit?"

"I'll admit, I almost had a bit of a meltdown this afternoon." Vanessa sighed, hating to reveal her weaknesses, "But I know this is just an endurance race. I mean, once the Shelter opens, things will slow down somewhat, and I'm sure I'll be a bit more level-headed and can get our last-minute wedding details squared away." She tossed Addison a smile, "It can be stressful at times, but I can handle it."

"Actually, I don't imagine things slowing down anytime soon. After the Shelter opens, your job is going to get even more demanding. There will be more paperwork, more staff to oversee, and a ton more records to keep. As amazing as this expansion is, it isn't going to happen without even more hard work."

"I know that, Addi." Vanessa reassured him, wondering why he sounded so concerned, "Things might get intense, but I'm a trooper. Trust me."

"Nessa, I don't want you to take this the wrong way." He grabbed both of her hands, hoping to reassure her that he didn't want to cause any kind of offence, "I know you can handle the workload that comes with your position. But I'm not sure if *we* can handle it. Our relationship, I mean. You're gonna be a full-time wife, and possibly even someday a mother, and well, call me old-fashioned, but I think that's a massive job in and of itself. I don't want you to feel like you have to keep working, plowing away at this position, when we're getting ready to start a life and a family together."

"So, you're saying that after we're married, you don't want me to work?" Vanessa asked slowly, attempting to uproot the core of what he wanted to express.

"No! Not at all. I mean, you have to do whatever God leads you to do." Addison added quickly, "All I'm saying, is that I want you to feel the freedom to do exactly that. If you need to let go of your position, to focus on other things, I would be all for it."

"I appreciate what you're saying, but I *love* my job at the shelter. I know our family income obviously isn't an issue, but I wouldn't be doing it for the money. I'm doing it for the people, Addi."

"I know." Addison nodded, "And that's what I love about you. It's just, remember that if things ever get to be too much, I'm not going to be disappointed in you or think that you're failing, or something crazy like

[73]

that. You set really high expectations for yourself, and I don't want you to think you have to be super-human and save the whole world all on your own. We're a team, you know."

"Speaking of teamwork, I have a meeting with Stacie, our wedding coordinator, tomorrow. Any special requests before we iron out this thing? Colors? Decorations? Cake flavors?"

"Cake flavors? Oh no, you can't be trying cakes without me! That's like, the best part of being engaged!"

"That's what Millie thinks, too!" Vanessa laughed, "She's already talked to Clark and made it absolutely certain that she will be in the room during our cake testing. So, don't worry. I won't deny you of that pleasure."

"Good." Addison grinned, "Other than the cake, do whatever you girls want! Oh, except for the music. I'd like to have a little bit of say in that... I'm really not a country music kind of guy. I don't want my wedding to be a hoe-down, throw-down."

"No worries there!" Vanessa grinned, "I'm not a country girl either. I've been thinking about music a little bit though, and I have kind of a silly request."

"Oh yeah? What's that?"

"Now, this is shamefully sappy and sentimental, but the day that you called to offer me this job, and Millie was acting as your little secretary, I was cleaning out my closet, listening to this song, and now every time I hear it, I just kind of shoot through the roof with all these giddy feelings of girlish crush and mush."

"Vanessa, this is our wedding. We can be as disgustingly sappy as we want to be!" he laughed. "What's the song?"

"*Hope,* by *Kennetic Energy*. Think we could play it at the reception?"

"We might be able to do better than just play it. *Kennetic Energy* has always been down for attending our events. Maybe they could perform live?"

"That would be amazing!" Vanessa squealed, "Ahh! I can't wait to dance with you."

"Neither can I." Addison told her, truly meaning every word.

Chapter Seven

Prince on Trial

Addison attempted to loosen his tie without fully undoing it. Anxious fingers fumbled around his collar, wishing he could remove his heavy suit coat and cool down. He shifted his back on the hard bench, attempting to make himself more comfortable, but his attempts were fruitless. The seat was like a stone.

The ancient courthouse was aged several hundred years and hadn't been updated with an AC unit. The stale air was dry and suffocating, as a blanket of unwelcome heat settled on each sweaty body. Although the windows were open, there were no cross breezes. Addison wasn't sure if his damp armpits came from the heat, or the intense stress and anxiety that plagued him.

Addison glanced at his father, who sat beside him with a fixed frown. Steve appeared just as concerned as he was. They had been trapped in the muggy courthouse all day, and things were *not* going well.

"Your Honor, if I may object, young Prince Asher had absolutely no way of knowing what was in that link!" Mr. Lee, his frustrated attorney, argued with flushed, angry cheeks. "He was taken completely off guard, innocently thinking his gaming friend sent him an app to merely mess with the lighting and such at the Coronation. Can't you see, it was a completely innocent action?"

The judge wore a thick mustache, and an even thicker frown. "From the documents presented to me, the conversations between Prince Asher and the warlord terrorist, as well as the testimony the Prince himself has shared, it is quite clear that there was a strong undertow of desire to harm His Majesty and the innocent people attending his coronation."

"I object!" Mr. Lee shouted, shaking an animated fist in the air. "Prince Asher confessed to having ill feelings toward his brother, yes, but he never said *anything* about intending to hurt anyone else attending!"

Addison's crystal eyes drifted toward the ceiling. He prayed fervently, asking the Lord to intervene, and for mercy to be released on behalf of his brother.

The dreaded court scene had been stretched out for several long, painful hours. A thick lump formed in Addison's throat, knowing that the verdict would soon be decided and the wooden mallet would slam down upon Asher's life, determining the course of his destiny. He glanced at his watch. It was nearing the dinner hour. Things had to end soon. If the judge didn't make his decision tonight, the torturous process would be drug into tomorrow. He prayed for a swift end.

He took a deep breath, knowing he had to trust the Lord with this. Addison gazed across the courtroom, his eyes lovingly watching his poor little brother. His chest swelled with a strange sense of pride, admiring Asher for enduring this challenging day like a humble champion. He patiently answered each painful question with brutal honesty, ready to claim responsibility for whatever his fate may be. Addison could scarcely believe how much the young man had matured over the past months. The old Asher would've whined and thrown a fit, claiming that this was all ridiculously unfair, and that he had better ways to spend his time than in a stupid courthouse. But Asher displayed great self-control and maturity, far beyond his years, as he endured false accusations and wild speculations venomously spewed against him.

Addison strongly desired to stand up, grab his brother, and ditch this life-sucking room. But he knew they couldn't leave. Not yet. There was no choice but to patiently await to hear the dreaded verdict.

Lord, I don't know what the judge is going to say, Addison told God once more, *but I trust You. I have to trust You. Help our family. Help Asher. Help me face the wild media beasts who are waiting outside this building like ravenous wolves, ready to tear into us the moment we walk out these doors...*

"Liam Henderson, stop splashing!" Bridget giggled between deliriously-happy squeals. She covered her eyes, hoping to keep the large amounts of water flying up, out of her face. "I'm not even wearing waterproof mascara!"

"Waterproof mascara?" Liam pulled his wet hand back inside their canoe and wiped it on his jeans. "I didn't know that was a thing."

"Of course, it's a thing!" She laughed, her cheeks sore from all the silliness, "And I should've known better, to put some on before getting in a boat with you!"

"Wow, so many things I never knew about women. I learn something new every day."

Bridget grinned, staring at him like a ditzy, starry-eyed lover. She knew it was ridiculous, but she couldn't stop her heart from admiring him so. She was officially head-over-heels. She scooted closer to the center of the canoe, attempting to re-center herself and keep from falling out. Liam had been rocking the boat and threatening to throw her overboard into the tiny pond. After the playful antics were over, Bridget adjusted her navy-blue frock and set her eyes back on Liam.

"Personally, I am quite glad to know you don't have any expertise in the area of the female studies." Bridget told him teasingly, "I'd really hate it if you were some kind of expert."

"That makes two of us." Liam revealed, "You're my very first, and Lord willing, my one and only first love."

Bridget wondered if it was humanly possible for a heart to burst of happiness. If so, she was teetering dangerously close to it. Moments spent with Liam were like rich frosting on her inner cake of celestial bliss.

All at once, she felt sheepishly awkward for getting so dressed up for their date. He told her they were going on a canoe ride, and anyone with half a working brain would've known better than to wear high-heels and a party dress while out on the water with Liam. But Bridget couldn't help but wonder if something extra special might happen on this date.

She had a sneaking suspicion that he might propose.

Bridget was trying her best not to think about it, but she couldn't keep her mind from secretly predicting when he might pop the question. Bridget knew a proposal was supposed to have a certain element of surprise, and she didn't want to ruin it for Liam. But Liam was a very predictable guy. And Bridget couldn't help but think that perhaps he was trying to recreate the first moment they truly talked and got to know one another–in a canoe in Alaska. It only made sense that Liam would ask on the water!

But then again, he might be waiting until all the hustle and bustle of preparing for Vanessa and Addison's wedding had passed. Was he going to hold out until after Vanessa and Addison left for their honeymoon? Or would he attempt a grand surprise and ask her right in the midst of all the busyness? Bridget chided herself for trying too hard to figure it out. She needed to quit thinking about it and embrace each beautiful moment they had to spend with one another. Still, she couldn't help herself from being a little bit bubbleheaded about it.

Just then, Liam's cell phone rang.

Bridget's giddy thoughts came to a screeching halt, just like a steam roller slamming on its breaks at the train station. She knew who the phone call was from. Liam had brought his cell with him, so that Addison could let them know the results of Asher's trial.

Bridget pressed her lips together nervously.

"Hello?" Liam's eyes flitted across the tree line. "Yeah. Mmm-hmm…mmm-hmm…"

Bridget wrung her hands, desperately hoping for a positive report. They had asked Addison to call Liam as soon as they knew what the judge's decision was.

"Oh man." Liam sighed, "Okay. Yeah. Right, okay. Mmm-hmm… we'll be praying, man. Alright. See ya."

Liam closed his flip phone, and Bridget looked at him in desperation.

"It's not good." Liam's eyes settled on her, hating to share the heavy news. "Asher has been charged with fourteen months in Juvenile Detention."

"Oh dear God!" Bridget lifted a shocked hand to her face, "Oh, Asher! Lord, help him!" She shook her head, "No, how can this be? He's just a kid!"

"Addison said they're not giving up yet. He and your dad are going to talk with the judge, to see if they can't work something else out. Such as community service hours, or military school."

"Oh Asher." Bridget's voice cracked, fighting back tears, truly wishing she *had* worn her waterproof mascara. "I can't even imagine what he's feeling right now. He must be devastated. Crushed. Absolutely defeated. And after he's been trying so hard to get his life back on track…"

"I remember the day the police came for me." Liam spoke quietly, his voice soft and distant, as if living in a foreign memory, "I was thirteen, so even younger than Asher. I had destroyed my step-dad's car with a baseball bat and was so close to destroying him too. Thankfully, my patrol officer thought I might do better somewhere *besides* behind bars, so they sent me to Donald and Becky's. God used them to change my life, forever. Man, I don't even know where I would be today without them. Don't worry, Bridget," Liam gently reached across the canoe and clasped her hand, "God had a plan of redemption for my life, and he does for Asher's too. This whole time, I've just been praying for God's will to be done, and if there's a better place for Asher to be than Juvie, I believe He's going to make a way for that."

[82]

"Do you think your parents might take him?" she asked in a hopeful tone, the idea hitting her all at once. "Up in Alaska, I mean? God used them to work wonders with you, maybe they could be an encouragement to Asher."

"I don't know how feasible that would be, seeing how this is all happening within the Tarsurellian court system." Liam scratched his chin, "I've never heard of them transferring teens internationally, let alone ones charged with crimes. I'm not sure if that would even be legal. I guess it all depends on what exactly they charged Asher with in the first place. Aiding and abetting a terror attack?"

"I don't know." Bridget shook her head, "This is all just insane. I mean, how wrong is it that we're even having this conversation right now? Asher is just a kid!"

"Sometimes the enemy can really screw up young people's lives." Liam spoke from a place of first-hand understanding, "But I know God has an amazing plan and destiny for Asher. In whatever ways the enemy has been messing around with that kid, once God truly gets ahold of him and captures Asher's heart, he's never going to be the same. Once Asher burns with that flame of fire from Heaven and his passion is ignited, he's going to be giving the devil a headache every day of his life. You have to believe that, Bridget. Someday, the enemy is going to deeply regret that he *ever* messed with this family."

Hope splashed her toes in the cool pool water, enjoying the refreshing feeling amidst the intense heat. She carelessly swirled her feet around while half-heartedly listening to the lively conversation among Vanessa, Mrs. Bennett, Bridget and Stacie, the wedding planner. They sat at a glass patio table just several feet from the pool, sipping cool beverages and

[83]

discussing dozens of important items on their wedding check list. Although Hope was more than welcome to be part of the conversation, she found the pool was a tad more enticing than their discussions loaded with the nitty-gritty particulars of the regal event.

As excited as Hope was for Addison and Vanessa's wedding, she had other thoughts occupying her mental space. Her last encounter with Luke was pricking her like an unwelcome stone wedged in the bottom of her flip-flop. Luke was moody and so unpredictable. She wanted to learn more about his political beliefs, but why did he have to be so melodramatic about everything? She had actually considered going to his silly top-secret meeting thing, but then he snatched the card right back out of her hand!

Ugh, he was so frustrating! She shouldn't even be wasting her time thinking about him. Yet she was. Why? Why was she so drawn to him, like the invisible tug of the moon pulling the ocean tide? It didn't make any sense. She had been praying a lot about her situation with Luke, and despite all the obvious frustrations on the surface, she felt as though there was a deeper purpose to it all. Somehow, she felt like it was her responsibility to discover what he had to say. Even though Luke was a bit of an unpredictable, uncontrollable spitfire, she knew God's hand was upon him. Maybe He was using him as an unpolished megaphone to speak some things her family needed to hear? Hope really didn't know. But she really wanted to find out.

Just yesterday, Hope had asked the Lord to reveal whether she should continue attempting to speak with Luke, or if she should just forget about everything and move on with her life. Just an hour after she prayed, she received a knock on her door. A friendly maid strolled in with a small box. "For you, Your Highness, special delivery from the kitchen!"

"Oh, I didn't order anything." She looked at the purple box, where a chocolate cupcake was tucked inside. "It must've been one of my sisters."

"No, Your Highness, it is for you," the maid insisted. "See, it has your name on it. It's a special treat from the kitchen staff. Just look at the card."

The maid plopped the treat into Hope's hand and scurried off. She slowly opened the lid, confused as to why the kitchen would randomly deliver a treat like this. Her thumb broke into the tiny envelope, and a business card fell out. Hope gasped. It was Luke's *Sons of Liberty, Media Movement* card.

Messy handwriting, scribbled on the edges, wrote, "Hope. I think U should come. Really."

Hope twirled her big toe around in the pool, shaking her head, wondering if she should dive in. Not into the pool. But into Luke's meeting. *The meeting is tonight, at the Town Hall. But before making up my mind, I really want a second opinion.*

"Though hamburgers and French fries seem *quite* American, I'll see if I can't come up with another way to make it a bit more… mmm…. shall we say, sophisticated?"

French fries caught Hope's attention. She glanced over her shoulder at the girls. *Is Vanessa actually thinking about serving hamburgers and fries at the wedding?* Hope's lips broke into a smile, *Go her! Way to break the stuffy traditions around here!*

"Thank you so much for your help, Stacie." Vanessa gathered a stack of papers, "Is there anything I need to do before our next meeting?"

"No, no, I'll arrange everything on my end. All you need to worry about is keeping that darling little complexion of yours free of blemishes, so you'll look fabulous in your wedding photos! Alright ladies, thank you for your time, I'll get to work on all of this, ciao!"

Stacie bid the girls goodbye and exited the scene.

"See, the meeting wasn't that painful, was it?" Bridget teased.

"No, I'll admit, it wasn't as bad as I thought it would be. I truly am thankful for all the help. I mean, without you and Stacie, and everyone pitching in, I would probably go mental! Who knew wedding planning could be such a massive undertaking!"

"Sorry I wasn't more help, but you girls seemed to have things well under control." Hope slowly arose from the poolside and joined them at the table, "But just so you know, I'll be more than happy to assist you when it comes time for cake testing."

"That's what everyone keeps telling me." Vanessa laughed, "I'll add you to the long, *long* list of volunteers in that department."

Bridget stood up, "Well, I guess I'd better go get dinner ready. Dad, Addison and Asher should be home soon. I want to fix a little treat for Asher. You know, something that'll lift his spirits. Care to join us tonight?"

"Oh, no thank you, I'll be dining with my parents," Vanessa told her. "But thanks for the invite."

Bridget bid the girls goodbye, leaving Hope and Vanessa alone by the pool. Vanessa continued sorting and stacking the papers before her, attempting to organize all the notes spread out on the table.

"Hey, I know you're busy, but do you mind if I talk to you for a minute about something?" Hope asked slowly.

"Of course! I'm never too busy for you. What's up?"

"What would you do, if say," Hope twisted her hands anxiously, fumbling to find the right words, "you grew up your whole life believing things were a certain way, simply because of the environment and the family you've been raised in, then one day you're offered an opportunity to hear about the world from a completely different perspective or point of view? Would you take the time to learn about this different perspective, or would you shy away from it, thinking it could be dangerous or could potentially put some kind of wedge between you and your family?"

"Hmm…. Why do I get the feeling this isn't just a hypothetical question?" Vanessa cocked her head slightly. "Have you been reading articles from rebellion leaders?"

"A little," Hope admitted, knowing Vanessa could be trusted. Because of Vanessa's differences in political opinions, she knew she would understand. "I haven't gone too deep into my research, just because I don't want to be deceived or led astray, but I have to ask what all the fuss is about. I mean, clearly these people are *not* worked up for no reason. Is there truly something of major concern our country is doing wrong? What if the way I was raised, thinking everything is perfect about our flawless little monarchy, is wrong? I want to find out. But at the same time, I don't want to make any waves, or cause Addison or anyone else in the family to be upset."

"I don't think there's anything wrong with doing research or asking questions. In fact, I think it's very wise of you! As much as I adore your family, and your brother, your country *isn't* perfect. Neither is your political system. The rebels do have some good ideas as to how we could bring positive change, and you're not crazy for wanting to learn more about those methods and ideas. Of course, I would caution you, as there are some radicals out there who really don't have a clue what they're saying and just like to make noise. But no, I don't think there's anything wrong with doing research and deciding what *you* believe for yourself."

"Do you remember Liberty Stone?"

"You mean the guy who leaked your family secret, and accused Addison of being a lying coward who was just trying to cover up truth to protect Asher? Yeah, I remember." Vanessa pursed her lips together tightly.

Hope bit her lip, not wanting to mention the fact that she'd been talking to him. She had been considering asking Vanessa to go with her to the meeting, but now she wasn't sure if that was such a good idea. Maybe she should skip the meeting entirely. "What do you think of his writings? I mean, does he seem too radical to you?"

"I think he's got some good points, but he goes overboard in some areas. Anyone who thinks Addison needs to be removed from power entirely is *way* too extreme in my book."

"Yeah." Hope nodded, disliking the fact that Vanessa was probably right, "I guess so."

Chapter Eight

The Bellington Derby

The following morning, Asher stared into his cold plate of bacon and eggs. He had been eyeing his food for so long, the flavors faded as they evaporated into the air along with the heat. His littlest siblings, Millie and Willie, had left the table, and now that they were out of earshot, the family was free to discuss the elephant in the room.

"Ash, I don't want you to give up hope yet," his dad spoke, his compassionate voice filling their kitchen. "Things can still change. Juvie doesn't have to be the final answer. Last night I spoke with our military commander. He is willing to work with the court, to see if they can't work out some sort of alternate deal. He's thinking that if we appeal for sixteen months of military school, they may accept it."

"Military school?" Asher's angry eyes shot up toward his father, "How is that supposed to be any better than jail!?"

[89]

"Son, there are a great many reasons why military school would be a huge advantage to you. Juvenile detention isn't going to do anything for you, other than scar your record. Military school would be a great stroke of providential grace, as you would be given a second chance to make something good of yourself for this world. I, myself, attended this same school, and it assisted me a great deal in my development as a young man. It instills vital skills into everyone who attends, girding your soul with admirable character qualities, humility, compassion, a hard-work ethic, strong integrity, a heart of service for others—"

"Why did you have to go to military school?" Jillian asked, her eyes wide with curiosity. "Did you commit some kind of crime?"

"No, Jilly." Steve shook his head, "But my father thought it would be a suitable choice for me as a teenager. And it turned out he was right. At first, I was a little cantankerous toward the idea, but looking back on it, I know I wouldn't be the man I am today without it."

"So, let me get this straight, my options are either rot in jail for sixteen months, or attend a stupid military school where I'll have zero free time and barking drill sergeants? Oh yeah, sounds like God's grace alright." Asher rolled his eyes.

"If we can convince the judge to change his sentence, it will be a great advantage to you." Steve spoke with conviction, "Not just for you, but for all of us. Asher, we do *not* want you to spend time behind bars."

"I get it." Asher set down his fork and crossed his arms, "Nobody wants to be related to a criminal."

"Ash, Liam was in the same position you are, when he was thirteen." Bridget quietly spoke up, attempting to bring some comfort to her hurting brother. She could see his heart was reeling with fear and pain. "But the Lord intervened and sent him to Donald and Rebekah's ranch. If He was that gracious to help Liam, I know God can do the same for you. He's no respecter of persons. Blessings can come in major disguises. Maybe military school could be your lifeboat."

Asher abruptly stood up from the table and carried his full breakfast plate toward the trash can. "Is everybody else just as sick of this conversation as I am? Don't we all have places to be?"

Addison sighed. He wiped his face with a napkin. "Asher's right. We've got a busy day ahead of us. Everyone be praying that the judge will change Asher's sentence this afternoon. We should know by the end of the day."

Chasity stood up, collecting several plates and joining her brother at the sink, where Asher rinsed off each dish before placing it in the dishwasher.

"The girls and I are going to the *Belington Derby* today!" Chasity spoke cheerfully, hoping to lighten the heavy mood. "*Pink Cotton* is running. He's a new horse that pretty much came out of nowhere, a total underdog. I think he might actually win, even though the competition is crazy stiff. Want to come with us?"

"As riveting as your offer is, it sounds like I should start packing for military school."

Chasity hated the disheartening negativity. "Well then," she kept her voice chipper, "why not take a trail ride after we get back? I've been working with Nic quite a bit, and it's such a gorgeous day, I'm sure he'd love to get out and about."

"Not really in the mood, Chas." Asher grumbled.

"Oh come on Asher, I know this whole situation utterly stinks, but you can't climb into your underground hobbit hole of misery again! We're *going* to have fun this summer."

[91]

"That sounded more like a threat than a suggestion."

"It's not a suggestion," Chasity spoke firmly. "You and I are going to find something to do, something that takes us back to being little kids again. I'm talking bare feet, wind in our hair, laughing deliriously, playing with sticks, capturing imaginary pirate ships kind of fun."

Asher rolled his eyes, even though Chasity detected the tiniest hint of a smile on his lips.

"The bottom line is," Chasity's voice softened as she looked her brother in the eye, "we don't know how long we're going to have left together as a family this summer. So, whether you go to Juvie, or a boarding school, or wherever it is that God might send you, I'm not going to let you leave without having made the most of our time together. Got it?"

"Right." Asher sighed, slowly surrendering to the fact that his sister wasn't about to give up on him.

Chasity ran her hand along the green railing, hurriedly bouncing up the steps, climbing to their luxury box-seat at the tip-top point of the outdoor racetrack arena. She felt like a little girl, all dressed up, excitedly climbing these same steps just as she had with her mother. She remembered attending her first race like it was just yesterday. As a bright-eyed three-year-old, Dad flung her up on his shoulders so she could see over all the towering hats. Her breath caught, as horses faster than lightening, thundered around the track, kicking up mud behind their wild hooves. Chasity didn't dare blink for fear of missing the winner. Since that inaugural moment, she had witnessed many wonderful races, but no matter how many she attended, that unbridled feeling of electric anticipation before the trumpets sounded never faded.

"If they award prizes for fanciest hat, you are going to win, hands down!" Vanessa told Bridget as they reached the top step.

Bridget giggled and struck a pose, framing her hands around her face and her ginormous, purple-velvet hat. "If you're going to a horse race, you have to dress the part! Like Mom always used to say, 'Make your hats big, or take your hats home'!"

Vanessa laughed once more and shook her head, slowly eying the other large hats below. From their private box seat, they had a spectacular view of both the track and the hundreds of spectators seated below them. "Is this VIP area just for us? It's huge." Vanessa spoke, noting that there were way more seats than they had need of.

"Oh no, there will be company," Bridget quickly corrected her. "And lots of it. People pay big bucks to sit up here with us. It's a reserved area for horse owners and wealthy socialites. Enjoy the peace and quiet while we have it, because it won't last long."

Vanessa nodded. "I wish Addison could've come. It would've been way more fun with him here."

"Oh posh, you'll have your boy-toy all to yourself once you two are married," Hope laughed. "But for now, you get sister time! Enjoy it, because once the kids come, you won't be able to get out and do stuff like this so easily."

"Kids?!" Vanessa gasped playfully. "Who said anything about kids?"

"Everybody!" Hope grinned, "We all know your kids are going to be the most adorable little munchkins on this planet. We've already got some names picked out." She winked at Bridget.

"In case you can't tell, we're stoked to become aunts." Bridget grinned.

"We'll talk about these assumed children later," Vanessa laughed. "But for now, can someone just explain to me how this whole horse-racing thing works? I mean, I know they run around the track a few times, whoever runs the fastest wins, yada-yada-yada, but I don't want to sound like a total newbie. Is there some important lingo, or rules I need to know about? If I'm expected to socialize with these people all afternoon, I'd like to at least be somewhat educated on the subject."

"This is just one of three very important races in Tarsurella," Chasity piped up, eager to share her knowledge. "The winner, depending on how many bets are placed, will win at least two or three million dollars in prize money. But far more important than that, they'll win the title of *Belington Derby* champion, which is one of the greatest honors in racing! The track is two and a half kilometers, which is pretty mind blowing, considering how fast they're going. Horse-racing isn't rocket science, so all you need to do is look at the odds, pick a favorite, and cheer for whoever you'd like to win."

"Or, you can order a lemonade, chat with your friends, and ignore the race entirely!" Bridget laughed, "Like I do."

Chasity rolled her eyes, brushing off Bridget's comment. "The predicted favorite is *Sundance Sauce*, but I'm rooting for *Pink Cotton*. I really hope he pulls through for the win."

After several moments, just as Bridget had predicted, the box seats quickly filled up. Dozens of women wearing fancy derby dresses and men in dapper suits flooded the area, greeting Vanessa and the Princesses.

"Why, if it isn't the woman who swept our dear King Addison off his feet!" A fluffy little British accent swept through the crowd. The girls instantly recognized her. It was Sapphire Scroonmaker, a flirtatious young woman who had hoped to weasel her way into Addison's heart.

Thankfully, Vanessa had come out ahead and beat all her competition, without even realizing what she had done. The last time Hope bumped into Sapphire, the girl seemed rather bitter about her loss.

"It's a pleasure to see you again, darling! My, my, so much has happened since we've last chatted! It was at the Coronation, wasn't it?"

"Sapphire." Vanessa pasted a fake grin onto her face, "It's nice to see you again."

"I declare, I never could have guessed *you* would be the one with that gaudy diamond on your finger, flaunting around your engagement to His Royal Majesty! Well, I suppose stranger things have happened." Sapphire's uppity tone rang through the air.

"I guess the surprise goes both ways." Vanessa gritted her teeth, attempting to stay kind and cordial, "I never imagined seeing you here either. When did you first become interested in horse racing?"

"Oh darling, I have no interest in those smelly animals." Sapphire laughed obnoxiously, "I am only here to watch the men. There's been a rumor circulating that James O'Conner will be attending, in support of his friend's horse, who is the favored to win. Oh, speak of the devil, look who just walked in!"

All the girls followed her gaze to where a group of dapper young men sporting tuxedos and ties had just entered. "Well, it was lovely catching up, truly a treat, but I must go make my rounds. Enjoy the race, ladies!"

Sapphire quickly strutted away, making a beeline toward James.

"That girl is the definition of a gold digger, if I ever saw one. She bounces from one rich boy to the next." Bridget shook her head, "It's sad, really."

"What's *sad* is that some people have the nerve to come to a race like this and call the stars of the show 'smelly old animals'. Ugh! Some people just irk me." Chasity watched Sapphire fling herself toward James. He greeted her with a simple hello, then politely excused himself and made his way toward the Royals.

"Afternoon, Your Highness," his thick British accent greeted Chasity. He then turned to say hello to the others, each in turn. "Lovely day for a race, isn't it?"

"Absolutely!" Chasity spoke eagerly. "The weather couldn't be more perfect. The track is dry, so that'll be great for traction. It makes me nervous when there's a lot of mud, as I always feel like one of the horses will wipe out and injure themselves."

"Do you have a moment to spare your sister's company?" James's lively eyes darted from Bridget, to Hope, then finally settled on Chasity. "I'd like to introduce you to a friend of mine, Nathaniel Wells. I don't know if you've heard of him, but he is a trainer and—"

"Nathaniel Wells!" Chasity burst out excitedly. "Of course I've heard of him! He's the one who worked with *Reckless Road Rage* last year*!*"

"I told him about your horse; Nic. He said he would love to meet you, and perhaps come take a look at the beaut."

"Nathaniel Wells?! Take a look? At Nic?!" Chasity was struck giddy by the thought. "For what purpose?"

"Why, for racing him, of course!" James laughed, "That's what trainers do. Train racehorses. Come, I'll introduce you."

Chasity slowly followed James, her mouth hanging open in disbelief.

Hope couldn't help but giggle. "Wow, somebody's a little star struck."

"I've never seen Chasity so animated and enthusiastic in a conversation with someone of the male persuasion," Bridget observed. "Come to think of it, James has been hanging around The Palace quite a bit lately. Do you think he might be interested in her?"

"The important question is, is Chasity interested in *him*?" Hope asked with a grin. "I've never seen her so much as look at a guy for more than three seconds, let alone get all flushed and excited in a conversation with one!"

"Well, he seems charming." Vanessa added her two cents' worth, taking another peek at where Chasity and James spoke with an older man with peppered grey hair. "Is he someone you guys have known for a while?"

"Yes, the O'Conners are old family friends," Bridget explained. "We used to visit their estate in England every summer. They have a beautiful herd of polo ponies. Chasity and James used to have a blast playing together as kids, and Dad always joked that someday they were going to end up falling in love."

"Well, in the famous words of Sapphire Scroonmaker" Hope slipped on a fake British accent, "'stranger things have happened.'"

Moments later, Chasity returned to her sisters.

"What was *that* all about?" Bridget asked with a sly grin.

"I can't even believe it!" Chasity shook her head in wonderment, "Nathaniel Wells wants to come and look at Nic!"

"We're not talking about your horse, we're talking about the hunky guy who set this all up for you!" Bridget giggled, playfully poking her in the arm.

Chasity's clueless expression told her sisters that she wasn't following.

"James!" Bridget finally spoke, revealing what she thought was the obvious center of their conversation.

"What?" Chasity asked, surprised to hear Bridget suggest such a thing. "You don't think that—oh no," she quickly shook her head, "it's not like that."

"Oh really? You sure looked *pretty* excited while you were talking with him."

"That's because we were talking about Nic! Do you not understand what this means?! Nic might have the chance to become a *real* racehorse!"

"That's Chas for us, always placing horses before guys." Bridget laughed.

"You people are hopeless." Chasity shook her head, wondering what their problem was. "I'm going to go get a snack," she grumbled.

Chasity left her sisters, wishing they could be at least a *little* bit excited for her. At this time next year, perhaps it could be Nic running in the *Belington Derby!* It sounded like a wild, inconceivable pipe dream, but Chasity knew Nathaniel could work miracles. As long as a horse possessed raw, natural talent, Nathaniel possessed the skills to bring underdogs to the top.

Chasity weaved her way through the cozy crowd, her sights set on a small snack vender. The tantalizing scent of roasted peanuts drew her forward.

"Good afternoon, Your Highness." A long-nosed man behind the counter handed her a menu, "How may I serve you? Champagne? Caviar?"

"Afternoon!" Chasity offered him a smile before glancing at the menu, "Hmm... oh, I don't know, everything looks so delicious, I—"

Chasity stopped, as something in the corner of her eye caught her attention.

Namely, *someone*.

Her eyes widened as surprise set in. Her heartbeat quickened.

Hanson Fletcher.

She attempted to keep a steady footing, a variety of strange emotions threatening to knock her over. He stood near the opening of the box door, dressed in a snazzy black tuxedo, chatting easily with another fellow. Chasity deciphered the clues, and quickly determined that he wasn't on duty. His relaxed shoulders and peaceful face set her at ease. A small, shy smile, slipped onto Chasity's lips, as she enjoyed his handsome features even from a distance.

She watched Hanson excuse himself from his friend and turn toward her. Her breath stopped for several seconds as they locked eyes, and he appeared just as astonished as she. The mesmerizing moment only lasted a few short seconds, and Chasity found herself fearful at the thought of losing him in the crowd.

Instead, he walked toward her.

Chasity lowered her menu and bit her lip. Her mind raced. He was coming to talk to her! What should she say?!

"Your Highness." Hanson greeted her with a slight bow.

"Hello," she managed to spit out, then racked her brain for the next practical thing that one might say in a situation like this. "I didn't know you were into horse-racing!" she blurted excitedly. "Unless of course you're in with the eighty-percent of people who are here just to mingle, and don't care whatsoever about the outcome of today's derby."

"Actually, I've got a little money bet on the winner." Hanson casually stuffed his left hand into his pocket, a small gesture Chasity used to secretly adore. "So, I'd say I'm pretty emotionally invested."

"Oh really?" Chasity almost smiled, "Who did you bet on?"

"*Sundance Sauce.*"

"Oh no." Chasity shook her head, "Bad choice. There's no way he's going to win."

"What do you mean there's no way?" Hanson argued playfully, "Isn't he the favorite?"

"*Pink Cotton* is going to dominate."

"*Pink Cotton?*" Hanson echoed. "That horse has terrible odds."

"I'd recommend changing your bet." Chasity was firm in her belief, "Or else you're going to lose some of your hard-earned cash."

"Well, I can't change my mind now," Hanson laughed. "*Sundance* is my friend's horse. I'm here for moral support."

"You know Carl Chesterfield? Is he here? I don't like to repeat rumors, but I heard that only a few of his family members would be attending." *Because he's in jail*, Chasity thought, choosing not to make the final thought audible.

Just then, as if perfectly on que, the bubbly, red-headed Lilly Chesterfield floated into their midst and clung to Hanson's arm. Chasity flinched. Lilly was one of Hanson's chummy little friends from school.

"It's so great to see you again, Princess!" Lilly gushed, then tugged at Hanson's arm. "Come on, I've got seats picked out for us!"

All at once, it made sense. *Of course, he knows Carl Chesterfield.* Chasity bit the inside of her lip. *Lilly's dad—duh!* Chasity resisted the urge to toss out a challenging, 'Your horse is going to lose today!' But Chasity had been raised to hold herself to a higher standard. As tempting as it was to start slinging mud, she wasn't going to stoop down to such a disgraceful level.

Hanson attempted to toss a smile onto his face, but he almost appeared irritated with Lilly's interruption.

"Enjoy the race, Your Highness," he told her with a polite nod before turning to leave.

Hanson followed Lilly's lead and sat down beside her in their reserved box seat. She chatted with several folks nearby, while Hanson retreated to his own thoughts. As much as he wished to stay and mingle with Chasity, he knew it was far more important to keep an eye on Lilly. Now, he was *her* security guard.

After whisking his mother hurriedly out of their house, he had raced to The Palace, explaining everything to Jackson, the head honcho of Security who doubled as Hanson's boss. He laid all his cards on the table, confessing that the same man who was responsible for the disappearance of Walter Akerly, had threatened him months previously, and now appeared as though he would cash in on those deadly threats. He explained Lilly's hair-raising situation, and how the frightful text came through, which Hanson interpreted to be a threat against his mother's life. Jackson nodded thoughtfully, soaking in all the information, attempting to make sense of it all. He told Hanson, Lilly, and Mrs. Fletcher that they were welcome to stay at The Palace, within their vacant guest rooms, until things were more secure on their end. They all greatly appreciated the offer, but Lilly was still deeply shaken.

"So, what am I going to do?" she had asked Hanson through tear-filled eyes. "Hide out here like a spineless coward? I have a life to live! I have school, and parties, and polo matches… I have to go out in public. Oh Hanson, I'm so terrified!"

"Shhh, Lilly, it's okay." Hanson attempted to comfort her with a warm hug, "I'm not going to let anything happen to you."

"But you can't promise that! You're not a superhero. You work for The Palace and have to be places that I can't… eventually, whoever this is will come back for me."

"Lilly, stop." Hanson hated the negative way she was speaking, "You heard Jackson. You can stay here for as long as you need. And I promise you, I'm not going to leave your side until I know everything is okay. Right now, I'm going to ask Jackson for time off, and I'll go wherever you need to be."

Hanson shook his head, jolting himself back into the current moment, checking his surroundings. He glanced at Lilly, who appeared relaxed and at ease, not at all worried about whoever made those vicious threats. Hanson sighed, not exactly enjoying his pledge to follow Lilly around for the next few weeks. She had already taken him to several yawn-enticing social events. As much as Hanson disliked his current lot in life, he was beyond grateful for Jackson's hand of assistance within their dysfunctional-family mess. His mother had been assigned a body guard from The Palace's Royal Security, something Hanson couldn't have been more thankful for.

Waves of chatter floated around him as Hanson's jaw grew tight, his thoughts returning to his weasel of a father, loathing him and all the crooked men who snuck around town doing his evil bidding. Hanson was determined that whoever made such numbingly-cruel threats against Lilly and his mother, wouldn't be given even an inch of opportunity to fulfill them.

Chapter Nine

Elephant Ears and Elated Tears

Jane Akerly sat on the porch with her knees tucked tightly to her chest. Her gaze was fixated on the zany mailbox decorated to look like a rooster, which stood firmly at the end of the driveway. Try as she might, Jane couldn't pull her eyes from it. It was Saturday. The last day of the week in which the winners of the Novelist Competition would be contacted. If the letter didn't come today, it never would.

Jane narrowed her eyes toward the box, wondering how such a small, inanimate object could hold such power over her. This week, her entire thought life had revolved around that box. She dashed outside every afternoon, running barefoot across the lawn, whipping the box open, only to have her heart fall with crushing disappointment.

Today was the last day. It *had* to come today. Her ticket to destiny. The letter that would unlock all her dreams and bring them into a head-on collision with reality. The letter *had* to be there. It just had to.

Jane glanced at Charlie, who sat beside her on the porch swing, immersed in a thick college textbook about Aerospace Engineering. Charlie was just as hopeless as she. He was having a love affair with science, and she was head-over-heels in love with a dream that had no chances of ever coming true. When she paused to think about it, they were both quite pathetic. Perhaps that's why they were one another's only living friends.

"I've got lemonade!" Aunt Cassidy announced as she burst onto the porch.

Jane continued to stare at the mailbox.

"Uh, didn't anyone hear me?" She looked at Charlie, "I'm serving sugar in a cup here, people!"

"Shhh, Aunt Cassidy, I can't think about consuming liquid at a time like this!" Not bothering to look up from his book, excitement soared through Charlie's high-pitched voice, "I'm just about to discover the principles of combustion behind rocket thrust, and how I can apply this to my inventions!"

"Oh how nice, dear." Aunt Cassidy sighed, "Just so long as you don't blow up the house. And what about you, Chickadee? Lemonade?"

"No, thank you." Jane sighed.

"What is with you two?" Aunt Cassidy asked, placing a determined hand on her hip. "This is the saddest display of teenagedom I've seen in my entire life! It's summertime! And it's a Saturday night! Shouldn't you be out doing something fun? Go to the mall, go see a movie, go play laser tag, something, anything!"

"Why?" Charlie asked, looking up at his Aunt with eyebrows raised.

"Because you're TEENAGERS!" Aunt Cassidy strained to get her point across. "These should be some of the most enjoyable years of your life! Aside from the zits, hormone changes, and embarrassing moments with your peers, high school summers should be a blast! And what are we doing? Reading and staring at the mailbox. Oh no, this is not acceptable."

Aunt Cassidy suddenly snatched Charlie's book.

"Hey!" he cried out in protest.

"You're not allowed to read anymore pages until tomorrow, do you hear me? Now, go put on some shoes, get on your bikes and find something fun to do!"

"Actually," Jane spoke up, "I wanted to stay here and see what came in the mail and—"

"No more excuses!" Aunt Cassidy grabbed her lemonade tray and turned toward the house, "Now I don't want to see either of you until *after* the dinner hour! I'm locking this door and you're not getting back in until you have some *fun*."

Aunt Cassidy quickly closed the door behind her. Charlie leapt up, reaching for the handle. But it was too late. The door was already locked.

"Oh blast it all!" Charlie huffed, sitting back down in the porch swing. "Is this even legal? Doesn't denying your children the privilege of eating dinner constitute as child abuse?!"

"No," Jane told him simply.

"Well, it should." Charlie lifted an angry finger, "And taking away their books should be a crime punishable by law!" He crossed his arms and released a frustrated sigh. After a few moments of quiet he asked, "Do you want to go to the library?"

"That's like fifteen miles away. Neither of us can drive."

"But they might have the book I was thoroughly engrossed in before Aunt Cassidy so rudely ripped it out of my hands!"

"There's no way you could bike fifteen miles. And it's gonna be dinner time soon. We can't eat books. We should at least think about where we're going to eat."

"What about the fair? I think it's in town this week."

"It's gonna be loaded with people." Jane wrinkled her nose in disgust.

"Yeah, but it's also gonna be loaded with food."

"Okay." Jane sighed, "Let's hurry up and go eat, so I can come back and check that silly mailbox."

Jane lifted the last bite of funnel cake to her mouth, then brushed off the remaining sugary dust from her fingers.

"These elephant ears are out of this world amazing!" Charlie declared before chomping into his third one. "I can't believe I've never had 'em before!"

Jane giggled and shook her head. Charlie got crazy-hyper whenever he had the tiniest amount of sugar. His little body could only process it so quickly, and Jane always knew there would be a show of spastic excitement when sugar and Charlie were together.

She looked up, eyes brushing the distant Ferris wheel. Pastel-colored seats floated through the air. Jane sighed. She really had no desire to ride it. She simply wanted Charlie to hurry up and finish eating, so they could rush home and check the mailbox.

"I think I'm going to get one more for dessert." Charlie rose, his eyes big as saucers.

"Funnel cakes *are* dessert. Hence the reason they're called cake. Come on, let's head back to the house. You'll feel better if you don't stuff yourself."

"But they're just so good!" Charlie expressed, unable to resist the sugary treat calling his name.

Jane sighed and plopped back down on the bench, as Charlie went to stand in the long line and order another. She stared at the Ferris wheel, imagining it was the famous London Eye. In London, she would stand on the sparkly streets and crane her neck toward the sky. Then, a handsome stranger would approach from behind, offering to purchase a ticket and treat her for a ride. She would shyly turn him down, but he would be kindly persistent, insisting that a lovely maiden like her shouldn't be—

"Well, if it isn't Jane Akerly and the shorty-boyfriend from Mars!" A cruel voice cut into Jane's fantasy.

She ripped her eyes away from the Ferris wheel, devastated to see a cruel troll standing several feet from Charlie. It was one of the hot-shot jockeys from school, with his posse of mean football players who highly enjoyed the sport of teasing.

"What are you doing out of the asylum? I didn't know they let you guys out this time of year!"

Jane wanted to speak up, but her mind was empty. She couldn't think of anything worth saying. Her colorful imagination froze, shutting down beneath their heartless comments. These same kids had teased her ever since middle school. There was nothing she could say to change their minds now.

"Come on Charlie, let's go." She quickly stood up and reached for his arm, hoping her presence could somehow defend him. She knew the bullies would find nothing intimidating about her tiny little frame, but at least there was strength in numbers.

"We're not leaving." Charlie stood his ground, puffing out his chest ever-so-slightly. "Not until I get my funnel cake."

"You heard your boyfriend—Short-Nye-the-Science-Guy isn't gonna leave until he gets his tasty treat!" The tall pack-leader grabbed Charlie's head and gave him a quick noogie on his hairline, harshly rubbing his knuckles over his head.

"Stop!" Jane demanded. "Don't touch him!"

"What, scared that if his fragile little nerd body breaks, he's not gonna take you to prom?" His deep laugh cut through the summertime air, causing Jane's throat to tighten with anger. "Well nobody's gonna take you anyway, freak, so you don't have anything to worry about." He released his grip on Charlie and pushed him backward.

Charlie tumbled over his own feet and fell hard onto the dusty fairground.

The guys laughed and sauntered off, pleased to have gotten such pleasure out of the disgrace.

"Are you okay?!" Jane asked, quickly leaning down beside him.

"Yeah." Charlie huffed while brushing his hands off on his jeans, "If only Aunt Cassidy could see us now." He shook his head, "It just goes to prove why people like us don't leave the house."

Jane slammed backward on her bike pedal, breaking just inches away from the mailbox. She panted, her chest rising and falling from the heavy exercise.

"This is it!" Charlie announced excitedly, "Open it, open it!"

Jane slowly stretched her fingers forward. All at once, she stopped. "I can't." She pulled her hands back. "I can't do it." She looked at Charlie. "You do it."

She quickly turned her bike around and closed her eyes, unable to bear whatever was about to happen next.

A pained look cast over Charlie's face as he slowly crept open the box. Jane could hear the old box lid squeaking on its hinges. She squeezed her eyes tighter, anxiously awaiting Charlie's news.

Only silence.

Jane could hear her own heart pounding within her chest.

Hurry up Charlie! She wanted to scream. If he didn't say something soon, she was going to explode!

"What is it?" she finally asked. "What is it?!"

Charlie didn't respond.

She slowly opened her eyes and looked at him. There was nothing in his hand.

"I'm sorry," Charlie spoke in a sorrowful tone. He cast his eyes toward the ground. He knew how disappointing this was for Jane.

Jane blinked. This couldn't be true! How could the mailbox be empty?! How could she have poured her entire heart into that story, and waited so long... all for this?

All for... nothing.

She wanted to cry, but she could not. She didn't have enough energy to shed another tear. She had to brush it off and come to the realization that this was her life. It was just another hauntingly-cursed reality of her pathetic existence. She should have known better. Things like *that*, midnight dreams coming true, just don't happen to people like her.

Her dad was gone. And now, so was her dream.

Jane couldn't think of anything worth saying. And so, she slowly turned and walked toward the house. Charlie kicked the mailbox with his shoe, angered over the heartbreaking results.

"How was your evening out?!" Aunt Cassidy asked excitedly as soon as Jane entered the living room. "Did you two have fun?!"

Jane didn't answer. She continued climbing up the stairs.

"Not a good time to ask, Aunt Cas!" Charlie scolded, following Jane up the steps. He couldn't let her be alone at a time like this. Surely, he could think of something to say that might cheer her up.

Jane reached her attic bedroom and wanted nothing less than to drop to the floor. But before she locked herself away in her bedroom, alone with her sorrows and her books, she addressed the young man behind her.

"Charlie. I want to be alone."

"But Jane, you need a friend! You need someone to support and encourage you and say there will always be a next time and—"

Jane abruptly closed the door. She felt cruel for doing it, but she didn't want him to see her cry. She didn't want to hear his empty, foolish, feel-good words. She didn't want to comfort herself with false hope that would never come through for her.

Jane's bottom lip quivered, and she tumbled backward onto her bed. As she reached her mattress, she felt something prickling her back. Curious, she flopped over.

All at once, Jane's heartbeat quickened. There was a letter on her bed.

She was almost afraid to touch it, for fear of it being a phantom, a soon-to-disappear figment of her imagination. Her eyes did a double take as she read the return address.

Young Novelists Writing Competition

6710 City Center Station,

New York City, New York

Her fingers trembled as she scrambled to open the letter. She struggled to read through her blurry tears.

Dear Jane Akerly,

We are pleased to announce, on behalf of Edison Ideas Publishing House, that you have been chosen as a finalist for our Young Novelist Writing Competition. We found your manuscript, London Love, to be both original and promising, and we are looking forward to having you fly to London and compete in the next leg of this competition. The official dates are–

Jane erupted with an ear-deafening scream.

The door flew open and Charlie rushed in. "Jane! Holy hamburgers, are you okay?!"

"Charlie! The letter! The letter, it's right here!" She bounced off her bed and rushed to show him, "I've been chosen as finalist! Me! I'm chosen! They chose me! ME! I'm going to London!" She screamed again, for she could not contain the pure joy and heavenly elation that overtook her entire being.

Chapter Ten

Secret Meeting

Jillian slipped out of the limousine, straightened her peach dress, and tossed an insecure stare toward the modest estate standing before them. Little Millie crawled out behind her. Everything about this situation was lavished in a thick jam of awkwardness. They were about to attend Deborah's daughter's birthday party. Jillian couldn't quite put her finger on it, but something about this situation felt incredibly unnatural. Was it the fact that she had never even *met* Pearl? The fact that she was several years older than her? Or was it that Vanessa suggested her dad might be 'interested' in Miss Deborah? None of those realities set right with her.

Two security guards escorted the girls to the front door, and Deborah greeted them with warm smiles. "I'm so glad you two are here! Pearl will be so excited to meet you! Come along, everyone is out back by the pool."

The girls followed Deborah around the house and to the backyard. Jillian observed the cluster of teens who excitedly chatted and giggled with one another. They were all circled around somebody. Jillian rose on her tiptoes, attempting to catch a glimpse of the birthday girl.

Deborah cleared her throat, and the chatter stilled. Several girls turned, their eyes growing wide at the sight of two buff security guards dressed in classy, black suits. The party guests instantly recognized the young Princesses. The grouping of teens parted, and Jillian caught her first look at Deborah's daughter.

Pearl wore a flirtatious-looking party dress, with red-lipped kissy faces splashed all across the calico print. Her tomato-red heels made her appear several inches taller than her peers, and her matching lipstick served as an unfriendly reminder as to how much more mature and sophisticated she was than them. Jillian wasn't even allowed to wear makeup yet.

"Young ladies, this is Princess Jillian and Princess Millie." Deborah looked at the Princess, "And *this* is my daughter, Pearl, as well as all her lovely friends."

"Happy Birthday, Pearl!" Millie quickly handed her a card.

Jillian bit her lip. Millie didn't have a single shy bone in her body. In Millie's eyes, this was all great fun. It wasn't everyday she got invited to leave the castle and attend a *real* birthday party.

"Mom, I thought you said the older Princesses were coming?" Pearl's voice was strained with a whiney complaint. "What happened to Bridget, Hope, and Chasity? You know, the *cool* ones?"

Jillian frowned.

"They were all busy darling, but isn't it just wonderful that Jillian and Millie were able to make it?" Deborah forced a smile onto her face,

[116]

coming behind Jillian and resting her slender fingers on her shoulders. "You girls have so much in common, I'm sure you'll hit it off right away! Now, I'll go tend to the snacks, and by the time I get back, I'm sure you'll all be the best of friends!"

Deborah disappeared. Jillian continued to stare at Pearl, unsure of what to do. What should she say? Should she compliment her dress?

Pearl lifted a disapproving eyebrow. She turned on her heel, setting her attention back on her friends. "So anyway, after this little shindig, Mom and I are going to Paris for the weekend! Mom requested some time off at The Palace just so we could have a little getaway."

"Ohhh, I love Paris!" one of her friends squealed. "Are you gonna go shopping while you're there? You have to go to the *Avenue des Champs Elyees*!"

"Duh!" Pearl exclaimed, "Mom promised to get me a Louis Vuitton bag!"

"Paris is alright, I suppose." One girl sighed, acting as though flying there on regular occasion was just as boring as taking a math test. "I much prefer to holiday in Greece."

"Oh, I've been to Greece!" Millie pipped up, excited to find a place to jump into the conversation. "Me and my sisters stayed with a really nice lady who had a big grape farm and—"

"Pearl, don't you already have like three Vuitton bags?" she interrupted, completely ignoring Millie.

"Four, actually," Pearl corrected her. "But I'm kind of addicted."

"What else are you getting for your birthday?" another girl asked.

"A new Chanel pallet, of course." Peal spoke as if the answer should be obvious.

"What's a pallet?" Millie asked. "Is that like for painting? I like to paint!"

Pearl shot Millie a disapproving stare, "How do you *not* know what a pallet is?"

"Hey, watch it. She's only nine years old!" Jillian spoke up, defending her little sister.

"And what are you, ten?" Pearl chuckled, obviously getting great pleasure from her little slam. "In case you didn't get the memo, this is a party." She looked at Millie once more, "Not a babysitting service."

"Apologize to her," Jillian demanded. "She's just trying to join in on the conversation. You're shooting down everything she says and acting like a snobbish jerk!"

"I don't have to apologize to anyone!" Pearl shot back, placing angry hands on her hips. "This is *my* party!"

"Some party!" Jillian huffed, "All you girls are doing is standing around discussing your stupid purses and makeup kits."

"Aw, what's wrong, you wish we would've set up Pin the Tail on the Donkey?" Pearl flashed a fake frown, "Maybe after we blow out candles we can play a rousing game of musical chairs!" Pearl rolled her eyes, "If you don't like the party, then leave."

Jillian snatched her card off the table, grabbed Millie's hand and proudly lifted her chin. "My pleasure."

And with that, Jillian stormed off toward the front yard.

"Vanessa, this library is wonderful!" Hope stood back from the creamy-white, built-in shelves, proud of their hard work. Every empty

[118]

space of the Library in the new Homeless Shelter had been filled. "Everyone who visits is going to be so grateful. My mom would be proud. She always said that giving someone a book is like giving them a ticket to a brand-new world."

"And hopefully, those who don't know how to read, or are struggling with it, can find all the assistance they need here." Vanessa sighed, satisfied with their accomplishment. "This room is just the beginning of producing more high school graduates, college students, and solid job opportunities."

"Vanessa, the press is getting very antsy to speak with you!" Deborah abruptly entered the room. "Interviews should've started ten minutes ago!"

"Okay, I think we're officially done!" Vanessa squealed as she clasped her hands together excitedly. She could linger in this room all day, basking in the glow of the dream come true. "I'm coming right now! Hope, can you put away all these boxes?"

"Sure, no problem," Hope nodded. "Go do your thing, girly!"

Vanessa gratefully tossed Hope a look of thanks, then lifted her legs over the empty boxes scattered throughout the room. She followed Deborah down the curvy hall and took a deep breath. "I can't believe this is actually happening! We're cutting the ribbon and opening today! Oh, how's my hair?"

The two paused in the hallway, and Deborah re-arranged several out-of-place strands. "You're radiant with beauty, as always."

"Radiant?" Vanessa laughed, "Hmm, you must mean the glow from my sweat. I'm so nervous! I sure hope I remembered everything! This is going to be the public's first look at what we've done. Oh no! I should've asked someone to make sure the bathroom mirrors were cleaned! There was still some caulking that hadn't dried yet around the sink and—"

"Vanessa, stop worrying." Deborah reassured her, "You've done everything to the best of your ability, but now time is up. You just have to leave it in the Lord's hands."

"Right." Vanessa sighed. Deborah was right. All the time on the clock had expired, and now the moment was at hand. She glanced out of the large windows in the lobby, noting the huge line of representors from media outlets, as well as dozens of local families who came for the opening celebration. "Well, ready or not, here we go!"

Back in the library, Hope collected the remaining cardboard boxes and stacked them on top of one another. She struggled to get them through the narrow library doorframe. She paused. *There has to be a better way to do this.* She pursed her lips. All at once, it dawned on her. *Breaking down the boxes will make them smaller. Perfect!* She quickly attempted to rip one apart, but the tough material resisted her iron grip. She tossed that one to the side, then tried a smaller box, from a different angle.

The struggle endured, until finally she released a frustrated groan. "Goodness gracious, WORK with me, boxes!"

"What's this, some kind of anger management class?"

Hope looked up in surprise. She didn't recognize the voice. Wild hair hung in her face, so she couldn't see who stood in the doorway. She threw her hair back and stood upright.

Luke.

"I guess attempting to rip cardboard boxes apart is cheaper than therapy," he chuckled.

Hope frowned. A sprinkle of pink pinched her cheeks as hot embarrassment rushed through her blood. She hated the idea of him seeing her struggling with such a simple task.

"Hope versus the boxes, and the boxes are winning." He laughed again.

"Okay, Mr. Macho," Hope challenged, feeling the familiar horn-butting attitude flair up every time Luke was present. She crossed her arms. "This isn't as easy as it looks, you know."

"Of course not!" he grinned. "Breaking boxes can take a lot out of a person." He swiftly slipped a box cutter from his back pocket and proceeded to slice the box in seconds. It fell onto the floor, flattened, and was ready to be carried to the recycling bin.

Hope wasn't amused. "You're totally cheating."

"Having the right tool isn't cheating. It's called street smarts."

Luke quickly sliced through each box, and Hope stacked as many as she could in her arms. Luke collected a pile as well, and then headed down the hall, through the kitchen, and out the back door to the dumpster.

"You know, for as much as you dislike my family, you sure do show up a lot to help out with things," Hope verbalized her observation after throwing the final load into the recycling bin.

"I don't have anything against your family. I just don't agree with the way your brother is running the country. And even then, there are still some movements and decisions made by the Crown that I *do* agree with and that I don't mind supporting. Like renovating the Homeless Shelter and adding all the new services and opportunities for those who are struggling? That's something I can totally get behind."

"Yeah, this was Vanessa's idea. She's all about projects like this." Hope lifted a nervous hand to scratch a non-existent itch behind her ear. "So, your Sons of Liberty card showed up in my bedroom the other day."

"And?"

Hope studied his poker face. He was nearly impossible to read.

"I want to come to a meeting." Hope continued cautiously, "But to do so, I'd have to have some kind of legitimate excuse for me to leave The Palace. I'd have several guards with me, and I really don't want to make a scene."

"So, you actually want to come and find out what we're all about?" Luke was unable to hide the hint of excitement in his voice.

"Yeah. I do. But it just isn't so easy for me to—"

"Hope. Look. Do you see any guards right now?"

Hope slowly peered over her shoulder in the empty backlot, realizing it was as quiet as could be. There was only one lone truck parked nearby.

"Yeah, but that's because they think I'm still inside and—"

Without warning, Luke lifted his index finger and placed it over Hope's mouth.

"I'm leaving for a meeting at my friend Todd's house." He removed his hand and offered a shrug, "You wanna come, or not?"

"Right now?!" Hope's heartbeat quickened.

"You've got five seconds to hop in the truck, or I'm leaving without you." Luke smiled then turned to walk toward his vehicle.

"Luke, that's crazy!" she called after him. "I can't just sneak away!"

"It's your choice." He shrugged, unlocking the truck over his shoulder, "But it looks like the coast is clear to me. Come on, we'll be back before they've even realized you're gone."

"I can't believe I'm doing this!" Hope gushed from the passenger seat of Luke's truck. She anxiously scanned the road behind them, wondering how many more minutes this tiny taste of freedom would last before the *entire* Royal Guard came looking for her. "If my family finds out I snuck off to a meeting with the rebels, they're going to freak!" She looked at him, her face as white as a sheet. "I've never done anything like this in my entire life!"

"Well, that is quite obvious." Luke grinned, fighting back a laugh. "Small piece of advice. When we get to Todd's barn—"

"The meeting is in a *barn*?" Hope asked, surprised with the new information.

"His parents are loyalists, so we couldn't exactly host it in his living room. Anyway, when we get there, stay low, and stay covered behind the hay bales to make sure no one sees you."

"Oh, right." Hope nodded, almost forgetting she was wasn't welcome at these functions. "Wow, I feel like some kind of criminal or something."

"To them, you pretty much are."

"Well, that's comforting," Hope huffed.

"Should something as uncontrollable as birthright be used as a scale to determine who has the power to make a difference in the world, and who doesn't?" Luke spoke, passionately sharing his thoughts with the group surrounding him.

Hope sat behind an itchy hay bale, her back pressed against the uncomfortable strands of hay poking out. She was safely tucked behind a wall of hay, close to the backdoor of the barn where no one would find her. At first, Hope's heartbeat pounded so loudly, she couldn't hear herself think, let alone hear Luke welcome the group. She felt as though at any moment someone would peek behind the bales and catch her red-handed. She couldn't ignore the racing fear. Panic arose as she thought of a dozen police cars rolling into the yard, her security guards dragging her back home to a frowning father and disappointed brother. Her conscience screamed, condemning her for sneaking out the way she had.

But now, sitting contentedly with her legs crisscrossed, every heavy layer of fear had evaporated. She felt a deep peace settle her heart as Luke opened the meeting with prayer. She was surprised to hear him do that. It was so strange for her to think that a movement which appeared to undermine her family, would begin by talking to the Lord. Was it possible that God was behind Luke's passion, driving him to say the things he did? Hope wasn't so sure.

She was also surprised by the number of people who sat in the barn, eagerly listening to Luke. When she first arrived, it appeared there were about thirty people present, and she had heard more enter since then. Although she couldn't see anything, she guessed that anywhere from fifty to sixty people were scattered across the large, empty barn.

"For centuries, our nation has been divided by a prejudice caste system, dividing the pureblood 'privileged' from the low, working class—the 'under-privileged'. We treat the Royals and their members of Parliament like they're some kind of lowercase gods, meanwhile the rest of us are expected to mindlessly submit to whatever they decide is right. For years, my father has worked in The Palace, but he and the staff are expected to address the Royal Family with lofty titles, curtsies and bows, following some old-fashioned protocol that our nation has ascribed to for hundreds of years, and nobody even knows why! They claim that this nation is founded upon the Bible, but I don't see anything Biblical about treating one man like a prince and another like a pauper! The Bible warns us against showing this kind of favoritism, and though the Bible urges us to honor those in leadership, sometimes there comes time for a change. A nation has no power without the power to govern itself! If we the people have no voice, no choice, no decisions to make, and no way to affect our government, then we have become slaves of the monarchy! Liberty should be a basic, fundamental right of everyone in this country! If we do not have the power of democracy, to vote on what happens in this land, and to make our voices heard, then what kind of future will the next generation have? Will they be forced to live in a society where they must conform to the opinions and decisions of *one* man?"

"We need to fight to get our voice back!" A young voice shouted from the crowd, "Every effort we make to express our opinions is shut down by the Crown!"

"But we have to be strategic in the way we go about this," Luke cautioned. "Protests, violence, and threats are not going to get us anywhere. Other than jail, maybe. If God is behind this movement, He will grant us wisdom and show us how to establish a new form of government. A free democracy will give Tarsurella the liberty for men to govern themselves! Our monarchy is affecting our reputation among global trade, and we're to the point that other nations aren't even taking us seriously! We're trapped in a happy little mirage of something that worked in the past. But it's *not* working anymore. Tarsurellian citizens are waking up and realizing things must change! This theocracy, though it can be applauded as 'safe' and 'moral' for some, is only going to cause more and more tension in our secular society. Just as we cannot force the citizens of Tarsurella to choose Christianity, the Royal Family should not force us to follow their political policies. If we continue to shove this theocracy down our nation's throat, we're just as bad any other religious powerhouse—such as radical Islam, forcing people to follow their ways. Jesus *never* forced anyone to follow Him. He always gave them a choice. And if Tarsurella doesn't allow the people to make their own choices about church, government, faith and religion… then we are nothing more than prisoners of a 'good idea' that no longer exists."

Hope closed the passenger door of Luke's truck and offered him a little wave goodbye.

"Hope!" Bridget called. She and Liam had pulled in the driveway at the same moment. They rushed out of Liam's car and bolted toward her. Bridget's forehead was tight with worry lines. "Thank the Lord, you're okay!" Bridget breathed a sigh of relief. "A whole troop of guards are out looking for you! We thought something happened!"

"Bridget, I can explain." Hope couldn't hide the nerves in her voice, "Just hear me out, okay? I'll tell you where I was, but you have to promise not to tell Dad or Addison—"

Luke rolled his window down. "Hey, thanks for running that errand with me! I never would've found the Ziploc bags Vanessa asked for." He tossed a small box of zipper bags out the window. Hope caught it, feeling uncomfortable in the wake of his lie. "Enjoy the rest of your day!" He nodded respectfully then backed up, pulling out of the lot.

Bridget's jaw dropped. "Was that Luke? Clark's son?" Her perfectly trimmed eyebrows towered to new heights. "Liberty Stone? The guy who leaked our secret and pushed for Asher to go to jail?!"

"Bridget, I said I can explain! If you'll just hear me out—"

"Mulan is in my sights! Mulan is safe, I repeat, Mulan is in the back lot of the Homeless Shelter!" An animated guard spoke as he burst through the backdoor, reporting that Hope had arrived. Several other guards, as well as Hope's father, were right behind him.

"Hope!" Steve rushed to her side, "What happened? Where were you?! Do you have any idea what you just put me through?!" He clutched a hand to his chest, "Oh, praise God you're safe, we thought someone had abducted you!"

Hope's throat tightened. Tears threatened to overtake her. She couldn't lie to her father. But how could she tell him she snuck out to attend a rebel meting? How could she express that she didn't think Luke was crazy, and that he might actually have some thoughts worth listening to? She was in a unique position to serve as a mediator for the two parties. But what could she possibly say right now that wouldn't send her dad through the roof? How could she encourage him to see things from her perspective?

"She was with us," Bridget quickly spoke, covering for her sister.

Hope's eyes flashed toward Bridget.

"We needed to pick up Ziploc baggies," Bridget added. "For Vanessa."

"Why didn't you report to one of the guards that she left?" Steve looked at Liam, "Didn't you get the notification that she was missing?"

"Yes, sir," Liam nodded. "Sorry, sir. It won't happen again."

Hope stared at Liam, quite surprised that he was going along with it.

[127]

Steve looked at Hope once more, then shook his head. "We'll talk about this at home. We're leaving."

Steve went back inside, and the guards followed.

Bridget exhaled angrily.

"Bridge, tha—" Hope started.

"Don't even say it," Bridget snapped. "Because I am *not* covering for you again. Hope, what in the world were you thinking?! Sneaking off with the enemy?! I get that things can get a little cooped up at The Palace, and you want to get out and do something exciting, live on the edge, whatever. But out of all the guys you could've chosen to do something stupid with, you chose him?!"

"Bridget, it's not like that!" Hope quickly attempted to explain, afraid Bridget was getting the wrong idea. "There's nothing romantic going on, and I promise we weren't doing anything stupid! He's been asking me to—"

The door opened once more, and a guard popped out his head. "Princess Hope, your ride is here. Your father wishes for you to leave with him."

"Go!" Bridget urged her, "Before you get into any more trouble."

Hope opened her mouth to protest, but it was clear Bridget wasn't in any state of mind to listen to her reasoning. Hope obeyed the guard, knowing that explaining things to Bridget would be much easier after she cooled off.

"I can't believe her." Bridget shook her head as soon as Hope was safe inside. "Sneaking out like that?! I mean, when I was her age, I wanted to leave more than anything. But I didn't. And I *especially* didn't sneak out with a guy like Luke!"

"I have a really bad feeling about that kid." Liam sighed, stuffing his hands in the pockets of his khaki shorts. "And what's weird is, he seems so familiar. I feel like I've seen him somewhere before."

"His face was all over the news once his secret pen name was exposed."

"No, it's not that." Liam shook his head, "I can't figure out what it is, but I could almost guarantee I've run into him somewhere before."

Chapter Eleven

Adventure Inquiry

"I just couldn't lie to you, Dad." Hope sighed. "That's where I went this afternoon."

Steve placed a thoughtful hand on his chin. A long silence passed between the two before he finally spoke.

"I appreciate you telling me the truth, Hope. I wish you wouldn't have fed me that bologna about picking up plastic sandwich bags, but right now, that's beside the point. The bigger issue is, yes, even beyond you sneaking out and not telling anyone where you were going, *why* in the blazes would you want to go to a meeting like that?"

"I know it might be hard for you to understand, but I want to express this in the clearest way possible." Hope took a deep breath, attempting to remain calm. She wanted her dad to hear her out and respect her opinion on the matter. But she was nervous about expressing her jumbled-up thoughts. How could she explain to her father what she was thinking, when she wasn't even sure of the truth? "I believe that Luke, as brash and ungraceful as he is in the way he goes about things, has some really important things to say. Although some of his ideas are challenging and controversial, I've also seen the hand of God on his life, and I've been impressed with his words of wisdom. I've known about these meetings for a while now, and really prayed about going. I wrestled with it in my mind, but I couldn't ignore the nudging of my heart. When the opportunity arose, I just couldn't turn it down. I knew it would be a risk, but there was no other way for me to truly hear where Luke's heart is at with all of this. And now that I've learned much more of the why behind his ways, some of it is starting to make sense to me. I think it would be beneficial for Addison to sit down with Luke and just calmly talk through some of these issues. Just because we've always done things a certain way for a long time, doesn't mean we should be afraid to listen to new ideas when they present themselves, right? We can't be afraid of change, Dad. So, that's why I went. Because I was curious, and in some strange way, I felt like God was urging me to."

"Hmm. Does this sudden interest in Luke's wonton perspective about things stem from a deeper attraction toward the young man?"

"Dad, no!" Hope frowned, "Why does everyone keep saying that? There's *nothing* romantic going on between Luke and me! I'll admit that yes, he's good looking, but I assure you that is not why I'm interested in his political perspective."

"I see." Steve nodded. "So, what is it specifically that Luke has spoken of that you're meriting as truth?"

"I'm not really sure yet." Hope replied with a gentle sigh. "I'm still sorting through a lot in my mind. I heard a lot of information today, and

[132]

it's a ton to process. I guess it's not so much one particular point that makes sense, but it's more just something in my heart that's telling me he could be right."

"Our hearts can be deceptive, Hope." Steve cautioned her, "And though you are old enough to make your own decisions concerning these matters, I would strongly discourage you from continuing to pour his perspective into your mind. Sometimes, when you listen to something for long enough, it can start to sound like truth, even if it isn't. Your mind is precious, Hope, just as your heart is, and you know that I've poured my whole life into encouraging each of my children to guard their hearts at all costs. I don't want you dumping toxic poison into your mind. Now I trust you, and I am confident in the young woman God has created you to be. You know who you are in Christ, and you've always had a strong Christian character. But even the strongest and purest can be deceived. It only takes a little bit of dirt to contaminate purity. I'm not going to forbid you from seeing this young man, but you're a smart girl, Hope. Don't go around playing with fire."

"Dad, can I ask you something?"

Steve smiled at his daughter who stood in the doorway. As a single parent, he was always in demand. But he didn't mind it one bit. Hope had just left the room, and now Chasity was waiting to speak with him.

"Of course, sweetheart."

Chasity entered his den and sat down on the sofa beside him. "I'm worried about Asher."

"We all are," Steve sighed, running a tired hand through his receding hairline.

"Ever since his trial, he's back to his old vice. Those stupid video games." Chasity's voice was heavy, "It's like he's convinced himself that he's some kind of criminal who deserves to go to jail."

"I've had several conversations with Principle Snyder, as well as with the judge. While I am still awaiting a confirmation call, I'm quite confident that our appeal for Asher to attend military school this fall will be accepted. Jail time won't be necessary."

"A few months ago, when that American girl—Jane, I think her name was—was here, I thought I saw something shift in Asher. It was like, for a few days he stopped thinking about himself so much and actually started caring about someone else's problems besides his own. It was almost like, he came alive." Chasity's eyes smiled at the thought, "But now, with the Walter Akerly case coming to a dead end, and there being nothing Asher can do to help that girl find her dad, I'm really concerned about him. He needs something else he can shift his mind and focus to. Something he can fix his attention on and forget about himself for a little while. He needs a distraction."

"I agree." Steve nodded, "But he sure doesn't seem interested in helping out with the Homeless Shelter, or any of the other projects Addison has suggested. What do you have in mind?"

Chasity took a deep breath. She hoped her father would be in favor of the idea. "I think we should go to England."

"England?" Steve chuckled, "That seems quite random. I'm assuming there is a greater purpose behind this suggestion?"

"Of course," Chasity nodded, scooting a little closer to him. Her voice picked up speed as excitement creeped out and increased her volume. "You know who Nathaniel Wells is, right?"

"Hmm, that name sounds vaguely familiar…"

"He's an amazingly-talented racehorse trainer!" Chasity nearly squealed, giddy with joy. "He worked with *Reckless Road Rage,* who completely came out of nowhere last year and won the *Belington Derby*! And this year, *Pink Cotton*, who he worked with as well, placed second! Dad, he's becoming a legend! Anyway, James introduced us, and he wants to come and look at Nic! James thinks he's got spectacular potential, and if Nathaniel comes to the same conclusion, he might decide to *train* him for the circuit next year!"

"As fascinating as all of this is, I'm confused. What does this have to do with England? And Asher?"

"Mr. Wells is hosting a racing convention for breeders, owners, and jockeys, in the English countryside, at the O'Conner Estate. It would be an incredible opportunity to learn more about the sport and see what the next year might hold for Nic and me, if Nathaniel decides to work with him."

"And how does Asher fit into this?"

"I think that a trip like this could be just what he needs. An opportunity to get out of The Palace, enjoy some fresh air, and reconnect with some old friends. We used to have such a blast at the O'Conner Estate as kids, and I think Asher needs to remember what it's like to be a child again. Carefree and simply having an enjoyable time. Besides," Chasity's voice softened, "if he's leaving for military school this fall, this might be the last chance I'd have to spend any time with him."

"That is a lot to consider." Steve nodded, "But I will take your words to heart. I agree, it would be good for Asher to leave The Palace and learn to enjoy life again. The O'Conners have been such good family friends, and I know with their high profile and security measures in place, it would be a safe little getaway. Hmm… let me pray about this, Chasity, and I'll let

[135]

you know soon."

Chapter Twelve

Welcome to London

The crystal blue skies rejoiced. Jane knew all of Heaven was celebrating with her. The fluffy clouds, from which her plane poked out its nose, murmured amongst themselves about the miracle. All of creation held its breath in elated anticipation: Jane was about to land in London!

None of it felt real. It was as if she was experiencing a most delightful bout of Deja vu. As the plane descended toward the bronze city, Jane knew she had been there before. Perhaps not in real life, but certainly in her dreams. Though the wheels had not yet touched the landing strip, she already knew she was home. London was one with her heartbeat. Surely this city would be everything she anticipated.

As the plane stretched its legs and attempted to brush its wheel-y toes on the ground, Jane pulled out her flip phone, prepared to let Charlie and Aunt Cassidy know she had landed. She had never own a cell phone before this trip, but Aunt Cassidy insisted that she carry one with her at all times while abroad. And so, they purchased a Jitterbug. Jane was quite confident that the thick-buttoned, large-numbered phone was intended for elderly folks who couldn't see well. Nevertheless, Jane didn't complain. How could she? She was in London!

Jane braced herself with her palms against the seat in front of her. The plane slammed on its breaks, attempting to slow the massive jet-liner.

The friendly stewardess spoke over the intercom, reminding the passengers of all the orderly rules they must follow before exiting the plane. Jane grinned. She imagined that those who flew frequently grew tired of hearing such messages. But Jane could listen to the stewardess chat all day. Her British accent was adorable. With the go-ahead to turn on their cellular devices, Jane did so and shot Charlie a quick text. It was strange not having him, Aunt Cassidy, her father… or anyone else for that matter, with her. She glanced at the empty seat beside her. She was completely alone. And she would be, until she connected with her YNC (Young Novelist Competition) chaperone, Laurie.

Jane's shoes tapped nervously on the plane floor. Couldn't they park this thing any faster?! Her senses churned with anticipation—she needed to get out and see her city! Jane smiled at the sunshine, knowing it would be a rarity. She knew rainy days were to be expected this time of year.

After several long, seemingly never-ending moments, the stewardess finally gave them permission to unfasten their belts and exit the cabin. Jane collected her luggage and cheerfully rolled down the catwalk, ready to face whatever was out there waiting for her! Jane had never felt this confident in her entire life. She couldn't help but wonder what was in the air. Was there leftover pixie dust floating around in the clouds, forgotten in the sky where *Peter Pan* had once flown?

Jane studied the busy terminal, searching for someone who looked like the woman in the picture emailed to her. She spotted a sign with her last name on it. "AKERLY."

Jane approached the woman.

"Are you Jane Akerly?" the woman asked excitedly. "I'm Laurie! Welcome to London!"

"I'm the girl." Jane smiled and shook her hand, slightly disappointed that Laurie didn't have an accent. Her words sounded boring—old midwest American, just like her.

"Well, congratulations! On behalf of the YNC we are thrilled to have you here as our United States finalist! Are you ready to raise your pen and go up against dozens of other talented writers from all across the globe?!"

Jane wasn't sure how to answer.

"Never mind that, I'm sure right now you're exhausted!" Laurie laughed, "Here, let me help you with your bag. Come along, we'll catch a taxi and get you checked in at *The Landmark London*."

Even though Jane didn't express it outwardly, she was electrified within. Contrary to what Laurie thought, she was *far* from tired. It was as if ten-thousand little Christmas lights had been turned on inside her soul, and she could do nothing but shine.

Jane rolled her luggage across the tan carpet, distracted by the blue and purple diamond shapes scattered across it. Her hotel room was absolutely elegant, boasting two French-door balconies, a fresh flower display, and two comfortable-looking queen-size beds.

"Your roommates will be arriving this evening. If you're hungry, feel free to take advantage of room service. There is a continental breakfast at 7:00 a.m., followed by orientation at 8:00. We expect everyone to be on time and dressed in a classy, professional manner." Laurie gave her the rundown, "Although we want everyone to have fun, this is not a free summer vacation. Anyone who breaks the rules, or behaves unprofessionally, will be disqualified and sent home immediately. We are here for the joy of writing, and we won't condone sneaking around, partying, or displaying any other questionable behavior. Although we will be busy with our writing classes, we will allow ample time for you to go and explore the city, as we know that will be a great source of inspiration for your soul!"

Jane glanced over her shoulder and stole a quick peek out the window. She couldn't wait for that.

"If you have any questions, please feel free to call me, or come knock at Room 305, as myself and several other chaperones will be right next door."

After Laurie left, Jane was alone again. She took advantage of the quiet to shower and change into her cozy pajamas. By the time she emerged from the bathroom, her room was full. Three teenage girls introduced themselves; a young woman from China, one from South Africa, and another from France. Jane was quite intrigued by the diversity of stories and backgrounds. She found herself growing even more thrilled about the upcoming week.

Jane floated onto the double-decker, cherry-red bus. She climbed to the second floor and took a deep breath of the wide-open air. It was finally happening! She was about to take a tour of the most whimsical, enchanting, history-filled city in the world! Orientation had ended, and now she and her roommates were free to explore Westminster Abbey, Buckingham Palace, and the Tower of London!

She slipped her Polaroid camera out of her bag, ready to snap images. She didn't care if she looked like a wide-eyed tourist. She was going to enjoy every moment of this experience.

As the bus lurched forward, Jane's thoughts left the morning meeting and flew forward as well. Now that all the kids had arrived, they were presented with a most-harrowing challenge: writing a captivating, excellent, superb piece of literature, in just two short weeks. Jane had never been any good at short stories, as her mind was far too excessive and drifty to condense her thoughts into something so choppy and concise. She had hoped the challenge would give them space enough to write an entire novel, but then again, it would be absolutely batty to think she could pull that off in two weeks either. She knew a short story was the most realistic option of the two, especially if she wanted any time to sightsee, eat, or use the restroom! Still, the challenge was quite unnerving, and she wasn't sure if her skills were up to par. The other competitors were harshly intimidating. Several of them boasted of winning various competitions, self-publishing their own trilogies, or having a huge fan following online. Jane didn't have any of that. All she had was an imagination.

But Jane wasn't going to worry. At least not right now. She wasn't going to allow the stress and pressure steal the utter joy of this moment. She was about to explore London!

"I cannot imagine having so much jewelry that you'd need to build a whole tower just to protect it!" Johannah, her South African roommate, commented.

[141]

"That place gave me the heebie-jeebies!" Laurie shivered, appearing as if she were trying to shake off the creepy feeling. "The Big Ben is much friendly than that stormy tower."

"But it has so much history!" Cha-Linn expressed, "It was almost as if you could feel the stories of the past, the blood of the innocent, those who had been wrongly accused and brutally executed, calling out to us. In fact, I already know what I am going to write about."

"So do I!" Johannah cheered. "I've never had so many ideas floating through my head! There's inspiration hiding beneath every cinderblock!"

Jane twisted her lip as the girls continued talking. She didn't have any ideas yet. She had crossed three most-exhilarating items off her bucket list: touring Westminster Abbey, witnessing the changing of the guard, and attempting to make a Royal Guard laugh. Yet, despite those activities she had always dreamed of, her inspiration resembled the Sahara Desert. How could these girls already have stories forming in their mind? Jane needed to think of something brilliant—and quickly—if she wanted any chances at winning this thing.

They crossed the busy street, Laurie leading the charge. "Now, go, go, go!" she urged, encouraging the girls to pick up the pace, not wanting any of them to get hit by busy traffic.

"You girls are going to love this place!" Laurie told them once they safely reached the sidewalk. It was nearly dinnertime, and the tourists had worked up ravenous appetites. Jane suppressed the desire to let out a squeal. They were about to dine at a real, authentic, Fish and Chips restaurant! After standing in line for a solid fifteen minutes, they finally ordered their meals, and Laurie suggested they take advantage of the time to brainstorm. "Our schedule this week is going to be quite demanding, with writing classes, special speakers, as well as various field trips and outings. You'll have to be aggressive when it comes to blocking out moments to write. Mealtime is ideal. How about we each sit at separate tables and meet back at the counter in an hour?"

"Sounds perfect!" Cha-Linn spoke, "That should give me enough time to create my outline!" She took her tray and confidently headed toward a table near the back.

Soon they all split up, and Jane smiled. That was one delightful advantage to being in a competition with so many deeply-introspective introverts. They all needed their space, and no one really cared to speak with one another. Too much socializing would take away from their time to write. Well, that worked just splendidly for her!

Jane sat at a counter near the front. It was terribly noisy. She wasn't sure how far any of the girls would get with plotting their tales. How could anyone think in a place this loud? Although Jane was typically pretty talented at blocking out the real world, there was far too much going on. She dove into her supper and contentedly watched the long line of people order their meals. Her toes swung happily on the bench, swaying with the music in her mind. Her ears smiled as she listened to their bustling British accents. She wanted so badly to have an accent. But her attempt at forging a British accent was painfully pathetic. She always told herself that when she went to London, she would speak with a faux accent the entire time and see if she could fool anyone. But she hadn't been brave enough to try it yet.

As the line ebbed and flowed, she noticed a young man nearing the front. His charming face struck her attention. His kind blue eyes shone, and Jane admired his distinguished jaw. London seemed to be swarming with handsome European fellas. Jane sighed, wondering what it was about British boys that were so entirely captivating. She had never wasted her time pining away over the young men at school; they were all heartless jerks. And even though Jane knew London had its share of cruel heartbreakers, she had to believe it was also hiding some authentic, caring, devastatingly-polite gentlemen. Jane thought of her main character in *London Love*, and even though he was very much a fantasy, she couldn't help but wonder if someone like him existed.

Jane turned back to her fish and chips and reached for a drink. Just as the straw reached her mouth and a fresh gulp of water traveled down her throat, that same young man sat down in the empty stool beside her.

"Good afternoon."

Jane choked, abruptly coughing. The water in her throat shot up and went down the wrong hole. Her face turned bright red as she coughed three more times.

Concern flashed across the young man's face, "Miss, are you alright?!"

Jane tried to reply, but she couldn't. She was still coughing. She waved an anxious hand in her face, trying to calm herself and catch a breath of fresh air. Finally, the coughing ceased and the redness decreased in her face. "I, I'm…" Jane finally managed to spit out, "fine."

"I am quite relived!" The young man chuckled, "I thought perhaps we'd have to rush you to the ER. Would be a great bummer indeed, for your first real meal of fish and chips!"

Jane tossed him a quizzical glance, "How… how did you know this was my first time in London?"

Jane felt her heartbeat quickening. Was this guy even real? Was she completely hallucinating? Had her flawless character come to life?

"Your American accent gave you away." He grinned, revealing a shiny line of perfectly white teeth, "As well as the fact you appeared quite delighted, tossing your feet back and forth like a cheerful little child,

[144]

immensely enjoying your fish and chips basket. You had the word 'tourist' written all over you."

Jane wasn't sure how she should feel. "Who are you?" she asked. The question was terribly forward and abrupt, but she had to know.

"Oh, forgive me for not introducing myself!" He smiled and held out his hand, "It isn't proper to speak so freely with strangers, I suppose. The name is James. James O'Conner. It's a pleasure to make your acquaintance. And you are?"

"Jane." She spoke slowly, shocked at the realization that this was indeed a real person sitting beside her. She grew sweaty as she shook his hand. "Jane Akerly."

"Well, welcome to London, Miss Akerly." James smiled and stood up, "I hope you have a truly wonderful time, and that our city is everything you dreamed and more. Oh, and do not worry about your tab, I've already taken care of the bill." He nodded his head politely and headed toward the door, "Consider it a welcome gift of hospitality. Enjoy your stay, miss!"

Chapter Thirteen

Losing her Carrots

"Miss Bennet, Miss Bennet! May I ask you a few questions?!"

Vanessa looked up from the selection of carrots, green beans, and sugar snap peas. A male reporter stood beside her with a massive camera hanging around his neck, and a pen and pad of paper in hand. Vanessa attempted to keep her irritation at bay. She was *not* in the mood to speak with the press. She had merely dropped by the farmers market with the purpose of picking up some items, in an attempt to make dinner for her parents. Vanessa wasn't the best cook, but stir-fry vegetables and rice seemed like something she could manage without burning her apartment down. "Actually, I'm really busy, and have an engagement tonight that I need to get home for."

"How are the wedding preparations coming?" the reporter asked, completely ignoring her polite refusal. "How are you feeling, with the pregnancy and all?"

"Excuse me?!" Vanessa snapped, nearly dropping her bundle of carrots on the ground.

"Well, isn't that why you and King Addison are getting married so soon?" he asked. "To cover up your pregnancy outside of wedlock?"

Vanessa could feel the veins below her eyebrows imploding. "You should be ashamed of yourself!" she told the crummy reporter. "Fabricating juicy stories that hold no ounce of truth whatsoever—stories that are loaded with made-up dirt, just so you can sell more magazines!" She turned and headed for the checkout line. So what if she had forgotten her peas and green beans! She was furious.

"Miss Vanessa, do you have any comments on Asher's trial? How do you feel about marrying into a family with criminal activity?"

Vanessa looked the other direction, but the man was right in her face. "I have no comment," she snapped. "Now if you'll excuse me, please respect my privacy. I need my space."

"Oh my lanta!" the college-aged girl in front of her spurted out. "I can't believe it! You're the girl King Addison is marrying!"

"What the heck!" A teen standing beside her, sporting a crop top and a belly button ring spat, "This market sells food to the Royals?! What a jip! See if I ever buy my vegetables here again!" She looked at the cashier, "I thought you said you were in support of the rebellion, Rod!"

"Huh?" Rod looked up from the cash register. His wide eyes told Vanessa he didn't want to get involved with this conversation. "I swear I didn't know Vanessa shops here! I've never seen her before in my life!"

Vanessa's jaw dropped. "I come here like every week!"

"If you sell to her, I'm never shopping here again!" Belly-button-ring girl threatened, "And neither is my *Green Girl* co-op!"

The reporter quickly jotted down each sentence on his note-pad, then flashed the camera at Vanessa.

"I told you, get that thing out of my face!" She held up her hand, covering the lens.

"Ohhh, future Queen throws a temper tantrum!" The reporter laughed, "That'll make a good headline!"

"She's not our Queen," the girl snapped, "and Addison isn't our King! You're a disappointment to women everywhere." Her fiery eyes flashed toward Vanessa, sparking just as vehemently as the words flying off her tongue. "Subjecting yourself to marrying him so young, telling girls that women are worthless until they've got a ring on their finger! People like you are the reason little girls think life is nothing more than castles and princes and stupid fairytales. Let me guess, you're gonna quit work, and have like ten kids?"

Vanessa glared at her. "You have *no* idea what you're talking about. Life with Addison is *not* going to be a fairytale, thanks to you people. And never once in my life have I said that getting married is the epitome of life, that I'm going to quit my job, or have ten children!"

"You don't have a job." The girl released a cruel chuckle, "Wearing a sparkly crown, parading behind your stupid fiancé, waving around your ring-bling in our faces is *not* a job."

"Ohhh, burn!" The reporter was getting great enjoyment out of the fight. "What are you gonna say back to that, Vanessa?"

[149]

"Would you just get lost?!" She dropped her vegetables on the counter. She turned to Rod. "And you don't have to worry about selling to me anymore, because I'm never shopping here again."

"Future Queen Loses Her Temper, Tells Citizens They're Ruining Her Fairytale." Addison chuckled, "Creative title."

"It's not creative!" Vanessa groaned, "It's a disaster!"

"No, no, listen to this!" Addison grinned. "Is Vanessa fit to be Tarsurella's next Queen? Just ask the man who nearly got hit in the head with carrots at the local farmers market!" Addison laughed, "I can just see it! You, flinging carrots at the cashier!"

"Stop reading that!" Vanessa sank into Addison's office chair, on the verge of tears. "This is terrible! I'm such a failure. Look at that picture, I look like I'm about to bite his head off! I'm a monster, I can't even look at it!"

Addison quickly set the newspaper down and rushed to Vanessa's side. He had no idea that this was deeply bothering her. "Ness, I was kidding!" He grabbed her hand, "Honey, it was just a joke. Can't you see, that whole article is completely laughable? Nobody's going to believe it. It's just tabloid garbage for people who have nothing better to do with their time."

"Addi, they think I'm pregnant! They think that I'm trying to cover something up, and that I'm a disappointment to humanity because I'm marrying you, and that I'm just going to be your slave, and do nothing but wash your clothes and clean up after the kids and—"

"Shhh, shh, shh, Vanessa." Addison welcomed her into his arms, and she collapsed beneath the pressure. Tears assaulted her. Vanessa's distressed emotions were too far gone to control. There was nothing to do other than cling to Addison and let the tears fall. "I know it's hard," he whispered, desperately hoping to comfort her. "I know they're cruel, and heartless, and publish all kinds of lies about us. But you *know* those words aren't true. It doesn't matter what they think. You know who you are."

"But it does matter!" She pulled away, her eyes puffy. "The entire world thinks I'm someone I'm not! Even some of my friends back home think—
"

"Ness, look at me." Addison gently touched her chin and turned it toward him, "You have to forget about everyone else. You have to block out the stories and the rumors. People who know the *true* you absolutely adore you, and that's all that matters. If your friends, or even your family, think those stories are real, well, then they obviously don't know you as well as they thought they did."

"It's not that simple," Vanessa sniffed. "I just… I'm not cut out for this. I can't be a Queen. I can't even go to the farmers market without blowing up! I'm not the soft-spoken, kind, submissive, polite woman everyone expects to be standing by your side. How am I going to represent you and your nation if I can't even have a conversation without feeling like I wanna smack someone?!"

"You've gotta give yourself some grace." Addison patiently reminded her, "You're in the middle of one of the craziest seasons of your life. This is going to take an adjustment period, and nobody is expecting you to be perfect. So what if you lose your temper here and there? You're carrying thousands of pounds of stress on your shoulders, trying to plan a wedding, run the Homeless Shelter, entertain your parents, and keep our relationship going strong—it's a lot, Vanessa. Don't except more from yourself than what is humanly possible."

"I just…" she sighed, "I didn't want it to be like this. I wanted to be—"

"Perfect?" Addison finished her sentence.

Vanessa nodded.

"Well, you're not." Addison smiled sweetly, "And you have to be okay with that. Hand me your cell phone."

"Huh?" Vanessa asked, unsure as to why he was asking such a thing.

He held out his hand, "Just trust me."

"But I've got a board meeting in ten minutes, and a whole bunch of calls I need to make and—"

"Hand it over, Missy," he demanded with a playful grin.

"But Addi!" she whined, feeling like a little girl who didn't want to obey.

"Hand me your phone, or else I'll tickle you until you relent!"

Vanessa's eyes grew wide as she suppressed a smile. As much as she didn't want to, a grin cracked onto her face and she reached into her back pocket. She handed him her phone. "There. You have my phone. Now what?"

He dialed a number and held the phone up to his ear. "Hello, Deborah? This is Addison. Cancel all of Vanessa's meetings for today."

"What?!" Vanessa's jaw dropped, "Wait, no! Addi, I have a really important meeting and a zillion things I have to do and—"

"Clear her itinerary and set up an all-day appointment at the spa."

"The spa?" Vanessa's lip curled. "Addi—"

"Okay, that will be all. Thank you, Deborah." Addison hung up. "And you're not getting this back until tomorrow."

"Addi, I appreciate what you're trying to do, but I have *so* much I need to get caught up on!"

"Which is why I'm doing this." Addison was firm in his resolve, "If there's one thing I've learned from being in The Palace, it's that you have to take time to stop and enjoy yourself. So that's what you're going to do today. No phone calls, no meetings, no computer, no typing, no wedding details... just rest and relaxation."

"But Addi, I—"

"Don't argue with me, Ness!" Addison laughed, "It's already settled. You might be frustrated right now, but trust me, you'll thank me later."

"My brother is brilliant! A spa day is just what you needed." Bridget lifted her right hand, "And my nails are also benefiting from the touch-up!"

Vanessa smiled. She took a deep breath, allowing her shoulders to settle into the chair behind her. She flinched slightly as the woman below her worked on adorning her toe nails. Vanessa always felt odd about the idea of other people touching her feet.

"I wasn't about to give up my schedule without a fight. But as always, Addi was right. I was on the verge of a mental breakdown."

"On the *verge*?" Bridget asked playfully.

"Okay, I may have already exploded a little bit." She glanced at Bridget sheepishly, "Did you see the article?"

"I did." Bridget giggled.

"It wasn't funny."

"Actually, it kind of was." Bridget grinned, "I now have this mental image of you throwing carrots at the cashier, and it's pretty fierce."

"It was awful!" Vanessa shook her head, her voice strained with emotion just at the memory of it all, "You should've heard that pestering news guy, egging me on, asking if Addison and I were trying to cover up some secret pregnancy? Ugh, it was disgusting. And then that girl who talked to me like I had single-handedly destroyed feminism and was dragging them back into the 1950's because of this ring on my finger. She accused me of quitting my job and having ten kids! What is it with everyone thinking I'm going to have a ton of kids?! We're not even married yet!"

"Ness, you can't let them inside your head." Bridget tried to reassure her of the truth, "All that matters is that you and Addison do what you feel is best. Just go wherever God is leading you, and none of their opinions hold any weight."

"I mean, in some ways I understand where those girls are coming from." Vanessa sighed, feeling stressed out just thinking about it. "I used to get totally frustrated with anyone who suggested getting married was the sole purpose of a woman's existence, and that we were made to submit to and serve our husbands. I loved my independence and the fact that I didn't need a man to do anything. I've always had this burning desire to prove everyone wrong and do things nobody thinks are possible. So, I never *ever* imagined I would be getting married this young! I wanted to travel the world, and make waves, and do all kinds of exciting things. It's a little strange for me to be giving all of that up."

"I know it requires a huge sacrifice to marry into this family. But it requires the same kind of sacrifice for any other couple out there, too.

Royal or not. But in my personal opinion, this wacky feminist movement has things all wrong. They think that getting married and 'depending' on your husband is a sign of weakness, but that couldn't be more of a lie! My mom used to say, 'meek isn't weak'. Meek actually means bridled strength, or power under control. And just because we as women *can* do everything guys can do, be the breadwinners, wear the pants of the house, fix the sink, and open our own car doors, doesn't mean we should shove the men out of the way and tell them to get lost. In fact, Mom always used to say that learning to serve, submit, and support your husband is one of the most powerful *strength*-required things you could ever do. Any old girl can climb the corporate ladder and plow through life, being crazy successful, smashing charts, breaking records—but how many women have the strength to surrender their own desires and do everything they can to support, encourage, and uplift their husbands? My mom was an amazing example of that. She put her family first, before anything else."

"You know how much I love Addison." Vanessa confessed, "But I can't help but wonder if I'm just not cut out for all of this. I don't know if I'm ready. I mean, me, a wife? Maybe… maybe we're diving into this too soon."

"I think having some doubts is normal. But what's at the root of all this? I mean, at the end of the day, what is it that you're truly afraid of?"

"I just don't know if I can be everything Addison wants me to be." Vanessa sighed, feeling those familiar tears surfacing. "My patience has been so short lately, I'm exploding at our citizens, I can't cook, my apartment is an absolute mess, I'm struggling to stay on top of everything at work, and I'm completely stressed about all these silly wedding details! Does any of that sound like Queen material to you?"

"No." Bridget was honest, "It sounds to me like completely *real* material. Ness, nobody is expecting you to have it all together! You have to give yourself a break here! Addi could care less about your cooking, or how messy your apartment is, or whether the flowers at your wedding are pink or red... he just wants you. He loves you. And you have to trust that his love is enough. The Bible says perfect love casts out fear. I know Addison loves you with the same kind of unconditional love that Jesus does. The only one expecting you to be flawless here, is you."

"Addi suggested that maybe I should quit my job." Vanessa sighed, hating to consider defeat. "But I feel like if I do that, I'd be giving up, saying that it's too much for me to run the Homeless Shelter, *and* be a wife. But I know women who do way more than that."

"But isn't being a wife a full-time job in and of itself? Not to mention being Queen, and helping my brother run a country! Ness, you have to remember, you two aren't just two normal college kids. Addison needs help with his mission. The country is in so much turmoil, and he believes that you're the one to help him with it. There would be absolutely nothing wrong with you resigning from your role at the Homeless Shelter."

"I guess you're right." Vanessa sighed again. Then she looked at Bridget, doing a double take. "How old are you again? And are you sure you're not secretly married? Because the stuff flying out of your mouth is like expert-level advice!"

Bridget laughed. "I've asked God a lot of questions over the past few months, and He just keeps revealing more and more of His amazing answers. With Liam and I moving toward the possibility of marriage, I truly want to be the best wife I can be. And it's required a lot of mental shifts for me. Like, moving to Alaska for example. When I was first struck with the thought, I wasn't crazy about it. But after I asked the Lord to help me surrender those desires to Him, Liam's dreams slowly started becoming my own. Now I can honestly say that I *love* the idea of living up there! I love Liam's vision to minister to children in foster care, and to continuing helping run his parents' ranch. Submitting to his mission isn't a burden, or even a sacrifice, because I think as two hearts become closer and closer, they slowly mesh into one. With each new day, it's like I'm thinking more like Liam, and he's thinking more like me, and there are less differences and disagreements between us. We're both heading in the same direction and have the same vision from God burning in our hearts, and because there's unity in where we're headed, I know our future is going to be blessed."

"Just stop, you guys are far too adorable!" Vanessa grinned, "Not to mention ridiculously unstoppable! I know God must be so proud of you two. So now the important question…" Vanessa giggled, "When is he going to propose? Do you have any ideas? Has he hinted at anything?"

"No." Bridget sighed, faking a frown, "I'm still completely in the dark. But I'm trying my best to be patient."

"Luke!" Hope called out. She pushed through the swinging kitchen door, attempting to catch him before he left.

He had just finished loading up the food truck and was prepared to take a load over to the Homeless Shelter.

"Hey, mister, I've been wanting to talk to you!" Hope smiled.

"Oh yeah, how'd things go after the meeting?" He jingled a pair of truck keys as he dug them from his pocket. "Did your dad blow up?"

"No, actually he didn't. But I've been thinking a lot about the things you said at that meeting, and I think you really need to meet with my brother."

"Right." Luke laughed, "Like he would ever 'have tea' with the rebel."

"Addison is far more thoughtful and understanding than you think he is. After listening to you the other day, I can see how there are some things our family might be wrong about. And I'm sure Addison would at least be willing to listen to your perspective. I'm not saying he would agree with it right away. But I know he would hear you out."

"So, what does this mean?" Luke grinned mischievously and crossed his arms, "Are you on our side now?"

"What? No!" Hope shook her head, "I'm not taking sides. I am the friendly, middle-ground peacemaker."

"Oh really?" Luke chuckled, "So you're a one foot in, one foot out kind of a girl?"

"I like to think of it as being diplomatic."

"Or, being too afraid to admit that everything you've ever known your entire life has been wrong."

"I didn't say that." Hope corrected him, "I said you might be right about *some* things. Not everything."

"In my limited experience of life, I've learned that there's no such thing as half-truths. Compromise is for people who are afraid to make up their minds. Either you're right, or you're wrong."

"I beg to differ. I believe there is such a thing as holy contradictions. I mean, God Himself is a holy contradiction. How can He be both the Lion and the Lamb? The Prince of Peace and the Mighty Warrior? Ecclesiastes 3 says there's a time for war, and there's a time for peace. Don't these things seem completely opposite from one another? Yet in God, they're one. How can both be right? I don't know. But somehow, they are."

"If you're trying to convince me that both I *and* your brother are right, then that was a really bad example. And as much as I know you'd love for me to sweep all the issues under the rug, and have a friendly chat with your bro, it isn't going to happen. If he wants to meet with me, I'm not going to sugar-coat anything. I'm going to tell him like it is."

"But would you at least listen to his side of the story?" Hope asked in an eager tone. "Have a teachable spirit?"

"I would listen," Luke nodded. "But he's not going to be telling me anything I don't already know. I was indoctrinated in everything you guys were—my dad believes all the same stuff. But true liberty isn't going to come from doing the same thing we've been doing for hundreds of years."

"Luke, I know you have a lot of good things to say, but you don't know everything either!" Hope could feel her irritation with Luke's pride mounting, "You have to be willing to know *why* we do things the way we do!"

"As much as I'd love to stay here and argue, I've got somewhere to be." Luke huffed.

"Fine!" Hope snapped. "Don't listen! Ugh, why is it so impossible to have a normal conversation with you?! It's like you're so consumed with your desire to have things your way, that you can't even pause to consider what life is like in someone else's shoes! You're so stubborn!"

"Stubborn? You think *I'm* stubborn?" Luke shook his head, "Says the girl who grew up in a bubble-wrapped zoo, overly protected, completely brainwashed, sheltered, tucked away from any kind of influence from the outside world! Talking to you is like talking to Siri. Your answers are pre-programed by things engrained in you from childhood."

"Whatever." Hope rolled her eyes, "I don't even know why I keep trying with you."

"Yeah, why do you keep trying? I mean, obviously there's something here that keeps drawing you back."

Hope was silent. She studied his face and considered opening her mouth, then she thought otherwise. She had no idea how to answer that question. What *was* it that kept her coming back?

"You know, it doesn't matter," she sighed. "Because it's clear you're not willing to listen to anyone but yourself. So, forget about the meeting with Addison." She abruptly turned on her heel and headed back toward the kitchen.

"Hey, Hope." Luke spoke quietly.

Hope stopped. She slowly turned her head around, unsure of what he might say.

"I'm kind of disappointed you didn't become one of us." A half smile inched across his face, "Because you would've made a really cute rebel."

Hope's eyes widened, and she quickly set her gaze toward the door. She picked up her pace and rushed inside.

Luke stood alone in the parking lot. He pressed his tongue against his lip. Okay, maybe he shouldn't have said that. All at once, Luke felt like smacking himself in the head, as he did many times after his interactions with Hope. He didn't know why he acted like such a jerk around her. It was as if her beauty had a strange, debilitating, melting effect on his brain, and sometimes he found himself saying the strangest stuff known to man. He shook his head, knowing he needed to forget about the gorgeous Princess. His feelings for her were just as pointless as attempting to meet with King Addison to discuss politics. So why get his hopes up... for Hope?

He started toward his truck. Even though he told himself to stop thinking about her, his brain didn't quite listen. A dull ache throbbed in his chest. Luke wanted so desperately for Hope to see things from his perspective and join their cause. He knew it was insane, thinking a girl like her would—

"Umph!" Luke released a surprised huff of air as a pair of arms slammed him against the truck. Luke attempted to fight, but the man had him pinned. It was Liam Henderson. Princess Bridget's boyfriend.

"Care to explain what you're doing here?" Liam asked in a firm tone.

"Picking up a food order—what the heck man, get off me!" Luke attempted to wiggle free from his grip, and Liam finally released him.

As angry as Luke was for the unexpected intrusion, he knew better than to toss a punch. The guy's burly arms were intimidating.

"You know that's not what I mean." Liam's voice was deep and full of warning. "What are you doing, talking with Princess Hope?"

"Exactly what it looks like." Luke straightened his shirt, miffed that the man would jump on him like that. "Talking."

"I finally figured out where I know you from," Liam told the kid. "A few months ago, when that mob rushed the *Agusto Zampini* Restaurant. Bridget was there. And so were you."

"We weren't going to hurt anybody." Luke's eyes narrowed. "We we're protesting."

"With a gun?!" Liam barked, "You could have killed Bridget!"

"Yeah, but I didn't!" Luke shouted back. "Just because I believe the monarchy has to be taken down, doesn't mean I think I'm the guy to do it!"

"Maybe not," Liam hissed, pointing a finger toward Luke's face, "but your rouge words have fueled the fire behind this rebellion, and if someone ends up pulling the trigger, even if your finger isn't on it, you will be held directly responsible."

"By who?" Luke huffed, "You?"

"God."

"You have no idea what God has called me to do!"

"Stay away from Hope," Liam warned. "If I find you anywhere near her, ever again, I will arrest you."

"Arrest me for what?" Luke laughed bitterly, knowing Liam had no legal grounds to do so.

"For harassing the Princess," Liam shot back. "I don't know what kind of lies you're telling her, but they end today."

"You can't ban me from being at The Palace." Luke shook his head, "I work here."

"Just stay away from her, and there won't be any trouble."

Luke wanted to fire back, but he kept his mouth shut. He abruptly left the conversation and hopped in the food truck. He whipped out of the lot and Liam stood standing, watching with intensely-protective eagle eyes.

Chapter Fourteen

Big Ben

Hope sat on her bed; legs crossed, and eyes closed, with her Bible in her lap. "Lord, I need direction. You have to speak to my heart and show me what to do. I don't want to be deceived, and I long to know the truth! You said Your Holy Spirit will draw me into all truth... I need to know what that truth is. Who is Luke, really? Is he a catalyst for much needed change, or is he nothing more than a charming wolf in sheep's clothing?"

Hope opened her eyes and stared at her Bible. She had been up most of the night, contemplating these questions. She's been straddling the line for too long...after her interaction with Luke yesterday, she went to bed with a burning desire for God to speak and make things clear. She needs to know who to believe. Was Luke right? Or was her dad right? Was Luke poisoning her mind with lies? Or was he following a strange and different path that God had set for the course of his heart?

She opened her Bible to the book of Isaiah, hoping to find something to help steer her in the right direction. Oftentimes, when her heart was exploding with questions and longing for a whisper from Heaven, the Lord would direct her to a passage that made everything clear.

Suddenly, a grouping of words leapt out at her.

"Do not call to mind the former things or ponder the past. Behold, I am doing a new thing. Now it springs forth. Will you not be aware of it? I will make a roadway in the wilderness, and rivers in the desert."

Hope's eyes widened, and she reread the passage.

Just then, her bedroom door flew open and Chasity burst in.

"Hope, guess what!?" Chasity proclaimed.

Hope looked up from her Bible, surprised by the interruption. Chasity's cheeks were bright red with excitement.

"The judge decided to excuse Asher from time in Juvie! He doesn't have to go to jail!"

"Oh my goodness, praise God!" Hope cried, shoving triumphant fists into the air, "He answered our prayers!"

"I am *so* relived!" Chasity flopped onto her sister's bed, "I just couldn't bear the thought of Ash being behind bars."

"Wow!" Hope was breathless with excitement, "So does Asher realize what an amazing example of the grace of God this is?!"

"I don't know yet." Chasity frowned, "He still seems pretty bummed. I mean, he's not completely out of the woods. He still has to go to military school in September."

"Oh." Hope looked down at her Bible, pondering the verse. Was this going to be a new beginning for Asher? "Well, I think it will be good for him." She smiled softly, "Like Dad said, maybe he'll learn more about responsibility, character building, and placing others' needs before his own. I'm sure God will work it out and use it all for good."

"Yeah." Chasity nodded, "I believe that too. Asher has so much untapped potential locked up deep inside, and whenever I catch a glimpse of it, it truly is spectacular. But I'm afraid it's buried pretty deep down beneath all that dirt."

"I think maybe…" Hope pondered, "the promise in him is like a seed. We all know it's there, but Asher can't see it yet. Someday those little sprouts will grow, and new life will push through the dirt. We just need to keep loving him and reminding him how much we care."

"Absolutely." Chasity nodded, "So, reason number two as to why I barged into your room like this: I asked Dad if we can go to England for a few weeks, and he agreed to it! James invited us to stay at his estate, and Dad thought it would be great for Ash to get away, as well as bring the little kids with us. With all the crazy wedding planning going on, he thinks it might be good for Millie and Willie not to be underfoot. Jillian wanted to stay here though. Do you wanna come with us? We're leaving tomorrow!"

"The O'Conner Estate?" Hope looked at her sister suspiciously, "Chas, is there something going on between you and James that I need to know about?"

"What? No!"

"You sure you're not interested in him?" Hope persisted.

"The only thing I'm interested in at James's estate is his spectacular racehorse trainers! Nathaniel Wells is going to be there, as well as dozens of other top trainers in the circuit! It's going to be incredible! So, are you coming, or what?"

[165]

"Tomorrow?" Hope pursed her lips, "Hmm… I guess I'd have to pray about it. I mean, I don't have anything terribly important on my schedule, and going to England is always a blast… but I've got a lot on my mind. I don't know, it might not be the right timing for me."

"Okay, I understand." Chasity shrugged, "Just pray about it and let me know in a bit. I'm going to start packing!"

In London…

Jane anxiously tapped her pencil on the cherry-wood desk. She stared at the wall, feeling her heartbeat increase with each passing second. She *had* to think of something. It had to be gleaming with resplendent possibility. It had to be witty and entrancing and smart. Her story needed to be timeless, entertaining, and classic. She wanted to bedazzle the judges. She had to win this thing.

"Alright, I've just finished my first draft!" Cha-Linn triumphantly announced. She closed her laptop and stretched her arms in the air.

"Overachiever," Johannah grumbled.

"I am so ready to get out of this stuffy room." Cha-Linn climbed off the bed. "Let's go downtown! The sun has just set, and I am sure the city lights will be beautiful!"

"I agree!" Phylicia, the blonde, French girl closed her notebook. "We've been in this room ever since writing classes got out. We need to take a break and have a bit of fun."

"Easy for you girls to say." Johannah rolled her eyes, "You two are further along with your stories than Jane and I."

Jane glanced at Johannah, wondering how she knew she hadn't written anything yet. Then she looked at her empty notebook. On second thought, it was probably quite obvious.

"Let's ride the London Eye!" Cha-Linn suggested. "It will be a spectacular view this time of night!"

"Ohhh, I bet you're right." Johannah sounded as if she was slowly warming up to the idea. She too closed her laptop. "Okay, I'm in. Enough writing for one day. Jane, are you coming with us?"

"No." Jane shook her head. As much as she wanted to, she couldn't afford the luxury. She was so far behind the other girls. They already had their tales mapped out and had begun their first drafts. Jane didn't even have so much as one good idea yet.

"Come on Jane, staring at the wall is not going to help you!" Johannah urged her. "I know we shouldn't be giving advice to our competition, but sometimes the only way to overcome writer's block is to go out and be inspired. And what could be more inspirational than riding a massive Ferris wheel over the city?"

"I hate heights," Jane confessed. "I mean, I don't mind airplanes, but that's only because they have a purpose of taking you to a certain destination. There is no purpose in riding the London Eye, other than making you feel woozy."

"You do not have to ride it if you don't want to. But you at least need to leave this room." Johannah pulled Jane's rolling chair away from the desk and spun her around. "Like it or not, I'm bringing you with us!"

Jane stood in her long, tan, button-up pea coat. She watched her friends climb into the glass capsule which would float them high into the air. Her stomach lurched. She was so relieved not to be going on it. She could only imagine how beautiful it was up there, high above the city with all the illuminating lights. But she didn't want to risk the possibility of throwing up, all for the sake of some good views.

She stuffed her hands in her pockets and sighed, desperately racking her brain for a good idea. The fact that she couldn't think of anything was absolutely unnerving. She knew she shouldn't have gone downtown, but they insisted, and Jane was never any good at standing up for herself. And so, she regretfully followed the crowd.

She stared up toward the sky, wondering which capsule her roommates were in. She shivered. There was a cool wind blowing through the evening air, and she wondered if perhaps she could smell rain in the distance.

"Beautiful evening, isn't it, Miss?"

Jane blinked. That same young man from the restaurant was standing beside her! His words surprised her, and she had nothing to say in return. It took her several seconds to realize she wasn't seeing a figment of her imagination, and he was actually staring at her, waiting for her to respond. She couldn't believe the moment. It was like something she'd always fantasized about, but never actually thought could happen. Why was this young man, James, talking to her?

"Oh, I'm sorry, we met just the other day, fish and chips, remember?" James added, sounding as if he were trying to jog her memory.

"Oh, no, I remember," Jane finally managed to spit out, "I just uhh… wasn't expecting to see you here."

"Nor I you!" James smiled, revealing his perfect teeth. "But, it is an ideal evening to spend downtown. Are you here with company, or out wandering the streets alone?"

"Company." Jane explained, "I mean, kind of. My friends are up there." She pointed toward the London Eye.

"And why are you down here?"

"Ferris wheels aren't exactly my thing," Jane admitted.

"That's a shame." James smile did not disappear, "The view is quite unforgettable. It is a must-do attraction for every tourist."

"Except this one." Jane shifted her feet nervously, "I prefer to stay on the ground."

"It's awful hard to have fun from down here, isn't it? Come along, I was just about to board. It's impossible for me to come to the city without riding the Eye. I'll pay for your ticket."

"Oh no, you don't have to do that!" Jane insisted, "And I never got to thank you for paying for my lunch either. That was too kind of you."

"My pleasure. Whenever I have the opportunity to treat someone to everything London has to offer, it is a joy to do so. Come, let's hop in line before it gets much longer."

Jane wanted to protest, but her mouth still wasn't working properly. As James stepped forward into the line, Jane's feet did the strangest thing. They actually followed him! She didn't know *what* she was thinking! It was as if she were no longer in control of herself and someone was orchestrating her every movement, like a captive in a dream.

"So, what brings you to London?" James asked. "Are you on holiday with family? Friends?"

"Actually, I'm in a writing competition."

"You're a finalist in the YNC?" James was impressed.

"Oh." Jane was surprised, "You know what that is?"

"Of course!" James nodded, "I've had several friends enter over the years. None of them won though. The grand winner gets a publishing contract, correct? Sounds like a very prestigious prize! What is your story about? If you don't mind me asking."

"I . . ." Jane anxiously looked at her shoes, "I don't know yet."

"Oh, sounds like you're in a bit of a pickle." James chuckled.

"Tell me about it." Jane groaned, "All the other girls are working on their first drafts, and I haven't even had one measly idea yet. It's quite pathetic, really. I mean, I worked so hard to get here, and if I lose it all because of a terrible bout of writer's block... I'll never forgive myself."

The line scooted forward, and next thing Jane knew, it was their turn to board the Eye. Her chest tightened as James paid for their tickets. She was *not* ready for this!

"Uh, uh, perhaps on second thought, I'll just—"

"Oh no, you've come too far to back out now!" James held out a hand to help her inside, "And who knows! Riding high above the city might be just what you need for your lightning strike of inspiration!"

Jane shyly took his hand, knowing he was only trying to be polite. She took a deep breath and forced herself to step into the swaying capsule. She quickly closed her eyes and held onto her stomach. "Oh dear. Oh dear, I am deeply regretting this already!" She stood up to leave, but the door had already closed, and the capsule was drifting into the air. She squeezed her eyes, allowing darkness to envelop her vision.

"If you don't open your eyes, you're going to miss the entire experience!" James chuckled.

"That's kind of the point!" Jane could feel her face turning green. "Oh dear, oh no. I think I'm going to be ill..."

James's eyes widened, realizing that the girl wasn't faking it. She really *did* look like she might lose her dinner. "Don't think about that!" James tried to coach her past the queasy moment, "Think about something, uh, relaxing. Tell me about something you enjoy. What do you like to do, back home in the States? Do you have any hobbies?"

"I, um…" Jane attempted to focus on his question. What could she say? Did she have any hobbies? "Writing, I suppose."

"What else?"

"Uhhh…" she bit her lip, realizing she had almost said *daydreaming*. What a terrible answer. "I live a very, very dull life."

James laughed. "Somehow I highly doubt that."

"No. Trust me, I do." Jane was firm, "I really don't do much of anything. I read, write, suffer through school, and only talk to people when it's completely, one-hundred-percent necessary. I don't go to the mall, or the bowling alley, or to school dances… I'm pretty much a social recluse, locked up like a hobbit in my bedroom."

"You must have great aspirations, though," James observed. "I mean, just because you prefer not to mingle at social happenings and mindless dances, doesn't mean your life is dull. Here you are in Europe, pursuing your dream of becoming a writer! That sounds quite fascinating to me!"

Jane's eyes popped open, feeling the need to set the record straight. She didn't want this guy to get the wrong idea about her. "Yeah, but these kinds of things never happen to me. Being a finalist in the YNC was like a once-in-a-lifetime, wish-upon-a-star kind of a thing. Before that day, I'd never won anything in my entire life. Not a school raffle, or a giveaway, or a T-shirt, or a game of cards… I always seem to be losing things." Her throat tightened up, as she thought of her dad.

[171]

"But you're here now, aren't you? Gifted with a spectacular opportunity to pursue your dream and write a story the world will never forget. You're a very interesting girl, Jane Akerly. And I'm quite confident we'll be seeing your name somewhere on the best-seller lists in the near future."

Jane studied the young man in front of her. Why was he saying these things? Why was he encouraging her in her wild dreams, when they'd only just met? Why did he think she would be a good writer, when he'd never even read her work?

"I appreciate your enthusiasm, but unless I get struck with an idea that can hold any weight in this competition, the only time anyone will be seeing my name is on my 'Welcome to Wally-Mart' name tag."

James laughed. "I don't know much about writing, but as I believe all the great authors say, 'Write about what you know.' They take the experiences that happen to them, or even things they wish would happen to them, change the names of all their characters, and write about their lives."

Jane couldn't believe how paradisiacal his accent was. She came to the sudden conclusion that she could listen to him speak to her all day in that harmonious voice of his, and she would never tire of it. "That might work for some people," Jane explained, "but again, my life is so unexceptional, I doubt anyone would want to read about it."

"Oh really?" James looked at her in a quizzical manner, "Look at where you are right now! You're four-hundred-forty feet up in the air, towering over the heart of London. Look, there's Big Ben!"

Her eyes turned toward the glass, and she gasped. Big Ben, the famous clock tower, sparkled in the horizon. Lights reflected on the water, doing a dance all their own. She sighed happily, nearly unable to process the beauty of the moment. It was far more spectacular than she could've imagined, even in the most vivid of her daydreams. In that second, she truly felt like she was on top of the world. She wished she could freeze time and remain in this moment for the rest of her life.

"Thank you again for the ride," Jane told him in a shy voice once they landed on the ground. "I'll never forget that."

"It was my pleasure." James bowed slightly, "And thank you for making the evening much more enjoyable. I was planning on going up anyway, before I return to the countryside tomorrow, but your fair company made the evening much more pleasurable. I wish you all the best on your endeavors." He shook her hand, "Once again, Jane, it was a delight meeting you, and I look forward to reading your many brilliant novels in the future."

Jane nodded, unable to speak once more. James was like a mist, appearing, then disappearing in the blink of an eye. His firm handshake reminded her that he was indeed real.

And with that, he turned and disappeared into the crowd.

"Oh my Eiffel Tower!" Phylicia squealed, "Are my eyes playing tricks on me?!"

Jane twirled around, seeing her roommates and Miss Laurie.

"Who was that handsome British hunk?" Phylicia fanned her hand in front of her face. "Did you get his number?! Did he get *your* number?!"

"That's enough," Laurie scolded. "Nobody is getting anybody's number. Jane, where did you run off to?! We told you to stay nearby and meet us at the lamp post!"

"Miss Laurie, I—" Jane's voice squeaked as she attempted to explain herself.

"I don't even want to hear it." Laurie shook her head, "Anymore disappearing acts like this one, and you'll be disqualified! You know the rules. Come along girls, back to the hotel."

Jane's mouth was still hanging open, but she hadn't been given ample time to respond.

As the girls walked ahead, Cha-Linn fell into step beside Jane. "Here's a tip. If that guy comes around, wanting to hang out again, go for it. Because you're so far behind, there's no way you're going to win anyway. You might as well just enjoy yourself."

Jane narrowed her eyes, wishing to say something to defend herself. But her silly brain couldn't think of anything. It was blank. Just like her story.

Cha-Linn skipped ahead cheerfully, satisfied with her hurtful jab.

Jane rolled her eyes. There was no way she was going to let Cha-Linn beat her. That mysterious stranger, James, was right. Her name belonged on the best-sellers list. And winning the YNC was the only shot she had at ever getting there.

Chapter Fifteen

Beware the British Boys

"And here we have the White Garden, a glorious display of lovely foliage in honor of the late Princess Diana."

Jane attempted to soak up the novelty of the moment, knowing she was standing on historical grounds at Kensington Palace. Jane stood patiently with the rest of the tour group and her roommates. Her eyes floated toward the stately building sitting in the distance. Though it didn't rival the grandeur of Tarsurella's unforgettable palace, Kensington had a cute little charm all its own. She wondered if perhaps the Duke and Duchess were home, and she felt a shiver of excitement run down her spine. It was quite spectacular to be standing so near such a historical landmark.

The dignified tour guide continued speaking, but Jane's thoughts drifted elsewhere. As much as she adored getting out and seeing the sights each day, her anxiety continued to grow. Her roommates were progressing with their stories, and Jane still hadn't even begun. It was so terrifying to think this might be her last time in London. This might be her last great adventure. If she didn't think of an amazing story, it would all be over for her. She would return home, heartbroken, forced to live in Charlie's attic and attend her stupid high school in the fall. There she would wait, being subjected to her trapping, devastatingly-dull life, forevermore.

Winning this competition could change her life. With a publishing deal, the course of her destiny could be set. Jane knew it was ridiculous, but in some strange, wild part of her obscure imagination, she thought that perhaps winning would bring her father home. She knew there was no correlation between the two. Writing an epic novel wouldn't change the fact that Dad was gone. But then again, maybe it could.

Jane sighed, tired of such oppressive thoughts tormenting her. The pressure was paramount. She needed an idea. She needed it more than her next breath.

"And thus, that concludes our tour of the palace grounds." The guide smiled, relived to be finished with her job for the day. "If you have any questions, please feel free to ask. Otherwise, the grounds close in forty-five minutes."

"Alright girls, that gives us just enough time to find a lovely place to eat our sandwiches!" Laurie told her group. "Then we'll board the bus, return to the hotel, and let the writing continue!"

"Well, maybe for some of us." Cha-Linn drew near to Jane's ear as she passed by. "Others will just stare at an empty sheet of paper."

Laurie's face held concern. "Is that true, Jane? You haven't begun your story?"

"I, um…" Jane anxiously scratched the back of her neck. She couldn't lie. "No. I haven't," she admitted ashamedly.

"Yikes. The clock is ticking." Laurie reminded her of everything she already knew, "Time is of the essence in this competition! I hope you'll take full advantage of it before the hour glass runs out."

Laurie left Jane with those troubling words and sauntered off to find a nice place on the lawn to eat her tuna sandwich.

Jane felt like falling into the ground. If only she could hide beneath these flowers and let the dirt swallow her up! She opened her brown bag and pulled out her ham and cheese sandwich. The *last* thing she felt like doing in that moment, was eating.

Jane found an empty space in the green grass beside Johannah. None of the girls were particularly chummy, but at least Johannah hadn't made any mean comments. Jane decided she could sit beside her without feeling threatened.

Johannah's notebook was wide open, and she was scribbling as quickly as her hand would allow. "This place is *so* inspirational! I could stay here all day and write!"

Jane bit into her sandwich. It was dry and tasteless, representing everything *not* happening in her usually-over-active imagination.

"Oh my heavens!" Phylicia suddenly squealed. "Jane, don't look now, but I think someone's stalking you!"

Jane looked up from her sandwich. What in the world was that girl talking about?

"See, he's over there!" Phylicia urged. "The same guy you were talking to last night!"

Jane allowed her eyes to travel past the garden area and settle on the other side of the double fountains. Her eyes widened. Sure enough, James was standing there. He was chatting with an older looking man. Jane's stomach did a nervous flip-flop. How was this happening? How did he keep showing up everywhere she did?!

"Are you two dating yet?" Phylicia asked. "Because if not, I volunteer as tribute!"

All the girls continued to watch him. Suddenly, without warning, James's conversation with the other man was over, and he looked their direction.

Jane quickly looked away, terrified to have made eye contact.

"Ohhh, he's coming this way!" Phylicia squealed. "Everybody act cool!"

Jane's heart rate spiked. Why was he walking toward them? Was he thinking about actually talking to them? Why, *why* was be being so friendly? People were never this friendly to Jane. It was starting to seriously concern her.

"Lovely afternoon for writing, isn't it ladies?" James's charming accent floated through the air.

Jane forced herself to look up from her sandwich. There was no avoiding this situation now. He was standing right in front of them.

"Absolutely," Phylicia quickly replied. "We're enjoying soaking in the sights, seeing everything London has to offer."

"Well, you haven't seen everything yet." James was outlandishly friendly, "Would you care to—"

"Uh, excuse me." Laurie stood up and confronted the young man speaking with her girls. Laurie's assertive tone reminded Jane of a protective lioness. "Who are you, and why are you distracting my group?"

"Forgive me, ma'am." James flashed his charming smile, "I am James O'Conner. I was just paying my cousin a short visit and—"

"Your cousin?!" Laurie suddenly burst out. "Oh my peppers, I know who you are! You're James O'Conner!"

"I believe that's what he just said, Sherlock," Phylicia mumbled under her breath. Several of the girls giggled.

"Oh, this is such an honor!" Laurie suddenly started fangirling, "Ladies, do you realize who we're talking to? James O'Conner, the *cousin* of the Prince of England!"

Jane looked at him again. So, the mysterious stranger is actually a purebred British Royal? Strangely enough, it made sense to her. He certainly looked the part.

"It's hardly anything to fuss over," James spoke humbly. "But I know who you are as well, ma'am. Laurie McIntire, student coordinator of the YNC."

"Oh my!" Laurie lifted an excited hand to her chest, "I'm flattered! However did you—"

"My father's a board member for the YNC Committee. He's been supporting this project for years and he's an activist for literacy programs among students on campuses across the country. He was quite sore when I didn't enter in high school, but my writing skills leave much to be desired and I knew I'd never have a chance in a competition like this. But I am very impressed with all of your students. I know they've worked very hard to come this far!"

Something inside Jane's heart fell. It's as if she could feel a little part of her breaking, smacking onto the ground below. *When I was in high school...*James's words were clear. How much older than her *is* he?

Mostly likely, he's in college. All at once, Jane's cheeks flushed with heat, embarrassed for allowing her mind to get wrapped up in the silly idea that he might actually be interested in her. Of course, he's not interested in her. He's the cousin of a duke, for goodness sake!

"Well, it is a true honor to meet you!" Laurie's defensive tone had melted away. "Do you mind if our girls ask you a few questions? Interviewing you would be great for learning more about the monarchy!"

"Actually, I have an appointment to which I must return home for, and I'm already running late," he politely refused, "But how would your group like to join me and some friends, this evening for dinner? How about, 5:00 p.m.? You can Google directions to the O'Conner Estate and let Gate Security know you have a reservation."

"Oh how delightful!" Laurie shook her head, "Wow, yes! What an honor! We will absolutely be there! Thank you, Mr. O'Conner, that will be just wonderful. You're too kind, really!"

"Splendid." He turned to the girls and offered them a polite bow, "I am looking forward to it. Enjoy the rest of your afternoon!"

And with that, he quickly dashed off, appearing eager to catch his car and return home.

Chasity watched in wide-eyed wonderment as a copper horse with thundering muscles pounded down the racetrack.

"His name is *Doctor Seuss*," James told her as they stood near the track. "Another rising star, to be sure. His parents were Thor and Winston-Salem. Couldn't have asked for a more perfect bloodline."

"Wow," Chasity breathed, blinking as the horse and its bouncing jockey flew by. "I'm seriously impressed. Are you going to race him next year?"

"No. The plan is to sell him this week, during the Convention. There will be an auction on Friday. Perhaps you should consider picking up a few new competitors of your own."

"Are you kidding?!" Chasity laughed, "I don't think my dad would be too crazy about the idea of buying new horses. I already have my hands full with Nic."

"True, but every owner who's interested in making money knows it's smart to have more than one racer. It's not wise to place all your eggs in one basket, or however that old saying goes. I can already tell you that if Nathaniel decides to work with Nic, it's going to be quite the gamble. It might be good to have another solid racer or two, in which you can be confident."

"But what fun is that?" Chasity lifted her hands up in question, "Dependability is over-rated. It's far more exciting to take a wild chance when all the odds are stacked against you, and nobody thinks you're going to win."

"You've always been an adventurous one, haven't you?" James chuckled. He glanced at his Rolex watch. "Perhaps we'd best head back and change attire before dinner. I've invited several friends to join us this evening."

"Do I have to dress up?" Chasity asked, not too fond of the idea. She glanced down at her muddy cowgirl boots and casual blue jeans. She came here to have fun with horses, not mingle at fancy dinner parties.

"You know how my parents are. They feel that every meal should be a suit and tie affair. They have very important guests frequenting the estate, and they ask that we do our best to represent England well."

"Don't take this the wrong way," Chasity told him as they slowly made their way toward the Stables, "but I kinda forgot how strict your family was. We've been getting more and more casual at The Palace. Ever since Dad passed the baton onto Addison, I feel like he's way more prone to wearing blue jeans and making it a fun pizza night upstairs. Millie isn't going to be very happy about getting dressed up. I think she and Willie are out catching tadpoles in the creek."

"And your brother? How is Asher doing?"

"Last I checked, he was just sitting up in his guest room, reading a comic book." Chasity sighed heavily, "He claimed to be tired from the flight, but I'm a little concerned. I think he's depressed. This is the last day I'm allowing him to hide away. Tomorrow, I'm forcing him to get out and take a trail ride with me, like it or not."

"He'll be coming to dinner, will he not?"

"Of course. He might be stubborn, but he's never too stubborn for food! Well, I'd better go find Millie and Willie, and make sure they're not completely soaked. Which, they most likely are." Chasity giggled.

"Very well." James nodded as the two split directions, "See you at dinner. You will look beautiful in whatever you choose to wear."

Chasity was surprised by his words. She acted as if they didn't affect her and continued walking. What was with the generous complement? Chasity pressed her lips together and continued down a dirt trail, which would lead to the shallow creek where Millie and Willie were playing. James was friendly to a fault. Perhaps he was just feeling extra polite today.

Chasity glanced at her muddy boots and smiled. It had been years since she and Asher ran around on these trails, but she still remembered where they led. Straight to adventure.

[182]

Chapter Seventeen

It's a Small World

"Why do we have to get all dressed up for dinner?" Millie huffed. She paused on the stairs and attempted to straighten out the waist line of the tights beneath her sparkly black dress, "These tights are strangling my legs!"

"I'm not hungry!" Willie wined, "I want to go back outside and play!"

"Yeah, we were just getting to the good part of our game!" Millie explained, "We were leaping across the creek, trying to escape the alligators, when a fire-breathing dragon appeared and turned the creek into LAVA!"

Chasity smiled. She fondly remembered those carefree days, when a simple stream of flowing water could be turned into the playground for dozens of wonderful games. "Mr. and Mrs. O'Conner have kindly allowed us to stay here for a few weeks, and when we're visitors in someone else's home, we have to respect their standards and traditions. Which includes dressing up for meals, and gracefully eating whatever they set before us."

They had nearly reached the bottom of the staircase, and she didn't want her little siblings to act up when they reached the Dining Hall. "Dad would want you to be on your best behavior and show off those fancy dinner manners of yours!" She looked at Millie, "Remember everything you've learned in Princess Lessons. Princesses are not picky eaters. Refusing to eat something just because you don't care for it is rejecting your hosts' hospitality. So be kind, graceful, and at least *try* everything that is on your plate."

Millie's eyes widened in horror as she thought of all sorts of putrid possibilities. "But what if they serve us snails? Or alligator?! Or a fish that still has its eyeballs attached to it! Surely you can't expect me to eat *that*!"

"Ewwwww!" Willie added a cry of his own personal disgust.

"Millie, you're not helping," Chasity grumbled. "Be a good example for your little brother." Chasity smoothed Millie's dress where she had gotten it all wrinkled from rearranging her tights, "Okay, come on, we're gonna be late."

The Royal Siblings landed on the floor then turned the corner down a long hall, mentally preparing themselves for the lavish dinner engagement ahead. Asher stuffed his hands into his dress pant pockets and released a frustrated sigh. He disliked this just as much as Millie and Willie.

Chasity felt like a mother hen. Without Hope, Bridget, her dad, or any of The Palace Staff here to help manage her siblings, Chasity felt like it was her responsibility to make sure they didn't totally embarrass their country. Even though Chasity was generally very lax about these kinds of things, she knew how nit-picky Mr. and Mrs. O'Conner could be, and Chasity didn't want to give them anything to scowl about.

"Ash, it looks like you got dressed in the dark!" Chasity suddenly noticed Asher's red tie. It was crooked. She stopped once more, attempting to straighten it.

"Chasity, quit!" Asher fidgeted beneath his sister's assistance.

Chasity managed to get it straightened out, as well as whisk a stray hair out of his face, before he wiggled away.

"There." Chasity huffed. She straightened her shoulders and took a deep breath. "Okay. Let's enter."

The foursome turned another corner and entered the wide-open doors into the O'Conners' Dining Hall.

"Good evening!" Mrs. O'Conner greeted the Royals as soon as they entered. The plump woman quickly set down her champagne glass and gave Chasity an airy hug. "Oh, we are so pleased to have you staying here with us, Your Highness!" She looked at the little kids, "And my, my, my, look at how grown up and sophisticated the two of you are!"

"Thank you." Millie curtsied politely, "It is nice to see you again too, Mrs. O'Conner."

Chasity smiled, impressed with Millie's manners. Apparently, she could be a gentlewoman when she wanted to.

"Chasity said we have to eat everything on our plates, but are you going to be serving anything gross? Because I don't think I could eat snails."

Chasity's eyes widened. *Well, there goes Millie's manners!* They derailed quite quickly.

Thankfully, Mr. and Mrs. O'Conner simply laughed, charmed by Millie's cuteness.

"And it is nice to see you again, Prince Asher." Mrs. O'Conner told the young man, "I hear you'll be attending Military School in the fall. What a fine ambition for a lad of your age."

Asher didn't reply. What was he supposed to say? '*Yeah, it's part of my legal punishment.*? Asher's cheeks grew hot. That wasn't a conversation he was ready to have. How was it that him going to military school as his Juvenile punishment, was a topic of small-talk conversation, all the way here in England? Then again, he knew media anchors all over the world had continued covering the story. 'The Asher Trials'. TNN gave them a catchy title and promised to keep everyone updated on the 'continuing saga'. Asher frowned. It wasn't just some stupid piece of interest topic to increase network views. It was his *life*.

His eyes drifted across the room, where a group of young ladies stood around in a causal circle, snacking on hors d'oeuvres and quietly chatting with one another. He blinked, doing a double-take. The young woman standing nearest to them looked strangely familiar. She wore a mustard yellow cardigan and a long, black and gray skirt. Her hair was styled into light, bouncy curls. Suddenly, Asher realized who it was. Jane Akerly!

Jane listened half-heartedly to the excited chatter coming from her roommates. It was hard to believe they were actually standing in such a fancy room. The ornate carpet, dazzling chandelier, and elaborately-decorated table were all stunning. It was no secret the O'Conner family was ridiculously wealthy.

As their little group stood near the window, Jane lifted a glass of sparkling grape juice to her lips. She wondered how many people would be dining here tonight. The table was massive. Although she still hadn't seen any sign of James himself, she hoped he would show up soon. Jane knew it shouldn't matter to her. It was clear that James was far too old for her, and nothing more than a handsome distraction. She needed to focus on what truly mattered. Writing her story.

"Can you believe we're actually here, girls?!" Laurie squealed excitedly, "I mean, look at this place! I've never seen such beautiful velvet curtains. This shade of blue is my absolute favorite and look at the porcelain dishes! And—" Laurie suddenly stopped, mid-sentence. "Oh my peppers." She lowered her voice to a near whisper, not wanting to speak too loudly, "Some members of the Royal Family of Tarsurella are here!"

Her words arrested Jane's attention. She slowly turned around, as all the others craned their necks.

"Don't all look at the same time!" Laurie scolded them "We're going to appear ridiculous!"

Jane couldn't help herself. Her gaze met Prince Asher's and her mind raced. How had this happened? How was he and Chasity here? How did—

"Jane?" Chasity suddenly burst out, realizing who was on the other side of the room. "Jane Akerly?!" She quickly erased the space between them and made her way toward the girl. Asher slowly followed.

"What in the world are you doing here?!" Chasity gave Jane a warm hug.

All of Jane's roommates' jaws were on the floor. Especially Laurie's.

"I was just about to ask you the same question!" Jane laughed as the Princess pulled away from her friendly hug, "What are you doing in England?"

"The O'Conners are old friends, and we're here for the Racing Convention." Chasity grinned. "But you didn't answer my question!"

"Oh." She glanced at Asher who remained quiet through the exchange, "Right! I'm here for a writing competition." She suddenly remembered to introduce the ladies standing behind her, "These are my roommates who are also competing. This is Laurie, our chaperone—"

"Oh, Your Highness!" Laurie released a dramatic bow, "It is such an honor to meet you! I, I can scarcely believe I'm standing in your presence! I've been a fan of your family for *so* long!"

"Oh good, I see you've all met." James entered the room. His captivating presence caught everyone's attention, as he stood a head taller than all the rest. "Having a good time, are we?" He smiled at Chasity.

"Are we ready to begin eating?" Mrs. O'Conner asked, appearing eager to get this dining event on the road.

James searched the room. "Mmm, not quite. I still have a few more guests coming."

Jane suddenly felt very overwhelmed. With everyone crowded around them, and so much conversation happening at once, she felt as though she needed to come up for air. James happily chatted with the group, but Jane found it hard to look at him. She felt so foolish for thinking he was some kind of fairytale. She should have known better. Things like that just didn't happen to her.

She slowly stepped away from the group, allowing all the happy chatter and loud laughter to fall away in the background. She neared the empty, white-washed-stone fireplace and placed her glass on the mantel. Finally, she could breathe. It was much quieter here.

But her quiet getaway didn't remain silent for long. Before she was even able to recollect her thoughts, Prince Asher stood next to her.

"Do you mind if I hang out over here?" Asher asked casually.

"Uh… no." Jane finally replied, not sure what to say. She anxiously opened her clutch and looked inside, pretending to be searching for something. What was she supposed to do now?

"It was beginning to feel a little claustrophobic." He laughed, attempting to make the mood lighter.

"I couldn't agree more," Jane sighed, anxiously looking toward the group. "Too many people make me nervous."

"Have you gotten any word?" Asher looked at her with eyes that held a whisper of concern and compassion, "About your dad, I mean."

"No." Jane gulped. Her throat tightened. "There haven't been any leads. Everyone thinks I should just…" it pained her to say the words, "give up. But I refuse to. They can't make me. I know he's out there somewhere."

Asher nodded. "Hope is good. Sometimes it's the only thing that keeps you going."

"Yeah," Jane spoke sadly.

"Jane, how much information about the case have they shared with you?" Asher asked.

"What do you mean?" Jane cocked her head slightly to the left, "I haven't heard anything. Other than the fact that every path is leading them to a dead end."

"They've framed two men as potential suspects. Carl Chesterfield and—"

"Well, if it isn't Lilly Chesterfield!" James's loud voice broadcasted the entrance of a new guest.

Chasity looked toward the doorway, shocked to see who had entered. The flamboyant red-head wore a flirty, plumb party dress and pointy black heels. A diamond choker adorned her neck, telling everyone in the room she had put much effort into her outfit choice. But the most shocking of all was the young man who was on her arm.

Hanson.

Chasity's breathing quickened as she started to put two-and-two together. It was devastatingly obvious. Hanson had been spending a *lot* of time with Lilly. And now, seeing the two here, together, grinning like Ken and Barbie, acting as if they were King and Queen of homecoming court—Chasity was struck with what she should have picked up long before now. They were a couple.

Her eyes met Hanson's, and he appeared just as surprised to see her as she was him. Lilly detached herself from Hanson's arm and greeted James with a friendly hug.

"I'm so relived we made it on time!" Lilly told him excitedly. "We had a flight delay in Tarsurella, and I just got to the hotel. I had to rush to get ready, but I'm here! So, what did I miss?!"

"Oh, not too much, we we're just giving introductions," James told her. Two more men entered the scene, and James greeted them as well, "Thomas! TJ! Welcome!"

"Well, it looks like everyone has arrived!" Mrs. O'Conner announced. "Everyone please find a seat. I'd like to get this meal started before it's time for dessert." She chuckled.

"Or maybe we could just eat dessert first!" Millie suggested.

The group slowly filtered around the table and found their seats.

"Lilly, I'm so pleased you could make it!" Mrs. O'Conner told her before sitting down. "How long will you be staying?"

"For the entire week of the Convention!" she revealed excitedly. "I'm hoping to purchase some horses for next year's circuit. From what James has been telling me, it sounds like there will be some true champions shown this week. I might even splurge on *Doctor Seuss*. Daddy said that any son of *Thor* is totally worth paying top dollar for."

"I might disagree with you there, Lilly," Chasity challenged. "I mean, just because horses have a strong linage doesn't mean they'll perform on the track. Famous parents don't mean everything. Sometimes a rouge horse can come from behind and win everything."

"What, you mean like *Pink Cotton*?" Lilly laughed, "He might have done okay in the *Belington*, but you have to remember that he still got second. *Sundance* was far faster."

"Let's face it, no matter how amazing the racer is, it's hard to compete with Chesterfield horses." James grinned, "Congrats on your win by the way! Your dad must've been pleased with that investment. Is *Sundance* going onto the next circuit?"

"Of course!" Lilly nodded. "Just because my dad's currently being questioned for a crime he didn't commit doesn't mean he's going to loosen his grip on our winning streak. You know how we Chesterfields are!" Lilly laughed, nudging Hanson playfully, "We *love* to win."

After dinner, a kind maid presented each of the dinner guests with a small ice-cream sundae shooter. Millie and Willie excitedly dove in, and Mr. and Mrs. O'Conner excused themselves for the evening. Their exit invited a more casual, less-structured flow to the evening. After Chasity finished her dessert, she stood up and lowered onto a couch near the window.

It was so strange seeing Hanson here. As much as she tried to make sense of the scenario, something just wasn't adding up. Why was he here with Lilly? Wasn't he supposed to be working at The Palace? How did he get a week off just to come to the Convention? She had tried her hardest not to think about him during dinner, but it was nearly impossible. She found herself sneaking shy glances, secretly admiring and missing so many things about him. Something ached deep inside her heart as she wished they could somehow spend more time together. She knew it was a foolish wish, especially now that he and Lilly were clearly together. Chasity knew she had to let go, once and for all. But her white knuckles didn't want to release the reigns.

Chasity sighed and examined her fingers in her lap.

James got up from the table as well and announced that the party would be moving. "I've got a new record ready to roll on our turntable in the Billiard Room. Anyone up for a game of pool?"

Lilly excitedly accepted the invite, as well as several of James's other friends. Millie proclaimed that she had never played that game before, so James invited her and Willie to come along. Chasity smiled. James was kind to include them.

Soon the table cleared, as Jane and her writing competitor friends, as well as Asher, all made their way to the Billiard Room. Chasity thought about standing up, deciding she should probably go as well. But Hanson lowered himself into the seat beside her.

"Hey," he spoke.

Chasity glanced at him. The room had thinned out, and there were only several maids present, clearing the table.

"Well, this is strange." Chasity smiled, "Seeing you without your uniform, out here in the 'real world', beyond The Palace walls." She giggled, realizing how odd that sounded, "How did you get so much time off?"

"Uh, it's kind of a long story. But I have to confess, I was crazy surprised to see you here."

"The feeling is mutual. I mean, I guess I should've expected Lilly to be here, with her dad as into racing as he is, but I guess I didn't know that you two were, uh…"

"We're not," Hanson quickly told her.

"Then why are you here?" Chasity wished to dig to the bottom of his mysterious ways. "Planning on purchasing some thoroughbreds for the circuit?"

"Yeah, right!" Hanson laughed, "I get a nice paycheck from The Palace, but it's not *that* nice."

Chasity continued to stare at him, awaiting his answer.

"It's complicated."

"Oh." Chasity nodded, clearly not satisfied with his response, "More vague, secretive answers. Great."

"Hey, I'm not the only one keeping secrets around here! I mean, when are you gonna come clean and tell the world about you and this O'Conner dude?"

"What?" Chasity laughed, "Oh no, not you too!" She shook her head, "What is it with everyone and their silly speculations?! It seems like everyone thinks something is going on between us, *except* for me and James."

"Or maybe it's just you. From what I've seen, James seems pretty into you."

Chasity's face flushed. The clanking of dirty dishes died down in the background as the final maid left the room. "What's that supposed to mean?"

"Have you forgotten where I work, Chasity?" Hanson continued, completely forgetting about Royal protocol. "I see and hear everything. I think I've got a pretty good handle on what's happening at The Palace."

"Well, that's not creepy." Chasity wrinkled her nose.

"From my vantage point, you appear pretty clueless about James's intentions. I wouldn't be surprised if he asks you about an official courtship soon."

"What?!" Chasity laughed again, "That is ridiculous! James and I are just friends. And I assure you, I've never given him any kind of indication that I'm interested in anything more than his horses."

"Wow." Hanson smirked, "You really are clueless. It's kinda cute, actually."

Chasity's hurrying train of thought slowed to a halt. *Cute*? Did Hanson just call her cute?

Hanson stopped talking. All at once, he realized what was happening. They were alone. There were no guards, no maids, and no little siblings. He had a wide-open shot to tell Chasity *exactly* how he felt. He could finally admit his feelings. He could open up and tell her everything on his heart. But where would he begin? What could he possibly say to express all the wild and wonderful things he thought about her? Hanson's forehead grew sweaty.

"Chasity," he spoke, just above a whisper. He reached for her hand.

Chasity's breathing slowed. She was locked into his eyes, and a flood of memories crashed into her like ocean waves. All at once, it was as if they were in Greece again. He was looking at her the same way he had on the beach. The day he admitted that something between them was real, and—

"Are you two slow pokes coming, or what?" A familiar voice suddenly broke into their moment.

Hanson quickly pulled his hand away from Chasity's, fearful that he might get in trouble. Chasity looked up. James was standing in the doorway.

"Yeah!" Hanson nervously launched himself to his feet. "We were just coming."

"Good." James grinned, his eyes sparkling at Chasity, "We wouldn't want you to miss out on anything."

Chapter Eighteen

Second Thoughts

"Well, the table sure does feel empty this morning," Steve commented as his family sat down for breakfast.

"I know," Hope agreed. "It's crazy how quiet things are around here with four of them missing."

"Most of the volume coming from Millie," Jillian giggled. "As annoying as she can be at times, I actually kinda miss the little sprout."

"And that's the way family should be." Steve smiled, proud of the fact that his children had all forged such strong bonds. "Happy when we're together and missing one another when we're apart. Let's pray."

After the 'Amen', Bridget reached for the platter of bacon and served her siblings.

"So, what's on the agenda for today?"

"Another press conference." Addison groaned, "Vanessa and I need to address the public and defuse the whole 'pregnancy rumor' thing."

"Seriously?" Bridget frowned. "They're still bugging you guys about that? Goodness, these people need to find a better way to spend their time! Or at the very least, report stories that are true."

"Oh, but that's not where the money is." Addison rolled his eyes, wholeheartedly agreeing with his sister. "What good is a story about a young couple who chooses purity and is saving their first kiss for their wedding day? That's not gonna sell magazines."

"I think it's wise of you and Vanessa to address them on this topic," Steve told his son. "There's no need to go running down fruitless rabbit trails, responding to each rumor that pops up, but this is just a beautiful opportunity to share your testimony with the world. I know it may not feel like it at times, but I am confident you and Vanessa are a shining example of light in this dark, dark world. I know there are many young people who look up to you. I'm sure your openness to share how God has orchestrated your love story, will encourage others to surrender their own dreams of romance and allow the Lord to do the same."

"It's true, Addi." Bridget smiled, "And even if nobody out there in the world was affected by what you and Vanessa have chosen to do, I know there are some little kiddos around here who are influenced by your example." She looked at Jillian.

Jillian resisted the urge to roll her eyes. She is *not* a little kid. When was Bridget going to realize that she was actually growing up? "I'm almost thirteen, Bridget!"

"I know." Bridget's eyes softened, "I'm sorry. That's not what I meant. You being almost thirteen is just all the more reason for Addison and

Vanessa to be proud of their standards and values. They're setting a great example for you."

"Thanks, Bridge." Addison told her before biting into a pancake, "I just hope Vanessa's gonna be able to handle all the stress. These rumors are really getting to her."

"Well, just make sure you don't have any carrots hanging around at the press conference, and you should be safe." Bridget giggled.

"As much as I try to remind her that it doesn't matter what other people think, all the negative backlash really seems to bother her. Bottom line is, she just wants everyone to like her. And sadly, anyone who marries into this family, isn't going to be liked by everyone."

"Speaking of wanting everyone to like you." Steve cleared his throat, "I have something I'd like to discuss with you guys. And to be completely honest, I'm a little nervous." He set his fork down, "I'm not sure how, uh, popular this is going to be, but I know it's important to be upfront and honest with you all about this."

Hope cocked her head, wondering what could be wrong.

"We're all ears." Addison urged him to go ahead.

"Well," he cleared his throat once more, then let out a nervous laugh. "Wow. I feel a bit like a bemused young man in high school." He laughed once more, "Okay, I'm just going to come right out and say this. Tonight, I have asked Deborah to grace me with her company for a dinner date."

Hope's eyes widened. Bridget and Addison exchanged bewildered glances.

"What?!" Jillian burst out.

"I know, I know, this might come as a bit of a shock to you all, but I have known Deborah for many, many years. She is a kind, caring, Godly woman, and I admire her Christian character very, very much. We greatly enjoy one another's company, and I would like to spend some time getting to know her on a more personal level."

"Dad, you can't!" Jillian made her thoughts on the matter heard loud and clear. "Her daughter is an absolute brat! She treated Millie like a clump of dirt, and all she did was brag about her stupid vacations and fancy hand bags! You can't marry Deborah, you just can't!"

"Whoa, whoa, whoa, honey, please calm down!" Steve attempted to keep her reaction at bay, "I didn't say anything about marriage. Deborah and I are merely going to spend some time getting to know one another better."

"Yeah, right!" Jillian snapped. "You've been teaching us our whole lives that dating without intention is just a waste of time, so don't try to tell me that you're not thinking about buying her a ring!" Jillian shoved herself away from the table and rose to a fiery standing position, "But I don't care how much you like her! Deborah is never, *ever* going to replace my mother!"

And with that, Jillian burst out of the room.

"Honey!" Steve called after her, hating that she had taken the news so hard.

"Don't worry, Dad, I'll go talk to her." Bridget quickly went after her.

Steve sighed, placing his elbow on the table. "Well, that could've gone better." He glanced at Addison, then Hope. "What are you guys thinking? Are you just as angry with me as Jillian is?"

"Wow," Addison breathed, trying to process everything his father had shared. "No, I mean, of course we're not mad. A little bit shocked, but definitely not mad. I'll admit, it does seem extremely strange to think

[202]

about you dating… but Deborah is an amazing woman. She's done so much to, I don't know, somehow fill that empty space that Mom left. So, I can see why you like her."

"What about you, Hope?" Steve asked.

"I'm with Addi." She started slowly, "I mean, yeah, it's a little strange, but who's to say we couldn't get used to the idea? It might take a while, but Deborah really is an amazing lady. I can't blame Jillian for reacting the way she did though. We all still miss Mom." Hope felt tears surfacing. "A lot."

"I know." Steve reached across the table and patted Hope's arm. "I knew that this wasn't going to be easy for you guys. I've been laboring with this in prayer and asking for God's perfect timing to share what's been on my heart. I thought that perhaps with Millie and Willie out of the picture, and with just you older kids here, it would be easier. I know it will be a challenge explaining things to the littles—I just don't want anyone to think I'm trying to replace your mom." He looked at Addison, "Because that would be impossible. She was, and always will be, my first love. No one can fill that role."

Addison looked down into his lap. He didn't always miss his mother this much. Sometimes life easily flew forward, and the pain was nowhere to be found. Yet other times, in moments like this, the ache returned, and all the old memories resurfaced.

"I know, Dad." Addison whispered.

"I just want what's best for this family." Steve sighed, "And I know Deborah feels the same about her daughter. We're both approaching this potential relationship with much caution, determined to place our children's well-being before our own."

[203]

"But it shouldn't be like that, Dad," Hope spoke up, suddenly feeling a strong urge for him to be happy. "You've sacrificed so much for us. And you deserve to do something for yourself, for once in your life! If being with Deborah makes you happy, then who are we to stop you? Everyone should have a chance at finding true love. *Especially* you."

"Hope's right." Addison agreed with a firm nod, "As much as we all love Mom, I know she would want you to move forward with life. The last thing in the world she would want is for you to be lonely."

"Aw, you guys, I'm not lonely." Steve smiled, "I have all of you!"

"But things are changing," Addison added. "We're all getting older. Millie's growing up, Jillian's almost a teenager, Hope graduated from high school, and I'm getting married. Bridget might be next. We're not always going to live under the same roof forever."

"You're right." Steve sighed, "Try as we may, we cannot stop the change that's adjusting the landscape of our lives with each passing day. Change is never easy, but stepping into the new thing that God is doing is always, always worth it."

Hope looked at her father. His words resonated with her. She took a deep breath, wanting to speak while she still had the courage. "Um, do you mind if I change the subject for a second?"

The two looked at her, so Hope took that as her que to continue.

"Addison, I have a request for you…"

"Vanessa! Tell us, how do you plan to continue your work with the Homeless Shelter, go to school, manage a family, *and* be the Queen of Tarsurella, all at the same time?"

"Do you think young women should get married at such a young age, or are you setting a bad example for girls out there?"

"Do you have any baby names yet?!"

"Vanessa, are you going to continue your studies at the university, or are you throwing away your career?"

"Vanessa!"

"Vanessa!"

Vanessa stared helplessly into the sea of flashing cameras and pointed questions. Eager media anchors raised their hands and shouted out questions. Vanessa could feel the pressure traveling from her heart to her head, and she felt as if her temples would explode. She couldn't think straight. How could she possibly begin to give the answers to these questions when she didn't even have them?!

Without warning, Vanessa abruptly turned around, nearly smashing into Addison.

He grabbed her shoulders, attempting to steady her. "Whoa, whoa, whoa, Ness, are you okay?"

"I can't do this," Vanessa told him, tears pressing dangerously close. "I—I can't!"

And with that, she rushed out of the press room, pushing past several security guards who blocked the door. She dashed down the empty hall, feeling like Cinderella running away from the ball.

"Ness, wait!" Addison called after her.

She didn't stop. She couldn't think of anything else, other than to run.

Addison quickly caught up with her. He stood in front of her and grabbed her hand.

"I can't do it!" she told him again. "It's too much!"

"I know it feels like a lot right now," Addison spoke gently and attempted to coach her through the uncharted waters, "but you *can* do this. We'll get through it. Together. We'll just take one question at a time and—"

"No!" She shook her head, feeling as though the water works were really about to break through. "It's not just that. I don't care about the stupid press conference! It's not just their questions, Addi. It's everything. I can't do it."

"Ness, I know—"

"Stop!" she told him. "You can't help me right now! I know you want to, but you can't!" She shook her head, "I'm being completely unfair to you. I can't be your Queen."

"*Yes,* you can," Addison insisted. "You—"

"Shhh." Vanessa lifted a finger up to his lips, the tears now pooling, ready to leak out at any moment. "Just listen to me for a moment. Addi, you know I love you. But that's why I can't do this."

"Can't do *what?*" Addison asked, his voice high with desperation. "The press conference? Running the Homeless Shelter?" His throat tightened. "Marrying me?"

"I think…" Vanessa spoke, her heart breaking with each word. "I think, I just need some time. I need to know if…" Vanessa whispered, unable to speak through the tears, "if this is really God's will for me."

"Vanessa." Addison felt himself growing angry, "Don't do this. You *know* this is God's will."

"I thought I did!" Vanessa cried. "But now…" she looked at the floor, ashamed to speak the words, "I'm not so sure." She slowly looked back at him, "I need to do what's right for me. And being Queen might not be it."

"So, what are you saying?" Addison couldn't suppress his anger. He threw frustrated hands into the air, "You're just going to throw everything away? One bad day comes, and you're ready to lay down and give up?!"

"I don't know!" Vanessa called back, unable to even express what was bothering her. "I just need to stop and think about things!"

"Fine!" Addison's volume increased, "Go! Go back to your apartment and question. Question everything you know to be true!"

"Addi, I need to do this," she argued. "For myself!"

"Of course." Addison crossed his arms, "Of course, it's for yourself. Because that's what it's been all about lately, right? Yourself."

"That's not true!" she snapped.

"Yes, it is!" Addison argued. "You're so wrapped up and consumed in worrying about what everyone thinks about you, that you're not even willing to make the sacrifices required for this relationship to work. So just go." He shook his head angrily, "Go ask your questions."

"You're not even listening to me!" Vanessa accused him. "I didn't want this to turn into an argument!"

"Yeah, well it's better now than after the wedding!" Addison couldn't believe the words flying out of his mouth. He took a deep breath, reminding himself to get a handle on the situation. *Addison, calm down,* he told himself. *Yelling at her isn't going to help anything.* "I hate arguing just as much as you do," he admitted quietly. "But if you seriously have so many questions about where this thing is going, then maybe you should take some time to figure things out."

Vanessa's throat constricted. She sniffed and wiped several tears from her eyes. "Yeah. Maybe I should."

And with that, she continued down the long hall.

Chapter Nineteen

Play to Win

"I blew it," Addison admitted as his head fell into his hands. "I completely, *completely* blew it."

"You didn't blow it," Steve reminded his son, placing a confident hand on his neck.

"You should've heard her!" Addison lifted his head and looked toward his dad, "It's like she hates everything about my life! And then, you should've heard *me*! I got all mad and told her I thought she should go home and think about stuff!" Addison felt like smashing his head into his desk, "Dad, what was I thinking?!"

"Addi, things are going to be okay." Steve tried to encourage him, "It's totally normal for couples to argue about things like this as the wedding day draws closer. You and Vanessa have been under a lot of stress lately! You have to give one another some grace."

"But, Dad." Addison's bottom lip quivered. "I think we went too far. I think it's over."

"If my memory serves me correctly, which it always does," Steve smiled, "I recall something similar happening this winter. Angry words, misunderstandings, threats to hop on a plane and return to the United States—Addison, it's going to be okay. You guys are going to work through this."

"Why do you sound so relaxed about this?" Addison asked, now finding himself growing angry with his dad. "How are you not even concerned that our entire engagement might be in limbo?!"

"Because, I was in your shoes once, remember?" Steve's eyes twinkled as he spoke. "Your mom and I got into a massive fight, the night before our Rehearsal Dinner. I was devastated. I thought our entire relationship had gone up in flames. She had a complete meltdown and told me she could never handle the stress of being Queen. I, very stupidly, told her I thought she was being selfish and wasn't willing to make the sacrifice required to govern this great nation." Steve laughed, "Ouch, what a mistake that was."

Addison gulped. He had just told Vanessa nearly the same thing.

"Addi, the last thing you want to do is make your woman feel like marrying you is going to be a chore. As men, things are black and white for us. We're duty-bound to our call as King, and anyone who questions that just seems ludicrous! We tend to think in very straightforward, military terms: 'either you're in or you're out!' That's what I told your mom, 'There's no middle ground! Either you love this country, or you don't.' But that's not how women think. Women like to color outside the lines." He chuckled, "They want to be romanced. They want to be cherished and adored and swept off their feet! They don't care so much about black and white boxes as they do about how you make them *feel* throughout the process. I came to the conclusion that marrying your mother should have nothing to do with duty, and everything to do with love. I told her I loved her and was willing to give up the entire country for her. I wanted to serve her, and cherish her all the days of my life, and I reassured her that she would *never* come in second place to Tarsurella. Once I got that 'other woman' out of the picture, everything changed for us. We based our relationship on love, and love alone, and as you well know, your mother turned out to be an *amazing* Queen. Once the pressure was off and she stopped thinking about her role as Queen being some 'job' she had to perform, she truly blossomed. I believe it will be the same for Vanessa."

"Well, I wish you would've told me all that *before* this afternoon." Addison lifted a frustrated hand to his head. Despite the agony of it all, he released a small chuckle. "Who knew this relationship stuff was so complicated."

"Indeed, it is!" Steve chuckled, "Want to know another secret?"

"What's that?" Addison asked, eager to get all the advice he could possibly receive.

"You're never going to get it perfect, either. You'll be learning how to love your wife until you're old and gray! But that's okay," he smiled. "Just so long as you're learning, and putting true, heartfelt effort into it."

"You decided to come!" Hope greeted Luke. There was no way of masking the pleasure in her voice. Seeing Luke always set off an unexpected spark of excitement from somewhere deep within.

"I'll admit, you were right about one thing," Luke told her as he plopped into a chair in the waiting area, just outside Addison's office.

"Ohhh, really?" Hope pretended to be surprised. "Do I get the pleasure of knowing what about?"

"As much as I didn't want to come to this meeting, if I had turned down your brother's request to see me, I would have no justifiable reason to keep running my mouth about stuff. Even though I know this is gonna be a total waste of time."

"Well, it's nice to see that you've come with such an open mind." Hope rolled her eyes then tucked her sarcasm away for another day. "Luke, do yourself a favor. Make the most of this opportunity, and really try to listen to what Addison has to say. I'm bending over backward, attempting to be a peacemaker between my family and Sons of Liberty. So, just please be respectful and remember that Addison isn't the enemy. He's our King, and he deserves to be treated with honor, whether you agree with the way he's running things or not."

"I know that," Luke nodded. "And Hope, it's nothing personal against your brother it's just—"

"Politics." Hope sighed, "I know that, too." She stood up, knowing that now there was nothing she could do other than leave the two to discuss things in private.

Chasity clicked her tongue and pressed the heels of her English riding boots into Manchester's sides. "Come on boy—go, go, go!"

Chasity urged her polo pony, determined to reach the ball before James.

Manchester raced down the field, just as eager to reach the ball as Chasity was. Chasity's tenacious eyes were fixated on the prize. She leaned into Manchester's mane, lowering her right arm along with her mallet. Just as she swung backward to smack the ball, James was right beside her, lowering his mallet to the field.

Chasity scrambled to smack it, but James had already wiggled in and stolen it from her possession.

"James, James, I'm open!" Lilly called from down the field.

James cantered forward, knowing Chasity would be right on his tail in the attempt to steal it back. James's horse was several strides ahead of Chasity's, giving him ample space to swing his mallet and make the pass.

With no one guarding Lilly, she happily accepted the pass and powered several gaits ahead. Then, with one swift swing, she launched the ball and brought forth a victory.

"Wooo-hooooo!" she cried as the ball passed the defensive line and rolled in for their much-needed points. "Win!"

Chasity slowed Manchester to a walk and released a frustrated sigh. This was the second game Lilly and James had won in a row. It was quite clear Lilly enjoyed winning. But Chasity hated losing just as much. She should have known their polo skills would be far beyond her own. Lilly competed locally, and James practically cut his teeth on polo saddles.

Chasity directed Manchester toward the sidelines, ready to call it a day. Polo was exhausting.

"What's wrong, Your Highness?" Lilly asked mockingly, "You're not giving up already, are you?"

"Of course, I'm not giving up," she snapped, feeling herself growing more and more irritated by Lilly with each passing hour. "You already beat us."

Chasity slipped off Manchester's high back and onto the ground. She unbuckled her helmet and removed it. She shook her hair. She knew it must be a horrendous mess.

"That's enough for today, Lilly," James told her as he rode up behind Chasity. "Polo can be quite challenging for beginners."

"Beginners?" Chasity snapped, "I've been playing for years!"

"Come now, can't you take a good joke?" James chuckled, "Surely you're not sore about losing. It was all in good fun!"

"Mmm." Chasity pursed her lips together, too frazzled to think of anything better to say.

James dismounted and reached for Manchester's bridal, "I'll take him. You go on and get rested before dinner."

Before Chasity could protest, explaining why she intended on doing *no* such thing, James had already led their horses off the field. Chasity frowned. She needed to defuse. She wasn't normally this on-edge after losing. But there was something about Lilly's impish grin that made Chasity want to pull her hair out.

Chasity ran tired fingers through her hair and attempted to rearrange her wild do. She spotted Hanson by the sidelines and approached him with a smile. "Hey, how come you didn't join us on the field?"

"You think I'd wanna get between you and Lilly hitting each other with sticks?"

"We were *not* hitting each other," Chasity argued, even though she felt like giggling. "And they're called mallets. Not sticks."

[214]

"Whatever." Hanson smiled, "From my vantage point, it looked like you girls were getting pretty violent."

"I could have used you on my team out there. We got creamed."

"I don't think me being on the field would've made any difference."

"What, don't you play?" Chasity was surprised with his response, "I assumed with you being such good friends with Lilly and all, maybe you were on the same competitive team back home or something."

Hanson laughed, "The closest I've ever been to polo, was wearing a polo shirt."

Chasity allowed herself to laugh this time. "I don't know why, but I find that kind of hard to believe. I mean, you're a security guard. I would think an intense sport like this would be right up your alley."

"Whew, that was refreshing!" Lilly announced.

Chasity looked up at the young woman who proudly sat on one of James's polo horses.

"It's a bummer you're scared of horses, Hanson. Polo is such a blast."

Chasity looked at Hanson. The tips of his ears were red. She bit her lip, restraining herself from saying something that could be embarrassing. Hanson was afraid of horses? How come she didn't know that? Then again, there wasn't much she *did* know about Hanson.

"Well, I'd better go get freshened up before dinner!" Lilly threw a handful of curls over her shoulders, "You coming, Hanson?"

"Actually," Chasity suddenly spoke up. She looked at Hanson, wishing for a way to spend more time getting to know him. "I was going to ask if you wanted to walk to the track. Several trainers are doing a few mock races in a couple minutes, and I thought it would be fun to watch. Maybe you could give a second opinion about some of the geldings. Care to come along?"

"You're asking Hanson for his opinion on thoroughbred horses?" Lilly laughed, "Yeah, not exactly his thing. Come on Hanson, I just need to cool London down and wrap his legs, then we can get ready for dinner."

Hanson wore a pained look. He glanced at Chasity, not wanting to turn her down. Her invitation was a wide-open opportunity for them to talk. But as badly as he wanted to take it, he knew he couldn't. His duty was to protect Lilly, and he needed to stay by her side. They still didn't know when or if his father would send someone to act on those dreadful threats. He couldn't run the risk of letting her wander around alone.

"I'm sorry," Hanson told Chasity, and his eyes truly confirmed that he meant it. "But Lilly's right." He glanced at his watch, "Dinner will be soon. See you then."

He quickly walked off, following Lilly on her high horse. Chasity felt a deep tear within her heart, wondering why he had rejected her. They had plenty of time before dinner. She bit her lip and decided to head back to their suite as well. She should at least check in on Asher.

"Asher, it's a gorgeous day out there!" Chasity proclaimed as she entered his room. "Never in the history of the English countryside has there been this many glorious days in a row without rain! Now I know polo isn't your thing, but we didn't come all the way here, just so you could stay cooped up in your stuffy room! After dinner we're saddling up, and I am forcing you to go on a trail ride with me. End of story."

Asher sat at the small desk overlooking the balcony windows. His determined face tore into his computer screen, and Chasity was confident he hadn't heard even a word she'd just said. She let out a frustrated huff, knowing that he was playing a stupid computer game. When he was like this, nothing could beak his concentration.

He held a nervous hand up to his mouth as he gnawed slightly on his knuckle.

"Asher, this is ridiculous, *no* computer game is that important—"

"Chasity!" Asher suddenly burst out as he broke away from the screen.

Chasity was taken aback with his dramatic response. He looked as though he had just witnessed a crime.

"You're not gonna believe this! I've been doing research on Frequency Advertising and the AA16." Asher excitedly poured out, "Scientists who've invented codes with a similar thread have been disappearing!"

"Whoa, Asher, slow down." Chasity plopped onto the bed. She was interested in what he had to say, but she was already completely lost. "What are you talking about?"

"Remember? The AA16?!" Asher rose to his feet and started pacing across the room. He was unable to sit still any longer. "The code Jane's dad invented! Charlie said that because of the impenetrable state of this code, if the wrong powers get their hands on it, it could be detrimental. Addison didn't think it was a big deal and the Secret Service just brushed it off, not seeing how this could be connected with Mr. Akerly. But I think Charlie was onto something. Jane's dad isn't the only guy working on this kind of elite technology! Scientists from all over the world have been reported as missing over the past few months." He rushed back to his computer and pulled up a web page. He motioned Chasity to take a look. "Look at this! A Norwegian scientist, a Japanese man... even a guy from Peru! Chasity, what if these disappearances are somehow connected?!"

"Wow," Chasity breathed, amazed to see her brother so worked up over something. "It looks like you've really been putting a lot of thought into this."

Asher ran anxious fingers through his hair. "I've been working on it all day. I mean, none of these disappearances have been obvious, and it's really taken some digging to find, but they all have a common theme! They're *all* experts in coding technology. Do you think that's just a coincidence? Or is someone with evil intentions trying to get their hands on what these men have been working on?"

"I dunno, Ash. But I'm sure the Secret Service is aware of all this. I mean, they have access to way-more information than you do. I'm sure they're working on it, bud."

"Are they?" Asher snapped. "Chas, it's been months! To the Secret Service, this is just another case stacked up among dozens of things they're trying to check off their to-do list every day. But this isn't just a name and a number!" Asher's face grew red as he spoke, "This is someone's dad! And to think she has to wake up every morning, with no word about what's been happening?! That's insane! Why aren't they updating her on this case? Why aren't they moving faster?!"

"Wow," Chasity breathed again, placing a compassionate hand on her brother's shoulder. "I've never seen you so passionate about something like this before."

Asher looked away, almost as if he was trying to hide his emotions. After a few moments, he finally looked back at his sister, his voice strong with a steadfast resolve. "Nobody should have to lose a parent." His throat tightened, "Ever. And if this was our dad, I'd want someone to do something about it. Now I have no idea if it's too late. For all we know,

Mr. Akerly could already be dead. But Jane deserves to know. And if Lilly's dad killed him—"

"Asher, stop," Chasity quickly spoke. "We don't know that. Mr. Chesterfield is just a suspect. He deserves the benefit of the doubt; he's innocent until proven guilty. But even if he did..." Chasity had trouble saying the words, "You know. Even if he did, we can't hold Lilly's father's crime against her."

"I need to go tell Jane." Asher shook his head, appearing as if he couldn't possibly wait any longer. He reached to unplug his laptop. "She needs to know about these other disappearances."

"Whoa, bud!" Chasity warned him, "Slow down! I know you're ardent about all this new information you've absorbed, but this is a really sensitive subject for her!"

"Nobody's told her anything! Except for the fact that she can't do anything about it, and she just has to wait! But what if they're wrong? What if there's actually a connection here with these disappearances, and we could get this process moving forward? Someone has to do something."

"I know you want to help. But I don't see how hearing a bunch of new conspiracy theories is gonna help her right now."

"They're not theories," Asher growled. "And if even half the stuff I'm reading online about the AA16 code is real, then Mr. Akerly's disappearance is the *last* our problems."

Asher stuffed his computer into his backpack and headed for the door.

"Wait, where are you going?" Chasity called after him.

"The Landmark London." He readjusted his backpack strap and tossed Chasity an unstoppable look of stubbornness. "I'm going to talk to Jane." He whipped around and opened the door.

"Wait!" Chasity called once more.

He turned on his heel, ignoring her badgering. He had already made up his mind. He was leaving.

"You need a coat." She tossed him his black leather jacket which had been sprawled out on his bed. Surprised, his hands caught it anyway. Chasity smiled. "It might rain."

Asher tried to hide his smirk, but it slipped involuntarily into his eyes. "Thanks, Mom." He rolled his eyes, pretending to be irritated with her motherly gesture. But Asher knew better. The coat was a symbol of Chasity's approval for his mission. She winked, and Asher knew that she believed he was doing the right thing.

Asher allowed the smile to spread all the way to his lips this time. Then he closed the door, dashed down the steps, and set out in pursuit of saving the world.

Chapter Twenty

Jane typed three careful sentences. She paused. Then she quickly slammed on the backspace button. No way. She couldn't just start writing about nothing.

And that was all she had.

Absolutely nothing.

"You sure you're not hungry?" Johannah asked.

The girls were getting ready to go down for dinner, but Jane refused to join them.

"I can't eat." She repeated, "And I'm not going to eat until I get an idea."

"Ohhh, she must be desperate." Phylicia giggled, "Food strike."

"Okay girls, that's enough!" Miss Laurie clapped her hands, "Let's head on down; we're already late. Let's leave Jane in peace."

The girls smugly left the room, but Johannah offered Jane a sympathetic pat on the shoulder. "Good luck. I do hope you think of something. I know how cruel writer's block can be."

Jane sighed, relieved to hear the door close.

She felt tears lingering dangerously close to the surface. All her ideas were awful. There wasn't a single thought that had floated into her head the past forty-eight hours which had any solid story potential. And even if she *did* think of something, like a crazy miracle happened and she was able to crank it out with minimal effort and miraculous ease, it still wouldn't matter. She was running out of time.

Jane pressed her hands to her eyes, allowing her elbows to rest on the desk. *You're going to lose,* she told herself. *You might as well give up.*

Her fantastical trip to London was nothing like she thought it would be. She was far too stressed to enjoy anything. And then, the one guy on the planet whom she thought might be, by some freak phenomenon, actually interested in her, was far too old to give her a second glance. His dashing British manners completely blindsided her. To make matters far worse, last night, seeing Princess Chasity and Prince Asher brought back so many terrible memories. It was like a stinging slap in the face, reminding her of the cruel reality that her father was indeed missing. Jane's London daydream was slipping out of her fingertips. Reality was not kind to her. Jane lost her dad, she lost her dreamy British boy, and now she would lose the writing competition.

Just then, a knock came to her hotel room door.

Jane regretfully pushed herself back from the desk, assuming it to be one of her roommates. Probably Cha-Linn. She kept forgetting to bring a key with her.

Jane whipped the door open, "Back so soon—" Her words caught in her mouth.

It was not Cha-Linn. It was Prince Asher! "Wha—" she tried to speak again.

"I can explain!" Asher quickly spoke up. "I think I might know what happened to your dad."

Jane quickly looked around the messy room. With the girls' busy schedules, they hadn't been the best at keeping things tidied up. Surely, it wouldn't be proper to invite the Royal into their trashed abode. "I would say come in, but…"

Jane couldn't help but feel strange about the situation. Where was the Prince's Royal Security? Had he come here alone?

"I know this is improper." Asher tried his best to explain, "But I've found some information I think will be of serious interest to you. I would recommend that we go somewhere to chat, but I don't want to cause a huge scene. Are you okay if I come in?"

"Uhh…" Jane's upper lip curled. "Give me five seconds." She quickly shut the door.

Jane thrust herself into action, collecting piles of dirty clothes off the floor and tossing them into the bathroom. She cleared Phylicia's makeup vanity and dumped all the contents into her unzipped suitcase. She shoved stray objects beneath the beds and pulled up the covers. She took a deep breath and placed her hand on the door handle. As improper as it was, she had to allow Asher in to speak with her. If had any further information about her father, she was desperate to hear it.

"We're good," she told him as the door flew open. "I just had to call the maid."

Asher smiled, despite the seriousness of the moment.

Jane stepped out of the doorway and invited him inside. "Maybe we can sit on the balcony. It's not quite so, uh…"

"Sure." Asher nodded, heading straight through the room and out the slider door.

Jane followed him and sat down in the wicker chair beside him. She clenched her hands together nervously and offered him a brave gaze.

"So, what do you know?" she asked, almost afraid to hear the answer.

"You remember what Charlie was talking about, right? About your dad inventing the AA16 code and how dangerous it could be if it fell into the wrong hands? It turns out, your dad's not the only one whose been working on developing that kind of technology. There's a whole group of underground scientists who have been conducting top-secret experiments for governmental projects. Have you ever heard of the GWSA? Governmental World Science Association?"

Jane shook her head. She had not.

"I'm not surprised. The scientists involved with it seem to be pretty undercover. But your dad is one of them. His involvement with the association means that every couple years he's entrusted with a massive assignment that's supposed to help develop new technology and improvements needed to assist specific countries and world leaders. I couldn't access all the records, but from what I saw, your dad has worked on a lot of those projects."

"But how do you know this?" Jane asked. "I mean, if it's some big secret, where did you get this information?"

"I may or may not have hacked into Tarsurella's GWSA database. Once I discovered the association existed, and that we have a chapter in Tarsurella, Google wouldn't take me any further, so I needed to break into their archives. But that's not really important. What's important is the fact that a handful of scientists from various countries have been reported as missing over the past few months. Scientists who are all members of the GWSA."

"I still don't understand how this is going to help find my dad. Does this give you any idea as to where he might be?"

"Not exactly," Asher admitted. "But these might be major clues into this case! If we can find out why all of these scientists are disappearing, and who is responsible for it, it'll just bring us that much closer to finding him!"

"This is such a mess." Jane shook her head, "My dad isn't the kind of guy to get involved with all this underground secretive stuff. There has to be some kind of mistake! The guy you're talking about, the man who invented your Wall of Fire and helps world governments out with problems—there's no way that's my dad. He's just a goofy, off-the-wall, quirky inventor from Ohio!"

"I know this probably all seems pretty insane, but you have to consider the fact that maybe your dad was hiding some things from you. The projects he was working on before his disappearance are so powerful, they have the potential to destroy nations if they fall into the wrong hands. By not telling you, he was protecting you. If you knew anything about these projects, your life could be at risk. Jane," Asher scooted closer and his eyes intensified. He was unable to contain the explosive information hiding inside. "I know this is going to sound crazy. But you have to hear me out. Your friend Charlie? I don't think he was just rambling about nonsense. The AA16 code is crazy powerful. We need to find out where your dad is, as well as all the other scientists, and make sure whoever it is doesn't unlock the power of the AA16 code. I don't know what they're planning to do with this code, but I have a really, really bad feeling about it."

Silence fell over the two as Jane attempted to process all the new information.

"So, what's the next step?" Jane finally asked. "I mean, you seem to know what you're talking about, but—"

"Jane!" A voice called from outside the hotel room. She could hear pounding on the door. "Jane, are you in here? Let us in, we forgot our key!"

Jane froze, her eyes wide with horror. It was Laurie! How could they be back already? They hadn't even had enough time to sit down, let alone eat an entire meal! She glanced fearfully at the Prince sitting beside her.

"You can't be here!" she told him as she flew to her feet. "If Laurie finds out you're in our room, she's going to disqualify me!"

"I can speak with her, I'm sure she'll understand," Asher told her calmly. Asher was used to people making exceptions for his family. And surely, in a situation like this, Laurie would forgive her the offence.

"No, you don't understand!" Jane hissed. "She's made it perfectly clear. Anymore acts of misconduct and she's sending me home!"

"Misconduct?" Asher echoed, wondering what a seemingly-innocent girl like Jane could possibly do to get herself on her chaperone's suspect list.

"Stay here!" Jane quickly closed the balcony doors and yanked the curtain shut. Jane flipped open her laptop, in hopes of appearing as if she was working.

She bolted toward the door and quickly opened it. Suspicion furrowed Laurie's brows.

"Who were you talking to?" she snapped.

"Huh?" Jane stuttered, terrified that Laurie could see right through her. She was no good at lying. "Talk-talking? I wasn't talking to anyone."

"*Righhhhttt.*" Laurie stepped into the room. Her eyeballs widened as she noted how clean the room was. "I wasn't even gone for ten minutes, and you already cleaned the room?" She sniffed, "It smells like cologne in here!"

"I can't write in such a messy environment!" Jane's brain desperately attempted to craft a viable excuse. Laurie couldn't send her home. She just couldn't! "I had to clean in order for my brain to think straight."

"Do you have to write in the dark, too?" Laurie crossed the room and reached for the curtains.

Jane suppressed a gasp, as she wanted to shout 'Nooo!' But that response would be far too obvious.

"Miss Laurie!" she suddenly burst out.

Laurie took her hand off the curtains and eyed Jane suspiciously.

"I need help," Jane admitted. "I'm having the worst bout of writers block ever known to man." She sat down on the edge of her bed, hoping to distract Laurie from opening the curtain. "I think I'm starting to go mental! I'm blocking out the sunlight, making my roommates' beds, and having conversations with myself, hoping something will catch fire in my mind! Don't you have any advice for me? I'm getting completely desperate!"

"Yes." Laurie's eyes softened, "Actually I do. Next time you want to enter an international writing competition, perhaps you should take some acting classes first."

"Huh?" Jane was stumped by her response.

"Because you are the worst liar I have ever had the displeasure of busting!" The curtains flew open and Laurie flung open the balcony doors.

Jane watched in horror as Laurie stepped onto the balcony. She cringed, dreading what was to come.

"Where is he?!" Laurie called out.

"Where is... who?" Jane asked cautiously.

"The boy you were hiding on this balcony!" Laurie called back.

Jane slowly stood up and stepped onto the small balcony. She glanced around, just as puzzled as Miss Laurie was. Where had Prince Asher gone? They're three floors high! Where could he have possibly escaped to?

"This is your final warning, Jane." Miss Laurie turned toward her with a deep scowl, "You weren't chosen to come on this trip, just so you could fake writer's block, miss our dinner meetings, and sneak around with British boys."

"But Miss Laurie, I—" Jane attempted to explain herself, but Miss Laurie wasn't in the mood to listen.

"Don't think I haven't seen this kind of behavior before," Miss Laurie barked. "I've been chaperoning this event for twelve years, and I know *all* the tricks in the book! Now forget your story, you're coming with us to dinner."

Miss Laurie stormed inside. Jane's shoulders fell. Her hand clutched the railing as she peered below. The height difference made her woozy. Surely Asher didn't climb all the way down from here!

She noticed a black limousine and a small figure with a blob of dark hair. A hand saluted in her direction, and Jane couldn't help but smile. It was Prince Asher. He hopped into the limo and was whisked away down the street.

Chapter Twenty One

Charismatic Wolf

Vanessa knocked nervously on Addison's office door. It quickly opened, and the kind face of Deborah was before her.

"Oh, hello, dear! His Majesty is just finishing up a call with France."

"Oh." Vanessa nodded. "I can come back later."

"That's not necessary, he's almost finished. Come on in, I'll get you some tea!"

"Thank you, but I think I'll pass on the tea." Vanessa timidly followed Deborah into the familiar office.

She sat down on the plush sofa which served as the designated waiting area and tossed a nervous glance toward Addison. They hadn't spoken since their massive disagreement. She had no idea how he was going to respond.

"Thank you, yes, of course," Addison told the man on the other line. His eyes smiled as he spotted Vanessa. "Mmm-hmm, we will take that into consideration, absolutely. Yes, thank you for your time, sir. Have a wonderful day. Au revoir."

Addison hung up, and his gaze met Vanessa's. "Hey."

"Hi." Vanessa rose to her feet and neared his desk. She anxiously clasped her fingers together. "Do you have a minute?"

"Of course," Addison spoke kindly.

"I'll go make copies of these files, Your Majesty." Deborah quickly found a reason to exit the room.

"I'm so sorry." Addison apologized as soon as Deborah left the room, "Some of the things I said the other day were so selfish and stupid, it's like I wasn't even thinking straight, I never should've gotten upset—"

"No, no, I'm the one who needs to apologize!" Vanessa confessed as she plopped into the chair across from him. "I was acting absolutely crazy and becoming a total bridezilla. I allowed the stress to takeover and start controlling me like a slave master. I thought I could handle everything, but I didn't even give a second thought about how it might be me making you feel. God really convicted me, and after praying and talking to my mom, I finally realized what my problem was. Addi, I didn't mean any of those things. You were right, all along, and I was so foolish not to listen to you. I have way, *way* too much on my plate, and I was so consumed with worrying about what everyone thinks of me and trying to perform with perfection, that I lost sight of the only thing that truly matters here— us! Our relationship. Addi, I'm so, *so* sorry. I love you with every part of my heart, and I am more than willing to make the sacrifices required to be your wife, and your Queen."

"But I don't want you to *have* to make sacrifices. I hate that there's so much stress and garbage that comes along with marrying into this family." He reached across the table for her hand, "Ness, I want this to be a fairytale for you. I don't want this to be hard. I want you to feel so completely and irrevocably loved, and never have to worry about anything a day in your life."

"I love that you want that for me, but it just isn't reality." Vanessa smiled softly, "As much a dream come true as it is for me to marry you, I know there are going to be some really tough challenges ahead. It's just the nature of life, Addi! But it doesn't matter how ridiculously unfair or painstakingly hard things get; as long as you're standing by my side, I know we can weather these storms. Together."

"I love you, Vanessa." He squeezed her hand, passion soaring in his voice, "No matter what happens, I never want you to doubt that. Ness, I promise to remind you of that truth every single day of your life."

"Oh Addi." Vanessa sighed, feeling as if she was swept into her unbelievable fairytale dream yet once more, "I love you, too." She squeezed his hand in return, "So, *so* much. Which is why I decided to resign from my position at the Homeless Shelter."

"What?" Addison questioned, having trouble believing the words. "Why? Ness, you love that job!"

"But I love you far more!" Vanessa's voice expressed her pleasure with her decision, "We've both seen how disastrous that kind of stress can be for me, and I don't want anything coming between us. Our relationship is the most important thing in the world to me, and I want to be one-hundred-percent focused on that. I want to be all in, Addi. I need to focus on my most important job—being your wife."

"Vanessa, you don't have to do that," Addison reassured her. "I would never want you to feel like I'm forcing you to—"

"You're not." Vanessa spoke confidently, "I've really prayed about this, and I feel like it's what God is asking me to do. As much as I adore working on the Homeless Committee, maybe it's time to give someone else that position. Besides, I don't know how much free time I'm going to have on my hands, while I'm helping you run the country and raise up an army of adorable little munchkins."

Addison laughed, "This is true. Little Addison Junior might be a handful."

Vanessa giggled. "So, this means we're good?" She grinned, "We're still on for that whole, crazy, getting married thing?"

"I dunno." Addison shrugged playfully, "I mean, it's on my calendar but my schedule has been getting pretty jam-packed." He winked.

"Well, you'd better make up your mind soon, because we have a cake testing session in two hours," she teased.

"Ohhh, they serve cake at those things?" Addison grinned, "In that case, I'm in."

Vanessa giggled once more, and Addison stood to envelop her in a warm hug.

"I'm *so* relived." Vanessa continued the playful banter as she rested in his arms, "I thought you were gonna make me attend the wedding all on my own."

"I would never do that to you." Addison squeezed her tightly, relived that all was well, and nothing would stop them from walking down the aisle. "We're in this together, Ness. The good, the bad, and the ugly. I'm going to be here for you. For everything, faithfully, forever."

[234]

"Hey, so how'd your meeting go with my brother?"

Luke's hands paused from where he frosted a purple cupcake. He looked up, already knowing who the voice belonged to. Princess Hope.

"Fantastic." Luke's sarcasm was evident, "The King decided to step back, reevaluate his life, and change all his wayward methods of leadership." He squeezed the end of his tube, hoping to press out more purple frosting. "How do you think it went?"

"I don't know, that's why I'm asking." She stood on the other side of the steel kitchen counter. "I haven't had the chance to talk to Addi since it happened; he's been in meetings all day. I wasn't expecting the two of you to become best friends or anything, but it went alright?"

"Well, besides the fact that he called me a toxic threat to society, a babbling fool who talks too much, and suggested that I leave the country immediately, oh yeah, it went great!" Luke flashed a fake smile.

"But I'm sure you completely kept your cool, were an absolute gentleman, and didn't say anything at *all* to be deserving of those comments, am I right?" Hope challenged.

"Yeah, just keep telling yourself that." Luke tossed a handful of sprinkles onto the purple top, then reached for another topless cupcake.

"But did you guys reach any kind of middle ground?"

"Hope." Luke's eyes delved into hers, "I'm trying not to be a total jerk about this, but don't you get it? Your family and I are *never* going to be friends. And what I don't understand is why you keep trying so hard. Why can't you just face the facts? I'm never going to be a loyalist and your

[235]

family is never going to care about what I have to say." He grabbed his tray of cupcakes and moved to a separate area of the kitchen.

Hope followed him. "Luke, that's not true…"

"Yes, it is!" Luke snapped. "Because if your family actually *got* it, they would have to give up everything for a new order of government."

"Then can you blame us for feeling threatened by your thoughts and proposals?!" Hope's volume grew, "You're telling our country that the only way for true change, is to betray our family and overthrow the monarchy? Then of course we're going to be mad at you!"

"I'm not going to stand here and argue with you!" Luke set his tray of purple cupcakes on the counter near a station of six dazzling wedding cakes. "You're like a dog chasing its tail, going around in circles and getting absolutely nowhere! Hope, nothing about you makes sense to me! Are you supporting Sons of Liberty, or are you not? Do you want to protect your family's monarchy, or are you ready for some real change? This middle ground thing is maddening—just decide which side you're on and stay there!"

"This is not a simple matter for me! You have no idea what it's like to be in my shoes! I get what you're saying Luke, and I hear you loud and clear! My heart believes what you're saying is right, and I have no idea why! Somehow, I *know* God has gifted you to bring change, yet I can't seem to see the full picture yet. But this is my family, Luke! I love them, and I would never want to do anything to hurt them!"

Luke's gaze softened. "You do? You actually believe that God is going to use me to bring change?"

"Yes," Hope admitted without hesitation. But once the words slipped out of her mouth, she doubted herself. Perhaps she shouldn't have said that? She took a deep breath and carried on anyway, "I don't know why,

[236]

but every time I pray about this, I feel like something is... right. It makes absolutely no sense to my natural mind, and to be completely honest, it frightens me. I have no idea why I trust you so much, but I do."

Luke couldn't believe his ears. He continued to stare at her as a stillness settled over the quiet kitchen. His heartbeat increased, as he desired to share what was on his heart. There were so many things he wished he could say, yet he knew it would only bring more chaos and confusion. He cared for Hope too deeply to steer her down the wrong path. Her fierce desire to have her family support everything she did would only cause them trouble. As strongly as Luke desired to express what he felt for the Princess standing before him, he knew opening his mouth could be disastrous. He had to protect her heart at all costs. Luke knew the road ahead wouldn't be an easy one, and the last thing Hope needed was to become entangled emotionally.

"I'm leaving," Luke admitted.

"What?" Hope stumbled over the simple word.

"That's all I can say." Luke shook his head, "I wish..." He bit his lip. "I'll always remember you, Hope."

"Luke, what are you talking about?" Hope's voice was shaky, "Where are you going?"

"This is my last day at work." Luke lifted a cupcake and handed it to her, "And this, Lord willing, is the last cupcake I'll ever frost." He smiled, but Hope didn't return the favor.

Hope was completely thrown off by his worlds. "You're not making *any* sense."

"I know." Luke could feel his emotions growing tender. He was careful not to look into her eyes, as he wasn't sure what kind of reaction might fall out. He had to stay steady. Luke placed the remaining cupcakes on the counter and took off his required apron. "Just promise you'll pray, okay?"

"Luke, I—" Hope couldn't even begin to make sense of her thoughts. She could feel tears surface as he headed for the door. What in the world was going on?!

"I'm gonna need all the prayer I can get."

And with that, Luke turned on his heel and left the kitchen.

"You know Millie's gonna be *so* mad at us for testing these cakes without her, right?" Vanessa told Addison as they headed for the Dining Room.

The cheerful couple held hands, swinging their arms back and forth in a carefree manner, acting as if they were giddy besties on the playground.

"Yikes. You're right. She had her heart set on doing this with us."

"Maybe we should save her a slice," Vanessa suggested.

"Or, we could have Clark bake us six *more* wedding cakes, and do this process all over again when she gets back."

"Oh, I like the way you think!" Vanessa giggled. The Royal couple pushed through the Dining Room doors and were greeted by Stacie, their wedding planner. Bridget, Liam, and Jillian were also present.

"Alright, the love birds have arrived!" Stacie announced. "Let the cake testing begin!"

"Hope isn't here yet," Vanessa observed. "Let's wait for her."

"Very well." Stacie sighed, perhaps wondering why the couple wanted to involve *all* their siblings with this simple decision. "As you can see, Clark has created six mock-up cake designs. You can observe them here, on the table. We can mix and match with whatever design you prefer, as well as the flavor of your choice! We have here ten different flavors, and I assure you, these flavors are all at the height of popularity! So, I will happily approve of whatever flavor you choose."

Clark handed each of the siblings a fork. "I'd recommend starting with the s'mores flavor. It's my personal favorite."

"Cake that tastes like s'mores?" Vanessa gasped, "Oh dear, Millie is never going to forgive us for this."

"That girl would be bouncing off the walls right now," Jillian added. "I almost feel guilty for doing this without her. She would be in cake heaven."

"Well, I guess that just means someone else needs to get married soon." Vanessa tossed a grin toward Bridget.

Just then, Hope burst through the doors.

"Addison!" she cried. Her voice was full of anguish. Everyone met Hope with wide eyes, astonished by her tornadic arrival. "What did you tell him?!"

"Excuse me?" Addison was completely lost. "What did I tell who?"

"Luke! What did you tell him in your meeting?!"

"Whoa, Hope, calm down." Addison attempted to pour a small cup of water on her blazing flames of furry. "I tried to listen to what he had to say, but the kid was a total whack job." He glanced at Clark, suddenly remembering he was Clark's son. "I'm sorry, Clark, but the things he rattled off were just insane." He turned back to Hope, "I simply shared

[239]

my opinions with him, and when he grew more and more irate, I told him he had no right to be running around spreading false information and that he needed to seriously consider reevaluating the purpose of his life, before he gets himself in even bigger trouble."

"You told him to leave the country, didn't you?"

Addison paused, as if trying to recall everything he said. "I highly recommended it, yes."

"Addison, you completely bulldozed his dignity! He probably thought you were threatening him, and now he just took off!"

"Your Highness, with all due respect, my son's not going anywhere," Clark jumped into the conversation. "Luke's going to continue working in the kitchen, until I see fit to release him."

"Oh really?" Hope was beyond frustrated, "He just told me, he decorated his last cupcake. Luke is gone."

A dark look of concern cast over Clark's face. He turned to Addison, "Your Majesty, may I—"

"You're excused," Addison quickly told him, sensing Clark's worries about what his son might be up to.

"Thank you, Your Majesty." Clark bowed quickly, "Enjoy your cake."

And with that, he rushed out of the room.

"How could you do this?" Hope was nearly on the verge of tears.

"First of all, you just need to calm down." Addison couldn't hide the frustration in his voice, "And secondly, what makes you think I'm responsible for this kid deciding to quit his job and leave The Palace? Yes, I was harsh with him in the board room, but a guy like that shouldn't even be working here anyway!"

"You don't even know him!" Hope snapped.

"Hope. Why are you so emotionally wrapped up in this? Do you have some kind of crush on the kid?"

Hope wasn't prepared to answer that question. Instead, she darted back out the door.

Addison was ready to go after her, but Vanessa stopped him gently by the arm. "I'll talk to her. I'm guessing you're the last person she wants to talk to right now."

"You're probably right." Addison sighed, attempting to deflate his frustration, "But this is so stupid! Hope is smarter than this! She knows better than to get involved with a kid like that!"

"Vanessa, let me come with you," Liam spoke up.

Everyone was surprised. Bridget tossed him a concerned glance.

"I think I know why he left," Liam revealed.

"Sis, can I talk to you?" Vanessa asked in a humble tone.

Hope sat alone in the Family Room. She looked up from where she sat quietly stewing on the sofa. Hope scooted over, offering Vanessa the non-verbal invitation to join her.

Vanessa entered, but Hope was surprised to see Liam follow as well.

She eyed him suspiciously.

"I need to talk to you, too." Liam lowered himself in the chair across from them. He clasped his hands together and leaned forward. Hope took a deep breath. It looked like the guy meant business.

"I know why Luke left."

[241]

"Because Addison threatened him?" Hope suggested.

"No." Liam shook his head. "I did."

Hope remained silent. As frustrated as she was, she wasn't about to blow up in the face of Bridget's boyfriend.

"He's bad news, Hope." Liam explained himself, "All around. He's a good-looking kid with a rotten agenda. Now I don't know how far your relationship has progressed—"

"We're not in a relationship," Hope snapped.

"Okay." Liam held up his hands in surrender, "How far your *friendship* has progressed. But as the ring leader of Sons of Liberty, his false ideology is spreading like cancer. Do you have any idea what the SOL plan on doing to this country? They're fixated on taking down the Crown. And even though Luke claims he would never resort to violence, he already has. He was there the night Bridget was attacked at the restaurant downtown. And even though he didn't pull the trigger, it's only a matter of time until someone in the SOL does. In your eyes, Luke may appear completely innocent because he's all talk and no action. But if their movement continues to gain momentum, it won't be long until they resort to taking this country by force. Can't you see the massive target you have on your back? It's only natural Luke would want you as an ally, just until he gets the information he wants, then twist it for betrayal like he did last winter. We all love you, Hope, and your family isn't just going to stand by and watch you get hurt by someone like that. You deserve better."

"I hear what you're saying," Hope spoke calmly. "And I'm not stupid. I know that to the natural mind, it seems insane to trust Luke. But I've prayed about this diligently for *months*, and I believe God is working in his life. Now I don't expect any of you to approve, or even agree with what I'm saying, but there's just something about Luke that I trust."

[242]

"I know how complicated these things can be." Vanessa placed an understanding hand on her knee, "The matters of the heart can be messy, confusing, multi-faceted, puzzling ordeals. But sometimes when we're attracted to someone, our judgement can become so clouded until we're not thinking clearly anymore—"

"This has nothing to do with me liking Luke!" Hope lifted frustrated hands in the air, "Why does everyone think I'm in love with him or something? Will you guys just *listen* to me for a second?! It doesn't matter what Luke looks like, I mean he could be an ugly sumo wrestler with a paper bag over his head! None of this has anything to do with how I feel or don't feel about him. I've prayed about this *so* much, and God is directing my heart to listen to what he has to say! It doesn't make sense to my natural mind, but something is just clicking in the spirit. I have to believe God has a purpose in all of this, and even though I can't tell you what it is yet, I know He's doing something in Luke's life. Something that is going to help all of us."

"You know, Hope," Liam spoke cautiously, "the scary thing about deception, is that we don't actually know if we're being deceived or not."

"I appreciate your concern." Hope's jaw tightened, attempting not to lash out at him. "But I know what God is speaking to my heart. And I'm not being deceived."

"Sis, I know God is going to reveal the truth about all of this," Vanessa told her. "If what Luke is claiming to be all about, really is of God, then you don't need to defend him. If God's Spirit is truly moving through Luke, then it will be like a lion and fight for itself. If God wants things to change so dramatically in this Kingdom, then you or me, your brother, Liam—not a single one of us will be able to stop it. But, if this *isn't* part of God's will, and Luke is just a charismatic wolf in sheep's clothing, then

[243]

it's gonna fall apart. And until we know for sure, try to do your heart a favor and let go of him."

Chapter Twenty Two

"Ew! Who eats poached eggs and asparagus for breakfast?! That is disgusting!" Millie vented, clearly appalled by what was displayed on the breakfast table.

Chasity was grateful they weren't sitting at the large table downstairs with the rest of the O'Conners. Thankfully, breakfast was far more casual, and they were free to eat in their suite upstairs. Which worked nicely for them, because there was no way Chasity was going to have the kids up and ready, dressed to the hilt by 8:00 a.m. for breakfast.

"Millie, we have to be grateful and thank God for the food set before us, even if it is asparagus." Chasity reminded her little sister, "There are some kids in the world who don't have *any* food and they would happily eat what you're rejecting."

"You mean, like the kids Vanessa is helping at the Homeless Shelter?"

"Exactly," Chasity nodded. "Okay, Willie, Millie, eat up, I've got to get out to the track." She did a little dance as she slipped into her black, slender riding boots, totally thrilled about what the day had in store. Today she would meet Nathaniel Wells and talk to him about working with Nic!

"If we eat, then can we go outside and play?"

"Yes, but only if you eat everything on your plate." Chasity was surprised by how much she sounded like their mother. She glanced out the window, "And if it starts raining, you need to come in ASAP."

"I want Asher to come play with us!" Willie suggested.

"I know." Chasity offered him a weak smile, "But it's still early for him. He'll probably be sleeping for another few hours."

"Can we go jump on his bed and wake him up?!" Willie was electrified by the idea.

"Morning!" Asher entered the small breakfast nook area, sounding as chipper as a springtime birdy.

Chasity couldn't hide her shock. "Whoa, someone's up early!"

"Yay, you can come play with us!" Willie cheered.

"What happened to sleeping in 'til noon?" Chasity questioned.

"Are you kidding?" Asher looked at her like she just suggested he go jump off a bridge, "I have way too much on my mind to sleep." He grabbed a piece of toast from the table.

Chasity lifted a questioning, yet highly impressed eyebrow.

Asher crossed the room and reached for the built-in, black phone on the wall.

Chasity wanted to ask what he was doing, but she decided to trust him. Asher had been behaving quite maturely lately, and Chasity didn't want to squelch that by being overbearing.

"Hello, yes, may I reach room 344?" Asher asked.

Chasity looked up from the table, trying to stay focused on breakfast, yet severely distracted by Asher's conversation. Who was he calling?

"Hello?" Jane picked up the ringing phone in their hotel room.

One Infection music blasted in the background as her roommates scurried about the room getting ready. Jane didn't have a clue as to who would be calling them this early in the morning.

"Is this Jane Akerly?" the voice asked.

Jane nodded. She then remembered that whoever was on the other line couldn't see her head movement. "Uh, yes."

"This is Asher, I wanted to—"

Jane quickly hung up the phone.

Her eyes widened as she realized what she had done. She just hung up on the Prince of Tarsurella!

"Who was that?" Johannah asked as she floated by, rocking out to the song blasting through their hotel room, while also attempting to attach her fake eyelashes.

"Nobody," Jane quickly spat. "I mean, it was a wrong number."

Johannah only shrugged and continued her dance through the room as she pranced back toward the mirror.

Jane stood up and took a deep breath. That was close. Way, *way* too close. Thankfully, Laurie was in the shower, and didn't know Asher had tried to reach her. She anxiously looked at the phone, desperately hoping he wouldn't try to call back. Then an idea struck her. She subtly reached behind the bed and unhooked the phone cord from the wall.

There, now anymore attempted phone calls wouldn't get her in trouble. They were just about to leave for their next sight-seeing expedition and would be gone the rest of the day. There was no way Prince Asher could find her.

At least, not today.

Asher's face expressed just how puzzled he was. He tried to dial several more times, and asked for the same room, but it was to no avail. Finally, he hung up and walked back toward his room.

"Asher, aren't you joining us for breakfast?" Chasity asked, wondering why he was acting so strange.

"I need a Plan B," he mumbled, then returned to his room, closing the door behind him.

"Does this mean Asher isn't playing with us today?" Willie asked sadly.

"Mmm... I wouldn't count on it." Chasity placed a sensitive hand on his shoulder, "But maybe tomorrow."

"Tomorrow will be too late!" Millie spurt out. "By then, the alligators in the swamp will have eaten Willie's last leg! He needs Asher to bring him the antidote as quickly as possible, injecting him with his hyper-immune superpowers before Willie is doomed!"

A knock came to the main door. "Room Service!" a kind little British voice called out.

"Ohhh, is she bringing us waffles?!" Millie could only dream it would be so.

Chasity smiled. She rose to her feet and opened the door for the friendly little lady.

"Good morning, Your Highness." The maid whom they knew by the name of Lydia curtsied, "Fresh towels, Your Highness, as well as a special delivery from Mr. O'Conner."

Chasity spotted the massive vase with a hodgepodge of blooming flowers colorfully popping out in every which direction, sitting on Lydia's cart.

"Oh, they're beautiful!" Chasity clasped her hands together and admired the arrangement. "But the Mr. and Mrs. did not have to do that— they're too sweet!"

"Uh, you may want to look at the card, Your Highness," Lydia suggested after she entered and set the vase down. "Not that I did," she quickly added.

"Right." Chasity laughed, "Thank you again."

"You're very welcome, Your Majesty." Lydia curtsied again before heading out the door, "It is my pleasure to serve! Please don't hesitate to let me know if you need anything, anything at all."

Chasity smiled once more before closing the door. She reached for the envelope buried amongst the fresh flowers, surprised to find the card was addressed only to her. She slowly ripped the seal, slightly nervous about what she might find inside.

Roses are red,

[249]

Violets are blue,

Posies are beautiful,

But not as much as you.

Yours Truly,

~James

Chasity quickly stuffed the card back in the vase and reached for her jacket. Surely James was just being overly hospitable. The flowers meant nothing romantic, Chasity was sure of that.

"Alright, let's finish up those breakfasts, kiddos!" Chasity raised her voice, hoping to forget about the flowers, "Looks like the sky is going to open up and rain soon! Let's take advantage of the sunlight while we've got it!"

"Oh my goodness, that's Nathaniel Wells!" Chasity whispered to James. "I think I'm actually nervous! Look, my hands are all sweaty!"

Mr. Wells heartily shook hands with several men near the track, and Chasity bit her lip. She couldn't wait to talk to him!

"Come, I'll introduce you." James smiled.

Chasity excitedly followed him toward the man, careful to wipe her damp palms on her jeans before approaching. Mr. Wells was clearly a very popular guy, as several others flocked around him. Lilly popped into the conversation just before they did.

"Mr. Wells, it's such an honor to meet you!" Lilly bubbled, "I'm a huge fan of your work!"

"Ahh, Miss Chesterfield." Mr. Wells offered her a smile, "Congratulations on the *Belington* win. Your father's horses always seem the ones to beat."

Chasity frowned.

"I'm flattered you would say that, but it's pretty clear here who the new celebrity trainer is!" Lilly grinned, "My father's willing to pay you top dollar, to begin working with Dr. Seuss. I'm gonna purchase him in the auction tomorrow. Are you interested in the job?"

"Actually, the training methods I use are quite different from your father's. I fundamentally disapprove of some of his practices. I don't push as hard as the traditional trainers do. I'm not interested in running the horses I work with into an early grave. So, if I'm training your gelding, it's going to be my way or the highway."

"Oh, of course!" Lilly nodded eagerly, "We would promise to ascribe perfectly to everything you recommend."

"What makes you so sure that Dr. Seuss is going to be your horse?" James asked, budding into the conversation. "There are dozens of men who already have their eyes on him."

"I know how to get what I want." She shrugged playfully.

"Mr. Wells, allow me to introduce you to Princess Chasity. She's the spirited young lass I was telling you about. She's interested in racing her horse, Nic, next spring."

"Ahh, yes, it is a pleasure to meet you, Your Highness." Mr. Wells nodded with a slight bow, "James has told me much about you. He believes your horse has a great measure of potential. I would love to take a look at him. Is he running this weekend?"

[251]

"Oh no, he's not here." Chasity quickly explained, "He's back in Tarsurella. But please, feel free to come and watch him anytime! He has no experience with the race circuit whatsoever, he just loves to run fast."

"Sometimes that's all a horse needs to win!" Mr. Wells smiled warmly, his eyes twinkling with love for the sport. "That and an owner who is completely dedicated to following the unique, one-of-a-kind, training schedule that I create for my clients."

"I can't wait for you to start working with Dr. Seuss!" Lilly jumped back in, even though it wasn't her turn to speak. She turned to Chasity, "But I'm sure it'll be fun for you to get your toes wet, and splash around in the world of racing a little bit. It'll be cute to see you run Nic!"

And with that, she turned on her heel and exited the conversation.

Chasity bit her lip. She wanted so badly to put that girl in her place. But she knew that wasn't her job. She had to trust God, continue to choose love, and keep her mouth shut.

"Well, Miss Chesterfield certainly doesn't struggle in the confidence department." Mr. Wells chuckled.

"Maybe I should think about getting a new horse." Chasity twisted her lip, "Just so I have the satisfaction of creaming her next spring."

James laughed as his eyes widened in surprise. "Nothing brings out the competitive spirit quite like racing!" He turned back to Mr. Wells, "Thank you for your time, we look forward to hearing you speak at the Convention this afternoon."

"Of course." He smiled, "And, Your Majesty, I am highly anticipating seeing what your Nic can do."

"Thank you," Chasity breathed, feeling as if she was floating on a cloud of celestial bliss. Nathen Wells was actually interested in working with Nic! "I so, *so* appreciate it!"

The conversation came to a close, and Mr. Wells carried on, to speak with several others. Chasity and James turned to leave.

"Can you believe it?!" Chasity squealed. "I feel like I'm floating through a daydream! Nic might *actually* be on his way to becoming a racing superstar!"

"I get quite tickled seeing you so animated," James laughed. "I've never met anyone so passionate about horses. If anyone deserves to win the next *Belington*, it should be you. I find your enthusiasm compellingly adorable."

Chasity kept her eyes centered on the path ahead. James's words made her uncomfortable. Why did he have to be so lavish with his complements? Chasity was beginning to grow concerned. Was his natural propensity for politeness turning into something more dramatic and defined? Was he this nice to everybody, or had she become the sole target of his flowery words? Was he actually interested in her? Chasity hoped it wasn't so. Those were awkward waters she did not want to wade through.

Chapter Twenty Three

Pretzels and Mopeds

"Ohh, I love this palate!" Phylicia lavishly obsessed over Johannah's makeup. "You're so lucky you can afford these things. Perhaps after I win and become a world-famous author, I'll be able to splurge on a set like this."

Jane sat at her desk, trying to block out the chatty girls. But it wasn't working. They were still getting ready for the day, *oohhhing* and *ahhhing* over one another's fancy makeup kits. Even though Jane wasn't the least bit interested in their conversation, she still couldn't seem to tune them out.

"What makes you think you're going to win?" Cha-Linn spoke up. "I just finished my final edits, and I couldn't be prouder. Some of you in this room have your work cut out for you. If you haven't already lost."

Jane's ears burned. She knew Cha-Linn was talking about her.

"Okay girls, five minutes and I'll be ready!" Laurie told them. "I'm just going to fill up my water-bottle with ice. Gotta stay hydrated!"

She left the room, and Jane attempted to refocus. But five minutes wouldn't be long enough for her. *Face it,* Jane told herself sadly, *five YEARS isn't going to be long enough for you. The girls are right. Your time is almost up, and you've already lost.*

Jane quickly closed her laptop. She didn't want to look at the blasted Word document anymore. Even the flashing curser had been mocking her. The vast whiteness of the empty page was giving her a headache.

Just then, a loud *thwap* hit the balcony door. Jane's head popped up, wondering if perhaps a bird smashed into the window. The other girls heard it too.

"What was that?" Johannah asked, nearing the balcony.

Curious, Jane opened the door and stepped outside. Her eyes searched but didn't find any injured animals. She couldn't seem to detect anything that was out of place. Finally, she saw a small, black, film canister near the foot of the wicker chair.

"What's that?" Johannah asked, picking it up. "Oh my! Is this one of those old film canister thingies? Like from the 90s? Before digital cameras? I haven't seen one of these in forever!"

"Looks like it," Jane agreed.

"How did it get up here?" Johannah was puzzled.

"Maybe a bird found it in the park and accidently dropped it," Jane reasoned.

"It's so cute! I forgot how nifty these little things are." Johannah shook it playfully. Then she paused. "Wait, it sounds like there's something in it." Johannah popped the top, and sure enough, there was a thin piece of paper rolled up inside.

"Oh my cheeseburgers, it says your name!" Johannah burst out, "It's a letter!" Johannah's eyes widened, "From a guy named Asher! Wait. Asher?!"

"Shhhh!" Jane shushed her, quickly bounding across the balcony and closing the door. She didn't want the other girls–or Laurie–to hear. "Huh? Give it to me!"

"I can't believe you got a secret note in a film canister from *Prince Asher!*" Johannah gasped, "I am totally freaking out right now!"

Jane quickly grabbed the note and started reading.

Jane,

We need to talk. Meet me on Cannon Row, near Big Ben.

I'll be waiting there.

-Asher

"This is so exciting!" Johannah squealed. "My jealousy is off the charts right now! How'd you get the Prince of Tarsurella to ask you to sneak out?! I mean, how much more romantic can this get?!"

"Shhh!" Jane hushed her once more. "Please, I don't want the other girls to know. And it's not like that. It's an important, governmental matter."

Johannah appeared even more impressed.

"And you don't have any good story ideas?!" Johannah's jaw was scraping the floor, "Girl, your life *is* an epic novel right now!"

Jane quickly stuffed the note in her pocket.

[257]

"We're going to the Big Ben today!" Johannah's wheels were turning. "Maybe I can cover for you when we get lunch. You can say you have to go to the restroom, then dash off and meet him," Johannah sighed in a dream-like state as she clenched her fingers to her chest, "The Prince."

"I can't sneak away from the group!" Jane panicked, "Laurie is already suspicious of me! One more mishap and she's sending me home."

"Jane, can't you see what's happening here?" Johannah tried to encourage her to see the big picture, "You're in the middle of a crazy-amazing adventure! Who cares about writing the perfect book, when you can be *living* it? Maybe this time you're not supposed to be the author. Maybe you're supposed to be the main character."

"It's too big a risk." Jane shook her head, afraid of getting caught. "If Laurie sends me home—"

"So *what* if she sends you home?" Johannah spoke with vibrant fervor, "Our time here is almost finished anyway! Writer's competitions come and go. But opportunities like this only happen once in a lifetime. Losing isn't the end of the world, Jane. There will be more chances to get published in the future, I'm sure of it. But dashing off on an exhilarating adventure, determined to save the world, or whatever this is all about? A moment like *that* is never going to happen again."

"This iconic clock tower safely holds our beloved Big Ben bell!" A spirited male tour guide told the group, "Old folk tales say that the bell was originally going to be named Royal Victoria. So how did they switch from Victoria to Ben? Who knows! But I'm quite surprised those fiery feminists haven't started a petition to change it back to Victoria!"

He laughed at his own joke, even though nobody else was amused.

He cleared his throat. "Anyway, the arrival of Big Ben was quite the elaborate ceremony! It was floated down the Thames River on a massive barge, and then taken across Westminster Bridge in a fancy carriage with sixteen beautiful, gray horses. Though some would argue that the horses were white, if we want to be politically correct, in the equine world there is no such thing as a white horse. I would know, as I was so rudely reminded by a tourist several years ago, right in the middle of my usual rigga-ma-roll! I argued with her for a good five minutes, then when I went home and Googled the matter, I stood corrected! To my surprise—"

Jane anxiously glanced over her shoulder. The unsettled feeling in her stomach grew ever stronger with each passing minute. Their tour was nearly over, and soon she would be faced with a choice. Should she follow Johannah's suggestion and slip away to meet with Prince Asher during lunch?

Jane hated the idea of breaking the rules. Getting busted would not only be embarrassing, but also heartbreaking. She wasn't ready to go back home. Even if there were just a few days left in the competition, she couldn't bear the thought of leaving early.

Then again, it appeared as though Asher had something really important to say. Jane struggled to make sense of all he had shared, and she didn't quite see how any of it would help find her father. But, it was clear Asher wasn't going to give up very easily. And if the Prince believed it was that vitally important, perhaps it was worth risking everything to hear him out.

Jane gulped as the physical anxiety she felt floated to her throat. Jane needed to be brave. She thought of her father and realized that this might be her last real chance at finding him. As frightful as it was, she needed to do it.

A good fifteen minutes later, the tour ended, and Laurie's group sat in a small café right beside Cannon Row.

Johannah sat across from her. Jane glanced at her helplessly, wondering what she should do next. Laurie already knew she was a terrible actress. Whatever excuse she chose to come out of her mouth had to be a good one.

Johannah slipped a small piece of paper beneath the table. Jane felt it reach her lap. She casually peaked at it. She attempted to make out Johannah's messy scribbles. The words suggested she order some sea food and then fake an upset stomach.

Jane took a deep breath. She felt terrible about behaving deceptively. But if it was going to help save her dad, she was willing to try.

Shortly after the waitress brought their food, Jane attempted to eat jellied eel. Yikes. Perhaps she wouldn't have to pretend to be sick after all!

After just a few bites, Jane was sure she couldn't stomach any more.

"Oh dear." Jane lifted a hand to her mouth. "Uh, excuse me." She quickly darted off toward the restroom.

"Oh no, she looks sick!" Johannah expressed her concern, "I'll go with her!"

In the bathroom, Johannah gave her a high-five. "Alright, girly! That was impressive!"

"I wasn't pretending." Jane shook her head and panted for air. "I really do feel like I'm going to hurl. That eel was awful!"

"Hurry!" Johannah urged her, "You don't have much time!"

Jane tossed her a concerned glance, wondering if she could truly trust her. Was Johannah as kind as Jane thought she was? Or was this all part of a devious plan to get her removed from the competition?

"Go! I've got your back!" Johannah reminded her.

Jane grabbed her purse and headed for the back door. She didn't have a choice. Like it or not, she would have to trust Johannah.

After sneaking out of the restaurant, Jane gasped for air. She was outside! She had made it through the restaurant without Laurie seeing her! She quickly headed for Cannon Row as a jolt of adrenaline shot through her veins. This was crazy! She was actually doing this!

It only took her a few moments to find and cross Cannon Row. But where was Asher? She glanced around, spotting the iconic firetruck-red phone booth, a favorite spot for tourists to snap pictures. She continued searching, wondering where he might be hiding.

Finally, she spotted a young man wearing a black leather jacket, with large black sunglasses, and a black baseball cap. *That must be him*, she told herself. *He must've snuck out as well.* She suddenly realized what a risk it was for him. *If the media finds him here, things could get crazy.*

She quickly approached him. "Film canister?" she asked. If it wasn't him, the stranger would have no idea what she was talking about.

Asher quickly took off his sunglasses and offered her a relived smile. "You came."

"I don't have long," Jane admitted as she sat down beside him. "Laurie is shrewd as a hawk. She'll be on to me soon."

"We need to contact all of your dad's scientist friends and find out what they know about the GWSA." Asher drove right in. "There's an agent who was on this case and he's staying at the O'Conners'. I'll find out if he has any more information. But the most valuable information is going to come directly from your dad's contacts."

"I don't know if Dad has any friends who are scientists. He's kind of a loner. I mean, he didn't really hang out with anyone." *Besides me.*

"I'm confident your dad is connected to an underground network far greater than anything you're aware of," Asher continued. "If we can get more information about the GWSA from anyone who's involved with it, maybe that will lead us to a suspect. I mean, there's gotta be someone with inside information. The GWSA is either forcing the staff to make something against their will, or threating those who refuse not to, at least, that's what I suspect."

"I don't know." Jane shook her head in doubt, "You were there when they raided our home for every kind of clue possible. Haven't they already traveled down those rabbit trails and still come up empty-handed? And what about the suspects, Mr. Chesterfield and Mr. Fletcher? Why haven't they gotten any information out of them?"

"The team Addison dispatched on this assignment isn't looking for anything past the surface. Their goal is to find your dad, and that's a super-important one. But I can't help but think that maybe this is all just a distraction. Maybe your dad's disappearance, and the framing of Mr. Chesterfield and Mr. Fletcher, were set up as a distraction to keep Tarsurella's eyes off the bigger problem."

"The bigger problem?" Jane echoed. What could possibly be a bigger problem than losing her dad?!

"Whatever the powers that be are doing with the AA16 code." Asher spoke calmly, "Though it's possible that Mr. Chesterfield and Fletcher were part of the initial kidnappings, from what I've researched about these two men, neither of them seem like evil masterminds set on taking over

[262]

the world. They were probably just in it for the money, doing someone's dirty work up front, and when they got caught, the greater powers at work were relieved. Instead of trying to stop the AA16 code from being applied to extremely dangerous frequency technology, everyone's just trying to find a missing man, and decide who to prosecute. Meanwhile, the larger plot is going on under the radar, completely undetected."

"Oh no." Jane's face suddenly turned pale.

"Yeah, that's what I'm saying!" Asher excitedly scooted closer, relived she was finally getting it. "The only way to stop—"

"It's Laurie!" Jane screeched, feeling her entire world crash down. She could see the angry woman arguing with a desperate Johannah, just several blocks away. "I'm dead!"

Asher glanced over his shoulder, suddenly realizing she wasn't talking about the AA16 code. His eyebrows shot up. He could see steam rolling out of the woman's ears, even from this far away. "I can talk to her," Asher reassured her. "Don't worry, you're not going to get dis—"

"Come on!" Jane suddenly grabbed his hand and yanked him to a standing position. "We need to get out of here!"

"But what about the writing competition?" Asher questioned, knowing that if they dashed off now, she would only be getting herself in deeper trouble.

"My dad is way more important than some stupid competition!" she told him fiercely.

"Follow me." Asher slipped on his sunglasses and took off in a sprint.

Jane stayed close behind him as they weaved through crowds of people. She was shocked by how fast the kid could run. Her chest was already tightening, and her feet were sore, but fear pounded in her ears and kept her moving forward.

If Laurie caught them, she would ruin everything. It would all be over. Jane would be sent home, her conversation with Asher would be aborted, and she wouldn't know how to help her father.

She anxiously glanced over her shoulder, and then instantly regretted it. Laurie was running toward them. Jane made eye contact with the woman, then she quickly turned forward again. "Faster, she's gaining on us!" Jane shouted.

"Jane! Jane Akerly!" Laurie hollered. "You stop right this instant, young woman! You're disqualified! Do you hear me? DISQUALIFIED!"

"Where's your cab?!" Jane desperately asked, short of breath, hoping he might have a car waiting nearby.

"It's all the way on the other side of Westminster Bridge!" Asher called back, careful not to crash into a group of three teen girls attempting to take a selfie together. "Excuse us, coming through!"

The girls screamed as they split apart from one another, hoping not to get run over by the speedy Prince. Jane was right behind him.

"Sorry!" she called out.

Asher kept running. His chest burned, but they needed to keep going. This Laurie lady was clearly not happy. Asher knew better than to think he could talk any kind of common sense into her. The whole scene looked really, *really* bad. Asher tried to think on his toes. Suddenly, he spotted a Vespa Rental shop on the far side of the street. He grabbed Jane's hand and yanked her in the opposite direction.

She let out a sound of surprise as Asher redirected her movement.

He practically pulled Jane across the busy street, careful not to get hit by cars flashing in front of them. Once they safely reached the sidewalk, Asher jumped on a black Vespa.

"Quick, get on!"

Jane didn't even have time to think. She quickly followed his lead.

"Hey, kid, what are you doing?!" the rental owner burst out.

Jane's eyes grew wide in horror.

Asher revved the engine.

"Hey! Wait! Wait! You need to pay for that!" the angry man shouted after them.

Asher directed the Vespa into the street. Jane gasped. She held on for dear life as they sped into busy traffic. Did they seriously just steal a Vespa?!

"Put it on my brother's tab!" Asher called back. Then he released a laugh. His tongue pressed against his top lip. There was no way that Laurie lady would catch them now!

"*That* was the craziest thing I've ever done in my entire life." Jane exhaled, relived to be on solid ground again. "We didn't even wear helmets! And are you even old enough to drive?!"

Asher laughed. He turned off the engine, and all was still. They had escaped the crazy traffic and reached a serene park. Happy ducks floated and quacked in the small lake nearby, and an elderly couple with their goldendoodle strolled by. Aside from them, there wasn't a soul to be seen.

"Nope," he shrugged. "But I'm a Prince. They make exceptions for that."

Jane's face was truly horrified. "And you didn't pay that poor old man for his Vespa! What were you thinking?!"

"Hey, you're the one who needed a quick getaway! Nobody forced you to hop on!" Asher defended himself. "Relax. My dad will pay him back. Maybe we'll buy him a whole garage full of Vespas, just for his troubles."

Jane shook her head. This entire fiasco was absolutely bonkers! She couldn't believe she had just done that. And now, after running away from her chaperone, throwing the entire competition away, she was in the middle of a stunningly glorious park, with the Prince of Tarsurella.

"You think she'll find us here?" Jane asked, already internally freaking out about what would happen when she did.

"Naw." Asher stepped away from the Vespa and strolled toward the lake, "Not unless they send the police after you."

Jane's eyes widened.

Asher looked back with a smile. "I'm kidding."

Jane's gaze softened. She looked around and decided to toss all her anxieties to the wind. Johannah was right. Moments like this didn't just happen every day. This was truly one of those once-in-a-lifetime kind of things. She followed him to the pond and took a deep breath. "So, now what?"

Asher picked up a small twig and flung it into the water. The splash caused several ducks to startle and release angry quacks. "First, I congratulate you for what you just did. I know that took some serious guts. But your dad would be proud. Sacrificing the writer's competition like that had to be hard."

"It was." Jane sighed and lowered herself to the ground. The soft grass felt warm and welcoming after running so intensely. "I wanted *so* desperately to win. Thinking about it now, it was absolutely foolish of me, but I just thought that..." her voice trailed off as she burrowed deeper into her own thoughts. "if I won, things would change. I thought that if perhaps I could be good enough, some sort of fairytale would take place. I know I'm not Cinderella, but I always dreamed of something euphorically magical happening to me in London. Like, somehow I'd meet my Fairy Godmother who could evaporate the hurt and miraculously make my dad reappear." Jane laughed, realizing how utterly stupid it sounded, "But I guess I should know better than to live in a fantasy world."

Asher continued to stand and stare across the gentle waves. As odd as her words were, strangely they struck a chord in him. Somehow, he could relate. "Sometimes fantasy is better than reality."

Jane looked up. She pondered the personality of the young man whose back stood before her. She knew the Royal Family had been through a lot. With the terror attack last fall, the unhappy street protests from fed-up citizens, and Asher's legal issues in court, it was no secret this family had their share of hard times. It was all over the news.

"I don't imagine you entertain completely unrealistic illusions about happy endings and silly scenarios about the way life could be if things were different. It seems to be more of a girl thing, I think."

"Maybe not," Asher admitted. He turned to face her, "But I have spent a shameful number of hours locked in my room, shutting out real life, refusing to leave the make-believe world of my stupid video games. And we all know where *that* got me. Opening up the backdoor of our palace to a psycho warlord terrorist."

All at once, Jane's problems didn't feel quite so large anymore. Asher and his family had truly been through some terrifying moments. She struggled to find the right words. "I'm sorry things have been so hard for you guys."

"I used to think I was the only person on the planet with problems." Asher plopped down into the grass beside her. "Boy, was I wrong." He looked at Jane, "Your life stinks just as much as mine does. Along with millions of others on this planet."

"Yeah." Jane sighed, "I guess there's nothing real about daydreams and fairytales after all. If anything, such false expectations of reality only leave us ill-equipped for reality, and heartbreakingly disappointed. If a guy who lives in a *castle* thinks that life is hard, then I guess happily-ever-after really *is* just an illusion."

"One of Mom's favorite, um," Asher could feel his throat tightening up. It killed him to talk about her. "Her favorite, uh, Bible verses, was Romans 8:28. She always used to tell us that if we just trusted God, no matter what, He would be faithful to work everything out and bring a good ending to the story He's writing with our lives. But after she died…" Asher looked away, careful not to reveal the intensity of his pain. "I wasn't sure if I believed that anymore."

"Do you believe it now?" Jane asked carefully.

"I don't know," Asher admitted. "I mean, I want to. But this world is just so messed up."

"What I don't understand, is why a God who claims to love us, would allow such terribly-cruel things to happen." Jane could feel her voice growing weak, "Why would God take our parents from us?"

Asher didn't have an answer for her question. And so, they both sat in silence.

[268]

The ducks continued to splash and play, acting as if they didn't have a care in the world.

"I'm going to military school soon," Asher revealed, turning toward her and speaking with fervency. "But before that happens, I'm going to do everything within my power to help find your dad."

Jane could feel tears coming to her eyes.

"I want to help you." Asher expressed, "Maybe God still has a happy ending for you. And I would never forgive myself if I didn't do everything within my power to see if He does."

Jane's chin quivered. "Thank you." She whispered through misty eyes. "You're the only person, throughout this entire process, who I feel truly cares." She sniffed, attempting to gain a reign on her emotions, "Why *do* you care so much?"

"I've made a lot of mistakes in my life, Jane. There were innocent people that—" Asher stopped himself. "I know it's not possible to bring them back from the dead." His mind flashed with the cold graves of each innocent life stolen in the terror attack. "But I figured, if one guy can do that much damage, just imagine how much I could do if I actually *tried* to make my life matter? I don't know how to explain it, other than I feel like it's my duty. I just want to help people now." He looked back at her, "I want to help you, now."

"I think you already have." She smiled. A slow and sweet sunrise started from somewhere deep within her heart. It was as if a cold, dead, painfully-dormant area that she never dared to give the time of day, was slowly beginning to warm with fresh rays of hope.

"How?" Asher asked quietly.

"You pulled me into real life." She glanced around, truly embracing the moment. "I was so consumed with trying to think of the perfect story that I was completely missing out on everything happening around me. I nearly self-destructed, ruining this entire trip, thinking I had to create something that was already right in front of me. But this is the first time in my *entire* life that something *this* fun has happened to me!" She suddenly laughed, in absolute disbelief as to what had just occurred. "I just snuck away from my chaperone and hopped on a Vespa with a Prince, *without* a helmet! I never do stuff like that! For me, living on the 'wild side' is having two cupcakes instead of one."

Asher released half a grin. "Two cupcakes? How insurgent of you."

He suddenly stood up.

"Wait, where are you going?" Jane was puzzled.

"Come on!" He encouraged her to follow, "We've only got so long until Laurie figures out where you are. And there's some more real life waiting to happen."

Jane gave him a concerned glance.

"It's pretty clear that you don't get out much." He smiled, "So, I think you should drive."

Jane popped up, ready for the challenge. "Really?"

"Yeah, as long as you promise not to kill us."

"Ohhh, I don't know," Jane laughed. "I mean, I'll try my best, but I can't make any promises. After all, this is real life! Who knows what's gonna happen next…"

"I am going to be in *so* much trouble." Jane laughed. Asher handed her a warm, soft pretzel. She took a deep whiff of the heavenly smell. "But this pretzel alone is going to be worth it."

"You think *you're* gonna be in trouble?" Asher laughed, "I ditched my driver back at Westminster Bridge and told him I was only going to be gone for two hours. It's almost 4:00!"

Jane laughed. She was having far too much fun. The only thing plaguing her mind was what would happen when it was time to say goodbye. She didn't want the day to end.

They maneuvered their way through the busy crowds and found an empty bench. Jane quickly opened her small, plastic mustard container. She couldn't wait to dip her pretzel and enjoy the epic yumminess.

Asher paused to pray.

Jane was surprised. From the way he spoke, he sounded as if he wasn't that crazy about his family's belief in God. But maybe she misunderstood him. She paused, waiting until he finished his silent prayer, then finished her mustard dipping.

"Oh yes!" Asher was overjoyed when the pretzel reached his mouth. "Now *that* is good."

Jane nodded excitedly in agreement.

"I'm gonna stock up on all the junk food I can before September."

"Why, what's in September?"

"Military school."

"Oh." Jane suddenly felt bad for forgetting. He had mentioned it earlier. "So, how do you feel about it?" she asked slowly. "I mean, are you okay with going?"

[271]

"Well, I'm not exactly looking forward to it. But it's better than prison, so I'm just gonna have to deal."

"I know this might sound stupid," she started slowly, "but maybe it will help you. With life, and your dream, I mean. Your desire to help other people. Maybe it will give you more avenues to do that."

Asher nodded slowly. He hadn't thought of it that way before. "So, what about you?" he asked. "What happens when you go back to Ohio?"

"School." Jane curled her upper lip, disgusted by the thought. "AKA, the most cruel, inhumane, unusual form of social torture that could be heartlessly bestowed upon a turtle-introvert like myself."

"You're an introvert?" Asher asked, surprised to hear the news.

"Oh goodness!" Jane laughed. "Don't look so surprised! I am probably the quietest, most socially awkward, ridiculed, 'real-life' challenged girl you'll ever meet. Remember? Fantasies are way more my thing. I usually fail at anything involving conversations with real people."

"That's crazy." Asher shook his head, "You don't seem like that to me at all! I mean, this whole day has been a blast! You're super entertaining and intellectual, and refreshing to be around. Anyone who labels you as 'socially awkward' clearly has a screw lose."

"Yeah, but see, I'm not usually like this." Jane smiled, "I'm different here. I don't know what it is about this city... but it's like today, for the first time in my life, I've actually been free to be..."

"Yourself?" Asher suggested.

"Yeah." Jane could feel her heart glowing.

"Me too." Asher looked down at his pretzel, clearly trying to hide a smile that snuck into his eyes. "I haven't been like this in a long time either."

"Oh my flapjacks!" Jane suddenly burst out. Dramatic flingers clutched her scalp.

"Uhhh... pretzels?" Asher held up his tasty snack, "Wrong food to express your current excitement here."

"I just got the most brilliant story idea!" she gasped, not even believing all the epic characters and plotlines coming to her. All at once, it was as if the heavens had opened and inspiration fell from the sky. "Quick, I need a pencil!" She stood up, calling out to the people who passed by, "I need a pen, a pencil, paper, somebody! Oh my flapjacks, this is amazing! I can't forget this!"

"Jane!" Asher leapt to his feet, hoping to stop her from calling out to the passersby. The last thing they wanted to do was draw attention to themselves. "Shhh!" He laughed, "Let the people pass in peace! Why don't you just use your phone?"

Her eyes widened. She looked at the boy like he had just suggested she won the lottery. "Brilliant!" She squealed.

Jane straightaway returned to the bench and started typing as fast as her fingers could go. "This is it! This is it! Oh, why didn't I think of this sooner?!"

"Planning on writing the whole thing right now?" Asher laughed. This was the first he had seen her so completely elated over something.

"Of course not!" Jane continued to text on her large-buttoned phone, "I'm just writing down the basic plot. Oh my goodness, this is gold! I'll be done in just a second. I'm sorry, let me just finish this, I have to jot it down before I lose it."

"No problem, take your time." Asher took another bite into his pretzel. He looked out toward the people, watching the crowds scurry past them.

[273]

He breathed a sigh of contentment. Today had been perfect. Nobody had discovered who he was, Laurie still hadn't found them, and the O'Conners' security team hadn't come looking for him yet. He looked back at the girl who appeared ten-thousand pounds lighter, and ten-thousand times happier than when he first met her. The deep sorrow had nearly evaporated from her eyes, and her laugh was genuine and cheerful. Asher almost smiled. No matter what happened to her dad, Jane was going to be okay. He was confident of that.

"There!" Jane announced triumphantly and stuck her phone back in her pocket, "I've got it."

"So, do I get to know what your story's about?" Asher asked.

Jane shook her head.

"Why not?" Asher gave her a questioning look.

"I wouldn't even know where to begin." Jane sighed, "I'm no good at explaining these sorts of things. Trust me, it'll be far better once it's all written out."

Asher stuffed the last of his pretzel in his mouth and wiped his hands on his pants. "Well, it looks like you got your story idea before getting kicked out of London, after all."

"Yeah." Jane smiled, "I guess I did. This whole real-life thing isn't turning out to be nearly as terrible as I thought it would be. And a lot more fun."

"Anything else you want to do before the clock strikes midnight, Cinderella?" Asher teased.

"Nope." Jane grinned, "I have officially done it all. I am now content to return home in my pumpkin, and happily reminisce about my trip for years to come. Except…"

"Except?" Asher wanted her to finish her sentence.

"This is going to sound so silly." She shook her head, almost ashamed to admit it. "But I was really hoping it was going to rain."

"Rain?" Asher echoed.

"Yeah, you know, those famous London rainstorms?" Jane giggled. "Where the downpours are so ridiculous that everyone needs to run around with their umbrellas and jump over puddles in order to get anywhere? I was secretly hoping the rain would start falling and the streets would sparkle from the crystal drops, releasing that sweet little splashing sound every time tires drive by." Jane sighed, "But it's been nothing but sunshine."

"I dunno, those clouds are looking a little bit ominous. You might still see rain before you leave this city."

"But it's okay if I don't." Jane smiled, truly meaning every word, "I think I'm slowly starting to learn, that sometimes reality, as out-of-control and unpredictable as it can be, is actually better than my dreams."

Chapter Twenty Four

Dancing in the Rain

"Asher!" Relief flooded Chasity's voice as Asher entered the suite. "Oh, thank the Lord, you're okay! Where in the world have you been?!"

"I was talking to Jane." Asher shed his jacket and headed for the mini-fridge. The pretzel had worn off, and he was hungry again.

"And you had to ditch the O'Conners' security team in order to do that?!"

"Chas, it's not a big deal, everything worked out fine. It was all good until the police showed up."

"The police?!" Chasity gasped.

"Yeah, Jane's chaperone sent them looking for her." Asher leaned forward and dug around in the mini fridge. "But I left before they spotted me. So, there's no need to freak out, it's not going to be on the news or anything."

Asher removed a bag of baby carrots from the fridge and attempted to pop one in his mouth. Chasity quickly yanked the bag away from him.

Chasity huffed, "Asher, what were you thinking?!"

"That I wanted some carrots?"

"Not about the carrots!" Chasity quickly placed them back in the fridge, "Come on, we're late for dinner. We need to get downstairs." She crossed the room and slipped on her pearl necklace. "I already sent Millie and Willie down. Ugh, Asher what am I going to do with you? I give you a little bit of freedom and you completely take advantage of it, sneaking around with Jane, getting *her* in trouble!"

"Will you let me explain before you tear into me like this?" Asher couldn't hide the anger in his tone, "I haven't even explained to you what happened yet! You're jumping to conclusions and assuming the worst-case scenario."

"Can you blame me?!" Chasity shook her head, "I believe I just heard you use the word *police*!"

"Chasity, I think I know what's going on with the AA16 code." Asher spoke quickly, "Talking to Jane couldn't wait, but her creepy chaperone threatened her into thinking that if we talked, she would get disqualified from the competition. We—"

"Ash, we've gotta go." Chasity didn't have time to stand around and listen to his story, "But you're going to tell me everything after dinner."

"What the heck, Chas, you're talking to me like I'm a six-year-old!"

"When you act like one, I don't see any reason not to," she snapped.

"Oh you're one to talk!" Asher added fuel to the fiery argument.

"What's that supposed to mean?" Chasity firmly planted her hands on her hips.

"You might be fooling everyone else with your goody-two-shoes, perfect Princess act, but I know what's really going on. You're secretly pining away over this Hanson Fletcher guy, dying to impress him, sneaking glances and getting whatever juicy conversations you can with him. Our family might be completely blind to the fact that you're into him, but I'm not. And honestly, Chasity, I can't believe you would go that low. Having secret conversations with the son of the man who kidnapped Jane's father!"

"What?" Chasity breathed, struggling to process everything Asher had just spoken. What did—how did he—*huh*? "Asher, I have no idea what you're talking about!" Her face was beat red. She wasn't sure if she was angry, embarrassed, or just plain confused. "Hanson didn't have anything to do with Mr. Akerly's disappearance!"

"Maybe not. But his dad did."

"Oh. Mrs. O'Conner, dinner was divine!" Lilly raved.

Chasity stared at her plate. She had barely touched her roasted duck. She knew she needed to set a good example for Millie and Willie, but her appetite was nowhere to be found. She was still shocked by the words Asher had spoken. How had he picked up on the fact that Chasity had a secret crush on Hanson? Chasity was mortified. Was it really that obvious? Had she been looking at him without thinking about it, or giving off some kind of unintentional body language that clued Asher in? Chasity continued to be amazed by her kid brother. For as quiet and moody as he was, he possessed an uncanny amount of intuition.

Chasity was careful not to look at Hanson all through dinner. She had to figure out what was happening here. How did Asher know who Hanson's dad was? How had Chasity missed the massive fact that Hanson's dad had been arrested for this crime, along with Lilly's? This revelation, something as simple as his last name and information about his family tree, should have been common knowledge. But it only served to remind Chasity that there was much she didn't know about Hanson. So why did she like him, anyway? Hanson was like one massive mystery. She didn't know his likes, hobbies, favorite foods, or even his favorite color. She didn't know a thing about his parents, his past, or his dreams for the future. She didn't even know if he was a Christian. The thought scared her. How had she allowed herself to become so emotionally intertwined with the stranger?

"Thank you, Lilly, I'm so glad you enjoyed it!" Mrs. O'Conner was beaming, "We have some of the finest cooks in England working for us, if I do say so myself. George," she turned to the server, "please bring out dessert."

Millie's eyes danced with delight. A silver platter loaded with small ice-cream sundaes were set before them.

"I know I didn't eat my peas," Millie's turned to Chasity, "But plllleeeease may I have dessert?!"

"Yeah, that's fine." Chasity's voice was low.

"All right!" Willie gave his sister a high-five. The two giggled mischievously, and Chasity glanced at Asher. She wondered how angry he was with her. It appeared as though his thoughts were far from the conversation happening at the table. Chasity sighed. She shouldn't have blown up on him like that. Perhaps he really did have a legitimate reason for sneaking around the way he did today. And like Asher reminded her, she surely wasn't one to talk. She had once exchanged secret messages with Hanson, breaking all sorts of Royal protocol. Chasity knew how Asher felt. His passion to help Jane find her father was admirable, and she shouldn't have squelched his desire to do so. If anything, she should've asked for more information and inquired how she could help.

"What have been your favorite moments of the Convention thus far, darling?" Mrs. O'Conner asked Lilly.

"Hmm… it's all been incredibly insightful and eye-opening, but I think I'd have to say, hearing Mr. Nathaniel Wells speak today was truly moving. You can tell that he deeply cares about each horse he works with, and he doesn't just want to run them through the machine. He's a true horse whisperer, if I've ever seen one."

"I think he's just the man for the job to work with Nic." James smiled, attempting to draw Chasity back into the conversation.

"If he isn't too busy working with Dr. Seuss." Lilly asserted.

Chasity narrowed her eyes. Why was Lilly sitting so close to Hanson? If they were truly 'just friends' surely they'd give one another a little bit more breathing room.

An awful thought struck Chasity. Perhaps they were partners in crime. Perhaps they stuck to one another like glue because they had their and their parent's reputations to protect and defend. Chasity's stomach sank to the floor. What if Asher was right? What if they really *had* somehow been involved with Mr. Akerly's disappearance? Hadn't Hanson been obsessed with digging up as much information as he could find about The Wall of Fire *right* before Mr. Akerly's kidnapping? What if the reason

Hanson had diligently searched the library for info, was because he was on an evil errand for his dad, to find Mr. Akerly?

"You know, it's very possible that someone might outbid you," James reminded Lilly. "Dr. Seuss is the horse everyone will be wanting at the auction tomorrow."

"You keep saying that, but I know I'm going to get him." Lilly laughed. "Dad gave me permission to spend whatever is needed. We're *going* to get that horse."

Chasity raised an eyebrow. *I wouldn't be so sure of yourself, Lilly. It doesn't matter how many underhanded strings you and your daddy pull. Sometimes the most unsuspecting competitor can come from behind and win it all.*

"Never, in the history of the YNC, have I had the vulgar dishonor of calling the police to report a runaway!" Laurie barked, still miffed about yesterday's outlandish events. "Until you, Jane Akerly."

Jane looked down at her clasped hands. She sat beside Laurie in the backseat of a cab. They were headed to the airport. The final curtain had closed, and her time in London was over. Jane couldn't help but feel guilty for everything she had put the woman through. She knew it was Laurie's job to protect her, and being responsible for a missing teen in a foreign country wouldn't be good for her resume.

"I truly am sorry." Jane apologized for what felt like the hundredth time, "It was very childish, immature, and selfish of me." She stole a careful glance at the woman, wondering if it would be okay to say these words. "I suppose you'll always remember me as the YNC student from Hades."

"Ha!" Laurie laughed, "You can say that again! But what I can't seem to understand is *why* you were so bent on destroying this opportunity for yourself! I read your application, Jane. Your initial story was one of the best out of this entire group! You have raw talent. But if you keep letting foolish, no-brained distractions such as handsome men get in the way, you're not going to get *anywhere* in life."

Jane stared on ahead in silence. She understood where Laurie was coming from. From the outside looking in, things must've appeared awful. But Laurie didn't know the full story. And it would be far too complicated to explain. So, Jane kept her mouth closed.

Jane pressed her forehead against the taxi window, knowing they were nearing the airport. She could scarcely believe she was about to go home. Yesterday had been one of the strangest, idiosyncratic, completely out of character, most marvelous days of her life. Nothing had gone as planned. Yet she knew that even years from now, that particular day would forever hold a most-historic monument of utmost importance in her mind. It would go down in history as the day she dashed around London with the Prince of Tarsurella. Every element of their raw conversation was parasitical. It was entirely selfish and unfair of her to think that somehow the day could've lasted forever. She knew better. The rich cheesecake of their intellectually-delicious time together slowly faded into bitter dandelion greens. Shortly after she finished her salty pretzel, sirens were seen in the distance, and Asher didn't waste any time saying farewell. He disappeared like Peter Pan, and Jane was in massive trouble for daring to fly with him to Neverland.

She doubted that a day like that would ever happen again, and now there was nothing left to do but cherish the fact that it happened. The very best part? It wasn't a dream. It was real. It was exciting, freeing, eye-opening, delightful, and painfully heart wrenching, all at once. Just like any good story should be. But it wasn't just a story. It was *her* story.

While sitting on the bench, smack dab in the middle of real life, Jane felt as if someone had downloaded a massive amount of heavenly revelation into her brain. Finally, it clicked. All she needed to do, was write about her life. She didn't need to go searching the four corners of the earth for the perfect story; the story she had so desperately longed for, had fallen right into her lap.

And so, when she returned to a hotel room full of giggly, gossipy, gasping girls who begged Jane to expound upon every detail of her day, she turned them all down. She grabbed her laptop and locked herself in the bathroom. She ignored their knocks and whiney cries. Jane's fingers flew. She typed, and typed, and typed some more. It was as if her fingers had a mind all their own, and it would be utterly impossible to stop them.

She watched in wonderment as words splashed onto the page. She fought back tears as she wrote about her father, and the gaping hole that his missing presence had left in her heart. She wrote about Charlie and his steadfast friendship. She released all the stress and despair concerning the heartless bullies who teased her. Her heart was unlocked, and everything dumped out. Like a waterfall, every last detail crashed out. Her trip to Tarsurella, Princess Chasity and Prince Asher's involvement with her father's case; as well as her plane ride to London, her colorful roommates, and her first encounter with James O'Conner.

Finally, at 4:47 in the morning, she was done. Her eyes burned, and her hands ached, but her heart was finally free. The heavy burdens she had been carrying for months, were finally gone. Now that all the trauma was out of her head, she felt as if she could breathe again.

All at once, the taxi hit a large bump, and Jane smacked her head on the window, yanking her back into the current moment. Jane straightened her back. Only a few more moments, and they would be at the airport.

"Miss Laurie," Jane spoke quietly.

Laurie met her with questioning eyes.

"I know I've been disqualified from the competition, but I want you to read this anyway." Jane handed her a small USB card. "It pretty much explains everything."

Laurie sighed. "You were up all-night writing, weren't you?"

Jane nodded.

"I wish I could accept this. But I can't." She handed it back to her. "The YNC would have a fit if–"

"No, it's not for them." Jane insisted and placed it in her hands once more, "I know I've been disqualified. But that doesn't matter anymore. I want you to be the first one to read that story."

"Why?" Laurie sounded puzzled.

"Because, I know you only had my best interest in mind. All along, you did what you thought was best for me, and I know that if my mom was still living, she would've really appreciated that. And even though it doesn't look like it, I appreciate it too. There are not very many people who care enough about me to get involved with my life in such a dramatic way. But you did. So, thank you."

"You are an odd young woman, Jane Akerly." Laurie shook her head, "And for as much trouble as you've given me this week, I can't deny the fact that I'm still rooting for you." She reached across the cab to give her a hug. "Good luck on everything, dear. I hope you end up getting everything you want out of life."

"You too." Jane smiled.

The taxi traveled through the massive airport roundabout, then pulled off to the side. It was time for Jane to get out. Laurie helped collect her bags from the back, then sent her off with a wave. Jane returned the favor and offered a friendly wave before reaching for her luggage and rolling on ahead. She took a deep breath as she crossed the busy, outdoor departures area and searched for the American Airlines door.

Suddenly, a quiet rumble was heard in the distance. Jane lifted her head toward the sky in wonderment. It was thunder! She stared upward like a little child in wide-eyed mystique. She squeezed her eyes shut, passionately believing for *one more* radical miracle.

"Dear God," she whispered, "I know I'm just one tiny little person on this massive planet of millions of people and I don't even know if you can hear me. But if You—"

Jane stopped. The words were caught in her throat. The smallest, sweetest, most gentle raindrop fell to her wrist. Jane could feel tears coming to her eyes. A tiny drip targeted her head. She now felt one on her cheek. Jane's eyes flew open. It was raining!

She flung her arms open and laughed, not even caring how foolish she looked to anyone who walked by. The raindrops came faster and faster, as the sprinkles grew in speed, size, and quantity.

Another rumble was heard, this time it was louder. Jane was trembling inside. Her miracle had happened! It was as if God was whispering to her heart, telling her that He cared.

She laughed and cried all at once, doing a happy twirl on the edge of her toes. God heard her! He *actually* heard her! All at once, she didn't feel quite so forgotten about. The vast, overwhelming, debilitating feeling of fear and abandonment was starting to flee.

With each new raindrop, it was as if God was washing the deepest places of her soul, displacing fear and restoring hope. Next thing she knew, she was basking in a full-blown rainstorm of His utterly overwhelming love.

Chapter Twenty Five

The astonished look on Vanessa's face was priceless. Jillian quickly snapped a picture with her vintage bubblegum-pink Polaroid camera. A pile of lavender and gold balloons rained down on Vanessa as soon as she walked through the door.

"Surprise!" Bridget called out between giggles.

Vanessa batted several balloons out of her face and let out a laugh of her own. "What in the world?" she gasped.

The Tea Party Room had been completely transformed. Adorable little tables were adorned with lilac tablecloths and gold glitter. Delicate mason jars filled with bouquets of Queen Anne's Lace served as the centerpiece. But even more than the charming decorations, was the fact that all her favorite women filled the small room. Her mother, her soon-to-be sisters-in-law, Deborah, and even some Palace staff members.

"Bridget!" She turned to the girl. Vanessa was confident she was responsible for coordinating the surprise. Nobody liked to plan parties as much as she did. "What is all this?!"

"It's your bridal shower!" she squealed. "Celebrating the fact that you're about to become Addison's wifey!"

"Oh honey, we're so excited for you!" Mrs. Bennett squeezed Vanessa tightly.

"Mom, you knew about this?"

"Everyone did a great job keeping it from you." Bridget chuckled, "Although, I'm sure if Millie was here, we would've had a much harder time keeping things under wraps."

Jillian smiled. Bridget was right. Millie would've blurted about the party the second she knew it existed. Thankfully, she and Bridget were able to plan a classy, elegant, and totally-sophisticated shower, without Millie underfoot. Jillian glanced at the delicious display of pink-fondue-covered strawberries. If Millie were here, she would've sneaked several already. Jillian sighed. Although she didn't want to admit it, she did *kind of* miss her juvenile kid sister.

"This is crazy!" Vanessa shook her head, "Aw, you girls are so sweet. I was not expecting a party."

"We know you weren't." Bridget grinned, "That's what made it so much more fun to plan."

"So, what am I supposed to do here? I mean, I've never actually been to a bridal shower, let alone had one thrown in my honor!"

"You don't need to do anything other than let us shower you with love!" Deborah touched her arm, "It's just a fun time for us ladies to get together, enjoy the cupcakes, and give you presents! And maybe a piece of advice or two," she added with a wink.

"Oh, perfect!" Vanessa clasped her hands together excitedly, "I'll take all the advice I can get!"

"It's also a time to relax before all the last-minute crazy kicks in before the wedding," Bridget added. "How are you holding up?"

"Honestly?" Vanessa smiled, "I'm doing amazing. After I had my complete mental breakdown, and Addison and I broke out in a radically-irrational agreement, the storm inside started to settle. It's like all the stress and worry I was feeling a few days ago has completely vanished. Now I can truly, *truly* say that I just feel a deep peace about everything."

"I'm proud of you, honey." Mrs. Bennett beamed, "I know your decision to resign from the Homeless Committee wasn't an easy one, but I think it was a wise one. You seem so much more at ease now."

"I am." Vanessa's eyes confirmed her words to be true, "It's kind of spectacular how good it feels to just let go and trust God. Now that I can focus completely on Addison, our relationship, and preparing for the wedding, I think there will be a few less bridezilla moments." She laughed, "Of course, I'm not shutting the Homeless Shelter out of my life completely. My heart is far too invested in that project to drop it entirely. I'm going to continue volunteering and being involved in whatever ways I can."

"How did Matt react when he found out you were quitting?" Bridget asked. She could only imagine how much the pesky guy would've lorded it over her.

"Actually, he hasn't said anything yet. Thankfully, I haven't bumped into him. I know he's gonna be full of those haughty opinions of his. He and the rest of the staff might think I made a stupid mistake, but this whole 'becoming Queen' thing is a major promotion in my book."

"You've got that right!" Bridget laughed. "Alright, let's fill up our plates and get snacking! These goodies aren't going to eat themselves!"

Jillian happily followed Bridget's lead and filled her pink plate with delicious treats. She poured herself some punch, then headed for a small table near the front of the room. It was nice having a small, intimate little party, without any press outlets present. Jillian appreciated the fact that they could get all dolled-up for the occasion, yet still control who was invited. It was a nice change of pace.

"Oh honey, I'm so glad you could make it!" Deborah called out.

Jillian's head popped up. Her eyes widened. Deborah's daughter, Pearl, entered wearing a long, elegant, rose-gold gown.

"Your Highness, I'd like you to meet my daughter, Pearl. I wasn't sure if she'd make it on time after her violin lesson, but it looks like it all worked out just as it was supposed to!"

Jillian's eyes narrowed as Pearl graciously curtsied.

"Hi there! It's so nice to finally meet you." Bridget's voice was kind, "Your mom has told us a lot about you!"

"Oh, my goodness, excuse me for my lack of class, but I am completely fangirling right now!" Pearl squealed, "I just can't believe I'm finally meeting you! I mean, you have been a *huge* example to me and my friends, we just adore everything about you! You're seriously one of my favorite people ever!" She turned to Vanessa, "And you too! My friends and I love your spunk and your style, and we think you're going to make an amazing Queen!"

"Aw, thank you." Vanessa blushed, "You're too sweet!"

Vanessa carried her plate to where Jillian was sitting, but Bridget continued to happily chat with Pearl.

Jillian frowned. "Who invited *her* here?"

"Who, Pearl?" Vanessa looked over her shoulder, then turned back to Jillian with a questioning look. "I'm guessing from the sound of your comment, you're not a fan?"

"The girl is an absolute brat!" Jillian hissed through a quiet whisper. "She completely disrespected Millie and I at her party! I don't care what's going on between Miss Deborah and Dad. That girl is *never* going to be my sister."

Vanessa's eyes softened. "Addison told me about your dad and Deborah. How are you doing with that?"

"They went on their first 'date' last night," Jillian huffed, using her fingers as air-quotes around the word 'date', "And Dad said they enjoyed themselves. It's a disaster."

"I know this is hard, but maybe you should give Deborah a chance. As well as Pearl. Perhaps if you talk with her more, you'll really grow to like her."

"Yeah, right." Jillian grumbled as she crossed her arms, "The only way I'm going to ever get along with her is if she goes back to Paris and stays there forever."

Hope sat down beside them. Vanessa glanced at Hope, wondering how she was doing. Since Luke's abrupt departure, she hadn't seemed quite the same.

[293]

"Hey Hope, I wanted to ask you about something."

Hope popped a strawberry into her mouth and gave Vanessa her full attention.

"Have you ever thought about working down at the Homeless Shelter?"

"What do you mean? I've been volunteering there like, every other day."

"I know, and you're amazing at it." Vanessa smiled, "Which is why I think you'd be *perfect* to take on my old position. There's a wide-open opportunity, you know! And who better for the job than you?"

"As flattered as I am that you would suggest that, following in your footsteps would be a dauntless task that I am in no way equipped for." Hope shook her head, "Anyone who has to take off where you left off is going to have a huge amount of work cut out for them."

"I've seen you with the families down there, Hope. You're amazing! Your passion and love for people is truly contagious. I've also been spotting some killer administration skills. I wouldn't be saying any of this if I didn't believe it. I think you'd be amazing at this job, Hope. The Shelter needs someone like you down there! Besides, I can't bear to think of Matt getting the job." She shuddered playfully.

"I don't know." Hope looked down at her plate and traced the remaining strawberry with her pointer finger. She looked back at Vanessa, "I'm kind of in one of those in-between, transition phases, you know?" She sighed, "I'm asking a lot of questions right now. So, I'm not sure this would be the right time to take on something like that."

The day after Luke left, Clark revealed that he knew nothing of Luke's plans to leave. "I don't know what that unreasonable, feeble-minded boy is thinking!" Clark had told Hope. "He broke his apprenticeship agreement with me, and this kitchen, and left without a word to his mother or me. We've been calling his friends, trying to figure out if anyone has clues as to where he might've gone. But it turns out six of his other rebellion buddies are gone, too."

Luke's decision to leave left Hope battling a tidal wave of emotions. None of it made sense to her. She wasn't sure which was more confusing, Luke's moronic behavior or her own short-sighted and ludicrous thoughts to trust him. After hearing what Liam had to say about the Sons of Liberty's potential underground plans to overthrow the Kingdom, Hope didn't know what to think. Who should she believe? Her family? Or Clark's fiery, spirited, seemingly-prodigal son?

"Hope, I know you're struggling with Luke's decision," Vanessa spoke, pulling Hope back into the current moment. "But I think this is just one of those things where you're going to have to be patient and see how things turn out. My mom always used to say, that sitting around waiting for Prince Charming is a total waste of time. We need to be productive, pursue our dreams, and keep pressing forward. Then, when the timing is right, God will allow our paths to cross with the right man. That's what happened with Addison." She smiled, "I never would've met him if I was just sitting around at home doing nothing. And I doubt God wants you just sitting around in this season of life as well. Trust me, Hope, if God wants Luke to be involved with your life, he'll be back."

Hope sighed. She knew Vanessa was right. As confusing and disorienting as this entire ordeal was, she would drive herself crazy if she just sat around and attempted to figure it all out. Nothing was making sense to her. "I know," Hope admitted. "I've never done anything as huge as running a Homeless Shelter," she thought, slowly warming up to the idea. "But maybe I'll pray about it. I've been asking God for months to help me find my true purpose. And I still have no idea what it is. But who knows, maybe this could have something to do with it?"

"Maybe so." Vanessa's eyes continued to smile, "And even if it's not, maybe serving in this capacity will just help open doors to more opportunities in the future. Being faithful in the little things God places in our laps helps build our character and equip us for all the bigger, crazier things that lie ahead."

"Yeah." Hope nodded. "Thanks, Nessa."

"Anytime, sis." She reached across the table and gave her hand a squeeze.

"So, speaking of helping out with the little things." Hope changed the subject, "Is there anything Jillian and I can to do assist getting ready for the big day?"

"Hmm…" Vanessa thought for a moment. "Between Stacie and Bridget, those two seem to have things pretty well covered. Oh! I just thought of something! The music! For the reception. How would you two like to choose some fun, celebratory party songs? I think we're having a DJ, but we're going to need a playlist. I know you two listen to a lot more music than I do."

"That sounds fun!" Jillian nodded, "We can totally do that for you!"

"Yeah, it does. Any special requests? Or do you just want us to choose everything and let it be a surprise?"

"Well, I think Addison and I would like to pick out a few of the slower, love ballads. You know, for our first dance and such. But beside that, I'd say you two are pretty much free to do whatever you like! Except for the Chicken Dance! I hate the Chicken Dance!"

"Dually noted." Hope giggled.

"What's the Chicken Dance?" Jillian asked.

"I'll show you later," Hope laughed.

"Oh! And we are going to have a live band for some of the songs," Vanessa added. "You know the group that was here during Addison's Coronation and played at the Fashion Show? *Kennetic Energy?*"

Hope's eyes widened.

Jillian's elated expression matched her sister's, "Duh! Of course, we remember them! Oh yay, Nessa, that's *such* a good idea, they will be PERFECT!"

Hope took a deep breath as her mind started to race. She attempted to slow her thoughts, but they were already too far gone. How would she react? What would she say? What would *he* say? Hope could feel herself blushing.

Pretty soon, she would be seeing David Carter.

Again.

"Well, I'd say that was a pretty successful party!" Bridget tossed a handful of gold, sparkly plastic party cups into the trash.

"For sure!" Pearl squealed, "Best party I've ever been to! And trust me, I've been to a lot of epic parties."

"I'm sure you have." Bridget giggled, truly getting a kick out of the young socialite. "Thanks again for staying to help me clean up."

"Of course!" Pearl tossed her long, straight locks over her shoulder, "It's an honor."

"Well, honey, I hate to say this, but we'd better get going," Deborah spoke up. "We don't want to be late for your ballet lesson."

"What are ballet lessons compared to hanging out at The Palace?!" Pearl shook her head, "My friends are not going to believe this happened. They're going to be *so* jealous."

"Well, I'm glad you could come." Bridget placed hands on her hips and decided the cleanup was almost over. "I can handle things from here. Thanks again for coming!" She gave the girl a hug, and Deborah's eyes shone with thankfulness. They said goodbye and left the small room.

Bridget removed a cloth from the table and beat the crumbs into the trash.

"Knock, knock," Liam spoke in the doorway.

Bridget looked up and grinned.

"Is it safe to come in?" he asked cautiously.

"Unless you're still scared that all this purple might rub off on you," she giggled.

"It's not the purple I'm worried about." He entered, "It's the glitter. That stuff sticks to your clothes for weeks. Need any help with clean up?"

"Always!" Bridget's eyes continued to smile, "Wanna take down that grouping of balloons? It's a little high for me to reach."

"Of course." Liam leapt into action. "So, did everything go okay? Is Vanessa ready to be the blushing bride?"

"She is *more* than ready. In fact, I think she was ready weeks ago. Reminds me of someone else I know," she added playfully.

"How is Hope doing?" Liam's question shifted the mood in the room, "Is she still angry with me for pressing Luke to leave?"

"I think she's managing alright." Bridget sighed, "I mean, she's clearly depressed about the fact that he up and vanished, but I think this is good for her." She paused to peer into Liam's eyes, "You did the right thing. I know from first-hand experience how dangerous it can be to open up your heart to the wrong guy. I'd hate to see Hope go through something like that."

"True." Liam nodded, "But in hindsight, I think I may have overstepped my bounds a little bit."

"No, you didn't." Bridget's voice was firm. "Hope should know better. But for whatever reason, she had a temporary lapse in mental judgement. You did what you thought was best; and even if she's angry with you right now, she'll get over it eventually. You were just trying to protect her. To protect all of us."

"I know." Despite Bridget's reassuring words, Liam's eyes still held a whisper of doubt. "But I can't help but wonder, if coming down so hard on Luke like that might not have been the best idea. I just don't want him to come back with some sort of vicious revenge."

"Revenge?" Bridget echoed. The word sounded cold. "What do you mean?"

"Bridge, I don't want to concern you, but the Royal Guard is really on edge about Sons of Liberty. Everyone is on high alert, especially with the wedding coming up. Jackson hasn't said it in so many words, but everyone's thinking the same thing. The current theory is that Luke and his guys left to prepare for an attack."

Bridget's heartrate picked up. She could feel the familiar fear and unwelcome trauma brought on by memories of Addison's Coronation, resurfacing. "You don't think they would try something at the wedding . . . do you?"

"Nobody knows for sure, but security measures will be intense." Liam told her confidently, "I know that God's Security Team is far greater than ours. If we pray and believe for angelic protection, I believe He will be faithful to equip us with that. No matter what happens."

Chapter Twenty Six

My Horse is Bigger Than Your Horse

"Our next thoroughbred is none other than the vigorous, strapping, young, two-year-old superstar, *Buckling Battlefield*! Bidding begins at twenty-five thousand, do I hear twenty-five thousand?" The excitable auctioneer began, "Twenty-five, I see twenty-five! Do I hear thirty? Thirty, we've got thirty, ladies and gentlemen, do we have forty? Fifty! Sixty, sixty thousand—"

Hanson watched the scene with hard eyes, scarcely able to keep up with the babbling auctioneer. A fine-looking horse pranced around the center of the ring, as dozens of people watching from the sidelines took turns raising their bidding cards.

Hanson couldn't believe the prices of these horses! The amounts of money people were throwing around was absurd! He knew horse-racing was a lucrative business, yet it still shocked him to see how much change these wealthy people had jingling around in their pants pockets.

"Maybe I should quit my job at The Palace and start investing in racehorses," Hanson joked, playfully leaning over and commenting to Chasity who stood nearby. "I don't think your dad is paying me enough."

Chasity released a musical laugh. "If you *really* want to get involved with racing, maybe you should start by helping me train Nic." She offered him a smile, "You could drop by sometime after work and see how he does on the track."

Hanson was surprised by her invitation. "You really think Nic is gonna beat out all these other horses? I don't have much of a clue about what's going on here right now, but it seems to me like these thoroughbreds have some pretty famous family lines."

"SOLD! For seventy thousand to the woman in the red hat!"

"Ugh, this sunshine is absolutely wicked!" Lilly broke into their conversation, anxiously fanning her face with her hand. "Hanson, would you be a dear and run back to the room and grab my hat? As well as my sunscreen, and a bottle of water while you're at it? You know how my skin does with this kind of exposure." She frowned, "I do *not* tan."

Chasity tossed Lilly a suspicious glance. They had been out here for fifteen minutes, and this was the first Lilly complained. Was she truly in need of protection from the sun, or was this just an underhanded way of getting Hanson and Chasity to stop talking? It seemed as though every time they had a conversation, Lilly had to burst in and break it apart.

"Oh come on Lilly, you look great with sunburn!" Hanson joked playfully. "It matches your hair."

Chasity stifled a giggle. Had Hanson seriously just said that?! *Go Hanson!* she thought, attempting not to laugh out loud. Chasity chided herself. She knew her frustration with Lilly was rude and not very loving of her... but still, the girl had weaseled her way into far too many of their conversations. Was it too much to ask for an honest discussion without interruptions?

Lilly wasn't happy with his comment. "Hanson, please." She pulled out her handy-dandy puppy-dog face, "If I burn, I'm going to be miserable."

Hanson hesitated, but finally softened. "Okay." He released his grip on the whitewashed fence and quickly dashed away. "I'll be back!"

Chasity almost smiled as she watched him run. It appeared as though he didn't want to miss any of this.

"Seems like you two are very..." Lilly stepped closer to Chasity, "friendly."

Chasity wasn't sure how to respond to Lilly's sly comment. What was she getting at? "Yes." She gritted her teeth, "We're friends. If that's what you mean."

"Good." Lilly straightened her back and continued to stare forward, "Because I'd hate to see someone get hurt."

"Enough with the games, Lilly," Chasity snapped. "I don't speak underhanded girl code. So, whatever it is that you're trying to get at, just come right out and say it."

"Fine." Lilly's angry eyes met hers. "You want me to talk turkey? Here it is. Just because you're the Princess of Tarsurella doesn't mean you can get everything you want. Some things in life are off limits. Including Hanson. So stay away from him."

It took everything within Chasity to keep her jaw from hanging on the floor. She bit her lip and turned her attention back toward the ring.

"And now, the moment you've all been waiting for!" The auctioneer cheered, "Our grand finale, the grand prize, highly coveted, sure to be the next breakout star of the racetrack–Dr. Seuss!"

Chasity could still feel her ears releasing steam. The sneaky young woman was far more vicious and cruel than Chasity imagined. Her breathing was heavy as she watched the tenacious, well-built, highly-durable horse, enter the ring.

"Oh, and as long as we're talking about things you can't have," Lilly leaned over and whispered into Chasity's ear, "Nic doesn't stand a chance racing against Dr. Seuss."

Chasity felt as though Lilly had removed the final straw from her card house of patience and grace. Chasity had been desperately trying to be kind, guard her mouth, and keep her lips zipped tight. But that was it! Insulting Nic was pushing things too far!

"Ahh, isn't he a beaut." James appeared beside Chasity. "We're sure to see the prices skyrocket for this one!"

"And the bidding begins at twenty-five, do I hear twenty-five? Twenty-five, we've got twenty-five!"

Lilly proudly held up her bidding card.

"Thirty! Thirty to Miss Chesterfield, do I hear forty?"

Without thinking, Chasity quickly reached for James's bidding card. She didn't have one. She hadn't been planning on purchasing any horses. She quickly popped it into the air twice, signaling that she had raised the price to fifty thousand.

"Fifty!" The auctioneer sounded pleased, "Sixty! Do I hear seventy? Seventy! Seventy-five, eighty! Eighty, do I hear eighty-five thousand for Dr. Seuss?"

The auctioneer's voice slowed down as those with smaller budgets slowly fell out of the running. A silence settled over the crowd.

Lilly raised her card. "Ninety thousand." She spoke out loud, wanting to affirm the fact that she was ready and willing to spend that much.

James eyes grew wide. He glanced at Chasity, wondering if she was going to let Lilly get away with it.

"Alright, ninety thousand to Miss Chesterfield! Going once, going twice—"

"One hundred!" Chasity suddenly called out.

She was almost sure she heard someone in the crowd gasp.

Lilly's eyes narrowed. She wasn't going to give up that easily. "One ten."

"One twenty!" Chasity was determined to win.

Lilly bit her lip. Her face expressed total frustration. She couldn't spend that much. Even if she wanted to.

"One hundred twenty thousand!" the auctioneer repeated, clearly enjoying such a large number. "Going once? Going twice? Sold, to Her Highness, Princess Chasity, for one hundred twenty thousand pounds!"

The man smacked his knee, and the crowd erupted with applause.

"Alright!" James cheered, "You've got a true champion on your hands now!"

Chasity took a deep breath, attempting to get a handle on everything that had just happened. Did she just buy Dr. Seuss?!

"That was some pretty intense last-minute bidding for a girl who said she wasn't interested!" James laughed.

Chasity slowly turned toward Lilly, not even sure what to say.

Lilly's face appeared as though Chasity had just run over her with a train. Chasity was shocked to see her heartbroken eyes. Lilly, on the verge of tears, quickly spun around and darted off.

All at once, Chasity's heart felt like led. What had she done?

"Hanson Fletcher."

Hanson stopped, surprised to hear someone speak his name. He had just turned the corner, prepared to leave the O'Conners' guest house and head back outside to where the auction was. Thanks to Lilly's 'emergency sunburn' errand, he had a floppy straw hat in his hand, a small tube of sunscreen, a bottle of water, and even a pair of sunglasses in his hands.

The figure standing behind him was surprising. It was Prince Asher.

"Yeah?" Hanson slowly responded, not sure what the Royal kid was getting at. "Can I help you with something?"

"Actually, you can." Asher stuffed his hands into his black shorts' pockets and took a step closer. "I need you to tell me about everything that happened the night you found Walter Akerly."

"Uhh... can this wait 'til later?" Hanson suggested. "I've really gotta get back to the auction and—"

"No, actually it can't." Asher's voice was firm, "Someone's *dad* is missing, and if we keep placing everything on the backburner, we're never going to find him."

"I was released from investigating Walter's disappearance several months ago." Hanson's voice was steady as he stated his case, "After we searched Walter's house in the States and didn't find any truly substantial clues, Royal Security released me from the assignment. So, I'm sorry, but I don't have any new information."

"Maybe not," Asher shrugged. "But I know you've got some old information. What happened the night that you found Mr. Akerly? At your dad's house."

Hanson's throat constricted. The memory made swallowing a challenge. "I reported everything that happened that night to the King. As sickening as it was to see Mr. Akerly there, tied up to a chair, I was confident Walter would be okay until the next day. I shouldn't have been, though." He shook his head, "Apparently they moved him that night, and nobody's been able to find him since."

"And by *they*, you mean your dad."

"Hey, there isn't a day that goes by that I don't regret my decision that night." Hanson's voice grew angry, "I had an open door to save him, and I didn't. You think I don't feel guilty about that?!"

"When's the last time you talked to your dad?" Asher continued to press the subject.

"Whoa, okay, now you're pushing into personal boundaries here!"

"Personal boundaries?" Asher echoed. "The way I see it, you have no personal boundaries. You were the last person to have contact with Mr. Akerly, which makes you a suspect for questioning."

"A suspect?" Hanson snapped, "What the heck? Now unless the King, or Jackson, or someone who has legal authority, comes along and arrests me for questioning, then whatever, I'll answer their questions. But you? I

[307]

don't have to answer any of your questions." He turned on his heel and attempted to exit the scene.

"Fine! Don't talk!" Asher called after him, "But if you think for a second that my sister is going to be okay with you keeping secrets from her, think again. She's far smarter than you give her credit for. And if you're hiding anything, she *is* going to figure you out, man."

Hanson continued walking, his chest pounding.

"I am such a dimwit!" Chasity announced as she entered their suite.

Asher sat at his laptop, immersed in research. "That's not news to me," Asher mumbled.

Chasity frowned. "I just bought a racehorse for one hundred twenty thousand pounds! How in the world am I going to tell Dad?!"

Asher didn't reply.

Chasity sighed and plopped down beside him. "Bud, I'm sorry. I know you're still mad at me about yesterday. I completely reacted and blew up in your face, and I shouldn't have." She looked down at her hands, "I didn't want things to be like this. I wanted this trip to be amazing, you know?" She looked up, hoping he would return the eye contact. "This is our last chance to spend time together before... well, you know." She sighed, "And I've been a total monster. Will you forgive me?"

Asher swirled around in his chair and stared at her for several seconds before responding, "Yeah." He pushed some stray hairs out of his face, "I mean, I can't blame you for reacting the way you did. Yesterday's events looked pretty suspicious. But Chas, you have to trust me. Everything Jane and I did was for her own benefit, and for the sake of trying to find her dad. I just don't get why nobody will believe me!"

Asher suddenly launched out of his chair and paced across the room, "Like yeah, I get it, I made some terrible mistakes in the past! But you guys are always talking about second chances, and now when I'm begging you to give me another one, nobody is listening! Chasity, I can't keep this stuff to myself!" His eyes were desperate, "I need you to believe me! We need to find Jane's dad, as well as the other missing scientists, and get to the bottom of this mess! We *need* to stop whoever's working on this AA16 code before it's too late!"

"I believe you." Chasity took a deep breath as she rose to her feet, "Bud, I believe you. I'm sorry. I can see that you're truly passionate about helping Jane, and obviously you feel an urgency to this. So, I'm all ears, Asher. Tell me whatever you need to get out."

"Well, don't you two look handsome!" Chasity gushed over her baby brothers as they entered the living room area of their suite. Both Asher and Willie wore matching black suits. Chasity giggled as Willie and Asher simultaneously adjusted their ties. There was no denying that they were related!

"This family is ridiculous," Asher huffed. "They demand that we get dressed up for *everything*."

"I like playing in the creek way better than this," Willie added to the mounting complaint.

"This is the last night of the Racing Convention." Chasity explained, "We received a formal invitation asking we wear our finest for this evening's party. James said it's pretty much like a ball."

"I hope they're gonna serve cake!" Millie chimed in. "Because a ball without cake is just a… just a…" She searched for the right way to end her sentence, "dull party."

"Alright, let's head downstairs." Chasity stood up and allowed the tulle skirt of her cream-colored gown to brush the floor.

Millie and Willie dashed out of the room. Asher and Chasity followed close behind.

"I don't know how easy it'll be to talk to Hanson tonight, but we need to get as much information from him as possible." Asher quietly reviewed the plan.

"Which would be far easier if Lilly wasn't glued to his hip," Chasity huffed.

"Chas. Try to keep your emotions out of this, remember?" Asher spoke matter-of-factly, "Right now, your top priority is to find out whatever Hanson knows about the AA16 and what his relationship with his dad is like."

"Right, the guy who hides his secrets in his eyes, and never wants to talk about anything." Chasity pursed her lips, "So, that should be easy."

The two descended the steps, then entered the elaborate ballroom. It wasn't nearly as large or as fancy as their ballroom back home, but it sure served nicely for the job. Expensive chandeliers hung from the ceiling, and happy conference attenders dressed in suits and fancy dresses mingled and easily chatted with one another. A small orchestra colored the background. Millie and Willie had already bounded off. Chasity hoped they would remember to behave.

"Princess, you look lovely this evening." James approached her and held out a hand, "As you always do. But tonight, you are glimmering with an extra sparkle. I am confident that every young man in this room will wish to dance with you. May I have the distinct honor of doing so first?"

"Uhhhh…" Chasity glanced at Asher. She didn't want to dance with James. But she knew it would be rude to turn him down. "Sure." Chasity attempted to smile.

James took her hand and led her to the center of the room, where several other couples slowly waltzed in time with the orchestra.

"So, tell me, what do you plan on doing with that expensive new horse of yours?"

"I'm probably going to have to sell him." Chasity bit her bottom lip, "I have no idea what got into me! I wasn't intending on buying him. But next thing I knew, I had charged one hundred thousand pounds to my dad's tab!"

"One hundred, *twenty* thousand, actually," James corrected her with a smile.

"Ugh, that's even worse!" Chasity shook her head, "I can't keep him."

"Why not?"

"Because, I don't know anything about managing a potential champion racer like him. With Nic, the newfound adventure of entering the racing world is going to be a blast. We're both newbies, and it's something the two of us can explore together. But I don't have any kind of history with Dr. Seuss. I don't know if we have a heart-to-heart connection or what it would be like managing his racing schedule. This is all so new to me! I'd be completely in over my head with him."

"Haven't you just spent an entire week at one of the finest Racing Conventions in Europe? Surely you've learned a thing or two that could help you manage Dr. Seuss."

"Well, yes, I mean, I've absorbed a ton of new information. But I don't have any real experience. I wouldn't even know where to begin."

"Oh, but isn't that the best place to be? Completely over your head?" James smiled, "I thought you would enjoy a challenge like that."

"Maybe." Chasity cocked her head, "But not right now. My heart belongs to Nic. I don't know if there's room in my heart for another horse right now."

"Racehorses are not so much about having a heart connection, as they are about making wise, business-savvy decisions. You don't need to fall in love with Dr. Seuss in order for things to work. Sometimes it is far wiser to do what makes sense in your head, then to haplessly follow your heart."

Chasity wasn't sure how to respond. Maybe James had a point?

"Perhaps you should at least give him a try." James grinned, "Just because he appears to be a stuffy, spoiled, well-bred, well-mannered, champion pedigree gelding doesn't mean you should throw him to the curb! In fact, most *normal* human beings would find that to be a good thing." He chuckled.

"Oh yikes, maybe I truly am crazy." Chasity laughed, "Turning down a nearly-guaranteed champion like Dr. Seuss, to invest all my time and energy in a horse that I don't even know is going to make it through the first round of qualifying trials? You're right. That doesn't make a lot of sense, does it?"

"Not at all." James laughed. "Do you know what else doesn't make sense, Princess?"

"What?" Chasity smiled.

"The fact that I have known you for so many years, and—"

"Ahem." Someone cleared their throat from behind.

Chasity and James paused from their dance. James wore a thick frown. Chasity's eyes lit up as she saw who had interpreted them.

"Excuse me," Hanson spoke, "may I have the honor of this dance, Your Highness?"

Chasity couldn't believe her ears.

"What a pity." James frowned, "I suppose I'm going to have to share you after all." James bowed out gracefully, leaving Hanson and Chasity standing alone. She stared at him, unsure of what to say.

Hanson extended a hand. Chasity slowly took it.

He appeared quite confident in his ability to lead the dance, so Chasity nervously followed him. She attempted to keep her head clear, but his handsome features were severely distracting. She fought the breathless feeling that desired to pull the very floor out from beneath her.

"Where'd you learn to dance like this?" Chasity asked with a shy smile. "I have to say that I never pegged you as a ballroom dancing kind of guy."

"Oh, I'm not." Hanson grinned, "Right now? I'm totally faking it. I don't have a clue what I'm doing." He leaned over and whispered playfully, "But don't tell anyone, it'll ruin my image."

Chasity couldn't help but laugh. "Well, you're pretty good at faking it, Hanson Fletcher."

"So I've been told." His eyes continued to penetrate hers.

"Hanson, I need to ask you something." Chasity took a deep breath. She didn't want to have this conversation, but she knew it was vitally important.

The warm glow from Hanson's eyes suddenly evaporated. Chasity sensed his unease.

"What is your relationship with your father like?"

All at once, the question tumbled out of her lips and smashed into the atmosphere, knocking the wind out of Hanson. His mind raced as the explosive words lingered in the air. Turmoil broke out within as a hidden area of his soul was unexpectedly bombed, now burning with the terrible fires of trauma.

After a few moments of silence, Hanson finally found the courage to speak.

"He's, he's..." Hanson stumbled over his words, "He's not my favorite person on the planet, let's just put it that way."

"It must have been devastating, finding out that he had kidnapped Mr. Akerly." Chasity cautiously pursued the matter, "It was your dad who had him tied up in the basement... wasn't it?"

"Why are we talking about this?" Hanson's jaw was tight, notably uncomfortable with the chosen topic of conversation.

"Because, you're the only one who knows what *really* happened that night." It hurt Chasity to speak the words, "And I think there's something you're not telling us."

"So, what, now you're accusing me of being part of this?!" Hanson's voice escalated with his anger.

"No!" Chasity whispered loudly, hoping he wouldn't explode right here in the middle of the ballroom. "Asher and I are just trying to learn as much as we can about the events, and look at things from multiple perspectives. You know your father better than anyone else, and I think you might know why or what he's planning to do with the AA16 code."

"Oh, you think *I* know him?!" Hanson suddenly stopped dancing, "You think an insane jerk, who walked out on us for years at a time, has any kind of relationship with this son?! I don't know what delusional planet you're from, but in the real world, just because you share the last name of a man, does *not* make him your father!"

"Hanson, I—"

But it was too late. Hanson had already stormed off.

The next day, Asher finally went on a trail ride with his sister.

"I'm so glad you decided to do this!" Chasity smiled warmly as their horses casually strolled through the winding gardens. "I was beginning to think you were going to spend this whole trip inside."

"Yeah, well it's our last day here, so I figured I might as well get out for a while."

Chasity glanced at her brother. She could tell his thoughts were elsewhere. She knew he was still concerned about Jane's dad, the missing scientists, and the AA16 Code.

"Ash, I know you're worried," Chasity sighed. "But we'll talk to Addison about this as soon as we get back. If you can tell him the entire story, everything you shared with me, and express the vital urgency you feel, I'm sure he'll take action."

"Yeah, right," Asher huffed. "He's got dozens of other, supposedly 'more important' things, piled up on his desk. And now, only weeks away from the wedding, he's going to be totally consumed with that. I just wish..." Asher hesitated. "I wish things were different. I wish that I was trusted enough to explore the case on my own and help Jane get her happily-ever-after. But obviously, that isn't going to happen. Not with stupid military school."

"Ash, Addison *will* help," Chasity reassured him. "I'm confident of that. As much as you want to run off and singlehandedly save the world, it just isn't your time. You have to believe God's got a plan in all this and that He's somehow going to work out everything, even your life at military school, for good. I wish things were different, too." She thought of Hanson and the way he reacted last night. "I wish a *lot* of things were different. But we just have to keep believing, and not become discouraged."

"Man, military school is going to be horrible." Asher grumbled, "Grumpy officers, a strict workout regimen, intense school studies, and absolutely *no* free time. How am I going to help Jane while I'm trapped behind invisible prison bars?"

"I don't want to read too much into this," Chasity started slowly, "but you seem to care an awful lot for this Jane girl."

"No, I don't!" Asher snapped, his face growing an adorable shade of pink.

"No, bud, it's okay, I think it's sweet!" Chasity smiled, "It's okay if you like her."

"Nobody said *anything* about liking her. I just want her to be okay, alright? That's not a crime."

"Of course not!" Chasity giggled, "I think it's really sweet. Just remember, you guys are still really, really young. Just because you had a blast running all over London together, and you have all these happy memories, doesn't mean you're destined to end up together. In fact, it's super rare that the person you like when you're fifteen ends up being your future spouse. So just remember to guard your heart, okay?"

"Oh right, like I'm gonna take relationship advice from the girl whose obsessed with her shady security guard she knows practically nothing about!" Asher rolled his eyes, "You haven't even told Dad about him, have you?"

"What?" Chasity shook her head, "Of course not! I mean, why would I? It's not like there's anything serious going on between us!"

"Uh-huh." Asher didn't sound convinced.

"Asher, I'm telling you the truth!" She attempted to remind herself of the painful facts, "He's never mentioned anything about being remotely interested in me, or even hinted at the idea of a courtship, dating, or long-term relationship." Chasity's mind quickly flashed to the moment of their almost-kiss in Greece. Uh-oh. Was she lying? Chasity's anxiety increased. Who was she kidding? She had formed a serious infatuation and strong heart-bond with the young man. The truth was frightening.

"That's because he probably doesn't even know what a courtship is." Asher laughed, "Most guys don't. Unless they've been raised in a culture similar to ours—which it's pretty clear that Hanson hasn't."

Chasity was ready to change the topic. "So!" She tried to perk up, making herself sound more cheerful than she felt, "What do you think I should do with my one hundred twenty thousand pound racehorse?"

Chapter Twenty Seven

"I still can't believe Princess Chasity swiped Dr. Seuss right out from under my nose!" Lilly huffed as her voice echoed through the empty barn. "Didn't she know how badly I wanted him? Didn't she know my dad had plans for that horse? He was going to be our next champion! That was the *entire* reason he paid for me to come to this convention! Ugh, he's going to be livid when he finds out I didn't get him."

"You haven't told him yet?" Hanson was surprised. Lilly stayed in fairly regular communication with her dad.

"No," Lilly sighed, "I know he's not going to be very happy. I just... I don't want everything to fall apart, you know? I mean, he's depending on me to keep things running smoothly and—"

"Hey, that's way too much pressure to put on yourself." Hanson attempted to remind her of the truth, "I know your dad wants to keep his business going, but he can't expect you to do everything. That's not fair."

"None of this is fair!" Her eyes were intense with emotion, "If life were fair, Dad wouldn't be in jail right now! Does he not realize how completely humiliating this is for me? I try to wear this big brilliant smile, attempting to convince everyone that life is grand and that it's totally normal to have a father behind bars. But I hear what they say about me. I see their disapproving stares and hear their vicious whispers and haughty giggles. I know what they all think. Like I'm some kind of black sheep, responsible for carrying on the tarnished reputation of the Chesterfield name. But I *know* he's innocent. How long until the court system figures that out?!"

Hanson bit his tongue, careful not to say anything he would later regret. Truth was, Lilly didn't know for sure if her dad was innocent. Hanson would like to think the best of Mr. Chesterfield, but he, too, had his doubts about the businessman's integrity. Nevertheless, even the most innocent of men could get cornered into a business deal with Mr. Fletcher, that they would later regret. Hanson wanted to give Mr. Chesterfield the benefit of the doubt.

"I know it's hard," Hanson sympathized. "But our dads don't define us. It doesn't matter how shady their pasts are, or even what people think they are doing or *not* doing currently. All I know is—"

"Hanson, look out!" Lilly released a terrifying scream.

But it was too late. Someone had already leapt on Hanson's back and was trying to tie his hands together. Struck with shock and adrenaline, Hanson attempted to knock the heavy man off his back. But the surprise attacker was larger than he and slammed him into the stable wall.

Hanson's eyes grew wide with horror as another man, wearing a mask, held Lilly in a tight headlock.

"Get your hands off her!" Hanson shouted.

The man who held Lilly pulled out a knife. Hanson's breath caught in horror as the knife glimmered in the sunshine.

"One more word out of you and she's dead!" the man barked.

Hanson froze. He knew there were no charades to the man's wicked words. He had seen the mafia kill innocent family members without even flinching. Hanson's breathing intensified, on the verge of hyperventilation. An avalanche of traumatic memories tumbled over him, and he felt as though he may suffocate beneath them.

Lilly's eyes were stricken with desperate fear. Hanson had seen that look before. The same look his aunt had just before she and his uncle were murdered in their living room when he was just eight years old.

"Your father misses you, Hanson," the man spoke in a gravelly voice. "Turns out he was still hoping you'd join him in the family business. But it appears as though you've made *other* choices. And now, he's asked us to return the favor. Delivering on a promise he made when you refused to do what he commanded." The man paused for a terrifyingly-dramatic effect, "It looks like this beautiful lady will be the first to go." The man raised the knife and Hanson shouted, "NO!"

Hanson felt a hard kick in his back as he fell to the ground, face first. The man who had been trying to tie him up finally achieved his mission and secured his wrists.

"I thought I told you to shut up!" the man barked, still holding the knife near Lilly's throat.

"Please, I'll do it!" Hanson called out. "I'll do anything, whatever he wants, just stop—don't hurt her!"

"Aw, isn't that touching," the man mocked. "The boss's kid is on his knees, begging for mercy. Well, it's a little late for that."

"Hello!" A British voice called out from the other end of the long stable row. "Who's in here?" James and two of his friends stood in the entryway, squinting their eyes, attempting to see what was going on down the aisle.

The masked men looked up, surprised to hear the voice. Hanson took advantage of the split second they were distracted, knowing it may be their only opportunity for escape.

"Arrggg!" Hanson kicked his leg into the air, knocking the knife out of the man's murderous grip. It flew over their heads, flinging into one of the empty stalls.

"Retreat!" the man shouted, realizing they were teetering dangerously close to being caught. "Go, go, go!" he shouted to his partner.

The man leapt over Hanson and followed his leader, dashing toward the exit at the opposite end of the stables.

"After them!" James shouted, leading the charge, commanding his friends to keep in hot pursuit. "Don't let them get away!"

His friends quickly obeyed, barreling toward the masked intruders.

James himself stopped to check on Hanson and Lilly, "Good gravy, are you two okay?!"

"Yeah," Hanson huffed, attempting to catch his breath after all the excitement, wriggling out of his wrist restraints "yeah, we're fine, but those guys need to be stopped!"

"We're on it." James bolted out of the barn as soon as he knew Hanson and Lilly weren't hurt.

Lilly quickly ducked into the empty stall, searching through the haystack for the knife that had nearly killed her. She picked it up, her hands shaking in terror. She ran to Hanson and released her grip. The knife dropped to the floor. Lilly lost the will to stand, as her knees gave out and she sank into the hay below. Hanson immediately caught her, his heart pounding.

Lilly sobbed, completely shook from the near-death experience. She buried her head deep into his chest and clung to him with a frantic grip.

"Shhh, Lilly, you're okay." Hanson was on the verge of angry tears himself. He attempted to keep his voice steady. "Everything's okay. It's alright. They're not going to hurt you."

"What if they come back?" Lilly cried, her voice cracking with emotion. "H–H–Hanson, I c-c-can't—"

"Shh, Lilly, they're not going to come back." Hanson held her closer, wishing there was a way to transport her to a world of guaranteed safety and bliss. "I *promised* I was going to protect you, and I am not going to break my word." Hanson slowly cupped her chin and turned his face toward him. "Lilly, look at me."

Lilly's tearstained face and horrified eyes revealed the frightened little girl that Hanson knew was locked up somewhere inside. Hanson felt the same way she did. But he couldn't show it. Her bottom lip quivered.

He carefully wiped a tear away with his thumb, "I am not going to let anything happen to you."

"This is a nightmare." Lilly sniffed, "I, I want to be brave, but I don't think I can... Hanson, I'm so scared that they're going to kill you."

"Me?" Hanson questioned.

"Yes!" Lilly cried, "Don't you know that I care about you more than anyone else in the world?! If anything ever happened to you I, I would—"

"Stop. Lilly, nothing's going to happen to me. And nothing's going to happen to you, either." Hanson wished he could believe the words as they left his lips. But he couldn't. Truth was, Hanson didn't know much of anything in this moment.

Lilly released one more sniff and attempted to rein in her emotions. She reached for Hanson's hands, "Oh, look at your poor wrists!" She held them in her own. She offered him a tender rub of affection, and Hanson's heartrate increased.

He continued to stare into the eyes of the beautiful young woman before him, determined to do whatever it might take to keep her safe. In this moment, he wanted more than anything to calm her fears and reassure her that all would be well.

Lilly slowly reached for his hair. Her subtle touch messed with Hanson's hormones, and he found himself slowly drawing closer to her. His heart continued to pound within his chest, as he wished there was a way to fix everything. Their faces neared, and Hanson thought she looked as if she might try to kiss him. All at once, the two were entirely enraptured in the moment. There was no room for rational thinking or common sense.

All at once, Lilly's lips were upon his.

Chasity and Asher ran into the barn opening. They came as quickly as they could, after James frantically reported that some sort of unidentified drama had broken out.

[324]

Chasity turned the corner, with Asher close on her heel. Her feet stopped moving, as well as her heart. It took everything within her to keep from toppling over.

There was Hanson, passionately sharing a kiss with Lilly.

In that very second, Hanson pulled away. His astonished, shocked, and guilt-ridden eyes tried to meet Chasity, but she couldn't bear to look at him. Before Hanson could speak, Chasity had already turned on her heel and broke out of the barn.

Asher bit his tongue, wishing to spew out some choice words. Instead, he shook his head and fed Hanson a glare so intense that Hanson was pretty sure lasers of death would soon shoot out of his eyes. Asher turned to chase after his sister.

Chasity ran as quick as her boots allowed, but the sluggish riding boots were only slowing her down.

"Chasity! Chas, wait!" Asher called after her.

But Chasity couldn't hear him. She couldn't hear anything. She couldn't see the path in front of her feet, or hear the birds chirping above. She broke away from the path and tore across the yard. A rude branch from a small sapling smacked her in the face as she galloped by. But Chasity didn't even feel that. She was numb. Completely and entirely numb.

Chasity's boots grew heavier. She didn't want to stop running, but she knew they were only slowing her down. She kicked them off and continued to press on harder. She didn't know where she was running to. But she didn't care. She just needed to run.

Unwelcome tears pooled her eyes, causing her vision to become blurry. Without warning, she suddenly ran into a small lawn decoration, a stupid little angel statue with a fancy little flowing fountain. Chasity fell to her knees and let herself cry.

Her shoulders shook as she clung to her stomach, rocked by such a deep pain that she had not known existed. As foolish as she felt for feeling so distraught, she couldn't help herself. Hanson had completely eradicated every one of her most fragile and deepest dreams concerning their future. Now, there would be no future. It was clear: Hanson was enraptured by Lilly.

Like a terrible replay loop that she couldn't get out of her head, the thought of their disgusting kiss was seared in the forefront of her mind. Each replay of the obtrusive scene caused a small dagger to rip deeper and deeper into Chasity's chest.

"How could he do such a thing?!" Chasity called out to the Lord. He was the only One she could trust with her unsteady emotions. Anyone else might call her silly or try to talk some sense into her. But Chasity knew the Lord completely understood. Jesus had been through every kind of pain during His time here on earth. He too was betrayed by a kiss.

"And even worse, how could I let my heart become so entangled?" Chasity sniffed. "I've given away so very much of myself, and the worst part is, I knew I couldn't trust him. Oh Lord, why have I behaved so foolishly?! Why have I thrown all father's advice out the window and lavished my affections on someone who I know isn't going about things in the right way? I've buried myself so deep in emotion, and now I'm in completely over my head. I'm not sure which way is up, and which way is down," she confessed. Her voice fell to a whisper. "But Jesus, I cannot change how I feel. Because the truth is…" She took a deep breath, prepared to speak what God already knew. "I care about him. I love Hanson Fletcher."

After allowing the words to tumble off her lips, Chasity's crying ceased, and she sat in the stillness of the settling storm. There. She admitted it. She finally said what she had been so fearful to confess, and desperate to cover up. She loved Hanson.

Chasity knew better than to hide her heart from the Lord, and she was confident that He was aware of this fact long before she was. Nevertheless, now that she confessed her true feelings, a strange peace settled over her. It was as if she finally removed a painful dagger from her chest. Chasity didn't know why, but admitting that simple truth, as shameful as it was, made her feel safe now. The eyes of her heart were becoming clearer, and the blurriness was starting to vanish. Perhaps now she would know how to get herself out of this mess. It didn't change the fact that Hanson had completely broken her heart. It didn't change the fact that her emotions were acting unwise and she never should've handed her heart to Hanson in the first place. Nor did it change the fact that Hanson clearly didn't feel the same way about her. Even so, Chasity found enough strength to stand up, wipe away her tears, and head back to the house.

And that alone, was a miracle.

Chasity sat on her bed, peering into her Bible, her heart aching to find more clarity and direction. Her heart felt like a dry, cracked desert, in desperate need of comfort and water from Heaven. She needed to hear God speak to her. She needed to know that He loved her. She needed to know that she wasn't just a washed-up, forgotten, second-choice reject when compared to the stunning Lilly Chesterfield. She needed her mind to be reassured of what her heart already knew. Casting her affections toward Hanson was a complete waste of time and mental energy. She needed a Word from the Lord that would give her strength to build her walls and reconstruct her barriers yet once again. She had completely failed at guarding her heart, and now she needed the strength to do what she should have done—and had tried to do—a long, *long* time ago. Let go of Hanson.

Her eyes soaked in the words of James, Chapters 3 and 4. She did a double take as the words almost jumped off the page, quickening something deep in her heart.

"Where envy and self-seeking exist, confusion and every evil thing are there."

Chasity looked up from her Bible. "Oh my," she whispered. "That's been me the past two weeks. Completely eaten up with envy and selfishness."

She looked back at the passage and continued reading.

"Where do wars and fights come from among you? Do they not come from your desires for pleasure that war in your members? You lust and do not have. You murder and covet and cannot obtain. You fight and war. Yet you do not have because you do not ask. You ask and do not receive because you ask amiss, that you may spend it on your pleasures."

Chasity allowed the words to sink deep into her soul.

"Oh, Lord, what have I been doing? Fighting Lilly for Doctor Seuss, knowing it truly had nothing to do with that horse, and *everything* to do with Hanson. I've been acting like a catty middle-schooler! Oh Lord, forgive me! This is no way for any daughter of Yours to be acting. I've been so, so selfish, anxiously thinking I needed to beat out Lilly to capture the prize. But Hanson isn't my prize." Chasity sighed, "Dad has always told us girls that when the right guy comes along, we won't have to pursue him or vie for his attention. Instead, he'll be pursuing us. At times I've felt like Hanson wanted to pursue me, and at other times I've felt like he's completely pushing me away. It's like he's sending mixed signals! Oh Lord, help me to let go."

A knock came to Chasity's door, followed by a careful head peeking in. It was Asher.

"Everything okay in here?" Asher asked. His voice was full of concern. Chasity smiled. It was so sweet of him to care so deeply about what had happened.

"Not really," Chasity sighed. "But it will be."

Asher opened the door the rest of the way and sat down on the edge of her bed. "Need me to go beat someone up for you?"

Chasity laughed. "As tempting as that offer sounds, somehow I don't think that's what Jesus would do."

"Naw, I guess not." Asher sighed, "I'm sorry this happened to you, though. That guy is a total jerk-face. Any loser who chooses Lilly Chesterfield over you clearly doesn't deserve you."

"Aw, thanks Ash." Chasity's heart grew warmer from his words, "But I've been acting just as ridiculous as Hanson has lately. So, it's not all his fault."

"On the bright side, at least you found out what kind of guy he is before things progressed any further, right? I mean, he's clearly got a past twisted with crime. It could've been you they were threatening with the knife."

"What?" Chasity questioned. "Knife? Asher, what are you talking about?"

"James explained everything that went down. I guess two hitmen came after Hanson and Lilly, seeking some kind of revenge. They almost *killed* Lilly." Asher's voice was serious, "Thankfully, James stepped into the barn just in time and scared them off. But as you can imagine, Lilly was really shook by it."

Suddenly, Chasity's thoughts flashed back to the moment Hanson had told her about the men who cornered him in an alleyway on his first day of work, and they had threatened to hurt him if he didn't get the Wall of Fire code. What if those were the same men?!

"Who were they?" Chasity's voice was frantic, "The guys who tried to kill them?"

"Dunno." Asher shrugged, "James called for backup right away and their security team nabbed 'em. I guess they just waltzed right onto the property, acting like they were here for the Convention."

"That's horrible." Chasity lifted a nervous finger to her mouth, "Ash, what if those guys were after the AA16 Code?"

"I thought Mr. Akerly was the only person with that information?"

"But the AA16 code is embedded into the Wall of Fire!" Chasity exclaimed, "And Hanson told me that on his first day of work at The Palace, several hitmen cornered and threatened to hurt him if he didn't get the code. He said he was tempted to do so, but he didn't."

"How do you know he didn't?" Asher asked.

"Because. He gave me the USB chip stating that it was proof that he would never betray the Crown." Chasity's voice quivered as she told the story, reminiscing of all the things they'd been through, "I kept it for several months, then in February he asked me for it again. I was suspicious, so I didn't give it to him right away. Finally, when I thought I could trust him, I gave it back. But this was all happening the same time that Hanson was researching about Mr. Akerly, and then he disappeared.

Do you think . . ." Chasity didn't even want to suggest such a thing, "Do you think he gave that chip to the bad guys?"

"It's possible," Asher contemplated. "But something's telling me he didn't. I mean, if he *had* handed over the code, why would the hitmen still be after him? When I confronted him the other day, he seemed pretty irate that I would ask him about his involvement with the case. But it wasn't a guilty kind of reaction . . . it was more of an embarrassed one, like he's still feeling sick about not setting Mr. Akerly free when he had the chance."

"It's me, I'm coming in!" a little voice chimed, and the door flew open. It was Millie. She launched herself onto the bed, completely disrupting their conversation. "Whatcha' guys talking about?!"

"Just some big people stuff." Chasity tried to smile.

"Hey, I'm not a little kid anymore you know!" Millie crossed her arms, "I'm nine! I'm losing my baby teeth, I don't cry when I'm scared anymore, and I don't sleep with all my stuffed animals! Well, I *do* still sleep with Mr. Pork Chops, but that's different. He's family."

"You're right, that's pretty grown up stuff," Chasity laughed. "But in all honesty, this is a conversation that *we* don't even want to be having right now. It's far too depressing. So, I'm glad you interrupted us."

"Good." Millie grinned, "Are you guys excited to go back home? Pork Chops and I sure are! We can't wait to see Daddy and Addi and Nessa and Clark, and go swimming in the pool, and decorate cupcakes, and most importantly–get ready for the wedding! My luggage is all packed up, and I'm ready to head to the airport! What about you guys?"

"Millie, we're not leaving for another two hours. Which is probably a good thing, because I am nowhere near packed."

"Are you ready?" Millie asked Asher.

"I was born ready." He smiled.

Millie turned back to Chasity. "Well, I'd better let you get packing! The sooner you can throw your junk in a suitcase, the sooner we can leave!" She launched off the bed then paused before leaving the room. "Oh, someone is at the door and wants to talk to you."

"Millie!" Chasity scolded, leaping to her feet, wondering who it might be. "Why didn't you tell us earlier?"

"I didn't think it was that important," Millie shrugged. "It's just James."

Chasity shook her head and tried not to laugh. She rushed through their suite and headed for the door. Her hand landed on the handle, then she stopped herself. She backtracked several steps and paused in front of the mirror. She frowned. Her eyes were still puffy from crying. She made a face and pinched her cheeks, hoping to add a bit of color. She didn't want to look like a complete mess.

Finally, she opened the door and James stood with a massive bouquet in his hands. Chasity's eyes widened.

"Oh wow, what am I going to do with all these flowers? Goodness James, you've been completely spoiling us."

"Oh, it's not much, just a simple going away gift," James grinned. "But I believe a Princess deserves to be spoiled, does she not?"

"Thank you." Chasity graciously accepted the flowers and set them on the desk inside, right beside the bouquet he had delivered yesterday. She looked back at him, "Was there something you wanted to talk to me about? Because if not, I really need to start packing."

"Yes." James fidgeted with his tie. He cleared his throat. "Actually, there is."

[332]

Chasity felt herself growing suspicious. She had never seen James act even the slightest bit of nervous before. This was a side of him she had never seen. What was wrong?

"Is everything okay?"

"Yes!" James reply was overly enthusiastic.

"Hi, James!" Millie bounded into the conversation, "Ohhh did you bring more flowers? You must really like my sister!"

James' cheeks turned pink. Chasity couldn't hide the surprise in her face.

"Why else would a guy bring a girl flowers?" Millie exclaimed. "You've been dropping them off every day and it's clearly a sign of your—"

"Okay, that's enough, Millie!" Chasity quickly stepped into the hallway and closed the door behind her. She gave James a bewildered glance, "I am *so* sorry. You know how little kids can be. Sometimes their imaginations can be crazy!" She laughed nervously.

"Ah, yes. Children are quite a joy, are they not?" James laughed as well. "Come, let's go to the Tea Parlor. Perhaps it will be a more conducive atmosphere for chatting than the hallway."

"Right." Chasity spoke, not sure of what else to do other than follow him down the stairs.

"That is one thing I admire about children. They're never afraid to speak their minds!" James noted. "I believe we could all learn a thing or two from them."

"And then there are people like me, who need to learn when to *stop* talking." Chasity shook her head, thinking about her mess with Hanson, "Millie and I are far too much alike."

[333]

"Ah, but that is just one of many things I admire about you." James eyes held a gaze of wonderment, as if he had placed her high upon the utmost pedestal, "Your gutsy fervor for living life! Like the way you snatched Dr. Seuss right out from beneath the nose of Miss Chesterfield. Nobody saw that coming! Your unpredictability is refreshing."

"Perhaps to some people," Chasity commented as they turned into the empty parlor. "But you're not the one who has to live with the consequences of purchasing such an expensive horse." She sighed, "I still don't know what I'm going to do. I can't ship him back to Tarsurella, as that would be far too long a ride. But I don't really want to sell him either."

"I have the perfect solution for your dilemma. He can stay here."

"Oh no, I would never ask you to do such a thing, your stables are already full and—"

"Princess, it wouldn't be any kind of inconvenience, I assure you of that! In fact, it would be an honor to have Dr. Seuss boarding here. We could hire a trainer to work with him in the spring, and it would give you a reasonable excuse to come visit more often."

"Really, I don't want to be intrusive and—"

"Princess." James voice was firm, "Allowing Dr. Seuss to stay here would be a blessing for us, a true benefit and joy to have a horse of such pedigree owned by the Princess of Tarsurella. We could even place an honorary plaque on the wall and tourists would come from far and wide, just to see the famous horse!"

"You make it sound like it would be such a massive benefit for your estate."

"It would be!" James reassured her.

"Hmm... I suppose that would solve my problem." Chasity considered his suggestion, "I could at least have him stay here until Dad decides if I need to sell him or not. Okay." She finally nodded, "it's a deal. Dr. Seuss can stay."

"Wonderful!" James poured a bottle of sparkling grape juice and handed her the thin-necked, crystal glass, "I'll drink to that!"

Chasity smiled and lifted the glass to her lips. James was so fancy and over-the-top. What kind of young man severed his visitor sparkling grape juice in the throes of a casual conversation?

"So, uh, what is it that you wanted to talk to me about? I really need to get back upstairs and start packing."

"Right." James set down his glass on the white-washed fireplace mantel. "Actually, I have something quite serious to speak with you about."

Chasity's thoughts immediately went to Hanson and the attack. Would James share more about what had happened? Did he have further information on how this might be related to the Walter Akerly case?

James cleared his throat. "There has been something weighing heavily on my heart and mind for quite some time, but you know me, the perfectionist that I am, I've been waiting for the perfect moment to talk to you about this." He wiped sweaty hands on his black pant legs. "Oh dear." He laughed nervously, "This is turning out to be a bit harder than I thought it would be."

Chasity's nervous hands clung to her cup. She had a bad feeling about whatever was about to come out of James's mouth.

"Your Highness, you are the finest young woman I've ever had the privilege of meeting. Your character is most amiable, and the way you

[335]

conduct yourself among social gatherings is both loving, full of tender kindness, and also captivatingly entertaining." He smiled, "I must say that you depict the most flawless image of a Proverbs 31 woman: graciously representing her family, her country, and most importantly, her faith and the Kingdom of God. We've been friends for quite some time now, and with each passing day, I find myself growing more and more—"

"James." Chasity interrupted. She knew where this conversation was going. She had to stop him before he said something he would regret.

"No, let me finish. I know this may come as a bit of a shock to you, as I have kept my feelings at bay. But the truth is, Your Highness, that my heart is quite taken with you, and I would like to ask you about the distinct honor of entering an official courtship."

Chasity's stomach dropped. It was too late. James had already said it! Her mind raced, searching for words, wishing for a kind way to tell him she wasn't interested. It hurt her to the core to think of how the rejection might shatter his innocent heart. Chasity knew far too well how it felt to be rejected.

"Oh James." She started slowly, already feeling guilty for the pain that she would soon inflict. "I don't even know what to say. The truth. The truth is, that I—"

I am not expecting an answer right now," James quickly explained. "I know I've sprung this on you, completely out of the blue, and you may need some time to think and consider my proposition. But I couldn't allow you to leave without knowing how I really feel. Chasity, I already know that my parents adore you, and both of our families would be in high favor of the match. As your friend, I know it might seem strange to learn that I think of you in this way. But perhaps, after you pray about and consider the words I have spoken here this afternoon, you may begin to feel the same way about me, after all."

"I have to admit that you're right," Chasity spoke gently. "Everything you've said is a complete surprise to me. You're such a dear friend, James, and you've been nothing but an absolute gentleman, and I would never want to hurt you. But it is true. I've never thought of you as anything more than a kind and thoughtful brother."

"And I understand that," James nodded. "But I do ask that you would at least consider and pray about what I've shared? I'll be returning to Tarsurella for the wedding. If, by that point, you have decided that you care nothing for me, and you only want our friendship to remain as it, then I will respectfully back down. But, if for some reason you find it in your heart to explore the possibility of this newfound companionship, I will happily accept your answer, and move forward accordingly."

Chasity strolled into the barn, her mind heavy with dozens of wild thoughts. Today had struck her with a myriad of potent emotions. She felt as if she had been on a rollercoaster, plummeting to the depths of despair as she saw Lilly wrapped up in the arms of the man she loved, then coming back to somewhat of a level ground while spending time with the Lord and learning her attitudes had been all wrong. The rollercoaster then threw her for another loop, as James turned on the overwhelming spigot of his adoration and showered his flowery, heartfelt words all over Chasity. She'd never heard anyone speak so highly of her. She could tell that each phrase and sentence he chose to use was carefully meditated upon and deeply considered. The saddest, most heart- wrenching part, was that James truly meant each word. James truly was a kind, caring, thoughtful guy. He deserved the best out of life, and Chasity could never wish him ill.

But a *courtship*?

Even just the word caused her head to spin! It was clear that James was over the moon about it! Yet, the way that he presented it almost sounded more like a business deal, or a negotiation made in in a board room. It severely lacked the compelling element of excitement and romance Chasity longed for. When she spoke with James, there were no fireworks. No tingly toes or playful banter. Nothing about him caused her to feel excited and cheeky. Nothing about him was… Hanson.

Chasity walked to Dr. Seuss's stall. She was going to say goodbye to the fella before they left for Tarsurella. Even though she hadn't spent any time at all getting to know him, she felt that he deserved a farewell. After all, he was her horse! She approached the muscular stud and stood back in wonderment, still completely shocked over the fact that he was hers.

"Hey buddy." She spoke gently as she reached out to rub his nose. "How do you like things here at the O'Conner Estate? Are you okay with the idea of me leaving you here for a few months? I'm sure you're going to get some of the finest treatment in the world. Delicious meals, lots of lovely paddock time—"

"Chasity."

Chasity instantly recognized the voice. It was Hanson. She didn't turn around. She knew he was standing behind her, but she wasn't ready to look at him. Not again. Not so soon. If she wasn't careful, she might start crying all over again.

"Chasity, I need to talk to you." He stepped closer, "Please just hear me out, okay?"

[338]

"Save it." Chasity whipped around. She couldn't bear to hear his pathetic little words, begging her for forgiveness, asking for a second chance. She didn't want to hear his apology. For she knew that if she did, it would be far too easy to let him back in again. "Your words mean nothing right now. But then again, they never have, have they? All this time, you've been claiming that there's 'nothing' going on between you and Lilly. But actions speak louder than words, Hanson."

"But Chasity, it was a mistake!" Hanson's voice was frantic. His fear-filled eyes were terrified by the thought of losing her. "That kiss meant nothing to me! I don't even know why I did it! Lilly was scared out of her mind, and I wanted to make her feel better, and next thing I knew we—"

"I told you, Hanson, I don't want to hear about this! Whatever is going on between you and Lilly is not my business. The only thing I care about is the fact that you lied to me with your smile. You led me on, causing me to think that there might actually be some kind of possible future between us, and I was actually stupid enough to fall for it! But don't you see how ridiculous this is? I know absolutely nothing about you! I don't know anything about your parents, or the house where you grew up, or what your favorite food is, or what your dreams are for the future! I don't know if you believe in God, if you're a loyalist, or what kind of dessert you like! Hanson, whatever's been going on between us has been absolutely shallow and imaginary. It's based on nothing more than a delusion conjured up by our selfish desires and diluted imaginations!"

"So, get to know me!" Hanson begged. "Chasity, I don't want this to be the end between us! I want to spend time with you. Can't you see that? What don't you get about the fact that I'm completely crazy about you? Chasity, I know we haven't done things in a traditional way. I haven't talked to your dad, or taken you out on a real date, or talked to you about the stuff that truly matters in life, but I want to. I really, *really* want to.

[339]

But in case you haven't noticed, my life is insanely complicated! Lilly's life is in danger, and it's my job to protect her because of the decision I made to disobey my dad's command to be part of his evil plot. My dad's trying to kill her, Chasity! And if he knew that you held any kind of special place in my heart, he would try to kill you, too."

"Hanson, this isn't going to work," Chasity spoke sadly. "And we both know that." She turned to Dr. Seuss and kissed him on the nose. "Goodbye, Champion." She turned to Hanson. She opened her mouth to speak, but she couldn't.

Instead, she quickly cantered down the aisle.

"Chasity, I love you!"

Chasity stopped dead in her tracks.

"I love you." He spoke again, sounding as if he truly meant every word. "And I'm going to prove it to you."

Chasity didn't turn around. But she was listening.

"I'm going to go to your dad, asking his permission to court you." Hanson's words attempted to smash through the thick, cement walls Chasity was frantically trying to erect against him. "And when he says yes, I'm going to show up in The Palace and escort you to your brother's wedding."

Chasity still didn't turn to face him. But she didn't run away either.

"I know you don't believe me right now. But that's okay. Because I'm going to make my actions louder than my words this time. I promise."

Chasity took a deep breath and continued walking. She didn't dare look back. For if she did, she feared that she might never turn away again.

Chapter Twenty Eight

Nitpicking Napkins

Back in Ohio...

"Would you prefer that I pick up pink notebooks or blue notebooks?" Aunt Cassidy asked. "Or, I could get five in each color! Or, we could go for the whole rainbow and get a different color for every class! Color coding always helped me stay organized in school! Ohhhh, I just love back-to-school shopping!"

Jane didn't share Aunt Cassidy's excitement.

She glanced at Charlie who sat beside her at the kitchen table, fully immersed in his latest invention. It appeared that he was attempting to rewire an old cassette player and turn it into something more useful. She didn't know what he had planned for it, but he was clearly determined to make it work.

"Oh, never mind, I'll just get a little something of everything. I'll surprise you!" Aunt Cassidy grabbed her purse and headed for the door, "Now are you *sure* you don't want to come with me, Jane?"

"Positive" Jane nodded. "Thank you, though."

The *last* thing Jane wanted to think about was going back to school.

The phone rang, and Aunt Cassidy quickly crossed the kitchen to answer it. "Hello?"

Jane watched the woman as her cheerful expression changed. Aunt Cassidy's eyes grew wide. "Yes, she's here." Aunt Cassidy carefully handed the phone to Jane, "It's for you."

Jane's mind immediately flew to her father. Was it a federal agent from Tarsurella? Had they discovered something?! Jane's hand trembled slightly as she held the phone up to her ear. Charlie looked up from his project, his eyes struck with worry.

"Hello?" Jane asked.

"Hi, Jane! This is Laurie!"

Jane didn't respond.

"From the YNC!" she added, just in case Jane didn't remember. But of course, Jane remembered. She would never forget anything about that trip, even the smallest detail, for the rest of her life. "How are you doing?" Laurie asked.

"Um…. fine." Jane's voice held a deep undertone of suspicion. Surely the woman didn't call her just to chat.

"So, listen, I read your story," Laurie started. "And you're right. It explained everything. Jane, I had no idea that your father was missing! Or that the Prince of Tarsurella needed to speak with you about such important matters! Jane, I wish you would have said something! If you only would've taken a few moments to explain what was going on, I wouldn't have acted so strictly, and I would've gone out of my way to make sure you got what you needed."

"No," Jane's voice was firm. "It wouldn't have been fair. I wouldn't have wanted you to treat me any differently. I'm not the only person in the world with struggles, and I would never expect any extra special treatment. You did exactly what you were supposed to, making an effort to protect me and enforce the rules."

"Jane, your story was incredible. I was completely captivated. At times you had me falling off my seat laughing, and at other times I was on the verge of tears! I passed your story onto Harvey, the judge of the YNC, and he was just as impressed as I was! Even though you were expelled, and there's no way for us to place you back in the competition, Harvey wants you to return to London and meet with him. We'd like to offer you a publishing deal."

Jane nearly dropped the phone. "What?!" she gasped, not sure she completely understood what Laurie was saying. Surely, she heard her wrong! Was she dreaming?!

"Your story contained the secret sauce great novels are made of!" Laurie insisted. "Internal struggle, unforgettable adventure, mountain-top triumph, exciting romance, and harrowing heartbreak—we want to publish your story!"

"But you can't!" Jane burst out. "*Nobody* can read that story! It's about my personal life!" Her mind started to race as she thought of Asher and what he might think if he found out she had written about him. Surely the Royal Family could sue her for making Asher a leading character!

"Please, Laurie, you can't! I'll write anything else, something completely different, but we *can't* publish that story!"

"Jane, please calm down, honey!" Laurie spoke gently, "I know, I know. We're not going to take the secrets of your heart and throw them out there for all the world to see. The raw form of what you've written isn't exactly what we want anyway. But what if you revisited the ideas? What if you spun the story into a more elusive, creative work of fiction? What if evil orgs kidnapped your dad, and you were a royal maiden who had to trek across the world in order to save him? And instead of your Prince riding a Vespa, he could ride a noble steed! Why, you could even make me the wicked witch who wouldn't let you out of her sights! Jane," Laurie's excited voice calmed down several notches, "You are an extremely talented young woman. The truth is, we would be crazy to turn down an author with as much potential as you. Though we don't often do this—extend deals to those who do not win our contest—every once in a while, we come across a young author who displays exceptional skill and a fresh dose of much needed imagination and originality, in a world of copy and paste formulas. So, what do you say? Are you ready to return to London?"

In Tarsurella...

And here is the monogram for your napkins." Stacie slid a gold napkin across Addison's desk. Vanessa and Addison exchanged amused glances, secretly reading one another's thoughts. The last thing they would be thinking about on their wedding day was their napkins. "We've designed a custom-made monogram which combines the A and V of your names to overlap and mesh together in this whimsical font. It speaks of sophistication and grace, yet contains undertones of deep symbolism, as the two letters become one."

"It's nice." Addison nodded, taking advantage of this moment to playfully tease their wedding planner. "But I was looking for something a little bit more upfront and clear about whose wedding this actually is. I mean, isn't A and V a little bit illusive?" His eyes twinkled with playful mischief. "These napkins look like they could be at anyone's wedding, Alice and Vinny, Andrew and Veronica… why not make it extremely obvious and print in big, bold letters 'Long Live Vaddison'?"

Stacie's eyes grew wide with horror.

Vanessa giggled. She knew Addison was only joking and they really shouldn't, especially with all the stress Stacie was under, but his eyes enticed her to join in. They were only several days away from the wedding now! And with each passing hour, she and Addison grew more and more giddy.

"Vaddison?" Vanessa shook her head, "No hun, that might be too long to fit on a napkin. What about 'Anessa'? Out of all our ridiculous celebrity couple names, I like that one far better. It's short and sweet. It definitely says 'wedding napkins' to me!"

"Uh, actually, Your Majesty," Stacie cleared her throat as she looked at Addison, "we, um, may not have enough time to—"

"Stacie, we're kidding." Addison smiled, "We love the napkins. We don't want you to change anything."

Just then, Addison's office door flew open and two little munchkins came running in.

"I'm home, I'm home!" Millie leapt over the threshold and blasted into their meeting. Willie was right behind her.

"Millie!" Addison stood, knowing she would soon launch herself into his arms.

"Addi!" she cried, hopping into his open invitation and embracing him with a massive hug. "Oh, I missed you so, so much! You should've come to England with us! You would've seen us play in the creek and dance around at James's party and see Chasity buy a horse! You missed everything, Addi!"

"Maybe so." Addison's eyes twinkled as he admired the little apple of his eye, "But I missed *you* the most!"

"Miss Vanessa!" Millie threw herself into Vanessa's arms.

Vanessa laughed, thrilled to hold the little girl close again. Millie brought so much life and laughter to The Palace; there had been such an empty void without her.

"I'm almost your sister, you know! Pretty soon you're gonna have to drop the 'miss' and just call me Vanessa!"

"Willie, my little man!" Addison embraced Willie and gave him a playful noogie. Willie released his infectious laughter. Vanessa continued to grin. Addison was going to make an amazing father.

"How is Clark? And Deborah? And all the other workers?" Millie asked eagerly, "Did everything run smoothly without me?"

"It was tough." Addison pretended to sound distressed, "But they pulled through."

"Clark!" Millie suddenly headed for the door, "I need to find out when we're testing out your wedding cake flavors!"

"Hey Mil, hold on." Addison leaned up against his desk, "Ness and I have something to tell you."

[346]

Vanessa took a deep breath, knowing this wouldn't be easy for the little girl to hear. "You know that preparing for a wedding is a huge, massive project that takes tons and tons of months to plan, right?"

Millie nodded.

"Stacie, our super helpful wedding planner here, suggested we try our cake options earlier in the month, while you were still in England." Vanessa spoke cautiously, "So we did. *But* we haven't made our final decision yet. And so, we need you and Willie to test out the two vying cakes, and make the final decision."

"Really?! Come on Willie, let's go! The cakes are waiting! Let's go save the wedding!"

"Alright!" Willie followed the fearless charge of his big sister.

The two bolted out of the room, and Chasity and Asher appeared in the doorway.

"Hey, sorry for the interruption," Chasity apologized on their behalf. "I told them you were in a meeting."

"No problem, we were just wrapping things up." Addison gave her a hug, "So, Millie says you bought a new horse?"

"Did she?" Chasity laughed nervously, "Yeah, that's kind of a long story. I'll explain it all later."

"Can't wait to hear all about it!" Vanessa embraced her, "We sure missed you guys!"

"We missed you as well!" Chasity smiled, "You have no idea how nice it is to be home!"

"Well, I suppose I'll leave you all to your reunion." Stacie stood up, "Tomorrow, we'll review the menu for your rehearsal dinner, finalize

[347]

your Thank You notes, and decide what we're placing in the gift baskets for your out-of-town guests. Have a lovely evening, Your Majesty." She bowed toward the King, then curtsied in honor of Vanessa, Chasity, and Asher, before exiting the room.

"Thank you, Stacie!" Vanessa called after her.

"I guess I'd better go unpack and grab a nap before dinner," Chasity spoke. "Is it possible to have jetlag from only flying two hours?"

Everyone laughed as she ducked out of the room. Asher lingered.

"Hey, man." Addison hugged him, "How was the trip?"

"There's something I need to talk to you about." Asher's eyes were struck with a deep sense of urgency. He glanced at Vanessa.

"Of course." Vanessa smiled, "I'm sure you two have lots to talk about and catch up on. I'll head on downstairs and make sure Millie paces herself and doesn't end up in a chocolate coma!" She laughed, then closed the office door behind her.

Asher left his brother's office with a deep sense of frustration. He felt like punching a wall. Why didn't anybody believe him?! Why couldn't they see the importance of cracking down and solving this case?

Despite all the new information, Addison spoke the same thing as before. "We're working on it, Ash. We've got agents dispatched on the assignment and they're doing the best they can."

The best they can? Asher was fuming inside. *Well, obviously these guys don't have a clue what they're doing, because their so-called 'best' is coming up with absolutely nothing!*

Asher's feet pounded up the stairs as he headed for the Family Room. He had to think of something. He had to do whatever he could before the sands of the hour glass ran out and his time was up. Once he was at military school, Asher knew he would be powerless to help Jane. But what *could* Asher do? His brother was the one with all the real power. If it were up to Asher, he would phone the UN and declare a national emergency because of the possible AA16 threat. But Addison didn't think that was necessary.

"If you had more proof or evidence that this was a threat to the general public, that might be a different story," Addison had told him. "But we can't just jump to conclusions and start shouting ideas that are built on nothing more than alarmist, conspiracy theories."

Asher needed proof. He didn't know how to get it, but he had to figure something out. Asher entered the Family Room. Maybe he could call Charlie and—

He paused in the doorway. He did a double take as he realized who was standing in the kitchen. Hope, Deborah, and—Asher would recognize the back of that head anywhere.

"Jane?!" he breathed.

The young woman twirled around, and Asher blinked. It wasn't Jane.

"Ash, you're back!" Hope hurried across the kitchen and gave him a hug.

Asher's eyes remained fixated on the young woman who stood beside Deborah. The resemblance was freakishly similar. Whoever this stranger was, standing in their kitchen, almost looked as if she could be Jane's long-lost cousin or something. Although her outfit was far more sparkly than anything Jane wore, the similarities had caused him to do a double take. Asher cleared his throat. The revelation that this *wasn't* Jane was surprisingly disappointing. Although it was foolish to think she'd just be standing around in their kitchen, Asher had secretly hoped to see her again soon.

"Welcome back, Your Highness." Deborah smiled, "Allow me to introduce you to my daughter, Pearl."

"How do you do, Your Highness?" Pearl offered a curtsy and batted her eyelashes. Asher tried not to show his displeasure with her obnoxious eyelid fluttering. What, did she have something stuck in her iris?

"Asher!" Steve entered from where he had been on the back balcony; grilling, Asher guessed. He wore his favorite 'Grill Master' shirt and a massive smile. "Aw, man, we sure missed you, bud!"

Asher returned the hug, then his eyes drifted back to Deborah. She wore a laid-back pair of khaki pants and a short-sleeved, blue, knit top. Asher had never seen her dress so casual. She leaned back with one hand against the counter. Even her customary high heels were missing. What was going on? Why was she acting so chill? And why was her daughter here?

"Have you met Pearl yet?" Steve asked.

"Yes, I just introduced them," Deborah spoke up.

Asher glanced at Pearl. She was looking at him with big, longing, suggestive eyes, and Asher resisted the urge to shiver. She hadn't stopped looking at him since he entered. That girl was giving him the creeps.

"Where is everyone?" Steve asked. "The burgers are almost done! And I've got an important family announcement to make." Steve's gaze met with Deborah's and they exchanged a smile. Asher felt his stomach drop as the puzzle pieces suddenly started to come together.

He studied Deborah, who glowed with an inner light of love and admiration toward his dad. Asher's breathing grew heavy. Surely it wasn't what he thought it was. Surely, they… no—they couldn't… that was impossible.

When his dad didn't break Deborah's gaze for several prolonged seconds, Asher's suspicions were confirmed. He suddenly lost all of his appetite. It was true. Dad was dating again.

Chapter Twenty Nine

Rehearsal Dinner

"Dad, your hamburgers are seriously the most delicious burgers I've ever eaten!" Vanessa raved.

"We don't call him the Grill Master for nothing!" Addison chimed in. "He worked hard to deserve that title though."

"Yeah, when he and Mom first got married, he couldn't cook anything." Hope laughed, "Not even toast! But he wanted to prove his skills to Mom, and he nearly set The Palace on fire the first time he tried to grill! She got him that T-Shirt as a joke, but Dad kept practicing and, hey, what do you know? Now he really is the grilling king!"

"That's why I always say, practice makes progress." Steve wiped his face with a napkin, "Don't ever say it's impossible to do something, because if you keep at it, eventually you'll get the hang of it."

"So, does this mean Addi needs to start practicing his grilling skills?" Vanessa asked.

"Oh no, is that one of the requirements on the 'How to Be a Good Husband' list?" Addison chuckled.

"Naw, that's just in the optional category." Vanessa shrugged playfully, "I think you have all the other criteria covered pretty well."

"Well, that's a relief." Addison pretended to wipe sweat from his brow, "Otherwise I know how I'd be spending the next few days. Grilling!"

"Oh, please no, let's not start a massive fire right before the wedding," Bridget joked.

"Well, I think I'm just about as stuffed as old Pork Chops!" Steve groaned as he stretched his arms into the air, "I don't think I could eat another bite, even if I wanted to."

"I'm full, too." Millie added. "But not too full for dessert! Do we have dessert?"

"Not tonight, Mil." Steve wiped a stray strand of hair away from his daughter's face, "I think you already had your fair share of sugar during your cake-testing session. Jillian, would you please clear the dinner dishes?"

"Yes, sir." Jillian stood up, relived to be excused from the table and have something else to set her mind on for a while. It pained her heart to see Deborah and her dad chatting and having such a good time with one another. Deborah fit into their family dinnertime conversation quite flawlessly, and everyone enjoyed her company. But Pearl? Pearl was another story. The entire time she was either making googly eyes across the table at Asher or chatting with Bridget about her latest shopping trip in Paris. Jillian couldn't stand being around her. Everything about Pearl's presence felt like nails on a chalkboard, screeching down the surface of Jillian's soul.

"Pitch in and give her a hand, sweetie," Deborah instructed Pearl.

"Of course." Pearl flashed a smile and stood up to assist Jillian. Jillian resisted the urge to roll her eyes. That fake grin didn't trick Jillian. She knew what kind of person Pearl really was.

"Oh. my diamonds, your brother is even dreamier in person than he is on the news!" Pearl exclaimed excitedly once they reached the kitchen and were out of earshot of the family. "My friends are going to freak out once they hear I had dinner with him!"

"Is that all you ever do?" Jillian scraped leftover food scraps into the garbage bin, "Brag to your friends about all the time you're spending with my family?"

"Of course not!" Pearl snapped back. "I happen to live a very sophisticated, high-class society life. My friends are jealous of my existence for lots of reasons, not just the fact that I'm becoming buddy-buddy with the Royal Family."

"The only reason you're here is because your mom happens to be an amazing woman and a kind human being. But apparently she didn't pass any of those traits on to you!"

"Listen, Pancake." Pearl sat down her stack of plates and took an intimidating step toward Jillian, "I don't like this little arrangement any more than you do. We both know that unless things seriously start to go south, it's only a matter of time before your dad pulls out a ring. I know how this family works, with fast proposals, and even faster engagement periods. But mark my words: I am *not* about to become Prince Asher's sister."

"Something we actually agree on." Jillian pursed her lips together tightly. She glanced toward the table where everyone was laughing and chatting happily. "So, what can we do to stop it? It's pretty obvious our parents are crazy about each other."

"I don't know yet," Pearl huffed, clearly just as stressed out about it as Jillian was. "But I'll think of something. Because no way am I going to become the step-sister of my future husband!"

"Husband?" Jillian laughed. She raised an eyebrow, "Yeah, right! Asher doesn't even talk to girls!"

"Ladies, why don't you come on back here for a moment?" Steve spoke up, "We have an announcement to make."

Jillian gulped. She and Pearl exchanged uneasy glances and stepped toward the table.

"What kind of announcement?" Millie asked.

Everyone was quiet.

"Well," Steve looked at Deborah, then back at Millie. "Miss Deborah and I have decided to begin getting to know one another better. We've enjoyed a nice friendship over the years and—"

"Daddy!" Millie gasped, "Are you in love with her?!"

Steve was speechless as his face went red. "Millie, I uh…"

"Miss Deborah, are you going to be our new mom?!" Without warning, Millie burst out of her chair and threw herself into Deborah's arms, "I would *love* it if you were in our family! You could get married, just like Addison and Vanessa, and our family would keep on growing!"

"Aw, you are very kind, sweetie," Deborah laughed. "But beginning a relationship doesn't always mean the couple is going to end up getting married. Right now, we're just enjoying getting to know each other better, and seeing how well our families like to hang out together. Does that sound good to you?"

"That sounds great!" Millie cheered. She gave Deborah another hug, and Jillian's heart fell. Poor, poor, Millie. She had no idea what this meant for their family. Millie was so quick to love and embrace everyone who came into their lives without thinking twice about the changes or consequences it would bring.

But Jillian knew better. If Steve and Deborah continued to build this relationship, *everything* was going to change.

One week later...

The butterflies in Vanessa's stomach were doing backflips. It was the day before her wedding! Tomorrow, she would become Addison's wife. Forever.

Vanessa could scarcely believe it was happening. The wild combination of thoughts and emotions were far too many to sort through with a rational mind. The delicious fruit punch of destiny she was about to drink was mixed with anticipation, surreal dreams coming true, bittersweet memories from the past, and wild unknowns for the future. But the chief emotion that ruled over her heart was the joyful anchor of love. Vanessa loved Addison far more than she could ever express. And because of that, she knew that all the questions, nerves, and frightful unknowns would be settled the moment their celebration began.

Tomorrow, they would pledge their love and faithfulness to one another before God and in the witness of all their dearest family and friends.

Tomorrow, they would be a real-life example of the unfading love between Christ and His Church. They would promise to care for one another in sickness and in health, on good days and bad days, and to build a God-honoring family together, for all the days of their lives. The thought was absolutely electrifying. Tomorrow, Vanessa would become Addison's, and he would become hers. 'Til death do they part.

"Stacie, the gardens look beautiful!" Bridget reaffirmed the slightly frazzled woman, "Do you need any help?"

"Oh no, dear, the rehearsal dinner committee is taking care of everything, nothing to worry yourself over." Stacie didn't sound too sure of herself. "Where is our silverware?!" she gasped. "Why do we only have one spoon on the table, are we not serving Clam Chowder as an appetizer?!"

"Don't worry, I'll run to the kitchen and grab more spoons!" Bridget volunteered. "And Stacie, please don't fret. The table displays are absolutely stunning."

With that, Bridget vanished out of sight, quick to set all the wrongs right.

"What can I do?" Vanessa asked.

"Absolutely nothing!" Stacie's voice was firm, "Miss Bennet, your only job is to stand around and look pretty!"

"And you, my dear, are doing a splendid job at that," Addison's voice came from behind.

Vanessa twirled around in her white, knee-length lace dress and soaked in the glorious sight of her groom to be. Addison looked dashing in a dapper, navy-blue suit coat and matching pants.

"And you look handsome enough to stand on top of your own wedding cake."

"Can you believe it?" Addison's hands met hers, "Only two hours until your dad walks you down the aisle."

"You know this is just the practice session, right?" Vanessa giggled, "We're not really going to be married until tomorrow morning."

"Bummer." Addison sighed and released a laugh. "We're getting closer. Does it feel real yet?"

"Not at all." Vanessa smiled.

"Yeah, me neither. But it's happening. The Main Hall was loaded with guests this morning when I came downstairs, all checking in for this thing."

"And not one of them nearly as excited as I am," Vanessa giggled.

"You think you're excited?!" Addison teased, "I'm the one who gets to marry the girl of his dreams!"

"Okay, so we're both excited. But just for the record, I think I'm getting the far better end of the deal."

"Not a chance." Addison desired to pull her close and tell her ten thousand more times more how much he loved her. The strong, magnetic pull to kiss her grew stronger with each passing day. It was a good thing they were getting married tomorrow because Addison wasn't sure how much longer he could wait. The closer their hearts grew, the closer they desired to become. But they were almost there. Tomorrow, all their patience and self-control would finally pay off, as they honored God with their very first kiss at the altar.

"Hey, there's one of my good-looking groomsmen!" Addison called out to Liam. "You clean up nice, man."

"So do you!" Liam chuckled. He glanced around nervously, and Vanessa wondered why he appeared so apprehensive. Was he concerned about possible security breaches this weekend?

"So, is the plan still on for tonight?" Addison asked.

"Shhhh!" Liam hushed and lowered his voice to a whisper, "She might be around here somewhere."

"What's going on?" Vanessa was suspicious, "Wait." She gasped, "Are you going to propose to Bridget?!"

"Shh, shh, shh!" Liam was fervent about keeping this a secret. "There are little ears everywhere! If Millie catches wind of my plan, the surprise will be scrubbed." Liam smiled and reached into his pocket. He pulled out a small box and Vanessa clasped her hands together excitedly.

"Ahhh!" Vanessa couldn't help but rejoice, "Bridget is going to freak out! And how perfect! This is the last time she'd ever expect it!"

"That's the idea." Liam's eyes shone with anticipation and delight, "She's completely zoned in on making sure everything runs smoothly for you, it'll be the last thing on her mind." He stuffed the ring box back in his pocket. "Now I just have to act cool and remain calm until seven o'clock."

"Good luck with that." Addison laughed, "The day I proposed to Ness, I was an absolute mess! Thankfully, I only saw her for a few minutes before popping the question. Otherwise, I think she would've gotten suspicious."

"It looks like everything worked out for you guys, though." Liam winked.

"And it will for you and Bridge." Addison smiled, "I can't wait to see how the Lord is going to use the both of you to further His Kingdom."

"I've gotta admit, Chas, you're the last person in this family I'd ever imagine losing her brains over some guy!" Hope continued their conversation as they walked through the Greenhouse.

"I can't say that I'm proud of it," Chasity sighed. "It's just, everything with Hanson has been such a mess. Yet we have all these unforgettable memories, and here I am clinging to them like a childhood blanket that's fraying at the edges. It's like I'm in this battle between my heart and my head. My head says we haven't gone about anything in the right and proper way, and now after seeing him with Lilly, I know that any sensible person would let go and move on. But that's the problem, Hope. My heart still loves him. Why? Why would I put myself through this kind of self-inflicting torture, when a perfectly good, kind, and proper human being has just offered another path? Even though I've never felt that spark of connection with James, everything about him makes sense. Our families have been friends forever, we have common interests and hobbies, and we come from similar backgrounds."

"I don't know what to tell you, Chas," Hope admitted, secretly facing a very similar battle. "I wish I had the answers, but I've been asking myself a lot of those same questions. As Christians, are we called to be led by the Spirit and step out into the unknown, even when we're not sure of where He's leading? Or are we supposed to stick to the safe roads of wisdom and common sense, only moving within the realms of what we already know to be true? It seems like two completely different, conflicting ideas to me. Dad's always told us to be wise and guard our hearts at all costs. And look where that's led Addison and Vanessa, and Bridget and Liam? They've safely reached their happily-ever-after's because they followed all the rules and precautionary measures Dad has instilled in us. So maybe there's something to be said for the path of common sense and wisdom."

"Does this mean, you're letting go of Luke?" Chasity asked.

Hope had opened up and shared everything that happened while Chasity was gone, and Chasity did the same. The sisters had processed through their individual struggles and came to the same, sad conclusion. Their loosely-titled 'love lives' were an absolute rodeo!

"I still believe God is working in his life," Hope spoke slowly. "But just because He's doing something in Luke's life, doesn't mean that *I* need to be a part of it. Maybe I've already played my part in his story, and he's finished playing his part in mine. Vanessa shared some really good advice the other day. She said that if what Luke and the Sons of Liberty movement are doing is of God, it will be proven and affirmed for everyone to see soon enough. But if it's of the enemy, then they're going to fail. As hard as it is to let go and trust Him with the question marks, I'm going to have to for the time being."

The glass doors parted before them, and the girls stepped out into the Garden. Chasity knew their conversation was over. It was time to focus on the task at hand, preparing for Addison and Vanessa's wedding rehearsal. It was a most joyous occasion. The last thing they wanted to do was damper the mood. It was time to set aside all distractions and embrace the moment for what it was–a celebration.

"Grandma!" Millie called out from behind. Chasity glanced over her shoulder, surprised to see Millie and Willie right behind them. Neither she nor Hope had known they were following them. Had they been playing their little spy game? Millie bolted forward, pushing a path between Chasity's and Hope's legs.

"Whoa!" Hope called out, nearly losing her balance.

Willie was right behind Millie. Millie shot like an arrow toward the woman she was so elated to see. Grandma Patricia, Steve's mother, stood chatting with Vanessa, Addison, and Liam.

"Millie!" Grandma called back, sounding just as excited as the little ones. "There's my grand adventurer!"

Hope grinned. The thin, fragile woman sported a floppy purple hat and flowy sundress. But Hope knew better than to let her dainty image deceive; Grandma was a lively spitfire, an adventurer at heart. She was the only grandmother in the history of grandmothers that Hope knew to ride a motorcycle, go scuba diving in the Caribbean, and hike across the Grand Canyon. It was no secret that the retired Queen immensely enjoyed herself.

"I'm an adventurer, too!" Willie called out.

"Of course, you are!" Grandma gave him a hug, "The two of you make an unstoppable team!"

"We were just tracking down hippopotamuses in the Rain Forest! They can be dangerous creatures, you know! If you're not careful, they'll eat you for lunch!" Millie informed Grandma on the latest, important updates happening in the realm of her imagination.

"And there's two more of the adventurous women after my own heart!" Grandma's blue eyes shone as Hope and Chasity approached with open arms.

"Are you still riding that wildly fast horse, Nic?" Grandma asked as she embraced Chasity.

"Absolutely." Chasity giggled.

"And you, my dear Hope!" Grandma hugged her next, "Are you still running around being your beautiful, bad self, breaking the hearts of all the young male popstars?"

Hope's face turned colors as everyone's eyes widened.

"Oh, don't think that I'm not down with the times!" Grandma explained to her bewildered audience, "I am hip and happening, keeping up with all the rumors reported about my grandchildren. Don't think I didn't hear about that song Mr. Carter wrote for you!"

Hope's face continued to increase in redness. She wasn't sure what was more embarrassing: the fact that her grandmother knew one of *Kennetic Energy's* songs was about her, or the idea that this revelation was just hitting everyone else who was within earshot. Addison and Vanessa exchanged glances.

"Excuse me," Stacie gently barged in, "I don't mean to break up this happy little reunion, but if you don't mind shifting this conversation into the East Garden that would be greatly appreciated. You're right in the middle of our walkway for setup.

"You heard the woman!" Grandma told her grandchildren. "Come along now, let's make ourselves scarce. This team has work to get done."

"Should we show her the chapel?" Vanessa suggested, unable to pull her starry-eyed gaze away from Addison.

Hope smiled. Addison and Vanessa were floating around on a different planet entirely. Their hands were stuck together like magnets and their eyes whispering all sorts of romantic secrets with one another. As cute at it was, Hope couldn't help but shake her head. The soon-to-be, happy honeymooners had clearly lost their minds over one another. And if they kept this behavior up for much longer, Hope might have to release a small gag.

[364]

"Of course!" Grandma took a large step forward and started singing a famous wedding tune. "We're going to the chapel, and we're gonna get ma-a-ar-ried . . ."

"Oh boy, that was intense."

Vanessa looked up and smiled at her father. She wasn't sure if he was joking around or being serious. She knew this was an emotional time for him. Although she wasn't expecting to see tears, the macho, yet fun-loving man she had known her entire life, appeared as though his eyes may sprinkle a little. She clung to her dad's arm as they strolled down a path leading to the East Garden. Blazing tiki lights, as well as adorable little candles hiding in mason jars, lit up the evening with a romantic ambiance.

The mid-summer night's air was set at a flawless temperature. It was as if God had predetermined the outdoor thermostat to perfectly match Vanessa's desires. Then again, it could have been raining and thirty-three degrees, and Vanessa still would've felt like the evening was flawless.

"It's okay, Dad, you survived the rehearsal," Vanessa reassured him. "Although tomorrow, when the Priest says it's time to give me away, you're actually going to have to let go of my arm."

Mr. Bennett frowned, "That's what I was afraid of."

"I know you love your daughter, Mr. Bennett, but you can't keep her forever," Addison called from where he walked behind with the rest of the family. "I'd really, *really* appreciate having her for the rest of my life."

Vanessa continued to smile. She felt like her face might be permanently plastered in this gleeful position. The anticipation was nearly too much to bear! Even though they were headed for a delicious dinner, Vanessa knew she wouldn't eat much. She was far, *far* too excited to think about food.

Hope tossed Chasity a dramatic look as she attempted to cross her eyes. Chasity giggled. She heard Hope loud and clear. Vanessa and Addison's love-bird antics were getting a bit over-the-top. Although Chasity couldn't blame them. They had every reason to be excited. What girl wouldn't be?

Hope inhaled, catching her first sniff of delicious flavors floating on the wind. Her stomach was grumbling. She was ready to dive into their rehearsal dinner feast. Her ears strained to make sense of the melody she thought she heard. She didn't know the staff would be playing music in the gardens. She listened further, and her heartbeat quickened. It wasn't just a CD. It was live music. And Hope knew *exactly* who that voice belonged to.

She slowed, and Chasity paused to ask what was wrong. "Are you okay?"

"Yeah!" Hope quickly tried to cover up. She didn't want to act like a total weirdo. She had to keep her cool. She had to be okay with the fact that David was playing in the gazebo just a few feet ahead. "I just wasn't expecting *Kennetic Energy* to be playing until tomorrow, that's all."

"I thought it would be fun to have them play for a while tonight," Addison spoke up. "Is that okay, Hope?"

"Of course!" She forced a smile onto her face, "Why wouldn't it be?"

"I'm sorry," Vanessa quickly glanced over her shoulder. "I didn't even think about the fact that this might be awkward for you!"

"Awkward?" Hope laughed nervously, "Who said anything about awkward? David and I are good friends. It's no big deal."

"Speak for yourself," Jillian mumbled.

"I don't get it." Millie looked at her, "What's going on and why is this no big deal?"

"You're too young to understand," Jillian spoke in a sophisticated tone.

"I am not!" Millie argued.

"Fine." Jillian pursed her lips, "David wrote a song for Hope, she told him she just wanted to be friends, broke his heart into a million pieces, and now things are awkward between them. Meanwhile, there's another young Royal here who would probably face plant into the wedding cake if someone like David Carter was interested in her." Jillian sighed.

"Boys are disgusting," Millie announced. "And you're not old enough to get married anyway."

"Thanks for the reminder, Einstein," Jillian huffed. She crossed her arms and sped up, quickly finding a table that wasn't beside Millie.

Hope's high heels paused. She bit her lip and stood nervously on the sidelines. As everyone found their tables and mingled happily, Hope dug under her nail, attempting to look busy. When she was sure David wasn't looking at her, she allowed her eyes to drift toward the small, twinkle-light-adorned gazebo.

David's sweet, comforting radio voice floated across the airwaves. The gentle, acoustic rhythm came from Justin, the long-haired guitar player who sat on a speaker. Zac, the eccentric young man who usually pounded on the drums, softly bobbed his head and played the maracas. The first song in their quiet dinner music playlist was an original called *Starlight*. Hope had heard Jillian play the romantic ballad on her iPod many times.

Laney joined in with skillful harmonies and Hope almost smiled. Hope might've actually enjoyed the moment if it wasn't for all the conflicting

[367]

emotions she felt rising up inside. It had only been a few months since she last saw David, but he had grown even more handsome since their last encounter.

Suddenly, in an unexpected moment, David saw her. His soft eyes met hers and Hope quickly looked away. She made a beeline toward the nearest table, snagging the first empty chair she could find. Her table company was Jillian, Asher, Pearl, Deborah, and her father.

Jillian's attention was fixated on the gazebo, and Hope took a deep breath as she reached for a roll. She had almost forgotten how much of a fan her little sister was.

"Lovely music choice," Deborah commented.

"Yes, the kids did a wonderful job planning this." Steve smiled, "I think Bridget inherited her mother's love for event planning. Let's just say, it was a good thing I wasn't in charge of this little shindig!"

"Oh nonsense, I'm sure you could've scrounged up some hamburgers for us to eat!" Deborah joked. "It all would've worked out just fine."

Hope buttered her roll and stole several shy glances at David. She gulped. His hair was shorter, his skin was tanner, and his arms were bulkier from all the guitar playing and demanding touring activities. She needed to stop thinking about him. This was just getting ridiculous. She needed to enjoy her dinner in peace, keep her cool, and remain level-headed in case he tried to talk to her at some point. His whimsical lyrics about floating on a magic carpet ride beneath the California starlight were ridiculously cheesy, yet every bit of lovely.

After the song ended, everyone applauded politely, and Bridget grabbed the microphone. She explained how the buffet line would work, asked Liam to offer a short prayer for the meal, then invited everyone to dive in.

Steve and Deborah stood up in the same instant. "After you, my lady." Steve bowed playfully.

Deborah giggled, causing both Jillian's and Pearl's eyes to widen in alarm.

Asher and Hope followed the group to the food line, and Pearl shook her head.

"We have to do something." Her voice was desperate, "Our parents are becoming more and more obsessed with each other by the second."

"I know," Jillian agreed. "But what *can* we do?"

"Have you ever seen that old movie, *The Parent Trap*?"

Jillian nodded.

"All we have to do is think of a plan! Instead of causing our parents to fall *in* love, we need to make them fall *out* of love. Surely it can't be that hard. What are some things your dad hates? Qualities in women that drive him absolutely batty?"

"I don't know. The only woman he's ever been in love with was Mom, and he adored everything about her."

"Well, my mom hates when men wear socks with sandals, don't clean up after themselves, and drive like maniacs. You could start dropping hints, telling my mom that if it weren't for his style coordinators, your dad would be a wardrobical nightmare."

"I can't do that. I'm not going to tell lies and sabotage their relationship. Surely there's got to be a better way."

"Like what?!" Pearl snapped. "Being upfront and honest? This isn't the 1950's anymore! I can't just be like, 'Gee Mom, you know, I really don't want you to ruin my life by getting married. Thanks, love!'"

[369]

"Why not? I know it sounds crazy, but it might be the only option we have! Dad always told us kids that we can talk to him about anything. If their relationship is bothering us, he's going to listen."

"I guess it's worth a shot." Pearl shrugged. She stood up, ready to prepare a plate of food for herself.

"Hey."

Hope paused from where she scooped a slice of cheesecake onto her plate. She slowly twirled around, already knowing who the voice belonged to.

David stood in front of her, hands stuffed into the pockets of his khaki pants.

"Hi." She spoke sweetly, truly excited to see him. She didn't know what else to say. And so, they continued staring at one another. Miraculously enough, there wasn't even the smallest trace of awkwardness in the air. Somehow, his eyes felt familiar and comfortable.

"Great job tonight," Hope finally spoke, aware that someone had to say something. "I mean, I know you're not finished yet, but all your songs sound great. As usual. It's fun hearing the acoustic versions of your album. How's tour going?"

"Great!" David's voice was bright, "We actually just had a little bit of time off, two weeks back home, which was nice. It's a blessing having some downtime before all the crazy kicks in again. We're launching our sophomore album next month, so we'll be doing the whole media circuit again. We weren't really supposed to have any shows scheduled for this time, but we couldn't say no to your brother. You all feel way more like

[370]

family than business at this point, anyway." David smiled. "So how are things with you? Keeping busy here?"

"Of course! Everyone at The Palace has been completely obsessed with preparing for this wedding." Hope laughed, "Bridget's a bit of a slave driver, so she's kept us super busy. It's hard to believe it'll all be over after tomorrow! I'm not really sure what I'm going to do with myself after everything settles down. I kind of thrive off the busyness and activity. The silence will be strange."

"Oh yeah?" David teased, "Come on tour with us then! Never a dull moment on the road."

"Oh, I bet! Actually I—"

"Hi!" Millie popped onto the scene. She reached for a slice of Oreo cheesecake. "Are you Mr. David Carter?"

"Yes, I am." David beamed.

"You're the same guy who was just up there singing, right?"

"Same guy." David nodded.

"Hmm…" Millie examined him, "I don't see why my sisters make such a big deal out of you."

Hope's eyes widened. She quickly grabbed Millie's hand, "Whoa, slow down there, missy! Is that already your second piece of cake?"

"It's my third!" Millie grinned, "I'm practicing for tomorrow!"

"Yikes, okay, I think that's enough sugar for one night, hun." Hope handed her the plate and shooed her away. Hope laughed nervously. "Sorry about that, Millie doesn't know what she's talking about. Sugar can make her act a little loopy."

David smirked, "Well, I guess I'd better let you get back to your dessert. Talk to you later."

"Right." Hope smiled, "See ya."

Steve and Deborah chatted easily, while Jillian and Pearl exchanged nervous glances.

Pearl nodded in her direction, as if giving Jillian the silent prompt to begin speaking.

Jillian gently shook her head, as if to say, 'I'm not going first!'

Pearl subtly kicked her under the table, hoping the nudge was strong enough encouragement to get Jillian started.

"Ow!" Jillian gasped.

Steve looked at his daughter, "Jilly?"

"She has something she wants to talk to you about!" Pearl quickly spoke up.

"We *both* have something," Jillian corrected her.

"Fine, whatever." Pearl rolled her eyes. She turned toward her mother. "Mom, there's no easy way to say this."

Deborah cocked her head, then anxiously reached for her mouth. "What? What is it? Do I have something in my teeth?"

Pearl's eyes pleaded toward Jillian for help.

Jillian took a deep breath. "Dad, Miss Deborah, we don't want this to sound bratty or hurtful . . . but something is really bothering us."

"What's that?" Steve set down his fork.

Nobody spoke.

"Come on girls, you know you can share with us," Steve prodded.

"Yes, Pearl, what is on your mind?" Deborah reached for her hand.

"We don't want you to get married." Jillian allowed the bold words to march out of her lips. There. She had said it.

"Neither of us are ready for you guys to move on and start this new relationship." Pearl quickly added, "Even though we've been trying to act mature and be supportive, we're just not comfortable with the idea of you guys being together. *Especially* if it means me giving up my life at school, moving into The Palace, and becoming a Royal step-daughter."

"I think you girls are jumping to conclusions." Steve spoke thoughtfully, "I know this isn't easy for any of you, but we've only just started dating. Believe me when I say we are taking things very, very slowly."

"I know, you already said that," Jillian sighed. "But we all know you wouldn't be dating just for the fun of it. Eventually, you'd want to get married, then we'd be forced to adjust to a whole new reality that we're simply not ready for! And we never will be ready for it, either. Dad, I don't want a new mom. Not now. Not ever."

Deborah glanced at Steve and took a deep breath. "Thank you for sharing that, Jillian." She offered a half smile, "And you too, Pearl. It isn't easy for us to hear these things, but we made it very clear from day one that our children's lives are top priority. As much as we care about one another, we care about you kids far, far more."

"Does this mean you're going to break up?" Pearl asked slowly, wondering if it could be that simple.

"No." Steve's forehead was tight, "It doesn't. But, as your mom has said, we will seriously take into consideration what has been shared here tonight. We would never want to make choices that wouldn't be in the best interest for everyone involved. I appreciate the way the two of you have gone about things. You've been upfront and honest, having this discussion in a very mature, rational way." Steve reached for Jillian's hand, "I'm proud of you, Jilly."

"Thanks, Dad," Jillian replied slowly. She glanced at Pearl. Now that they had made their point, why did she feel so bad? Shouldn't she feel relieved? Happy even, that things might go back to the way they always were?

"We've got a lot to pray about." Deborah's voice was tight, void of it's usually joyous, airy tone. Jillian's heart dropped as she caught a brush of sadness within Deborah's carefully guarded eyes.

Chapter Thirty

Hiding in a Shoe Box

"May I have everyone's attention please?" Bridget grasped the microphone and held it several inches from her lips.

The small crowd came to a hush as clanking forks and easy-going chatter slowly faded. Bridget's sequin-embossed dress sparkled beneath the light of the full moon above.

"We have officially come to the part of the evening where I am seriously going to regret not wearing waterproof mascara."

Vanessa smiled from the table near the front, and everyone else laughed.

"It's an opportunity to honor the beautiful bride-to-be and express how much we, her family, love and appreciate everything about her." Bridget took a deep breath and attempted to keep her voice steady. "When Vanessa first came into our lives, she was seen, by me anyway, as nothing more than a tiny little chick with a whole lot of spunk and sass! I mercilessly framed her as being a sneaky, underhanded American with a hidden agenda of stealing my brother's heart."

Everyone laughed.

"The Lord knows we didn't kick things off with a very good start! But as time went on, God did a miracle in my heart, and once He removed the massive plank of bitterness from my own heart, I was able to see Vanessa through a true and pure lens. And wow, was I wrong about her. Vanessa," she turned to speak directly to her soon-to-be sister, tears glistening in her eyes, "you're so much more than my friend. You're a shining example of a heart on fire for Jesus, you're passionate about the Kingdom of God, and you're intentional about your relationship with Addison. You know that love isn't just warm fuzzy feelings or fireworks, but that love truly is all the qualities of First Corinthians Thirteen. Love is patient and kind. It suffers long. It is not proud, it does not boast, and it keeps no record of wrongs. It doesn't rejoice in evil but rejoices in the truth. Love believes all things, hopes all things, and endures all things. Love never fails. And because the King of Love, Jesus Christ, lives inside of you, I am confident that love will continue to grow in your hearts as you and Addison set off on this amazing journey together. The task of becoming the Queen of Tarsurella isn't an easy one. But I can truly say with all my heart, I don't believe there is anyone better for the job then the girl sitting right here in front of us tonight. Vanessa, it is an honor to call you my friend, and now I am so blessed to be able to call you sister."

Bridget quickly scurried down from the gazebo stage and embraced Vanessa. The two hugged one another tightly as applause erupted. Addison was glowing. It was such a blessing to see that his sister and his soon-to-be wife had formed a deep and special bond.

"Okay, I guess it's my turn." Liam stood up.

Bridget handed him the microphone.

"First of all, I just want to say what an honor it is to be here tonight." Liam started with a humble nod toward His Majesty, "I give all the glory to God. I am truly humbled by the way He has caused our paths to cross, and the fact that I'm with all of you tonight is truly a miracle. When Addison first asked me to stand up at his wedding tomorrow, I was deeply honored. But then, when he asked me to serve as his best man, I was pretty speechless. At first, I wasn't sure if it was because of the special connection I have with his sister, or if Addison actually wanted me in his wedding. 'Cause, you know, this girl has been known to pull a few strings when she wants things to happen her way."

Steve laughed loudly. He could attest to that!

"Seriously, guys, you should've seen this girl the past few weeks, rushing around and attempting to whip everyone into shape, getting all the details set for Vanessa and Addison's big day."

Bridget crinkled her nose and tossed Vanessa a look of exasperation, hoping Liam wouldn't tell any embarrassing stories about her. It sounded as if he was getting sidetracked. He was supposed to be talking about his friendship with Addison, not spilling about Bridget's personality flaws!

"Liam, stay focused." Bridget corrected him with a gentle touch on the arm.

"No, no get this!" Liam's hands flung around as he talked, matching the animated expression on his face. "I've never seen a woman so passionate about picking out shoes before. Vanessa, you truly chose the right lady for this job. She had six different styles to choose from for the bridesmaids' footwear, but to Bridget, it wasn't just shoes. Oh no! To Bridget, it was like the most important decision of her life!"

"Liam," Bridget laughed and shook her head, "I wasn't *that* bad."

"Really?" He echoed, "You think two hours comparing shoes isn't that bad?" He chuckled then looked back toward the small audience, "This was us, trying on shoes. Here," Liam grabbed Bridget's hand and pulled her into the gazebo. "We'll act it out."

"Nooooo!" Bridget laughed. Her cheeks were turning pink. But she didn't resist him. She would follow Liam anywhere.

"It was so bad, she made me stand there and give my opinion on each style." Liam grinned, "Bridge, act like you're trying on shoes, and I'll show them what my face looked like."

Bridget's family members laughed.

"Liam!" she scolded, wondering why in the world he was acting like such a goofball.

"Fine, *I'll* act it out." Liam gently touched her on the shoulders, "You be me. Stand there, yeah, there you go, look completely uninterested."

Bridget giggled.

Liam acted like he pulled a pair of shoes out from thin air and made an excited face.

"Oh wait, you need a real shoebox!" Vanessa jumped out of her chair and ran a shoebox to the front.

Bridget laughed even harder as Liam accepted the odd prop. "What in the world, you guys?!"

"Yes, props!" Liam grinned.

Bridget shook her head, but she couldn't stop laughing. Liam leaned over, performing the charade of trying on the shoe. And then, as he leaned on one knee, he looked up toward Bridget and stared at her for several seconds. He slowly reached for her hands. Bridget blinked, fighting back confusion. Was this part of the charade?

"Bridget." He removed a small, dazzling diamond ring from within the shoe box. Bridget gasped. His kind and gentle eyes penetrated hers as he spoke from the bottom of his heart the sweetest, simplest, yet most sincere words Bridget's ears ever had the privilege of hearing.

"I love you. Will you marry me?"

Bridget's heart nearly ruptured with joy. She squealed with delight as she desired to fling herself into his arms. "Yes," she whispered, scarcely believing the moment was real. Her voice grew in volume and excitement, "Yes, yes, YES!"

Liam rose to his feet and embraced Bridget as she launched into his hug. Her feet flew into the air as she clung to him with all her might. She inhaled deeply, wishing to memorize his scent and never, ever let go. Bridget's family members cheered wildly in the background.

It took a moment for Bridget to realize anyone else was present. As their hug ended, Liam's eyes soared with confidence and joy. It was official. He had asked to take the next step in their relationship! They were engaged!

"Now Liam's gonna be in our family next?!" Millie called out above the noise, "Goodness, we're going wedding *crazy* around here!"

Everyone laughed. Bridget couldn't stop smiling. Vanessa stood up to hug her, and Bridget squealed again.

"You little sneak!" Bridget scolded her. "You were in on this?!"

"I just found out a few hours ago, I promise!" Vanessa threw her hands up in innocence. Then she added with a giggle, "But this guy has known for weeks." She poked Addison playfully in the stomach.

"Addi!" Bridget gasped.

Addison drew her into a hug, "Congratulations, sis. You deserve a man like Liam. He truly is the best you could find."

"I just can't believe this is real!" Bridget brought a shocked hand up to her face. "This is seriously the last night I ever would've expected something like this!"

"Speaking of real, where's your ring?" Vanessa asked eagerly.

Liam and Bridget exchanged glances. They both burst out laughing in the same instant.

"Oh right!" Liam grinned, "The ring." He dug back into his pocket, "I knew I forgot something!"

"Ptshhh, who needs a ring." Bridget laughed, "I was way too distracted by your sparkly eyes."

"I know this is just a diamond," Liam's smile was steady as he reached for Bridget's hand once more, "and its value is nothing compared to the value of the golden heart of the woman I'm giving it to. But it's my prayer that this precious stone reminds you exactly what you are to God, and to me." Liam slowly slipped the ring onto her finger. "Priceless."

As the party gently dwindled to a close, Stacie directed the putting away of tables and chairs. Grandma kissed her grandchildren goodnight and reiterated her excitement for the big day. Everyone hugged Vanessa once more before parting ways, and Liam and Bridget finally unglued their magnetic hands.

Hope lingered near the gazebo as David and the *Kennetic Energy* crew tore down their makeshift stage. She secretly hoped David would speak with her once more. But he appeared quite busy, rolling up skinny black cords and placing his guitar safely in its velvet case.

Laney approached and chatted with Hope for a few moments, then Justin and Zac offered hellos. Just when Hope was about ready to leave, David finally approached her with a small grin.

"Excited for tomorrow?" David's question was simple, but something about the way he asked ignited Hope's joy.

"Of course!" Hope grinned in return, "Vanessa is a gem. We couldn't have asked for a more perfect addition to our family. What about you? Are you nervous?"

"Not really." David shrugged, "I mean, don't get me wrong, playing here is like the highlight of my entire career! But I'm not nearly as in my head and anxious as I used to be. After playing hundreds of shows, I don't know, performing just kind of gets into your blood. You go on auto-pilot and performing is just like second nature."

"That makes sense." Hope nodded. Her heart felt refreshed in the wake of his words. It was as if the fresh smell of a sweet rainfall tumbled over her soul. Somewhere inside, she had been secretly aching for a conversation like this with David for months. Even though their small-talk wasn't anything overly thought provoking or interesting, the simple sound of his voice had a soothing effect on her heart. "Your tour schedule has been all over the place. Where's your favorite place you've played so far?"

"Wow, that's a tough question." David scratched a non-existent bug bite on the back of his neck, "Europe is amazing, but so is South America. Our fans back in the US are the most over-the-top though, so those shows are always fun. Playing in my hometown, Cross Creek, is always pretty crazy, too. But honestly…" he hesitated, "I think I'd have to say here."

Hope searched for words. The busy sound of tables and chairs folding, and heavy speaker systems rolling past them, served as a reminder that their time was nearly up. Hope knew it wouldn't be appropriate to linger much longer, but she sensed that neither of them wanted to leave.

"Hope." David suddenly found the courage to say what he'd been attempting to suppress. All at once, he couldn't wait another moment. He couldn't let the day pass without attempting to aptly express how he felt. He finally decided. He would do it. He would speak up and rise to the challenge at the batting plate. Perhaps this would be his third strike. Perhaps Hope would completely reject him, and whatever he dreamed they might be, would be over forever. Perhaps this would completely destroy all his chances and soil his reputation among the Royal Family. But he had to know. Had things changed? Was she finally ready to give him a chance? "I, um…" he stuffed hands into his pockets and glanced at the ground. He thought of Liam and his fearless proposal to one of the Princesses just moments ago. David inhaled deeply, praying for courage, and looked back up at Hope, "This 'just friends' thing isn't working for me."

Hope's eyes grew wide. Her heart tumbled within her, as did her stomach. Oh no. The words she had secretly longed to hear from him were finally out. A moment she'd imagined playing out dozens of times in her mind, was finally happening. But unlike the dialogue in her daydreams, Hope found her mind fearfully empty. What should her response be? What could she possibly say? What *should* she say, now?

"David!" Laney's voice traveled through the dusky air, "Come on, we're hauling all this junk back to the bus! We need your muscles, boy!"

David desperately glanced over his shoulder, then looked back at Hope. Confusion and fear dominated his eyes. Was Hope going to say something? Was she just going to leave him hanging like this? Had he

[382]

gone too far and completely stepped over the line? Just when he thought things were looking up, had he foolishly made things awkward for them, all over again?

Hope was just as panicked internally. Her heart pounded, but she couldn't get her mouth to work.

David hesitated, then turned, disheartened by her silence. His mind raced as he took careful footsteps toward Laney and the group. *What in the world just happened?!* David struggled to recalibrate after the disaster. *Why didn't she say something? What was she thinking? Aw man, I blew it.*

As David left to help the band with their equipment, Hope's heart fell with a devastating crash. All at once, she wanted to smack herself in the face. What was wrong with her?! Why hadn't she spoken up?! Why hadn't she told him how she truly felt?!

Hope quickly turned on her heel, anxious to abandon the scene as quickly as possible. Could she be any more embarrassing? Why hadn't her mouth worked properly? Why did she hesitate to encourage him in the possibility, unlock her heart, and reveal her thoughts?

She quickly entered the Greenhouse Room, her mind reeling. *Hope, what is wrong with you?! Now tomorrow is going to be even MORE awkward, thanks to you! Lord, what is going on here?* She quickly directed her thoughts toward Heaven, *Why does it seem like every interaction David and I have is so fragile? It's like we're walking on delicate egg shells. We're immensely interested in one another, yet too shy and confused to actually take a step forward. Why do I keep pushing him away? He's an absolute sweetheart, and he clearly cares for me. So why can't I just embrace him with open arms?*

"Hope."

Hope's feet stopped. She slowly twirled around, half expecting to see David standing behind her.

But he wasn't there. Her shoulders rose, then fell, as she inhaled and exhaled slowly.

Was she was just hearing things?

"Psst. Over here!"

Hope turned to the left. All she saw was a grouping of tall, leafy-green indoor plants. She squinted. The squint turned into a full-blown blink, then popped open, as her eyes did a double-take.

Someone was hiding behind the overgrown shrubs.

All at once, the mysterious figure stepped out.

Hope gasped. "Luke!"

"That proposal was the most adorable thing ever!" Laney proclaimed as *Kennetic Energy* rolled their oversized speakers down the tiki-lit path, toward the parking area where their tour bus rested. "And I can't believe we were actually here to witness it!"

"I don't get what the big fuss over proposals is." Zac revealed his thoughts on the matter, "It's like, some dudes go totally over-the-top, hiring a sky-rider, or jumping out of a monstrous, seven-tiered cake. I'm just like, whenever it's time for me to propose, I'm just gonna rent a dolphin costume. I mean, what girl doesn't love dolphins?"

"Reason number 310 why you're *never* going to get married." Laney shook her head, the gesture declaring how ashamed she was to be associated with such a character.

"Or have a girlfriend," Justin added jokingly.

David stopped. "Um, I'll catch up with you guys in a second."

And with that, he turned on his heel and bolted back toward The Palace.

"Whoa, what's his problem?" Zac asked.

"Dang, I haven't seen him run that fast in a long time!" Justin observed. "What's the motivation?"

"I *think* maybe he's going to catch a Princess." Laney grinned knowingly.

David's feet pounded forward, stampeding down the sidewalk like an unstoppable herd of wild elephants, mid-stampede. David's heart was determined. He wasn't going to lose her this time. He wasn't going to let stuttering lips and quiet misunderstandings cause any further distance between them. He would make himself heard, yet once again, loud and clear. And this time, he would get an answer. He wouldn't leave Tarsurella until he knew exactly how Hope felt.

David knew this would be a monumental moment in his life. He could almost hear electric guitars churning in the background of his mind; an intense and encouraging tune, cheering him on, pressing him to seize the day and conquer Hope's heart. He had invested far too much of himself into the young woman to give up on her this easily.

His chest pounded, and his lungs burned. He reached the Greenhouse Room doors within seconds. He flew inside as the automatic doors parted, desperate to catch her before she disappeared upstairs.

Suddenly, his shoes screeched to a halt. David's heart fell to the floor. There, standing beside Hope, was another young man. David's face turned beet-red. In that moment, he knew. The beautiful Princess was completely captivated, and entirely engaged with the words coming from this other guy. David struggled to breathe properly. Before the scene could turn any worse, David quickly turned and escaped out the back doors.

Chapter Thirty One

Another Day, Another Story

"Dad, have there been any, uh . . . calls for me?" Chasity asked her father.

Steve had just plopped onto the Family Room's sofa. As tired as he was, he always had time for conversation with his children.

"Calls? What kind of calls?"

"Oh, I don't know." Chasity quickly swept her hand through the air, hoping to dismiss the subject. She knew it was foolish to ask, but a part of her had hoped, wondering if Hanson might actually act upon the lofty, yet pathetically-frail words he had spoken. Chasity should've known he wasn't going to ask her father to court her. He wouldn't show up at the wedding tomorrow. He had only spoken those things from a guilty conscience, to make her think there was still a chance of something happening between them. But there wasn't. She quickly shook her head. "Never mind."

Chasity turned to leave, but her father's words stopped her.

"Are you referring to a particular young man whom you spent a great deal of time with in England?"

Chasity's hopeful eyes met her dad's.

"James just contacted me this morning, actually." Steve's eyes wore a smile. He patted on the sofa beside him, inviting Chasity to come and sit. "I've been meaning to talk to you about this. But, with all the busyness of wedding preparations and the whirlwind of the day, it nearly slipped my mind!"

Chasity slowly lowered beside him. James was *not* the young man she was hoping he'd hear from.

"Millie is right," Steve sighed. "Things are shifting and changing far too quickly around here. First Addison, now Bridget, and who knows? Lord willing, you might be next!"

Chasity gulped. "What did James ask you about?"

"Well," Steve placed an arm around his daughter's neck, "he very fervently expressed to me how much he admires and appreciates your Christian character, your faithful and loving heart, and the various qualities he has seen expressed through you over the years. He apologized for not checking with me first, stating that he blurted about his feelings while you were at their estate. But he asked my blessing for the beginning of an official courtship."

"And what did you tell him?" Chasity couldn't stop fidgeting with her hands as anxiety rose from within.

[388]

"I told him I greatly admire him and his family. They've been fantastic friends for a great many years, and I am quite pleased with the young man he is becoming. But I also told him I had never heard you speak of him in any manner other than friendship. Chasity, I'll admit that I feel a little hurt here. I had no idea you and James were interested in one another. I mean, I know things have been busy, but I've always made it my top priority to stay in touch with each of my children's hearts. Is there a reason you haven't told me about this blossoming affection for James?"

"But Dad, I'm *not* interested in him!" Chasity's voice grew louder than she intended, "He sprung this courtship idea on me from absolutely out of nowhere!" She bit her lip and tried to steady her voice, "I've never given him any reason to think that I'm interested in anything more than just friendship."

"Oh." Steve was quiet for a moment, then nodded. Chasity wasn't sure, but she thought she sensed a trickle of relief in her father's voice, "Well have you told James that? Because he sure sounded quite committed to the idea of pursuing an official relationship with you."

"Yes. No. I mean, sort of? He wants me to think about it. We agreed that I would give him an official answer at the wedding."

"And are you confident as to what your answer will be?"

"Dad, I'm so confused." Chasity could feel tears surfacing. She wasn't sure if they came because of the deep loss she felt over Hanson, or the guilt she felt over the fact that she had allowed herself to become entirely caught up with him. "I've been trying to seek God, I really have. But He doesn't seem to be giving me a direct answer. It's like my head is telling me one thing, and my heart is telling me another. But I don't know which path I should follow."

[389]

"These kinds of decisions can be challenging, indeed." Steve sighed, placing a gentle hand on Chasity's shoulder. "Relationships can be terribly messy things. There are so many factors to be considered. What is it about James that you feel is confusing?"

"He's perfect." Chasity spoke quietly, "He's kind to everyone, an absolute gentleman, and he embodies everything that an admirable and trustworthy Christian man should be. He's been a great and caring friend. I would never want to hurt him. So, in theory it would be foolish to turn him away. But I don't think I can do this. He might be perfect, but he's not perfect for *me*." Chasity took a deep breath, ready to reveal what she should have told her father long ago. "Dad," she started slowly, "I think I'm in love with someone else."

Jane, Charlie, and Aunt Cassidy stepped off the plane. Jane smiled and gazed upward, as if she shared a secret with the starry sky. She was back in London again! The feeling was quite surreal. After her last, abrupt goodbye with her favorite city in the world, she never could've imagined returning so soon.

The threesome rolled their luggage bags forward, then attempted to catch a taxi in the dark. Their flight landed them in London at 11:00 p.m. They had a meeting with Miss Laurie; and Harvey Dunvuker, the head of the publishing house, early tomorrow morning. Jane was already nervous about the meeting, but she wasn't about to let that steal her enjoyment of this trip.

"Can you believe we're really here?" Aunt Cassidy spoke in wonderment as they piled into the backseat of a cab, "London, England! My, my, we are becoming quite the world travelers!"

"Jane seems to have a fond attachment to Europe," Charlie observed. "Have you considered moving here someday? Might save you a bit on airfare."

"Thank you two for coming with me." Jane smiled, "I know this trip was a bit abrupt and unplanned—"

"Oh nonsense, Jane!" Aunt Cassidy gave her arm a quick squeeze, "We're happy to support you in all your endeavors! It's not every day a girl your age gets offered a publishing contract! Your father would be so proud of you."

Jane leaned her neck on the seat rest. Oh, she would give anything for her dad to be here right now! Or to simply know where he was, for that matter. Jane sighed and attempted to keep her thoughts in order. The devastating reality was that he was nowhere to be found. As terribly upsetting as that truth was to grasp, Jane was slowly starting to come to terms with it. She couldn't change the fact that her father was missing. As wrong as it was, it appeared as though God was going to make her wait awhile before making things right again. As the pain racked her chest, a quick temptation surfaced; the thought of slipping into a fantasy world and abandoning her present reality. In the past, Jane would've caved all too quickly. The pain was too much. But this time, Jane resisted. Even though many elements about her current lot in life weren't very pleasant, some things still were. And those were the blessings she would choose to focus on. She was in London with Charlie and Aunt Cassidy! She couldn't let her father's absence steal that joy from her heart.

Just then, Aunt Cassidy's phone rang. She dug around in her crowded, pink-and-white polka-dot purse before finding it. She squinted her nose as she read the foreign number, but she answered it anyway. "Hello? Oh! Yes!" She quickly handed Jane the phone, "It's for you. It's from Tarsurella!"

[391]

The puzzled expression in Jane's eyes told Aunt Cassidy she wasn't expecting a call.

Jane slowly accepted the phone. "Hello?" she squeaked out in a timid voice.

"Hey." Jane instantly recognized the voice, "This is Asher."

Jane's eyes smiled. "Hi."

"Listen, I know it's kind of late, but I couldn't wait any longer to update you. I spoke to Addison."

And?! The pause in Asher's speech was just long enough for Jane's mind to race with possibilities. *What did he say?! Did they fi—*

"He doesn't believe me."

Jane readjusted the cell phone beside her ear. "Doesn't believe you about what, exactly? The AA16 Code?"

Charlie's ears perked up. His gaze shot toward Jane.

"The code, the missing scientists, the fact that they might all be connected somehow… everything!" Asher spoke quickly, "He said he's got too much on his plate, and he doesn't want to go digging around, making a mountain out of a mole hill."

"Isn't the King getting married tomorrow?" Jane asked slowly, finding it odd that the busy Prince would call her the night before such a huge occasion. "It's no surprise that he has a lot on his mind."

Asher knew Jane had a point. Addison couldn't very well postpone his wedding and cancel his honeymoon, just to listen to a conspiracy theory coming from his kid brother. But Asher almost wished he would. "I'm sorry." Asher's voice was thick with regret and apology, "I wanted to do more. But the answer I keep getting from Addison, as well as everyone else involved with this case, is that their hands are tied and there's nothing we can do but wait. I would gladly do anything I can to help, but after I leave for military school, time is gonna be up for me as well." Asher sighed, "This isn't fair to you, Jane. I wish things could be different."

"Don't. Don't wish, I mean. I used to feel the same way. Always wishing my dad would show up, wishing my life would change, wishing for a miracle to happen. But I got so caught up in all my wishes that I failed to appreciate the gift of what was happening right in front of my face. I think this moment is called the *present*, for a reason. As much as I miss Dad, and want to see him as soon as possible, I'm determined to make a real effort to embrace every moment that comes my way, and to appreciate it for the gift that it is. As much as my mind wants to wonder into tomorrow and daydream about what might happen, tomorrow will be here soon enough. Everything is going to be okay. Somehow, this wild mess will work itself out. I don't know how, but it will. And until it does, we're just going to have to be okay with waiting."

Asher was impressed by her wisdom. As much as he didn't want to believe her, as much as he wanted to provide an immediate answer and save the day, Asher knew this wasn't his time. He had to wait, just like Jane. They must wait for another day. For another story. "Well, that sounded incredibly smart and mature." Asher smiled. The smile was quickly replaced with a frown, hating that he had to resign to the fact that her words were true. "But as much as I hate to admit it, you're right. Waiting is all we can do."

"Maybe not *all* we can do," Jane added as she glanced at Charlie. "We can get ready, preparing ourselves for whatever may come next. Charlie and I can continue doing research on our end, discovering whatever clues we may find, and you can keep your eyes and ears peeled for things on your end as well. Just because we're trying to be patient and attempting to embrace the moment, doesn't mean we can't prepare for what we hope will happen someday."

"The answers are gonna come." Asher spoke confidently, "We *will* find your dad, Jane Akerly. I promise."

"Thank you. But only God can make promises like that. He knows where my dad is, and if it's in His will for us to find him someday, then we will. Otherwise…" Jane bit her lip, not even wanting to speak the alternative. "I'll have peace and be content anyway."

"I, uh, I'm not going to have phone service and stuff at school." Asher spoke awkwardly, not quite sure how to finish their conversation.

"I understand." Jane gulped. She knew what Asher was saying. This might be the last conversation they would have for quite some time. "Take care of yourself at school, okay? I'm sure the skills you'll learn there are going to enable you to assist many people throughout your life. You have a kind and caring heart, Asher. Don't let anyone or anything ever take that away from you, or make you bitter, okay?"

Asher's throat tightened. "Yeah. You too, Jane. Tell Charlie I said hey. So, uh, until next time?"

Jane sensed that he didn't want to say goodbye. "Of course!" Jane attempted to keep her voice chipper, "Thank you, again." She blinked back a stray tear, "For everything."

Asher attempted to keep his voice steady as he bid her a farewell. "Bye."

Hanson laid wide awake in his bed. He kicked the sheets off his hot and sticky legs, oppressed by the thick humidity in the air.

He could hear his mother's gentle breathing across the room. Hanson wished to sleep, but his mind simply wouldn't settle down. Tomorrow was the wedding. The day he had promised Chasity that he would show up and ask her to enter an official courtship.

Hanson couldn't help but feel like he was going insane. There were so many reasons why this was a terrible idea. So many reasons why Chasity wouldn't say yes. But how could he blame her?! Hanson was a selfish, lowlife, heartless worm with no self-control, and he knew it. Chasity deserved far, far better than him.

Hanson's conscience ate at the edges of his heart like a slow, acidic cancer. He knew he had betrayed Chasity's trust. Kissing Lilly was despicably low. It was an impulse decision made in a split second of thoughtlessness. He hadn't seen it coming. One moment he was in complete control of the situation, cool-headed and collected. And the next, it all vanished. He allowed his hormones to man the driver's seat. How could he have done such a thing? What possessed him to do it? Why had he allowed himself to be drawn into Lilly's emotional distress and alluring charm? Sure, Lilly was beautiful. He cared about her. He wanted her to be safe. But he had no intentions of pursuing a relationship. Regret gnawed at his gut.

See, this is just like what I warned her about on the beach in Greece! Hanson's head continued to pound, *I said that if she got too close, I would only end up hurting her. And I was right.* Hanson flopped over in bed, battling the torment in his mind. *But then again, it runs in my blood. Fletcher men have a family tradition of hurting those they love the most.*

Hanson rose to a seated position. He couldn't do it. He couldn't ask Chasity to start dating him. Hanson would only prove to be a disappointment. The complicated elements of his shadowy past and tricky life would only damage her deeper. Hanson was no good for Chasity, and he knew it. And somehow, Hanson sensed that Chasity knew that as well. Yet despite all the warning signs, Chasity continued to give him the time of day. The spark between them was undeniable, and somehow Chasity was willing to risk much in order to explore the possibility of what could happen between them.

Hanson almost smiled at the thought of it. Chasity was such a free spirit, always aching for more, and believing for the impossible. How many Princesses took up thoroughbred racing? How many Princesses believed that their wild, untamed and completely untrained horse could come from behind and win it all? For a split second, Hanson almost wished that Chasity wasn't a Princess. She didn't belong in this stuffy, strict, regimented society. She shouldn't be hanging around people like James O'Conner and attending stupid cocktail parties with people who don't appreciate her spunk and spirit. Hanson couldn't bear to think of James, the smug British chap, sweeping Chasity away. He knew that James didn't truly love her. The freakishly polite man was only concerned with keeping up appearances. Thanks to the uppity society he was raised in, finding and marrying someone for the purpose of 'good breeding' was just as ingrained as pairing up the perfect racehorses with flawless pedigree, with the shallow goal of selling their foals for hundreds of thousands of pounds. Hanson knew Chasity was a wild mustang. She didn't belong with a thoroughbred like James. In order for Chasity to be happy, she needed to be free. Being locked up in a paddock of high-class society would break her spirit. Perhaps that's why Chasity was drawn to Hanson. Perhaps Chasity knew that life with Hanson would be adventurous, unpredictable, and without limits.

Chasity needed liberty. She needed room to breathe, and someone who loved her enough to give her that much. Someone who wouldn't try to control or manipulate her, but would simply step back and enjoy the wonderful woman she was. Hanson's heartbeat intensified. James shouldn't have her. He couldn't have her. *There's no way I'm letting that happen.*

Hanson was determined. He would fulfill his promise to Chasity. He would show up, tomorrow morning, and knock on the retired King's door. He would ask for his blessing. And if, by some wonderful miracle from the Heavens above, the King said yes, Hanson would approach Chasity.

He would ask for a second chance.

Chapter Thirty Two

Wedding Bells

Vanessa Bennett did her best to steady the shaking curling iron. Her jittery little nerves caused her hand to tremble.

"Oh no, you are *not* going to curl your own hair on the morning of your wedding day!" Bridget dove into action, removing the hot iron hovering near Vanessa's cheek. "That's what we're here for." She smiled warmly. "Besides," she added with a giggle, "we wouldn't want you to burn yourself."

Vanessa sighed and regretfully gave up control. There was no use in arguing with Bridget. Bridget was determined to see to it that Vanessa had absolutely *no* responsibilities today, other than enjoying the unfolding moments.

Vanessa placed an anxious hand on her stomach. She hadn't changed into her wedding gown yet. There were still a good three hours in which they would have to wait. Until then, Vanessa needed to keep her nerves at bay. She felt as though her emotions were in the driver's seat, calling the shots, and Vanessa was merely along for the ride. Her silly emotions couldn't seem to make up their mind, either. One moment they were gleefully excited, desiring to giggle and twirl and spin around like a goofy little schoolgirl, entirely elated to be marrying her best friend! The next, her stomach clenched and turned into cement, thinking of all the thousands upon *thousands* of people who would be watching their ceremony. Strangers from across the planet would be critiquing every detail, turning up their noses and squawking like dimwitted seagulls at any mistake Vanessa made. What if she tripped down the aisle? What if she was so choked up that she couldn't even speak when it was time to say her vows? What if she and Addison totally goofed up their first kiss? Her face flushed warm as she thought of it. She couldn't wait to kiss her husband.

Husband, Vanessa thought as a goofy smile ate up her face. *Today, Addison is going to be my husband. And I'm going to be his wife!*

Vanessa shook her head, unable to contain the joy she felt. Despite all the nerves, jitters, and subtle worries, the chief emotion she felt was joy. Soul-bursting, heart-illuminating, firework-exploding kind of joy. Today marked the first day of the rest of her life, spent adventuring with Addison.

"Hold still!" Bridget warned her, as she carefully turned the curling iron toward Vanessa's rosy cheeks. "I know you're over the moon, but can you stay down on planet earth for just a few seconds longer? I don't want to burn you!"

"Sorry." Vanessa giggled. She looked at Bridget's reflection in the vanity mirror and spotted her dazzling diamond ring. "How are *you* so calm? The morning after Addison proposed to me, I was like a hot air balloon! I was so scatterbrained and loony, everyone in the office thought I had gone mental."

"Oh, I remember." Bridget laughed. "And trust me, I'm completely freaking out inside. Every time I look at this diamond, I don't even feel like it's real! But today isn't about me. It's about you, and Addison, and making sure the two of you have the most perfect day *ever*. But tomorrow? I'll totally go back to fangirling over Liam."

"Vanessa, Vanessa!" Millie burst onto the scene, plowing through the Dressing Room doors. Little arms flung around Vanessa's waist. Her adorable, shoulder length hair was curled in tight ringlets. She was still in her pajamas. But the spunky flower girl had plenty of time to change before the ceremony. "I've got a special delivery for you!"

"Oh yeah?" Vanessa smiled, wondering what the little girl could have in store.

"It's a secret message from Addison!" Millie pulled out a letter she had been hiding behind her back, "He's not allowed to see you before the ceremony, but he asked me to sneak this in anyway." She offered Vanessa a playful wink. "I think it's a love note."

"Either that, or he's simply reminding me not to trip when I walk down the aisle," Vanessa teased.

"Oh, don't worry, you won't trip!" Millie reassured her. "Weddings are all about true love. And since you and Addison already have that, you've got nothing to worry about."

"The smart little cookie is right, you know." Bridget added, "Being nervous is only going to steal your enjoyment of the moment. Try not to

[401]

get wrapped up in all the extra stuff. Stay focused on the most important thing. You and Addison making your vows before God, promising to love and cherish one another for the rest of your lives." Bridget sighed gleefully, "You're going to look back on this day and cherish it forever."

"Yeah!" Millie added cheerfully. "And the guys are *way* more nervous than we are, anyway! They're all fumbling around, trying to figure out how to put on their ties." Millie giggled, "Willie looks like such a little man! I've never seen him so dapper-looking! He makes a great ring bearer."

"Aw, I can't wait to see him!" Vanessa grinned, "I'll bet he's adorable. With those suspenders and that fedora hat, he's probably going to steal the show."

"Donuts!" Hope burst through the door, followed by several maids rolling in carts of goodies. "Praise the Lord, I've got donuts!"

"Yay!" Millie tore across the room, eager to dig into the treat.

"There." Bridget added the final curl and admired her masterpiece. "Vanessa, you look gorgeous. As always." She unplugged the curling iron. "Now if you'll excuse me, I'll leave you alone with your letter." She winked.

Vanessa smiled and clutched the letter to her chest. She was going to start crying. She just knew it.

Bridget watched as Vanessa carefully popped open the seal, then Bridget turned to head toward the donut trays. She didn't want to invade Addison and Vanessa's special, intimate moment. Even though they weren't in the room together, Bridget knew Addison must've done his best to express the fullness of his love through a pre-wedding letter. The reading of it would be emotional, words spoken in a secret language for no one to know but him and Vanessa.

"Good idea, Hope." Bridget reached for a vanilla-flavored, sugary, glazed treat. "I hadn't even thought of what we were gonna do for breakfast. My main concern was keeping everyone on schedule. But it looks like we've got plenty of time. I don't want to jinx anything, but everything's running really smoothly so far."

"Actually, it wasn't my idea." Hope licked the icing off her chocolate eclair, "It was Clark's. When I dropped by the kitchen this morning, he said he wanted to do a little something extra to help out."

"What were you doing in the kitchen?" Bridget asked carefully, "Looking for... someone?"

Hope bit her lip. She wasn't sure how to respond. "Luke's gone, if that's what you mean," she snapped. Bridget's looming suspicion about her being somehow emotionally attached to Luke was really starting to grate on her. "But yes," she attempted to soften her tone, "I was looking for someone. Clark."

Hope reached for a second donut, cherry flavored this time. She knew her words toward Bridget had been sharp, but she didn't think her sister should be the first to know the whole story. It would only add more fuel to her growing flames of a conspiracy theory against Luke. The truth was, Hope wanted to speak with Clark about his son's abrupt exit from Tarsurella.

Last night, when Luke had showed up in the Greenhouse, Hope was utterly shocked. She fired an endless string of questions, but his explanations were vague. "I had to see you before I left the country," he had told her, his eyes intense with the usual passion and fire. "My parents don't know where I'm going. But someone needs to know. Hope, you have to promise me you won't tell them. I don't want them storming after me, dragging me back home."

"Luke, this is crazy! You can't just disappear off the map! Your parents will be worried sick about you! Me not telling them? I can't make that promise."

"Whatever. My mistake for thinking I could trust you." Luke turned to leave, and Hope grabbed his wrist.

"Stop!" She scolded, "Quit acting like a moody two-year-old! You came all the way back here to tell me something, which indicates that you thought it was important. Now I *know* that you're doing what you believe is right, but your immature, boyish behavior has you doing it all wrong! I know God has chosen and destined you for great things, and I want to believe that what God is doing in your life is true and genuine. But the way you storm around, disrespecting your parents, treating people badly, and shooting off whatever fiery thing pops into your head, isn't going to get you anything in life, except more trouble. Now *what* did you come back here to tell me?"

"There's a group of guys who have been secretly meeting and rallying for several months now," Luke revealed. The rainstorm of information came faster than Hope could process. "I've spoken with their leaders, trying to convince them that violence isn't the answer. Now I'm all for peaceful protests, but some things are starting to get out of hand. Even though I agree that your brother shouldn't be ruling, I don't think it's our place to forcefully remove the power from his hands. But not everyone in the rebellion agrees with me, and they're starting to follow the doctrine of other, more violently-inclined leaders. Hope, I've tried to keep talk of war at bay, stating that it is *not* the right way to go about things. But there's a sect of rebellion leaders who have people believing that it is. My buddies and I don't want to get caught up in this mess. So, we're leaving. I had to tell you, so that in my absence and silence, you don't think I'm somehow responsible for this."

"War?" Hope echoed, feeling frightened by his words. "You don't think they're planning some kind of," she gulped nervously, "attack, do you?"

"At this point, there's no way to know for sure. It might just all be talk. But me and the guys aren't going to take that risk. We don't want to end up in prison, being framed for something we had no association with. Hope, you can't tell anyone where we are. We're going to Bella Adar."

"How long will you be gone?" she asked with wide, concerned eyes.

"I don't know." Luke shrugged, "But just let my parents know that I'm okay, alright? I *don't* want them coming after me. But I can't have them thinking I'm guilty for crimes I didn't commit, either."

"But what if you are?" she asked quietly. "What if someone does attack, because of your words? Aren't you the one who started all this madness in the first place?"

"Hope, I've got to go." Luke anxiously looked around as voices stirred from the far end of the Greenhouse.

"But Lu—" Hope wasn't finished. Their conversation couldn't be over. Yet it was. As Deborah and several other Palace staff approached, Luke vanished out of the scene. Hope's heart sank as her mind raced. Was Luke telling the truth? Was he really as innocent as he wanted Hope to believe? Or was he simply running away in order to not be connected with a possible looming disaster?

Hope's heart felt stale as she bit into her doughnut. She hated the fact that such heavy thoughts vexed her on such a beautiful day. She was at a compete loss. Should she tell her dad? Was it her responsibility to warn Addison that there may be an attack secretly looming in the near future? The anxiety gnawed within her gut. If Hope shared what she knew, more questions would be asked, and she would have to share everything Luke told her. Clearly, he wanted his hideaway destination to be a secret. He

[405]

had trusted her with such lofty information. Surely, she couldn't just turn on him. Telling Addison what was going on would only give him all the more reason to distrust and dislike Luke.

Chasity plopped down beside Hope in the window seat. Hope studied her sister's tired eyes.

"Long night?" Hope asked.

"Yeah, I guess I didn't sleep too much," Chasity admitted quietly.

"Thinking about Hanson?"

"I know it's foolish," Chasity sighed. "But part of me almost hoped that he meant what he said. That he would show up today and ask Dad permission to court me." Chasity laughed bitterly and shook her head, "But I don't see that happening now."

"Hey, you never know." Hope gently touched her sister's hand, trying her best to encourage her. "The day isn't over yet."

"I just wish I didn't feel this way about him, you know?" Chasity admitted, "Things were *so* much easier before he came along. All I cared about was reading and horseback riding! If only I could go back to the good old days."

"Yeah, life is a lot less complicated without guys, that's for sure." Hope laughed as she glanced at Millie. "That little girl is *truly* living the dream. A world that revolves around chocolate, stuffed animals, and imaginary adventures. I remember when that used to be us."

"Love sure is a strange thing." Chasity continued in a thoughtful tone, "I never quite imagined that it would be so painful. Then again, I suppose it all depends on what, or who, the object of your affection is. Everything worked out just wonderfully for Vanessa. Addison was her first date, her first boyfriend—her first everything. And their happily-ever-after makes love appear so sweet and kind. But I fear I may have made a terrible mistake." She sighed, "Hanson isn't husband material. And I've known that from the very beginning, yet I haven't allowed myself to fully let go. I guess I've made him an idol, of sorts; clinging to him, desperately hoping that things are going to change, when I know full well that they're not."

"I guess the one nice thing about love," Hope added, "is that it always seems to be handing out second chances. Bridget and Liam are a prime example of that. Remember how heartbroken Bridget was after Jacob? She was convinced she would never fall in love again. And look what God did? He healed her heart and then brought along somebody who was worthy of having it. He'll do the same for you too, Chas." Hope smiled, "I'm confident in that."

"Thanks, sis." Chasity smiled, "The human heart is amazingly resilient, that's for sure."

Hope nodded, "We put the little dears through so much, it's a wonder they hang in there so well!"

Chasity laughed, "I'm just thankful that we have events like this to celebrate. Joyful reminders of God's goodness, grace, and abundant blessings. I'm determined to enjoy the day and celebrate alongside Addison and Vanessa, no matter how yucky my heart is feeling."

"Amen!" Hope nodded in firm agreement, "I second that! We don't need to let our emotions rule us. We can rule our emotions. If we just hang in there and continue to believe for our happily-ever-after's, I know they'll come someday."

Hanson tied his red bow tie. He fidgeted with it nervously in front of the mirror.

"My, don't you look dapper this morning!" his mother commented. "What's the occasion?"

"I'm going to a wedding," he revealed nervously.

"The King's wedding?" his mother questioned. "Have they put you back on duty for extra security? I thought you still had more time off."

"No, it's not for work." Hanson wasn't sure how much he should tell her. He glanced lovingly at the woman still dressed in her forest-green bathrobe. The Royal Crest embroidered into The Palace robe reassured Hanson that she'd be safe while he was away. "I'll tell you more later, okay? If everything goes well . . ." He couldn't hide his smile. "Well, I may have some big news."

Hanson kissed his mom on the cheek then headed for the door. "Love you. Be back later."

"Stay safe, Tiger." She tousled his hair.

Hanson quickly tried to put his hair back into place.

His mother giggled. "No matter how old you get, some things never change."

Hanson smiled one last time, then opened the door. He left their temporary hotel room within The Palace and headed down the hall. He took a deep breath, mentally preparing himself for all to come.

Okay, you can do this. He exhaled, *Just be real. Be bold. Express your true feelings to her dad and...*

Hanson's hands were damp. His nerves pounded, and his mind attempted to race in the opposite direction, reminding him of all the reasons why the Royal Family would never approve of him. Even, if by some miracle in Heaven, the retired King allowed Hanson the honor, there was no way Chasity would give him a second chance.

Despite the mental conflict raging war, Hanson's feet continued on. He landed in the Main Hall, where a flurry of media men with large cameras and expensive-looking equipment stood in line at the Front Desk. Hanson assumed they were getting their credentials and preparing to cover the wedding. The entire Palace was buzzing with a conspicuous energy. The electric current of anticipation fueled Hanson's steps forward.

Suddenly, his phone buzzed within his pocket. He pulled it out, curious to see who the text would be from. His mouth went dry as he read the words.

"60 days. Time is up. We've got Lilly. Come to the Tarsurella U football field and we'll make a trade. If you bring help, you're both dead."

The blazing sun caused beads of sweat to break forth on Hanson's brow. He ran as quickly as his bulky dress shoes allowed. His heart pounded. The long-sleeved, midnight-black tuxedo now proved to be a foolish wardrobe choice. His armpits were damp, and Hanson felt as though he may lose several pounds from sweating beneath the heat. But he didn't have time to change. He ran onto the empty football field, expecting to find Lilly and the wicked men who held her captive.

But the field was empty.

His footsteps slowed, as well as his breathing. He placed tired hands on top of his head, attempting to catch his breath. He looked around cautiously, searching for signs of an ambush. He noticed movement from beneath the bleachers. He sucked in a fresh gulp of air and mustered up every ounce of courage he possessed. He had no idea what was waiting for him under there. But he was determined to end this, once and for all. Lilly needed to be free from these antagonizing death threats. And, so did Hanson. He needed to be liberated in order to move on with his life. There was no way he could pursue a relationship with Chasity if his shadowy past continued to follow him into the future.

Hanson neared the end of the bleachers. Sure enough, there were three men beneath the bleachers, all the way at the opposite end. Hanson squinted his eyes, trying to see if Lilly was there. He slowly closed the space between them.

"So, he decided to show up after all." The stranger broadcasted Hanson's arrival. This time, the man wasn't wearing a mask. Neither were his partners in crime. Hanson didn't recognize them, but their voices were vaguely familiar.

"Where is she?" Hanson demanded.

"Now hold your horses, Fletcher." The man who stood a head taller than all the rest, spoke in a commanding tone. "We've got the girl. And we were ready to take care of her this morning. But your dad asked us to give you one last chance. He wanted to play some kind of mercy card." The man chuckled, "I guess because you're his son or whatever. If you come with us, we'll let the girl go."

"Where *is* she?" Hanson took another bold step forward, his face nearing the man.

"You've got five seconds to decide, Fletcher. Either you get in the car, or I make one phone call, and she's dead."

Bridget gently grasped her bouquet. Beautiful piano music floated from the Royal Chapel. She could hear the excited buzz of delighted guests finding their seats and fanning themselves with the Royal Wedding Bulletins.

"How long until we go on!?" Millie asked excitedly. She could scarcely wait to perform her duties as flower girl and toss petals down the aisle. Willie tinkered with the ring box and Bridget quickly scolded him.

"Put that back in your pocket, bud! You don't want to lose that!"

Willie stuffed the box back and adjusted his hat.

"Your job is very important!" Millie told him. "We can't have a wedding without the rings!"

Bridget smiled at the pair. Millie looked like a miniature bride herself, carelessly twirling around in her puffy white dress. She wore a dainty flower crown upon her head and the most darling smile which completed her ensemble. "The two of you look like you're cute enough to stand on top of your own wedding cake," Bridget giggled.

"I'm happy that Addison is getting married, but I am *never* getting married," Millie broadcasted.

"Me neither!" Willie added, "Girls are yucky!"

"I'm sure you'll change your mind someday." Bridget winked. She turned to Hope, Chasity, and Jillian, who stood nearby. Each bridesmaid stood by in elegant chiffon dresses. Their slender gowns fell to the floor, and though they were identical, each sister wore a different hairstyle. Hope's long, straightened locks hung over her shoulders; Chasity wore a tight, high-bun; and Jillian sported lose curls.

Just then, Vanessa emerged from the Dressing Room, shining in her glorious gown. Everyone watched with proud, watery eyes. Mrs. Bennett dabbed her eyes with a hankie, and Bridget squealed excitedly.

"Oh Ness." She quickly adjusted Vanessa's long, flowing train, and stood back to soak in the beautiful sight. "There are no words. How do you feel?"

"Like I'm in the middle of a dream." Vanessa fought back happy tears of her own. "It's here. It's now. It's actually happening! I can't wait to see Addison."

Stacie clapped her hands together excitedly and ordered that the entire wedding party gather in a formal line to prepare for their entrance. "The ceremony begins in five minutes!"

Willie and Millie stood in the front; then Jillian, Hope, and Chasity lined up behind them. Bridget stood behind Chasity, and Vanessa behind her. Vanessa's father took her arm, and the two shared a happy side hug. Mr. Bennett was careful not to squash her beautiful dress, nor wrinkle her lacy train.

"My dear, Nessa." Mr. Bennett choked, "There are no words to express how happy I am for you."

"Dad, don't cry!" Vanessa giggled, "You're going to make me cry, too!"

"Sorry!" Mr. Bennett laughed, "I'm doing my best to keep myself put together! But I can't make any promises."

"Well, neither can I." Stacie handed Vanessa a hankie, and she carefully dabbed around her eye makeup. Vanessa sniffed. "Can we pray?"

"I was hoping you would ask." Mr. Bennett grabbed his daughter's hands and invited everyone around to join in. Bridget placed a gentle hand on Vanessa's shoulder.

"Dear Heavenly Father," Mr. Bennett spoke quietly, "we thank You for such a special, special day. We thank You for answering a prayer—a prayer that we've been praying ever since Vanessa was a little girl. For You to prepare the heart of a Godly young man to whom she would someday meet and marry. And God, we can hardly believe it is happening!" His voice cracked, "It's a happy day, yet bittersweet, as I let go of my little girl. But it is a day to celebrate. A day to celebrate love, and to celebrate the fact that this couple has chosen to place You in the center of everything. Bless this day, Lord. Calm Vanessa's nerves, and Addison's nerves, and help them to truly enjoy every second of this ceremony. Bless everyone as we celebrate with the happy couple. Smile upon their holy union, and may their marriage be richly blessed as they continue to seek You first. In Jesus's name, Amen."

"Amen!" Everyone joined in agreement.

Stacie grinned, "Okay, come on people, we've got a wedding to attend! Willie, you're first, just like we rehearsed. As soon as I open the door, you know what to do. Remember: slow, sweet, patient steps. Think like a gentleman!"

Willie nodded excitedly.

Bridget clenched her bouquet. She offered one last smile toward Vanessa, then set her eyes forward. She took a deep breath. The wedding was finally happening!

Graceful piano music mingled with the singing of strings and floated across the airwaves as soon as Stacie opened the Chapel Door. Willie stepped forward, and Millie waited patiently for her turn. Bridget could hear everyone inside the chapel *awww*-ing when Willie entered. He was such a little charmer.

"Your turn!" Stacie whispered to Millie, "You go, little Flower Princess!"

Millie stepped forward. Bridget couldn't stop grinning.

Next, it was the bridesmaids' turns. The girls each entered, one at a time. Lastly, it was time for Bridget to enter.

Bridget took a confident step forward, careful not to trip in her high heels. The ancient Royal Chapel, which was the same place where their ancestors worshiped, and their family met on Sundays for church, smelled strongly of sweet cedar. The high ceilings and towering wooden rafters gave the atmosphere a most holy feeling. Sunshine streamed in from stained glass windows. Every wooden, red-cushioned pew was filled. Glowing faces met Bridget as she took slow, careful steps down the red carpet. A glorious display of flowers flooded the alar. But Bridget's eyes were focused somewhere else.

At the very front of the Chapel, standing right next to Addison, was the love of *her* life, Liam Henderson. His eyes shone as he smiled at her, and Bridget couldn't help but wonder what it would feel like when it was her turn to walk down the aisle as the bride. She smiled at Addison, who held his breath in anticipation. In just a few short seconds, his bride would emerge.

Bridget quickly found her place at the front next to her sisters and took a deep, contented breath, smiling blissfully. She couldn't hide the giddy emotions she felt as their family and friends gathered together to celebrate such a momentous occasion.

Suddenly, the piano shifted keys. The orchestra followed, and everyone stood up from their pews with bated breath. They turned toward the Chapel doors and fought back delighted tears.

Vanessa floated onto the scene. Bridget glanced at Addison who stood in wonderment. His Adam's apple tightened, as he fought back tears. Seeing her brother in such an emotional state of utter happiness caused Bridget to sniff as well. It was all so perfect! Addison and Vanessa had waited so very long for this moment. And now, it was as if Heaven collided with earth as Vanessa gracefully approached her groom. Bridget was positive she could feel the warmth of God's smile upon them.

Mr. Bennett gave his daughter one last hug, then let go. Addison was more than ready to receive her. He squeezed her hand, and the two stood facing one another at the altar. The song ended, the crowd was seated, and the pastor cleared his throat.

"Dearly beloved, we have gathered here on this blessed morn, to celebrate the holy matrimony of our young King, and his highly-favored and soon-to-be Queen." He smiled kindly at Vanessa. He opened his Bible and asked that they begin the ceremony with prayer.

As the ceremony continued, every word which floated out of the pastor's mouth was elegant and weighty. It was full of joyful celebration, yet heavy conviction. The commitment Addison and Vanessa were making to one another was a commitment for life.

"What God has brought together, let no man tear apart! You are committing your lives to one another, pledging your very selves. Marriage is a display of covenant, a prophetic act which in a most humbling and awe-invoking sense, points us to the foreshadowing of Jesus, the Holy Bride Groom, and His Bride, the Church. One day we shall see Jesus face to face at the Marriage Supper of the Lamb. It is challenging for the human heart to scarcely imagine that God would love us in such a manner, and we shall not know the fullness of His love until we see Jesus face-to-face on that joyful and blessed day. But until then, we are blessed with the opportunity to see the love of Christ portrayed through the example of our brothers and sisters in Christ, as we all strive to be the hands and feet of Jesus, loving one another just as God has commanded us.

"We know that love is the most powerful force in the universe. We know that love is what causes the world to stop and say, 'There is something different about them.' Love is what draws us to the heart of God and miraculously transforms our lives. Love overcomes evil. Love endures. Love never fails. Your Majesty, King Addison, you have been admonished by God to 'love your wife, just as Christ loved the church, and gave Himself for her.' And Vanessa, you have been commanded to 'submit to your husband, as unto Christ.' As the two of you make this choice and commitment here today, in the presence of God and all these witnesses, you are offering us a glimpse into the amazing love of our Savior. As we celebrate with you today, this is just a small inkling of all the wonderful celebration to come at the grand wedding in Heaven! But we know that marriage is so much more than a party. It is more than flowers and tuxedos and a delicious banquet. Marriage is a *lifetime*. Marriage is always placing the needs of others before your own. Marriage is saying, 'I'm sorry', and 'I forgive you', and 'I love you', even on the hardest and most challenging days. Marriage is making the decision to daily pursue the one you said yes to. Marriage is making the unstoppable, determined decision to choose love over, and over, and over again."

The Pastor continued, asking for Willie to share the rings. Everyone smiled and suppressed their laughter as Willie stuck out his tongue as he dug into his pocket, a gesture that proved it wasn't a simple task. Finally, he removed the rings from his snug pants, and appeared very proud as he handed them to Addison.

Addison's hands shook with anticipation as he and Vanessa repeated their vows and slowly slipped rings onto one another's fingers. Addison pledged his lifetime promise and eternal devotion, and Vanessa did the same.

Bridget's eyes met Liam's and she knew he was thinking the same thing. *Someday, this is going to be us,* she thought, scarcely able to even imagine how Vanessa must be feeling right now. In just a few short moments, she would kiss her groom for the first time *ever*. Bridget's toes tingled with delight as she thought about what it would be like to finally fall into Liam's arms and experience what they'd been waiting for, for so long.

"And now, the moment we've all been anticipating." The pastor chuckled, "Although I am sure they are far more excited about it than we…"

Addison squeezed Vanesa's hand once more, and Vanessa continued to glow. Bridget nearly squealed out loud. It was too much cuteness to handle!

"By the authority invested in me by the Nation of Tarsurella and by Almighty God, it is with great honor and pure joy that I officially announce to you, His Royal Highness, King Addison, and his beloved Queen, Vanessa, as husband and wife!" The Pastor closed his Bible and grinned, "Your Majesty, you may kiss your bride."

The entire church stood up and cheered as Addison met the patient lips of his beautiful wife.

"Woo-hoo!" Bridget called out and clapped her hands together with all the rest.

The beautiful kiss was perfectly timed. It appeared as though the flawless couple had been doing it for years. Bridget giggled, and Millie tossed another handful of petals in the air.

"Alright, Addison!" Millie cheered, "That's the way you kiss your lady!"

This brought on more laughter from the entire congregation.

Chapter Thirty Three

Here Comes Forever

Vanessa floated through the gardens, hand-in-hand with her husband. She knew her feet were touching the grass, but her heart was soaring high above the clouds. She had never experienced this much carefree joy and intense level of heavenly ecstasy! She was far more in love with Addison than she was the day before. And though she wasn't sure it was possible for her little heart to love him anymore than it already did without bursting entirely, she was quite confident that this was just the beginning. Their love story had officially begun! Vanessa knew that this wasn't their "happily ever after." Instead, it marked a brand-new chapter of their lives. "Once upon a time" was just beginning.

The Master of Ceremonies announced their arrival in the East Garden and dozens of press outlets flashed photos. Addison waved at the crowd, knowing it was now time to offer the public a few words.

She clung to his arm and stared at him in a love-struck manner. She knew that from the outside looking in, her doe eyes had to look utterly ridiculous. But none of that mattered. She was married now! She could fawn over her hunky, handsome husband all she wanted to!

Addison was just as captivated as she. If not more. Vanessa was always beautiful. But seeing her in her spectacular gown, her eyes shining brighter than the stars themselves, had nearly knocked the wind out of Addison. What amazed him the most, was that he knew Vanessa's heart was even more stunning. How had he found such an immaculate gem? How had the Lord brought everything together so perfectly? Addison was in absolute wonderment. He clung to his wife's hand and addressed the press with a huge grin. He answered several quick questions, then posed for a few photos and continued on their way. They had a banquet to attend! Addison's siblings and the rest of their guests were already out back, getting seated and undoubtedly chatting about what a lovely ceremony it had been. But now, he and Vanessa had a few moments alone as they walked slowly down the path.

"Can you believe it?" he asked her.

"Not even one bit." Vanessa shook her head and laughed, "The day is going by so fast! I mean, I used to think this day wouldn't come fast enough; and now that it's here, I'd like it to slow down! Gotta give this girl a little bit of time to process! I mean, the fact that I get to spend the rest of my life with you?! And that starts *today*?! Like, what?!"

"I know." Addison laughed as well. "It's all so surreal. But I like it." He winked.

"Very much so." Vanessa melted beneath his gaze.

"You know what else I like?"

"What?" Vanessa asked playfully.

"This kissing thing. Not to brag or anything, but I think we're pretty good at it. Not to say we won't need more practice."

"Oh no, practice is good." Vanessa nodded then giggled once more, in spite of the silliness of the moment. "We'll *definitely* want to keep at it."

"And we get an entire lifetime to do so." He quickly pecked her with a sweet kiss on the forehead and continued down the trail.

All too soon they had reached the banquet tables and their precious alone time was over. As much as Addison halfway wished they could just run off on their honeymoon right now, he knew that celebrating with family and friends was just as important. They'd have plenty of alone time later. Two weeks of it on a private island in the Bahamas! So long as Vanessa was by his side, he knew he would enjoy every moment of the day's festivities.

The lawn was covered with a large, white, party tent, deep stakes driven into the ground and the white sides flopping in the subtle breeze. Vanessa could smell delicious foods wafting through the air. The loud chatter of their guests rose and fell in the gentle summer air. The temperature was unbelievably perfect. A balmy seventy-five degrees.

The Master of Ceremonies announced Addison and Vanessa's entrance, and everyone cheered once more. Addison and Vanessa were all smiles as they made their way toward a long table covered in a white cloth, decorated with an abundance of flowers set in trendy mason jars. The table which waited for them, propped up on a wooden stage above the rest of their guests, was where their Wedding Party sat. Vanessa and Addison slipped into the white chairs which were center stage, right beside Bridget and Liam.

"Congratulations, you old married couple, you!" Bridget teased playfully. "How does it feel to be a *wife*?"

"And how does it feel to officially be a husband?" Liam asked with a genuine smile.

Addison and Vanessa exchanged glances then burst out laughing, as if they knew what the other was thinking.

"I don't think it's really sunk in yet," Vanessa admitted.

"Yeah, so far it feels pretty much the same. Except, not?"

"Miss Vanessa, Miss Vanessa, you're finally my sister!" Millie ran toward her and hugged her legs. Vanessa scooped her onto her lap and kissed the little girl on her head.

"I know!" Vanessa's voice was loaded with excitement, "Ugh, I'm so thrilled, we've been waiting for this for so long!"

"Do you want to have a sleepover party with me tonight?!" Millie's wide eyes suggested a new idea as it floated into her mind, "We could play with my doll house, and then we could stay up late and look at the stars in my telescope!"

"Mil, Vanessa's going on vacation, remember?" Bridget spoke up. "She and Addi are going on their honeymoon. They're going to be gone for a few weeks."

"Can I come too?!" Millie asked eagerly.

"Nope," Bridget answered for her, "honeymoons are exclusive. Married people only."

"But I want to go on a honeymoon!" Millie continued. "They sound fun!"

"In that case, you'll have to get married." Bridget smiled as she leaned toward the table for a sip of her ice water.

"No way!" Millie shook her head. "Forget the honeymoon. I'm going to go on a single-moon instead."

"Ladies and gentlemen, if I may have your attention," the Master of Ceremonies spoke up. A gentle hush fell over the bubbly crowd. "We will begin serving our banquet in just a few moments. But before we do so, we would like to invite His Royal Majesty and His Royal Queen, to come to the stage and perform the first dance."

Addison and Vanessa locked hands once more, and Addison led her toward the small dance floor.

"After you, madam." Steve stepped backward and allowed Deborah to scoot into the buffet line just before him.

"Thank you." She smiled kindly and took a deep breath. "Ah, today has been just glorious, hasn't it? Goodness, Vanessa is such a beautiful bride."

"Indeed, she is." Steve smiled, "And are you enjoying the day off?"

"You know how much I love serving your family." Deborah reached for a dinner roll and set it on her plate. "But it has been nice just to sit back and enjoy the morning, without having to run around like a chicken with my head cut off."

Steve reached for a roll of his own.

Deborah looked up. "Steve." She took a deep breath. Her voice sounded nervous. "There's something I wish to speak to you about."

Steve's eyes held concern as he gave her his full attention.

"This will be my last month working for your family. I submitted my two-week notice this morning."

"You did?" Confusion rang in Steve's voice. "Whatever for? I thought you enjoyed your job? Is there something wrong? Has the Personnel Department adjusted your wage without my knowledge?"

"Oh no, it's not that. I love working here!" She smiled weakly, "It's just, that… Pearl. I don't think it's best for her with us, you know…" she lowered her voice to a whisper, in case of any lingering ears. "Dating."

Steve was quiet. It was quite clear that her daughter was upset by their decision.

"You know how much I care for you. But I must place Pearl's interests before my own. The idea of me dating again, let alone being involved with your family in such an intimate manner, has been very, very hard on her. I'm so sorry. If I had known she would respond in such a troubled manner, I never would've allowed things to go this far in the first place. I hope I haven't hurt you." She kindly touched his arm.

Steve sighed heavily. "I must admit, I've been having some of the same thoughts. I know this has been a challenge for Jillian, but after hearing her worries so clearly expressed last night, I fear that perhaps you are right. It isn't fair to ask your daughter to be transplanted into a life such as this, nor is it fair to ask my children to make room in their hearts for a new mother. Perhaps it's just too soon. I truly am sorrowed over this. I appreciate your companionship, Deborah. Very much so. But why do you feel the need to resign? Surely, we can mend our relationship and return to the stately, business-like manner that it was before. It would be a great loss to not have your services here. You're such an irreplaceable member of our team!"

"I know." Deborah spoke sadly as her eyes drifted toward the dinner rolls, "But it would be too hard for me to stay." She sighed, then looked back at Steve. "I care very deeply for you, and if we cannot—" she bit her

[424]

tongue. "At any matter, Pearl is reaching an age where she needs a full-time mother. Why, with all this newfound interest in boys and dating and drama at school, I'm prayerfully considering not going back to work at all. My mom has a home in the countryside in Bella Adar. We could go live with her there. Besides, it might be good for Pearl to have a break from all this high-strung, fast-paced, big city life."

Pearl's eyes grew wide. She had been passing by the outside of the tent, returning from the restroom, just in time to hear her mother speaking. She knew eavesdropping wasn't polite, but here on the other side of the tent there was no chance of them knowing she was listening. Her jaw dropped as her mind started to race.

Move?! She thought frantically, *To another country?! What?! No! We can't move!*

She quickly set out to find Jillian. They needed to create a new plan. And fast! Their plan from last night was completely destroying her life!

It didn't take her long to track down the Princess. She, Prince Asher, Millie, and Willie were playing in the lawn just beside the buffet tent. Millie laughed with glee as she and Willie chased bubbles. The large, translucent bubbles floated out of the bubble-machine, glistening in the sunshine. Jillian and Asher stood nearby, chatting with one another.

Pearl strutted across the lawn, careful to look her absolute best in Prince Asher's presence. Just as Jillian made eye contact with her, Pearl tripped in her high heels, her left ankle bending slightly. She waved her arms frantically in the air, attempting to catch her balance. Her face turned bright red, embarrassed by the fact that Asher had seen her nearly fall.

"Jillian." She spoke in a serious tone as she approached the siblings, "We've got a major problem! Our parents are breaking up!"

"And this is a problem, why?" Jillian was confused.

"No, I mean they're seriously, completely, for-real saying goodbye, burning their bridges and cutting off all communication with one another!" Pearl's voice was frantic, "Mom is resigning! She's talking about moving to my grandmother's house in Bella Adar! I can't move! I can't give up my entire life here and live in the countryside in some foreign country!"

"Wait, why would they be breaking up?" Asher asked. "Dad and Deborah are crazy about each other."

"Oh no, this is all our fault!" Jillian released a small gasp. Pearl's panic spread to Jillian, as her mind raced for a way to fix it. Her eyes met Asher's, "We were so stupid! Last night, we told them we didn't want them to get married. We thought maybe it would help slow things down a little. You know, give them a few years before they decide to get married or whatever. But we didn't want to destroy the relationship completely!"

"Jillian, how could you?!" Asher shook his head in disappointment, "Dad hasn't been this happy in years! We watched him lose Mom, now he should *not* have to lose Deborah." He offered a glare toward Pearl, somehow knowing that she was behind it. It was likely Pearl had influenced his little sister in the wrong direction.

"Hey, it was a mistake!" Pearl threw up her hands in defense, "It completely backfired and blew up in our faces!" She turned back toward Jillian, "We have to think of something. Before it's too late."

Chasity stood by the outskirts of the dance floor, smiling. Addison and Vanessa swayed back and forth, happily grooving to the catchy Big Band music filling their ears and their hearts. Bridget twirled around with Liam on the crowded dance floor as well. Bridget threw her head back and laughed as she nearly crashed into Vanessa.

Chasity giggled. Seeing the carefree dance moves from so many happy couples was bittersweet.

Several hours had passed and the hot afternoon sun inched nearer to the horizon. A cool breeze blew through the tent, and Chasity knew the joyous party would stretch late into the evening. She glanced over her shoulder. Her eyes spotted the empty space near the tent opening, half-heartedly waiting for Hanson to appear. She dug anxiously beneath her finger nail, wondering why he hadn't showed up. She tried her best to keep thoughts of Hanson out of her mind and focus simply on the happiness of her brother and her new sister. But it was a challenge seeing her older siblings in such joyous relationships. She couldn't help but wish for someone special to dance with on this beautiful night.

"Excuse me, Your Highness."

Chasity's heartbeat quickened. She twirled around, feeling completely twitter-pated. Seeing Hanson would be—

Suddenly, her heart fell. Her breath caught amidst the disappointment. It wasn't Hanson.

It was James.

"Oh." She tried to mask her devastation but didn't do too well. "Hello."

"I've been trying to make eye contact with you the past two hours, but it seems as though you've been avoiding me."

Chasity didn't know what to say. Actually, she had been. Was that absolutely terrible of her?

"It's good to see you, James." She smiled, attempting to be polite, "I'm glad you and your family could celebrate with us."

[427]

"As am I," James nodded. "Vanessa is going to make a fine Queen, I am sure of that. But, that's not what I am most excited about this evening." He wore a huge, very sweet smile, "Would you care to dance?"

"Um," Chasity hesitated. She bit her lip. She thought of the words her father had spoken the day before.

He held out a friendly hand. Chasity couldn't help but take it. The playful music was compelling, and even though James wasn't Hanson, he was still someone kind and caring to dance with.

He led her onto the dance floor, and the two swayed seamlessly back and forth.

"So," James asked the dreaded question, "Have you thought anymore about the future? About *our* future?"

"Yes." Chasity sighed, hating to break his heart. James was such a kind and friendly fellow, it would be so cruel of her to disappoint him like this. But she had to be honest. She had to be fair with him. She couldn't lie, especially about such an important matter of the heart. "James, you are incredibly kind. Your heart for others is truly sweet, and you've always been so encouraging to me. You're a true friend! But I must be real with you... I can't court you." She spoke sadly, "It simply wouldn't be fair to you. You're ready to dive headfirst into the ocean of commitment, and I'm still floundering on the shore somewhere, attempting to heal from a painful experience. I can't use you as a rebound. Saying yes to you at this point in my life would be far too cruel. For both of us." She sighed, "I hope we can remain friends though?"

"I'll admit, I'm disappointed by your words. But I can't say that I'm surprised. It's no secret that you're quite taken with Hanson Fletcher. I guess I had just hoped that perhaps things might be different." He smiled weakly, "Nevertheless, I respect your thoughts on the matter. And I will

[428]

gladly continue to be your friend, Your Highness. Besides, who else is going to help you get that crazy beast ready for the Spring Circuit?"

"You mean it?" She smiled genuinely, "You're still going to help me with Nic?"

"Of course." His eyes glowed, "I am a man of my word, and we O'Conners never go back on a promise."

"Thank you." Chasity truly meant every word. "For understanding. For caring. For being there. For everything. You're a true friend, James."

"Attention ladies and gentlemen of the Court!" The MC announced as the song ended, "It is time for the traditional tossing of the bouquet! May we have all of our single ladies, young and old, line up! That's it, don't be shy, step right up, ladies! Now is your chance to see if true love is in your future!"

Several of the girls giggled with excitement and dashed toward the front of the stage. Vanessa laughed and kissed her husband once more, pained to be parting from him for a few short moments. Bridget handed Vanessa her bouquet, and the stage was quickly filled with single hopefuls. Even Millie was up there.

"Good luck." James winked.

Chasity laughed and headed toward the front.

"Alright, is that everyone?!" the MC asked, scanning the crowd for any stragglers who were too shy to join in on the fun. "Ah, you ma'am!" He pointed toward Deborah, "Come on, we can't have anyone missing out!"

Deborah laughed as Pearl yanked her arm forward.

Vanessa turned around, careful to make sure she wasn't facing the crowd.

"Now on the count of three, Your Majesty, release the bouquet into the air!"

"One!" the MC called, and the audience joined in on the count.

"Two!"

"Three!"

Instead of releasing the bouquet, Vanessa twirled around and headed for Deborah. Deborah's eyes widened as Vanessa approached her, and the bouquet fell into her arms. She gasped. Everyone laughed.

"And the bouquet toss winner is," Jillian spoke into the microphone in an excited tone, "Miss Deborah!"

Deborah laughed awkwardly, unsure of what else to do. All eyes were on her.

"Ms. Deborah, we love you." Jillian continued speaking, "And so does my dad. I know that I speak on behalf of all us kids when I say that you are one of the most amazing women we've ever had the privilege of knowing. And we would be honored if God saw fit for you to someday be part of our family."

Pearl bounded onto the stage and spoke into the mic, "I love you, Mom! And I just want you to be happy!" She glanced at Asher, "And Prince Asher is right! We haven't seen our parents this happy in a really, really long time. And if you guys love each other, which we know that you do, then us kids are willing to figure out a way to make it work."

"What we're trying to say is," Jillian added, "stay. Ms. Deborah, we don't want you to leave. We want you and Dad to be happy. We're sorry for butting in and making everything so complicated. Whatever God is doing in your lives—whatever He's doing in *all* of our lives—we don't want to mess it up. So, if you two love each other," she smiled at Pearl, "we'll learn to love each other as well."

The audience released a sappy, "Awww!" and everyone laughed and smiled once more as Steve reached for Deborah's hand.

"So, what do you say?" Steve asked sweetly. "Will you stay?"

Deborah looked up at her daughter who offered her two excited thumbs up. "Yes." She smiled, fighting back tears. "Yes! I will stay."

Steve grinned and gave her a quick hug, which brought a release of applause from everyone in the tent. Millie squealed excitedly, wondering if this meant that there would be another wedding happening soon.

Chapter Thirty Four

Broken Promises

Hanson struggled against the entrapment of his wrists. They were securely fastened together, his back against a metal pole. The abandoned parking garage served as a dingy cage for the captive.

Hanson's chest heaved, and his heart pounded with anger. His captors had been holding him here for hours. His throat was dry, and his mouth parched. Although it was cooler underground, Hanson still longed for a drink. Even more so, he longed to be free. Every moment he spent here was another second he was away from Chasity. Another moment in which Chasity would believe he had forgotten about her, that he wasn't going to show up. That he had lied. And those thoughts were far more agonizing than his physical discomfort. If he didn't get out of this mess, it could be the end between him and Chasity.

Lilly had been released. Hanson agreed to play the hero and stand in Lilly's place. Even though Lilly had begged him not to, Hanson wasn't about to watch her be murdered. And so, Lilly was sent off, with the promise that she wouldn't be harmed. But her departure wasn't all roses and teddy bears. Her goodbye was reinforced with another threat. A threat that forbid her from speaking. If she told anyone about what had happened, or the fact that they had Hanson, the promise would be revoked.

Hanson didn't know why the men were still holding him here. Why hadn't they made a move to kill him yet? The two strangers paced back and forth, as if waiting for someone. They carelessly drank their ice-cold sodas that they had retrieved from the cooler in the back of their getaway car, taunting Hanson with their loud gulps.

"Are you guys actually gonna come at me, or just sit around and drink soda all day?" Hanson challenged them, unable to keep his feisty thoughts to himself. He was so sick of this waiting game. He needed to know what was going to happen. He needed to fight them. He needed to return to the wedding, before it was too late.

"Boss said to wait for him." One of the men took a final gulp, then crushed the soda can on his head. It deflated perfectly beneath the impact. He tossed it through his open car window, into the front seat.

"Your boss is in jail," Hanson told them, knowing full well that they worked for his dad.

"Correction." The man smiled wickedly, "*Was* in jail. He just broke out this morning."

A jolt of debilitating fear shot through Hanson's body.

"You didn't think some metal bars were gonna keep Mr. Fletcher down, did ya?" The man laughed, "The man always wins. And he told us to tell you that unless you abandon your job at The Palace and join the family business, you're gonna be on the losing team."

"Family business?" Hanson barked. "Don't you mean the family *mafia*?"

"Those are some pretty tough words for a man who's about to DIE!" the man shouted back.

Just then, the sound of distant sirens broke through the thick humidity.

The man cursed. "It's the cops! Get'm in the car!"

The second man quickly untied Hanson and attempted to shove him in the back seat. But Hanson wasn't about to give up that easily. He threw several punches, only to be greeted by a hard hit in his gut.

"Umph!" Hanson released a sound of distress, and the man reached for a handful of Hanson's black mane and pulled him backward. The distant sirens grew louder. Hanson continued to fight, but the two men quickly overpowered him. They tossed him in the back seat and locked the doors.

"Go, go, go!" the passenger shouted to the driver, "I can hear 'em! They've entered the parking garage; they're coming up on our tail!"

Hanson craned his neck to see backwards as the car lurched forward. The dingy parking garage was filled with bright blue and red lights. A string of five police cars closed in behind them.

Their little black vehicle blazed ahead at seventy kilometers an hour, dangerously whipping around the corners of the garage, too close to the walls for Hanson's comfort. He flinched as they nearly crashed into one, on the end of a hairpin turn.

A roaring police car squeezed between them and the right wall, attempting to speed ahead and force them to stop, but the crazed driver wasn't ready to surrender.

A wild look of insanity burned in the driver's eyes, as he made a sharp jab on the steering wheel. Hanson gasped as he slid across the backseat. The loud screech of metal hitting metal echoed through the garage as their car tagged the police vehicle. Hanson's cheek smashed against the closed backseat window, which had just rammed into the police.

"You're gonna get us killed!" the passenger warned the driver.

The driver merely laughed and pushed his lead foot deeper onto the gas pedal. Hanson scrambled to put his seatbelt on. The sirens continued.

"Watch out for the—"

Hanson's hands flew up to guard his face. He clenched his jaw and squeezed his eyes tight, bracing for the sudden impact. The sound of glass shattering as the front end of their car crunched into the taillights of a red SUV jolted Hanson's soul.

The men in the front seat shouted from shock and pain, as airbags flew in their faces. Now that the car had stopped, Hanson scrambled to get out.

Hanson was greeted by six police officers, all climbing out of their cars. There was a seventh figure with them—Jackson, the head of Palace Security!

The armed men dashed toward the accident, eager to place the criminals in handcuffs.

"Fletcher, are you okay?!" Jackson's voice of concern felt like velvet on Hanson's cuts. "You're bleeding! Quick, I need a dispatch of medical services!"

"I'm fine," Hanson quickly huffed, still panting from the adrenaline of the moment. He felt something odd on his face. He reached upward, wondering if it was a bug or—"Argh!" He winced in pain.

"Stop, you've got a huge gash!" Jackson grabbed his hand. Hanson looked down and realized his arms were peppered with tiny cuts as well. He could now feel the effects of the shattered glass.

"Oh no." Hanson was suddenly afflicted with a disturbing thought. "Did Lilly tell you I was here? Is someone watching her?! The mafia—"

"Hanson, calm yourself." Jackson spoke in an even tone, wondering if he was still in shock from the dramatic toll of the crash. "Miss Chesterfield is just fine. She's perfectly safe at The Palace."

Hanson's eyes continued to express grave concern.

"So is your mother," Jackson reassured her. "Son, it is our *job* to protect people. There's no way anyone is going to get through our sanctuary of safety. I just wish you would've told us about all of this mess sooner. I could've had some men on the assignment. Perhaps you would've slept easier at night. Hanson, why didn't you tell us the fullness of what was going on?"

Hanson suddenly felt uncomfortable beneath Jackson's questioning gaze. "I don't know," he murmured, looking awkwardly toward his shoes, then back up at the man. "I didn't think it was right to bother you guys with this. I mean, your priority is to safeguard the Royal Family. Not random people on the street."

"You're right." Jackson nodded, "Our priority is always to put family first. But Hanson, you've been with us for ten months now. You're family."

Hanson nodded, suddenly feeling the brick of tension dissolve from his shoulders. Another guard approached them, handing Hanson a towel and a bottle of water.

"Thanks." Hanson offered his simple words of gratitude and lifted the towel to his face. He tried not to appear uncomfortable when it made contact with his cut. He dabbed at the wound, then untwisted his water bottle and took a huge gulp. "Can I catch a ride?" Hanson asked. "My car is back at the football field. I need to get back to the wedding."

"The Wedding?" Jackson chuckled, "Do you see what kind of a sorry state you're in? Beat up lip, a purple cushion around your swollen eye, and a nice bright slice on your cheek?"

Hanson shook his head, "It doesn't matter. I have to get there before the reception is over and talk to—" Hanson stopped himself.

"And talk to?" Jackson's eyes twinkled with mischief.

Hanson cleared his throat. It was time to come clean. He couldn't keep trying to deceive his fellow security agents. His feelings for Chasity were real. So, it was about time he chose to be real as well. "Princess Chasity."

"Ah, yes." Jackson smiled. "About that."

Hanson was taken aback by his knowing response. Jackson placed a surprisingly-fatherly hand on his shoulder and continued speaking. "Her Highness is a delightful young woman. She'll make a treasured catch for whatever special young man she ends up with, and I can see how you would be drawn to her."

Hanson gulped. Uh, oh. Did Jackson know he was interested in her? Was he going to lose his job?

"But it's quite clear that your life right now is a little bit, muddled, to say the least. Your family history, though I don't understand or know the full extent of it, might be a tad bit unfitting for Her Royal Highness, well, you know, with a mafia coming after you and whatnot. I know these words are probably not what you want to hear right now, but I strongly

[438]

urge you to consider and hear from another's perspective. Sometimes, when we truly love someone, we must place their own interests and well-being above our own passions and desires, no matter how intense or genuine they may be."

Hanson's throat tightened. Was Jackson forbidding him from asking her to enter an official courtship? "So are you, like, uh…" Hanson struggled to speak, for fear of breaking down emotionally. It shook him to hear the words come out of his own lips, "Are you saying it's against the rules for me to be with her?"

"This is not a matter of rules, Hanson," Jackson continued gently, "as it is so much a matter of doing the right thing." His eyes softened, "I know you care for the Princess. But is it really appropriate to show up at the reception, bruised and tattered as you are, and introduce yourself to His Royal Majesty for the first time, as the young lad who's interested in courting his daughter? And when he asks you to give an account for your appearance, are you ready to explain the entire story? Your father's criminal record? The threat against Lilly's life? The reason you couldn't attend the wedding in the first place? It's not exactly a casual, cake-and-tea kind of conversation."

Hanson's heart sank. As much as he hated to hear Jackson's words, he knew they were right. The reality of this situation was just as ugly as the wounds on his face.

Storming into the happy reception right now could be disastrous. But if he didn't show up, it would appear as though he was breaking his word to Chasity. He couldn't do that to her. What if there was still a small part of her that actually wanted him to show up? Hanson's throat constricted as he realized he had come to the end of the line.

Who was he trying to fool? Things between him and Chasity—the *Princess,* for heaven's sakes—would never work out. Guys like him just didn't get happy endings like that. Why had he allowed himself to think that it ever could be? Hanson had lost sight of reality. After months of wrestling with his emotions, he had to end this once and for all. She was already mad at him. There were already ten-thousand reasons why she hated his guts! And rightfully so. He had been an absolute worm. Trying to make things up to her was an impossible dream.

A dream which Hanson would never have the luxury of pursuing.

He regretfully followed Jackson toward a police vehicle. His body ached just as intensely as his heart. He was exhausted. The emotional and physical toll placed on him this afternoon had been extreme. His trembling heart resigned to the fact that it was time to check on his mother and change out of his tuxedo.

Hanson slipped into the police car and stared out the window. His emotions were raw as they pulled out of the parking garage.

I hope she knows, Hanson thought as he clung to one last string of nonsensical hope. *I hope she knows how much I cared. I hope she can look back at these times and somehow find a way to forgive me. I hope she truly finds happiness. That all of her dreams come true, and that there's someone who cares for her far more than—*

Hanson stopped the string of torturous thoughts. He took a deep breath. His neck leaned backward onto the headrest. He closed his eyes, knowing the prolonged chapter between Chasity and him had officially come to an end.

Chapter Thirty Five

Sparkling Hope

A great blast of techno music penetrated the party tent. The crowd let out an excited cheer as Addison grabbed Vanessa's hand and tugged her toward the spotlight. Streaks of pink, blue, and purple lasers glimmered through the air, and Vanessa giggled. The heavy down-beat of the drums and bass guitar caused the audience to respond with joyous clapping.

"Oh no!" Vanessa giggled, "You know how much I can't stand this song!"

"Ness." Addison's eyes were playful, "You know what I'm gonna say." Addison got into groove with the popular song and opened his mouth just in time for the lyrics to be released, *"No excuses just dance with me!"*

Vanessa laughed wildly, as did the crowd. Millie bounded to her feet and joined them near center stage. Willie was right on her tail, bouncing up and down, appearing as though he was riding a hyped-up bucking bronco.

"That's it, get your groove!" The MC encouraged their goofy antics through the microphone. He then flashed the spotlight on Steve. "A little bug told me this is your favorite karaoke tune. We wanna see your moves!"

"Come on, Dad!" Bridget popped out of her seat and floated toward her father, tugging on his arm.

"Bridget, I'm not about to get up there and make a fool out of—"

But Steve's words were left hanging in his mouth as Deborah appeared and pulled on his other arm. "Listen to the song lyrics, Steve!" Deborah encouraged him, *"No excuses just dance with me!"*

Bridget laughed as her dad moved his hand and his hips in unison, like it was a 1970's disco party. Next thing Bridget knew, her father, Addison, and Liam were performing some kind of awkward line-dance showdown. With limbs flying, the crowd laughing, and family members snapping pictures, the carefree laughter just wouldn't stop. And it was nearly midnight!

"Where's Asher?" Pearl asked above the noise, "He needs to be up there!"

Asher's face turned beet-red as the spotlight fell on him.

Bridget smiled, "Come on, Ash! It's your big brother's wedding! Once-in-a-lifetime opportunity to dance until your feet fall off!"

"I think I'll keep my feet, thank you very much."

"Twenty bucks says he won't do it," Pearl taunted.

"Asher, puullleeease!" Bridget begged. "It would make such a cute picture! Dad and all the guys grooving it out! Just dance for like two seconds!"

Asher released a groan. He hesitated, but finally took heavy steps forward.

"Oh, my goodness, he's actually doing it!" Pearl's jaw dropped.

Bridget was just as surprised. When was the last time she'd seen Asher dance?

Asher slid onto the stage like a pro, causing the crowd to erupt in a wild cheer. He glided effortlessly through the moves, causing Bridget to wonder if he was some kind of secret closet dancer.

"That boy is full of surprises." Pearl shook her head in wonderment.

"Tell me about it." Bridget giggled, snapping as many quick pictures as she could.

The men's dance routine was quickly over, and Liam fetched Bridget. She excitedly danced beside him, laughing as she watched Pearl approach Asher, and Asher turn her down flat.

"Oh no, you're not done yet, mister!" Chasity grabbed her brother and yanked him back onstage.

The joyful moves continued as everyone bounced up and down, twirled, glided, or did whatever kind of strangeness their giddy little hearts desired. Asher grabbed his nose and pretended to dive under water. Mille pulled out some glorious ballet movies. Willie banged his head back and forth with the music, his curls bouncing every which way.

Hope stood on the sidelines, grinning. It was so delightful to see everyone enjoying themselves. She peered past the bouncing bodies and flashing lights, and accidenty made eye contact with David. He stood on the far end of the floor, wearing black dress pants and his white dress shirt.

[443]

But if it weren't for that stinkingly-cute, red bow tie—

Hope's eyes smiled as David's face expressed a full-blown grin. Her heart quickened as she realized he was making his way through the maze of dancers. His black dress shoes crept closer.

"Nice party," he commented when he had finally reached her.

"My mom would've loved it." Hope smiled, "She was all about us doing karaoke and having dance parties in the living room."

"I wish I could've met her. She seems like a really amazing woman."

"She was." Hope nodded in a reminiscent tone. She then spotted Deborah, who was twirling Millie around. A deep sense of peace washed over Hope. It was nothing like the unsettled feeling she had before, whenever she thought about Deborah possibly joining her family. As much as she missed her mom, Hope knew that seasons changed. And if this new change meant that Deborah was going to become a closer member of their family, Hope was okay with that. Deborah really was a phenomenal lady.

"So are, uh," David started nervously, "friends allowed to ask other friends to dance?"

Hope was surprised by his question. She was even more surprised by her answer. "Huh? Of course!" She grinned, "That's what weddings are for! Dancing with friends!"

David's eyes lit up just as brightly as the spotlight, and Hope pulled out some of her dorkiest moves. She didn't feel too awkward, though, because David was just as terrible as she was. If not worse.

"Yikes!" Hope giggled, shouting slightly to be heard above the music, "I would've expected something a little bit smoother from a popstar!" she teased.

"Says a girl who's supposed to be the posterchild of grace and poise?" He grinned, "Yeah right."

The two continued to dance and laugh until the end of the song. Everyone applauded, and Hope's chest heaved from moving around so much. She felt a trickle of sweat on the back of her neck.

"And now, ladies and gentlemen, as we are nearing the midnight hour, we ask you all to step outside and get ready for the fireworks!" the MC announced.

"Fireworks?!" Vanessa peered at Addison excitedly, "I didn't know you planned fireworks!"

"Surprise, love!" He grinned and kissed her on the forehead, "I know how much you adore explosives." He winked.

"Sparklers for everyone!" Bridget skipped around like the sparkler-fairy, dubbing everyone with long glorious wands of glitter and glow, all to be illuminated at the perfect moment.

"I guess I'd better go." David regretfully excused himself, "We're doing the next song."

"Awesome." Hope continued to grin, truly looking forward to hearing them play one last time. "So, uh, will you guys be around for a while?"

The bright light in David's eyes dimmed, "No. We're leaving for Tokyo first thing in the morning."

"Tokyo?" Hope was surprised.

"Yeah, I guess our last single is pretty big over there."

"Oh." Hope was disappointed to see him leave. Again. She tried her best to mask her true emotions, "Well, that's cool. Good luck in Japan!"

"Thanks." David smiled then bowed out gracefully, headed to catch up with the rest of his band.

Hope sighed, wondering what in the world she was going to do with herself until he returned. Would he ever return? Or was he just like Luke, suddenly vanishing from the scenes of her life forever?

Chasity stood beside her sister. "You okay?"

"Not so much." Hope offered her a weak smile, "But I will be. What about you?"

"I'm okay," Chasity nodded. "I've officially come to the bittersweet realization that Hanson isn't going to show up. But I'm finally alright with that. Truly. I'm not sure I was ready for all that drama anyway. Things are better this way, you know? I can just focus on Addi and Nessa and having a good time with the family." Chasity squeezed Hope's hand. "We'll get through this. We always do."

"This is true," Hope smiled back. "And nothing helps us through hard times quite as much as dancing... and chocolate." She giggled, "Which we have a lot of tonight!"

"And sparklers!" Bridget handed them each a long stick. "Come on, let's head out to the lawn!"

The girls smiled and followed their eldest sister. Just outside the tent, everything was dark, except for the soft glow coming from scattered tiki lights. Vanessa and Addison held hands on a small platform, surrounded by family and friends. Hope took a deep breath, inhaling the sweet summer evening air. Today had been quiet blissfully perfect. She knew Vanessa's and Addison's hearts were singing together in a seamless harmony, ready to dive into whatever God had for them next. Hope was eager to see what was coming next as well. How was the story of her life going to play out? Hope shook her head. Tonight, none of that mattered. All that mattered, was living in the moment, unwrapping this gloriously sweet gift from Heaven called the present. All of her senses were engaged as she heard crickets singing softly in the background and smelled the dew settling on tall grasses. Her feet were tired from the long day, but her heart was fully awake.

A sudden crackling was heard in the distance. Hope looked upward toward the dazzling starlight. A zigzag of electricity burst through the clear sky, and Hope held her breath. Once the hidden firework reached its predetermined destination, it opened up its heart and burst out in all of its glory. Flashes of pink, red, green, and gold decorated the sky.

Hope smiled at Millie who squealed with delight. Her eyes drifted toward her father, who slipped a gentle hand into Deborah's palm. Even Pearl appeared to be enjoying herself. Hope continued to study the faces of those staring upward. Asher wore a small smile as he admired the show above. Lastly, her eyes settled on Addison, who wasn't watching the fireworks at all. He was staring at his wife, watching the shards of color reflect in her eyes and dance on her hair.

Thank You, Lord. Hope prayed silently, her heart overwhelmed with words of thanksgiving to the One who had gifted them this moment. *Thank You for faithfully bringing Addison and Vanessa to their happily ever after. Thank You for caring enough, for shepherding us, and for seeing to it that we've all arrived safely in this breath-taking moment of beauty and grace. Thank You for Your faithfulness. Thank You that even when we can't see what's going on, You've still got a plan. Help me to trust You. I know that if things aren't good, it isn't the end. Help me to hang on, until You do bring about that beautiful ending.*

The fireworks continued to erupt. Nobody dared to speak, as only the gentle hush of *ohhh*'s and *ahhh*'s were whispered in wonderment.

Finally, the subtle sound of acoustic guitar strings floated through the

[447]

speakers. Hope instantly recognized the chords. David's milk-chocolate voice provided the velvet soundtrack behind this flawless moment.

"Just a small-town boy who's been on a ride,

midnight dreams flash before my eyes,

blinded by the bright lights of a Hollywood party at twilight,

I blink twice to make sure that she's real,

'Cause the vision before me is so surreal,

Now I've never seen an angel before,

Until she stepped through that open door."

Hope took a deep breath. She knew what was coming. Nevertheless, a deep wave of peace washed over her. She glanced once more at Addison and Vanessa who clung to one another in pure joy. She knew that this song was special to Vanessa. It held a special place in the hearts of thousands of girls all across the planet. But those lyrics would always mean the most to the girl it had been penned for.

Hope didn't know what the months to come would hold. But she knew she could trust the One who held them. She didn't know if she would ever end up with the one who sang her song in sold-out auditoriums all over the world. Nevertheless, no matter what happened, she somehow knew that in the meantime, her name was safe upon his lips.

"She'll think that I'm absurd, but I've gotta say these words,

Baby, you have to know I've lost all hope.

I've lost all hope, I've lost all hope."

Dear Reader,

You might be thinking, "Ahhhh!!!! This can't possibly be the end, can it?!"

You have a point.

Which is why I'm so excited to announce that this is NOT the end of *The Tales of Tarsurella*!

If it's not good, it's not the end.

-Livy.

Looking to the Future...

The Tales of Tarsurella

The Revolution

Bridget Henderson's fingers tapped impatiently on the chestnut desk. She stared at her computer screen. The green "loading" bar couldn't move any slower. Bridget let out an impatient huff. Trying to use the internet in her new home was a most-painstaking experience. Thanks to the spotty connection, Bridget's capacity for patience had been enlarged enormously. But learning to endure snail-like internet connection speeds wasn't the only shiny-new character trait Bridget developed over the previous year. In fact, so much had changed, Bridget could only recall a handful of things about herself that *had* remained the same.

Bridget pulled her crystal eyes away from the energy-draining screen and allowed them to settle on a nearby photograph. Her heart smiled as a flood of girlish feelings and giddy emotions washed over her. The image displayed a laughing version of herself, playfully climbing the back of her ruggedly handsome husband, Liam Henderson. It was hard to believe an entire year had passed since he got down on one knee and asked her to be his wife. Their sudden engagement in August led to the unfolding of their fairytale wedding in November. After enjoying their first winter together in Alaska as newly-weds, the calendar pages continued flying forward and brought them to the current date: August fourth.

Bridget anxiously glanced at the clock. She needed to leave. Like five minutes ago. But the lazy internet didn't seem to care about her hectic schedule.

Bridget gave her computer an intimidating glare. After trying to upload her digital photographs three times, Bridget wasn't in the mood to start the entire process over from scratch. This time, it *had* to work. She had already wasted much of the day fooling around with her blog page. She was not in the mood to begin again. The green progress bar moved another centimeter. Bridget was eager for the images to finish uploading. The carefully chosen pictures displayed trendy renovations and creative tweaks she'd been making to their home the past several months.

All at once, the green bar flashed to the finish line and disappeared. The page refreshed, and Bridget let out an excited squeal. Her desired results had come to pass. She quickly scanned the page, making sure that everything was set to her standard of excellence. She proofread each caption, careful to spot any typos.

Sage throw pillows are my current muse. I adore the splash of color they bring to our living room. They tie in perfectly with our vases sitting on the birch tree stump end tables.

Bridget's eyes traveled to the next caption.

May I take a moment to brag on my husband? His craftsmanship is STUNNING. See the floating shelves on our entry wall? These home-made, hand-carved pieces took this space from drab to fab. This little nook is one of my favorite places, because not only is it cozy and welcoming, it also adds more storage space!

Bridget smiled in sweet recollection, loving the way these photos pulled her back to the decorating phase of their home renovation project.

After saying "I Do," Liam had carried Bridget over the thresh-hold into one of his parents' very tiny hunting cabins, nestled in a pine-filled forest. Even though they were living on Mr. and Mrs. Henderson's land, their cabin was three miles away from his folks. Liam's wedding gift from his father was a huge plot of land on their Alaskan ranch. It was a benevolent surprise, as Liam had been planning to purchase a few small acres on his own. The extravagant gift was yet another symbol of the Hendersons' selfless heart toward their adopted son. The dozens of acres gifted were more than enough space to begin building their dream home. The temporary hunting cabin was more cozy than claustrophobic. It served as a nice newlywed nest as Liam sketched out plans for a six-bedroom, four-bath, three-story-dream home. Both Liam and Bridget were thrilled about their building project. But the more they planned, the more they realized the vision would take several years to fulfill. So, they agreed upon constructing a smaller, ranch-size, three-bedroom, two-bath home. After Liam worked with their contractors to make the all-important functional and foundational framework of their home, it was time for Bridget to pull out her magic design wand and have some fun!

Liam suggested they document it, to show the progress to her entire family back home in Tarsurella. Her sister-in-law, Vanessa, suggested she set up a blog. Liam encouraged Bridget in her pursuit, voicing the fact that he believed there would be a greater purpose in her blog than to just talk about trimming and DIY coasters. What she intended to be a cute little photo-album for her family had snowballed into something much larger. Millions of readers caught wind of Bridget's blogging adventures and anxiously sat on the edge of their seats as they watched Bridget's fairytale dreams unfold. Readers all over the world were obsessed with Bridget's real-life fantasy. What could be more whimsical than building your first house with the man of your dreams? Devoted fans couldn't wait for the next word from Bridget.

What I've continued to learn, with each new can of paint, bolt of material, and sparkly faucet fixture; is that the old saying is true. A house is just an empty building with four walls, until you make it your own. A family, and the love dwelling inside, is what makes it a home.

Bridget pushed the "publish" button, launching her newest post out to every eager soul who wished to receive it. But Bridget didn't have time to bask in the glory of the moment. She quickly switched her computer off and snatched a pair of car keys off the counter. If she didn't hurry, she would be late!

She slipped on a navy-blue sweater, grabbed her purse and bounded through the entry way into their garage. She lifted her small frame into the forest-green Jeep.

Bridget didn't waste any time zipping out of the garage and down the muddy terrain, which they generously referred to as their 'driveway.' She skillfully maneuvered around potholes and smelly presents left from Mr. Henderson's cows.

Soon, she approached the Main House where Mr. and Mrs. Henderson lived. A real driveway formed ahead. The Jeep wheels breathed a sigh of relief as they met solid pavement. Bridget cautiously slowed, aware that there may be people, dogs, or horses nearby. The working ranch was always busy, and Bridget knew better than to zoom through their property. Even if she was late.

After traveling several feet, Bridget spotted a familiar face. Mrs. Henderson. She waved, so Bridget slowed even further.

"Going to pick up your special visitors?" Mrs. Henderson asked excitedly.

"Yes, but I'm late." Bridget reported the frustrating news, "My blog was being a stubborn little thing. I couldn't leave until it finished uploading."

Mrs. Henderson laughed, "There's nothing I hate more than trying to do computer work! Especially up here where the connection is so spotty. That's why I have Donald handle all the book keeping. Oh, here!" She suddenly remembered and handed Bridget a pile of mail, "A few items for you."

"Thanks." Bridget placed the pile on the seat beside her, "See you soon, Mom!"

Tasurella Fans!

Want to be the first to know when

The Revolution **is released?**

Sign up for Livy's free email updates at www.livylynnblog.com

Come Connect!

One of my favorite things about writing these stories is hearing back from you, the reader! So please, feel free to drop me a line! Let me know what you thought of *The Wedding*, and what you're most looking forward to in *The Revolution*!

You can email me at: livylynnauthor@yahoo.com

Or you can find me here:

Goodreads: Olivia Lynn Jarmusch

Instagram: @livylynnglittergirl

Twitter: @livylynnmusic

Blog: www.livylynnblog.com

Let's talk soon!

~Livy Lynn

Team Tarsurella:

THANK YOU!

A special shout out to all the beautiful souls who made this book possible!

Theresa, Ellie, Sarah, Holly, Faith, Macie, Khylie, Emily, Tori, Sunshine, Karis, Ella, Victoria, Sarah-Grace, Bella, Rachel, Tabitha, Hannah, and Beloved! Your generous support has made this book a reality!

Thank you to everyone else who has shown their support as well, it would take far too long to list all of you in this book. :)

Please know that every time you share your honest review on Goodreads and Amazon, recommend these stories to a friend, or request them at your local library, you're part of Team Tarsurella!

Made in the USA
Columbia, SC
19 November 2024

46438256R00278